WHEN ALL THE GIRLS HAVE GONE

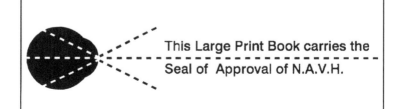

This Large Print Book carries the
Seal of Approval of N.A.V.H.

WHEN ALL THE GIRLS HAVE GONE

JAYNE ANN KRENTZ

LARGE PRINT PRESS
A part of Gale, a Cengage Company

GALE
A Cengage Company

Farmington Hills, Mich • San Francisco • New York • Waterville, Maine
Meriden, Conn • Mason, Ohio • Chicago

LIBRARY OF CONGRESS CATALOGING-IN-PUBLICATION DATA

Names: Krentz, Jayne Ann, author.
Title: When all the girls have gone / Jayne Ann Krentz.
Description: Large print edition. | Waterville, Maine : Thorndike Press, 2016. |
    Series: Thorndike Press large print basic
Identifiers: LCCN 2016043146 | ISBN 9781410493286 (hardback) | ISBN 1410493288
    (hardcover)
Subjects: LCSH: Missing persons—Investigation—Fiction. | Private
    investigators—Fiction. | Large type books. | BISAC: FICTION / Romance /
    Suspense. | GSAFD: Mystery fiction. | Romantic suspense fiction.
Classification: LCC PS3561.R44 W48 2016b | DDC 813/.54—dc23
LC record available at https://lccn.loc.gov/2016043146

ISBN 13: 978-1-4328-3430-2 (pbk.)
ISBN 10: 1-4328-3430-4 (pbk.)

Published in 2017 by arrangement with The Berkley Publishing Group,
an imprint of Penguin Publishing Group, a division of Penguin Random
House LLC

Printed in the USA
7 8 9 10 11   28 27 26 25 24

For Frank, with love

CHAPTER 1

The killer waited patiently for the target to emerge from the cabin.

There was no great rush, after all. The waiting allowed time to savor the prospect of revenge.

It was rather pleasant sitting there, propped against a mossy tree, rifle at the ready. High summer in the Cascades was a very enjoyable time of year. True, the tourists clogged the narrow mountain roads and insisted on stopping at every lookout point to take photographs. They left their trash behind at the numerous picnic sites. But come fall they would be driven away by the heavy rains and high winds of the early storms. In winter, snow would make the roads treacherous.

In the meantime, the warm, gentle breeze stirring the branches carried the scents of the trees and the vegetation that thrived in the short growing season.

Now there was time to contemplate the past and all the injustices that could be laid at the feet of the man inside the cabin. While making preparations the killer had worried that when the moment finally arrived, there would be at least a few qualms. Instead there was only a great sense of certainty.

The door of the cabin opened. Gordon Greenslade came out onto the porch. He had always been a good-looking man and he was aging well. His hair had turned an attractive silver-white, not dull gray. He was still lean and fit, and his aquiline features had softened only a little.

He had a mug of coffee in his hand. The killer recognized the mug. It was several years old, handmade and hand-painted. Like everything else in the rustic interior of the cabin, it was worn and faded.

These days Greenslade used the cabin primarily for hunting and fishing and when he just wanted to get away from the pressures that came with being the town's leading citizen. He owned the company that was the second-largest employer in town — the college had taken first place in recent years. But more to the point, he owned the local politicians, the authorities of Loring College and a couple of state representatives. If the rumors were true, he also had at least one U.S. senator in his pocket.

Everybody in Loring respected Gordon Greenslade and a lot of people owed him in one way or another. He was a rigid, self-righteous pillar of the community. But no one really liked him. It would be entertaining to see how much effort the police put into investigating his death.

The killer rose and picked up the rifle. There was a clear line of sight. It would be easy to take the kill shot without being seen. But that would defeat the purpose. When you set out to walk the path of revenge, you wanted your target to know who was pulling the trigger.

The killer moved out into the clearing in front of the cabin. It took Gordon a moment to notice that he had company. When he did, he was startled, but only briefly. Irritation soon replaced the surprise.

"What are you doing here?" he asked.

The killer did not bother to respond. It was, after all, pretty damn obvious what was about to go down.

Belatedly Greenslade realized the rifle was aimed at him. Rage and panic flashed across his face.

He tried to retreat back into the cabin where he no doubt had a gun. But he didn't move fast enough. The bullet took him in the chest.

A head shot would have been too easy because death would have been instantaneous. This way there would be time for the killer to watch the target bleed out; time for Greenslade to comprehend that this was all about revenge.

The death of Gordon Greenslade was front-page news in the *Loring Herald.* There was genuine shock — Greenslade had, after all, been the biggest mover and shaker in town — but not a lot of genuine mourning. Still, everyone made a point of displaying the appropriate degree of respect for the deceased, because Gordon Greenslade's death had not changed the economic and political reality. The Greenslade family still controlled the second-largest employer in Loring and, indirectly, Loring's largest employer, the college. It existed solely because of the Greenslade endowment.

The police did their job and conducted an investigation. But in the end they came to the conclusion that the killer had anticipated: Gordon Greenslade had been killed in an accident. The shooter had been hunting out of season and probably hadn't even been aware that his wild shot had killed a man. In any event, it was unlikely that the person who had pulled the trigger would ever be found.

Everyone who lived in the area knew that the mountains were inherently dangerous. In the fall, heavy rains flooded the rivers to dangerous levels, sweeping away those who were unlucky enough to get caught in the rushing waters. Landslides blocked roads. Strong winds felled trees that could crush vehicles. In the winter, backcountry avalanches invariably took the lives of a few skiers and snowboarders every year. In the summer, it was inevitable that a hiker or two or three would fall into a crevasse or simply go missing forever.

And hunting accidents happened all the time in the mountains.

CHAPTER 2

" '. . . And then I killed him.' "

Ethel Deeping looked up from the page she had been reading from her memoir. She smiled proudly, clearly anticipating a round of applause from the audience.

For a few seconds the other members of the Write Your Life memoir writing group were shocked into a state of speechlessness.

Then the muttered complaints began rolling across the room in a wave that crested to full-blown outrage.

"You can't put that in your memoir," Hazel Williams announced from the back of the room. She banged her cane on the floor for emphasis. "We're supposed to be writing our life stories, not fiction. The fiction class meets on Wednesday evenings."

"Hazel's right," Bob Perkins grumbled. "It's a memoir. There are rules. You want to write mysteries, go join the fiction writers' group."

Ethel narrowed her eyes. "It's my life story. I can tell it any way I want."

Charlotte Sawyer, seated at the front of the small classroom, raised her hand, signaling for silence. The grumbling subsided. Everyone looked at her.

She was far and away the youngest person in the room. The Thursday afternoon meeting of the Write Your Life group was a popular program at the Rainy Creek Gardens Retirement Village. It had been one of the first workshops she had introduced upon accepting the position of director of social and educational activities. That had been a year before, when, after bouncing from one boring, dead-end job to another in Portland, Oregon, she had taken her stepsister's advice and moved to Seattle. Her first interview had been at Rainy Creek Gardens. She had landed the job immediately. Five minutes into her new career she had concluded that she had found her place in the world.

Overseeing the busy schedule of workshops, events and programs at Rainy Creek Gardens lacked the glamour and sophistication that her stepsister, Jocelyn, enjoyed as a fund-raiser for a wealthy entrepreneur's foundation. Jocelyn frequently traveled to exotic locales and mingled with the rich and famous — all in the name of convincing them to donate to the foundation. Nevertheless, Charlotte had no desire to trade places. She found her job far more satisfying than anything else she had tried to date.

The only real drawback — and admittedly it was a big one — was having to walk past the memorial board in the elevator lobby on her way to and from her office. Rarely did a week pass without a new name being posted. Because of her position on the staff, she was usually acquainted with the deceased. She often knew some of their family members, as well.

She had attended more memorial services in her year at Rainy Creek Gardens than most people did in a lifetime. And somewhere along the way her attitude toward the inevitability of death had begun to change.

Lately it had dawned on her that until she had come to Rainy Creek Gardens, she had spent her life living mostly in the future. As a child, that had meant looking forward to holidays and birthdays and, most of all, becoming a grown-up. Upon achieving adulthood she had discovered that being a grown-up wasn't nearly as satisfying as she had anticipated. What was more, the future was uncomfortably unpredictable.

At Rainy Creek Gardens she had finally

begun to realize that, no matter your age, when you looked back it always seemed that your life had passed in the blink of an eye. The past could not be changed and the future was unknowable. The residents of Rainy Creek Gardens were teaching her that the real trick to a good life was to learn to live in the present.

She smiled reassuringly at Ethel Deeping and the other people in the room.

"Ethel makes an excellent point," she said. "She is allowed to write her life story any way she wants. And it's certainly true that there have been a number of very successful memoirists who have, to put it mildly, embellished their memoirs."

"Makes 'em more interesting," Ethel said.

"But it's wrong," Ted Hagstrom thundered.

Ted was a retired engineer. He tended to be a stickler for the rules.

There was another round of disgruntled murmuring. Once again Charlotte signaled for silence.

"Before we critique Ethel's essay, I think we should ask her why she chose her rather unexpected ending for the chapter on her marriage," she said. "Ethel?"

Ethel beamed. "It's more exciting that way."

"Well, yes," Charlotte agreed. "But are you certain that it fits with the rest of what you have told us about Mr. Deeping? You've made it clear that your husband was an excellent provider and well respected in the community. You said he was a churchgoing man. You mentioned his military service and you said that everyone liked him."

"Good golfer, too," Ethel said. "Seven handicap."

"Right." Charlotte cleared her throat.

"Looked good in his uniform," Ethel said. She winked. "Never could resist a man in uniform. That's how I met him, you know. We were both in the military. I was a nurse. Left to get married and raise the kids."

"Yes, you mentioned that. You also made a point of saying that after his death you struggled as a widow with two young children to raise."

"Yep."

"Is it possible that, as much as you loved your husband, deep down you perhaps felt some resentment toward him because he left you and the children alone?" Charlotte suggested gently.

"Well, it certainly wasn't easy making ends meet after he was gone," Ethel allowed. "But we managed." She beamed. "My son is a doctor, you know. My daughter is a lawyer."

"You already told us twenty or thirty times that your kids are all successful," Hazel Williams muttered, not bothering to conceal her resentment.

Hazel Williams had raised three children, but she had included only two of them in her memoir — a daughter who was a teacher and a son who worked in construction. Although she had dutifully recorded the birth of a second son in the family tree chapter, there had been no further mention of him. Every family had a few secrets, Charlotte thought. It was an unwritten rule in the class that the members of the group were entitled to their secrets. No one had a right to pry into another person's past.

"I'm just telling you that we did all right after Harold was gone," Ethel said.

"That's obvious," Charlotte put in quickly, hoping to change the topic. "It was a tremendous accomplishment, raising two children on your own and working full-time. You have every right to be proud."

Stan Barlow snorted. "Why is it that when a woman raises kids by herself, everyone thinks it's some kind of big deal? But if a man raises a family without a wife, he doesn't get any credit."

Mildred Hamilton, seated at the desk in

front of Stan, turned in her chair. "I don't know any men who raised a bunch of kids on their own. All the men I know who lost their wives or got divorced were married again within six months. Take yourself, for instance."

Stan reddened. He had recorded three marriages.

"I'm just asking a reasonable question," he said.

"I think we're getting off topic here," Charlotte said. She rose to her feet and made a show of looking at the large clock on the wall. All the clocks at Rainy Creek Gardens had big, easy-to-read numerals. "I see our time is up and it's almost happy hour in the Fireside Lounge. The assignment for next week is to work on the section of the booklet titled 'My First Job.' "

Most of the memoirists pushed themselves upright, collected their canes and walkers and filed out of the classroom at a brisk pace. Happy hour was another popular activity that Charlotte had implemented. Management had voiced some alarm at the start, but Charlotte had pointed out that many of the residents were already in the habit of enjoying a predinner glass of wine or a martini in the privacy of their own apartments. She had convinced her boss that an organized happy hour was a better alternative. It not only enhanced socializing in a segment of society that was at high risk for loneliness, it was safer than drinking alone.

The reaction to the introduction of happy hour had been so enthusiastic that Charlotte was fairly certain the residents would revolt if it were ever terminated. But it was highly unlikely that the event would be removed from the schedule of activities because there had been an unexpected upside. It turned out that featuring a daily happy hour had proven to be a highly successful marketing tool. The business of selling the retirement community lifestyle to seniors was a highly competitive industry.

Ethel waited until the others had left. Then she levered herself up out of her chair, gripped her walker and fixed Charlotte with a determined expression.

"I still say killing off Harold makes for a better ending," she said. "More dramatic. Sort of like you getting left at the altar a couple of months ago."

Charlotte tried not to wince.

"It's dramatic, all right," she said. "But keep in mind that you are writing this for your children and your grandchildren and your great-grandchildren. This memoir will become a permanent family legacy that will probably be handed down for generations. It will be uploaded online. If your descendants question the reality of some parts of your story, they might decide that you made up other elements, as well. It could call into question the authenticity of your version of your family's history."

"Huh." Ethel squinted a little. "Hadn't thought about that angle."

"I suggest you do consider it," Charlotte said. "Writing a memoir entails certain responsibilities."

"Good point." Ethel nodded. "Okay, I'll think about it. Now, I've got to go change for happy hour."

Charlotte smiled. "Enjoy it."

"Always do." Ethel paused at the door and wrenched the walker around so that she once again faced Charlotte. "You got lucky, you know."

"Lucky?"

"Just think how you'd be feeling now if you'd married the bastard."

"As a matter of fact, I have given the issue considerable thought and you're absolutely right, Ethel. I had a very narrow escape, didn't I?"

"Yep. Remember that when it comes time to write your own memoirs."

Charlotte smiled. "I will."

Ethel maneuvered her walker through the doorway and disappeared.

Charlotte listened to the soles of Ethel's sturdy shoes clumping down the hallway. Ethel was not the first person at Rainy Creek Gardens to point out that she had dodged a bullet. Everyone in the community — staff and residents — knew about the fiasco with Brian Conroy because they had all been invited to the reception.

Charlotte had booked the Fireside Lounge for the festivities. Jocelyn had been shocked by the choice. She had even offered to pay for a more elegant setting as a wedding gift. With her charitable foundation connections, she had access to any number of high-end venues. But Charlotte had been adamant. She had pointed out that she was new to Seattle, so most of her friends and acquaintances were connected to Rainy Creek Gardens. It had made sense to hold the event there. Besides, as she had told Jocelyn, most of the residents would have had a difficult time getting to an off-site location. Very few of them still drove.

The upcoming wedding reception had been the talk of the community for weeks. The sudden cancellation five days before the nuptials had stunned everyone. There was no getting around the fact that it had been the most dramatic thing that had happened at Rainy Creek Gardens since the last earthquake drill, when several residents had mistakenly believed it was the real thing.

She had, indeed, been lucky, Charlotte reminded herself. But the knowledge that she had come within a hairsbreadth of marrying Brian Conroy — aka Mr. Perfect according not only to her own criteria, but to Jocelyn's, as well — sent chills down her spine.

When she went through her list of desirable traits in a husband, it seemed as if she could put a check mark in each box. Brian was a friendly, outgoing, well-mannered man. He had appeared to be thoughtful and kind. He was intelligent and interesting and he had a good job teaching social sciences at a local college. He was easy to talk to and the two of them had enjoyed many of the same things, including long walks, the symphony, blah, blah, blah.

Mr. Perfect. Right. What could possibly be wrong with this picture? Oh, yeah. Nobody was perfect.

But as devastating as the canceled wedding had been — dealing with the sympathy from others had been the hardest part — she knew she could not blame Brian, at least not entirely. She knew exactly why he had gotten cold feet at the last minute. Her therapist had made it clear that she had to accept a large portion of the responsibility. She had tried to play it safe, as usual. The bottom line was that at some point Brian had awakened to the realization that she was boring.

You need to push yourself out of your comfort zone, the therapist had said. *You need to try new things, open yourself to new experiences.*

She'd given it a whirl with a class in kayaking — and quickly discovered that she did not like getting wet, especially when the water was cold. She'd also experimented with skiing lessons, only to find out that she really hated falling down in snow. As a last resort she had bought a bicycle, determined to bike to work for the sake of the environment. That plan had been shelved when she had nearly been crushed under the wheels of a delivery truck.

In the end she had settled for lessons in meditation. The therapist had not been impressed.

The truth was, now that the trauma of the canceled wedding was fading, Charlotte was aware that what she felt was a surprising sense of relief. Ethel was right. She'd had a very close call. But that didn't mean that she wasn't still pissed at Brian. A woman had her pride.

She gathered up her papers and notebook and headed for the door. When she passed the Fireside Lounge she was pleased to see a large crowd. Music from a bygone decade played in the background. Voices were raised in conversation.

She wished that she was looking forward to an after-work drink with someone. Usually she would have given Jocelyn a call and arranged to meet her at one of the popular downtown bars or restaurants. But Jocelyn was out of town for the month.

She paused at the memorial board to look at the faces of the recently deceased. The pictures on the board almost always featured the individual in the prime of his or her life. The men were often dressed in dashing military uniforms or well-tailored business suits and ties. The women were invariably garbed in the style of another era. Some were in wedding gowns, their eyes radiant with the anticipation of a blissful future.

Charlotte was pretty sure that none of them had expected to end up at the Rainy Creek Gardens Retirement Village. But the truth was that those on the memorial board had survived whatever life had thrown at them — tragedy, trauma, disappointment and heartbreak — and lived to tell their tales at Rainy Creek.

In the grand scheme of things, Charlotte thought, getting left at the altar was nothing more than a dramatic story that, with luck, she would be telling her friends and neighbors and, perhaps, her own grandchildren decades from now.

She went into her office, made a few notes about the next memoir writing session and then went over her schedule.

Sarah Jameson appeared in the doorway. She was in her late fifties, a trim, attractive woman who favored skirted business suits and black pumps. She lounged in the doorway, arms folded, and smiled.

"I hear there was a bit of a dustup in the Write Your Life group today," she said. "Something about Ethel Deeping wanting to end the chapter on her marriage by saying that she killed her husband decades ago."

"Word travels fast," Charlotte said.

"Blame happy hour."

"There appears to be some confusion in the class about the fine line between writing memoirs and writing fiction," Charlotte said. "Ethel says her husband was a successful, well-respected man who gave back to the community, but I think she carries some residual anger toward him. He died when their kids were young and Ethel was left to raise them on her own. I think she's using a fictional ending as a way of taking revenge. Also, she says it's more dramatic."

Sarah chuckled. "Well, she's got a point. Who are we to stop her from writing whatever she wants to write? Besides, you did say that memoirs are a kind of therapy."

"True." Charlotte glanced out the window. It was still raining. She retrieved her boots from under her desk and slipped off her heels. "The problem is that the rest of the class is upset with Ethel's decision to embellish her life story."

"I doubt if Ethel is the only one who is guilty of that."

"Well, a pattern is emerging." Charlotte tugged on the boots. "Most of the class prefers to write about the good stuff that happened to them and ignore the bad."

"Where's the harm in that?"

"I agree." Charlotte got to her feet and took her anorak down off the coatrack. "There is definitely something to be said for denial. I've learned that much from working here at the village. Some of the happiest residents are those who seem to have done an excellent job of rewriting their own pasts."

She took her handbag out of the bottom drawer of her desk and slung the strap over one shoulder.

"Any word from Jocelyn?" Sarah asked.

"No. Incredibly enough, I think she must be enjoying herself at that convent retreat. I never thought she'd make it through the first week, to be honest. Jocelyn is practically hardwired into the Internet. I bet her ten bucks she wouldn't be able to go a full month without checking her e-mail."

"Well, she's only been gone for a week. You might win that bet yet. Got plans for this evening?"

"Not really. I'm going to stop by Jocelyn's condo to water her plants and collect her snail mail on my way home today. That's probably going to be the highlight of my night. You?"

"No, but I'm looking forward to the weekend. My husband and I are going to drive over to the coast. There's another storm due in. I love the beach during storm season."

"Sounds great," Charlotte said. "See you tomorrow."

She made her way through the lobby, said her good-byes to the front desk staff and went out into the rain-drenched gloom of the fall afternoon. She paused in the wide, gracious entranceway and reran the conversation with Sarah in her head. She did not care for the ending.

I'm a single woman of a certain age and I've got zero plans for tonight and none for the weekend, she thought. That was ridiculous. No doubt about it, she had spent more than enough time brooding about the Brian Conroy disaster. She needed to get a life.

She pulled up the hood of her jacket — only tourists carried umbrellas in Seattle — and got ready to step out into the steady drizzle.

One of the many advantages of her job at Rainy Creek Gardens was that it was just a twenty-minute walk from her apartment. Actually, when she thought about it, everything she needed was within a twenty-minute walk of the apartment. Seattle had big-city lights, good shopping and all the other amenities of urban life, but it was still, in many ways, a small town. Brian Conroy and the rain aside, she was glad she had heeded Jocelyn's advice and made the move from Oregon.

An expensive-looking luxury car pulled into the small parking lot in front of the entrance. The driver's-side door opened and a man climbed out from behind the wheel.

He jogged toward the shelter of the covered entranceway. When he saw Charlotte, he smiled with just a polite hint of masculine appreciation.

"Really coming down," he observed. "But at least it's not too cold."

"True," she said.

"You look a little young to be a resident," he said. "Visiting a relative?"

"I work here."

"Yeah?" He glanced thoughtfully at the lobby entrance. "I was hoping maybe you had a family member here."

"Why?"

"Because I wanted to ask your opinion of the place. The family has appointed me to shop around for a retirement community for my grandmother. Since you work here, though, I guess your opinion would not exactly be unbiased, huh?"

"I work here because I like this community a lot," she said. "There's someone inside who can answer all your questions, but you really ought to bring your grandmother here to take a look for herself. Moving into a retirement community is a major lifestyle change. She needs to be involved in the decision."

Damn. She sounded way too earnest, even to her own ears. She could hear Jocelyn's

29

voice in her head.

That's right, Charlotte, a good-looking man flashes you a sexy smile and asks a simple question and you go straight into lecture mode. You've got to lighten up, woman.

The stranger's smile dimmed a couple of degrees.

"Right," he said. "The thing is, I'm just trying to get a feel for the options that are out there. Grandma has lived in the same house for fifty years. She's nervous about moving into a community full of strangers."

Charlotte felt herself on solid ground now. Forget trying to flirt with him, she thought. Just stick to business.

"Does your grandmother play bridge, by any chance?" she asked.

He seemed surprised by the question, but he recovered quickly.

"Are you kidding?" he said. "She plays killer bridge."

"Then she's golden," Charlotte said. "Trust me, as soon as the word gets out in the community that she plays, she'll have no problem making friends."

"Thanks, I'll let her know." He paused, as if trying to decide whether to engage in further conversation with her. "What do you think the in crowd will be playing when you and I are ready for a retirement community?"

"Video games, probably."

He chuckled and some of the warmth returned to his smile.

"You're right," he said. "Well, thanks for the info."

He went through the glass doors and disappeared into the lobby.

She went out into the rain and walked briskly along the sidewalk. She had managed to amuse him for a moment. That was the good news, she thought. The bad news was that she had not been trying to be funny. She had blurted out "video games" in answer to his question because it was the first thing that had popped into her head.

She hadn't exactly flirted with a stranger, but there had been a little whisper of the female-male vibe in the exchange and that realization boosted her spirits. Maybe whatever it was inside of her that had been crushed by the Brian Conroy fiasco wasn't dead after all. Maybe it had just been hibernating.

A little flicker of awareness prompted her to glance back over her shoulder. She didn't expect to see the man again. By now he would be at the front desk in the lobby asking for more information and perhaps a tour of the village.

She was surprised when she caught a glimpse of him on the other side of the glass doors. She could have sworn he was watching her.

The knowledge that he had apparently found her interesting enough to warrant a lingering glance should have given her another pleasant little rush of feminine satisfaction. But for some inexplicable reason, it didn't. Instead it sent a shiver of unease across the back of her neck.

Great. Now I'm getting paranoid.

Maybe the experience with Brian had affected her nerves, as well as her confidence in her own judgment.

That was not a cheerful thought.

She walked a little more quickly, very aware of the damp chill of the fading day. She suddenly wished she had been able to accompany Jocelyn to the secluded island convent. There was a certain appeal to the idea of going off the grid for a few weeks. But she had been on the job at Rainy Creek for only a year. There was no way she could have taken a whole month off.

She promised herself that when she got home she would use the meditation app that she had bought after completing the mindfulness class.

CHAPTER 3

Max Cutler stood in the middle of Louise Flint's living room and absorbed the sense of emptiness. It was always this way in the personal space that had once been inhabited by the dead — at least it was always this way for him.

Early on in his career as a profiler he had been told by colleagues that it was his imagination that conjured the sense of gloom. If he had not *known* that someone had died in that particular place, they said, he would not have experienced any particular vibe.

But he did know that Louise Flint had died in the condo in which he was standing and he did feel the emptiness. Of course, the steady rain and the unrelenting cloud cover didn't help matters, he thought. He had moved to Seattle six months before and he'd taken the notorious Seattle weather in stride. But today he was intensely aware of the atmosphere.

"The cops are convinced that she killed herself," Daniel Flint said. "But I don't believe that Louise OD'd, either deliberately or accidentally."

"You think she was murdered," Max said. He kept his tone neutral.

"Look around," Daniel said. He swept out his hand in an exasperated gesture. "It's obvious someone tore this place apart. Her computer and her phone are gone. I'm telling you that someone killed her and then stole her tech."

Daniel was a senior at a local college. Max had run a routine background check on him before taking the case. He had discovered that Daniel was working part-time at a restaurant and living the starving-student lifestyle. He had taken out far too many loans to pay his tuition and he was majoring in history, which meant he was going to be semi-unemployable when he finally graduated. That, in turn, meant he couldn't afford the services of a private investigator.

But two hours earlier Daniel had come through the doorway of Max's office looking sincere and determined; a young man on a mission.

Unfortunately, there was never any money in mission work.

I've really got to put up a sign. No Mission Work.

But it wasn't like he had any other clients beating down his door at the moment. He had finished the small insurance job the previous week with the usual unsatisfying result — the company had settled. The firm had paid out only a few thousand instead of the several hundred thousand that the lawyer had demanded, thanks to the information that Max had uncovered.

It had taken him less than fifteen minutes to discover that the dumbass threatening to sue the insurance company had helpfully posted photos of himself dancing half-naked at a party. Considering that he claimed to be wheelchair-bound with neck and spinal injuries, the company had held a very strong hand going into negotiations.

When confronted with the evidence, dumbass's lawyer had immediately lowered the number and the company had quickly accepted the new figure in the interest of making the problem go away. As was the case with most corporate and business clients, "Settling is cheaper than going to court" was the company motto. He couldn't argue with the financial logic.

But once in a while I need the mission work.

He surveyed the interior of the condo. It

wasn't a penthouse, but it was, neverthe-less, high-end real estate. Louise had been making enough money as a fund-raiser for a local charitable foundation to be able to afford a place in one of the new downtown glass-and-steel towers. The condo had undoubtedly cost a hell of a lot more than his little fixer-upper in one of the Seattle neighborhoods.

The interior of the unit was in shambles. It had been torn apart by someone who had been searching frantically for something. Max thought about that for a while.

The clothes in the closet all bore designer labels. Some of the jewelry looked valuable. According to Daniel, the car parked down-stairs in the garage was a luxury model.

"You're saying that whoever killed her took her tech but nothing else of value?" he asked eventually.

Admittedly it would have been difficult to smuggle a lot of clothes and jewelry out of the condo and it would have been risky to steal the car. But the thing that interested him the most was that the dead woman's Italian leather handbag was still sitting on the coffee table. Her wallet, complete with credit cards and a couple hundred bucks in cash, was still inside.

"The cops told me that the tech — laptops

and phones — is all that most thieves want these days," Daniel said. "That's the kind of stuff that moves fast on the streets. One of the officers said that most of the smash-and-grab guys are junkies looking to make enough for the next score."

"People like that are usually looking for drugs, as well," Max said.

He tried to say it without any inflection. Just an observation, not an accusation. But Daniel got mad anyway.

"I'm telling you, my cousin wasn't using," he said.

"Okay."

Daniel looked hesitant. "But there is one other fact that bothers me."

"What?"

"On the day she . . . died . . . she cashed in a bank CD. According to the receipt I found in her handbag, she withdrew ten thousand dollars."

"Huh. Check?"

"No." Daniel's jaw tightened. "Evidently she took the money in cash. I know that looks bad. Who needs ten grand in cash, right? People in the drug business, that's who."

"There are other reasons why someone would withdraw that kind of money in cash," Max said. "I assume you didn't find any of it?"

"No. The killer must have taken it."

"So he takes ten grand, but he doesn't bother with the cash in her wallet."

Daniel looked at the open handbag. "Maybe after finding the big money he simply ignored the little stuff. He would have been in a hurry."

"Maybe. Any theories about why she took so much money out of the bank that day?"

"No." Daniel shook his head. "I didn't tell the cops because I was afraid they would see it as more evidence of a drug connection. They would have assumed she was laundering cash for drug dealers."

"The police found an empty syringe next to the bed and a baggie filled with what they told you was probably some new designer street drug."

"Yes, but —"

"There were no signs of physical violence. Your cousin was not beaten or shot or stabbed. There was no indication that she'd had sex before she died. But ten thousand dollars and her laptop and phone are missing."

"Maybe she was set up," Daniel said quickly. "Maybe someone slipped something into her drink and then tried to make it look like an overdose."

There were no empty glasses sitting around, but Max decided not to mention that. It was possible, after all, that the killer could have taken time to wash a couple of glasses before leaving.

"What else did the cops say?" he asked.

Daniel's eyes narrowed a little. "They didn't actually say it, but it was pretty clear they think that Louise brought home the wrong guy. I think their theory is that she and her bad date did drugs and Louise OD'd. The bastard probably panicked. Instead of calling nine-one-one, he grabbed her tech, searched for any stashes of drugs she might have hidden, and then split. And that's the most charitable scenario because it doesn't include the missing ten grand."

"What's the other scenario?"

Daniel exhaled heavily. "It was suggested that Louise might have been working off the books as a high-end call girl. Drugs are often part of that lifestyle, they said. The conclusion would be the same — she OD'd and the client stole her tech and maybe her drugs, as well. Except that I know she wasn't doing drugs, she was not hooking and she wasn't laundering money for some dealer."

"Tell me about Louise and why you're so sure she wasn't into drugs and prostitution."

Daniel shoved his fingers through his hair. "She was my cousin, but I didn't see much of her until she was in her teens. She was raised back east. Her father died when she was just a little kid. Her mother married an asshole who molested Louise for a couple of years. When Louise's mother found out what was going on, she thought Louise was lying. But eventually she realized the truth. She divorced the creep and she and Louise moved out here to Washington. But Louise's mom told her that she shouldn't ever talk about the abuse."

"That advice usually backfires."

"Yeah. Louise was pretty messed up when she was younger, but none of the rest of us knew why at the time."

"Was she into drugs at some point in her past?" Max asked.

Daniel reddened angrily and looked as if he was going to deny it.

"For a while," he said finally. "In her late teens. She ran away from home a few times and finally just disappeared into the streets for months. I'm not saying she didn't hook or sell drugs to survive in those days. It was a bad time and I think everyone in the family just wrote her off as a lost cause. Looking back on it, I feel guilty because I didn't do more to help her."

40

"She was several years older than you, which means you were just a kid at the time," Max pointed out. "There wasn't anything you could have done."

"Maybe not," Daniel said. "But someone should have done something."

"Take it from me, you can't save someone who doesn't want to be saved."

"Yeah, Mom said that a few times, too."

"If what you're telling me is accurate, Louise did eventually get herself and her life together, right?"

"Yes, exactly," Daniel said. "She'd been doing great for quite a while — years. That's what I'm trying to tell you. She loved her work at the foundation. She got to travel and hang with celebrities."

Max decided not to mention that celebrities were notorious for going in and out of rehab because of drug issues.

"Anything else I should know?" he said instead.

"She volunteered several hours a week at a local women's shelter — because of her past, you see. She credited a shelter with saving her from the streets years ago. She felt very strongly about paying it forward. And she had good friends. Another sign of a stable person, right? She and a few of her pals formed an investment club. She was planning for her future. She wouldn't have put it all at risk by going back to drugs."

"Did she date? Was there a man in her life?"

For the first time, Daniel seemed uncertain. "I don't think so. I mean, Louise dated from time to time, but usually just when she needed an escort for one of her charity functions. To tell you the truth, I don't think she liked men. I know she didn't trust them — except for me. Please say you'll take this case, Mr. Cutler."

Max took another look around the condo, absorbing the gloom. Then he looked at the earnest young man who was waiting for a response.

"There are definitely some questions here," Max said. "I'm willing to see if I can find the answers."

Daniel looked as if a huge weight had been lifted off his shoulders.

"Thank you," he said. "I really appreciate this."

"One thing you should know before I start turning over rocks."

"What?"

"Sometimes, in situations like this, clients don't always like the answers I come up with. Are you sure you're okay with that?"

Some of Daniel's relief faded. "You mean

you might find out that Louise really had gone back to hooking and drugs?"

"All I'm saying is that sometimes people don't like the answers that I give them. Sometimes the dead take their secrets to the grave for a reason. I want you to be sure you can live with whatever I discover."

"Yes." Daniel shoved his hands into the pockets of his windbreaker. "What I can't live with is not knowing the truth."

"All right, I'll look into your cousin's death."

Daniel nodded once. "Thanks. About your bill. Louise left this condo and her car to me. I'm going to sell the condo. I'll pay you out of the proceeds."

Max decided not to point out that condos in which the former owners had been found deceased were sometimes very hard to market.

"All right," he said. "I need to be alone here in your cousin's place for a while. I want to take a look around. Make some notes. Take a few photos."

"No problem. I'll give you the keys to this place and the ones to her storage locker downstairs and the mailbox in the lobby. Stay as long as you want. I'll let the door staff know that you have my permission to come and go whenever you want."

"Probably best not to let them know I'm investigating Louise's death. That will make everyone in the building nervous and that, in turn, will make them uncooperative. Just tell the people at the front desk that I'm helping you settle Louise's estate."

"Right." Daniel nodded. "I can do that. And it's even true in a way."

"Whenever you're telling a lie it's good to go with as much of the truth as possible. Less chance of making a mistake that way."

"Makes sense."

"One more thing before you go," Max said. "I want to take a look at Louise's car."

"Sure. It's in the garage. I found the keys in her bag."

"Let's go take a look at the vehicle together."

"Okay." Daniel shot him a curious glance. "Mind telling me why you want me with you when you look at her car?"

"Condo owners and managers get very uneasy when they see strangers wandering around inside a garage. I'm not looking to get picked up for car prowling."

"Oh, yeah, I see what you mean," Daniel said.

He went toward the door, clearly energized now that someone was going to do something about his cousin's death. Max followed him out into the hall, pausing to lock the door.

A few minutes later they exited the elevator deep in the bowels of the garage. Daniel led the way to a dark blue sedan. Max used the remote to unlock the vehicle.

There was nothing of interest in the trunk. The glove compartment contained the usual assortment of vehicle paperwork, a small box of wipes and a spare pair of sunglasses. If you lived in Seattle, you could never own too many pairs of sunglasses, Max had discovered. When the sun did decide to emerge, it invariably caught you by surprise.

He sat quietly in the front seat for a moment, studying the odometer. "How long did Louise own this car?"

"It's fairly new," Daniel said. "She bought it earlier this year."

"Not a lot of mileage on it."

"One of the reasons she liked living downtown was that she didn't have to drive to work. The headquarters of the foundation isn't far from here."

Max cranked up the GPS and reviewed the last destination that had been programmed into the device.

"Who did Louise know in Loring, Washington?" he asked.

Daniel frowned at the readout. "I have no

idea. But she was a professional fund-raiser. I suppose she might have gone to Loring to talk to a potential donor."

"Whatever the reason, it looks like that was the last long drive she made in this car."

"Do you think it's important?"

"It's just a question. At this point that's all I've got. Questions."

CHAPTER 4

Charlotte unlocked the door of Jocelyn's condo and went through the ritual of deactivating the alarm system. Jocelyn was more than a little obsessed when it came to security. Not only had she installed a state-of-the-art system complete with discreetly concealed cameras in her own home, she had attempted to set up a similar arrangement in Charlotte's apartment.

Charlotte had agreed to the fancy locks and the alarm, but she had flatly refused to allow cameras to be installed. The thought of walking around her own apartment in her underwear knowing that there was a camera aimed in her direction was flat-out creepy. But, then, she was the one who had covered the built-in camera lens in her laptop with a Band-Aid.

We all have our little eccentricities, she thought.

She set the day's mail on the glass-topped

console and went through it quickly. As usual, there wasn't much that looked important — Jocelyn handled all of her bills and the majority of her other personal business online. The only item that didn't look like it was junk mail was a small padded envelope. It was postmarked Seattle, but there was no return address. Jocelyn had asked her to open any mail that looked like it might be important, so she put it on the hall table and reminded herself to check it before she left.

She dumped everything else into a paper sack and left it in front of the door to grab and drop into the recycle bin on her way out.

Next, she set about watering Jocelyn's plants. She was pleased to see that the large bamboo palm was thriving. The stately dracaena was also coming along nicely.

The plants were her idea. Shortly after moving to Seattle she had given the palm to Jocelyn, who had been distinctly ambivalent about accepting the gift. But Charlotte had insisted because it was clear to her that something was needed to soften the sleek, modern interiors of the condo.

Jocelyn's home was a sharp reflection of Jocelyn herself — cool and glamorous in the way of a classic black-and-white film.

The only touches of real color were the cobalt blue throw pillows and the dramatic cobalt blue wall behind the white leather sofa.

Jocelyn's decision to book a monthlong stay at the Caribbean island convent had been startling, to say the least. For one thing, the closest she had ever come to the concept of a retreat was the occasional long weekend at an exclusive spa. But she had been resolute about leaving most of her expensive vacation wardrobe as well as her tech behind. She had departed Seattle with only a backpack. True, the backpack carried a designer label; but, still, it was just a backpack. Jocelyn never traveled light.

Finished tending to the greenery, Charlotte ran some water in the sinks and flushed the toilets to keep things fresh and then she headed for the door, pausing in the hall to pick up the padded envelope.

She ripped it open. There was a smaller envelope inside. She could feel the hard shapes of a set of keys — three of them.

There was also a handwritten note on the back of the little envelope that contained the keys.

I'm probably just being paranoid here, but you know what they say — even paranoids have enemies — so I'm taking some precautions. In case it turns out that I've got a reason to be worried, I wanted to let you know that my copy of the file is in my condo storage locker. As we agreed, I didn't put any of the information online. Looking forward to buying you a drink to celebrate your return from the tech-free wilderness. Louise.

There was only one Louise in Jocelyn's small circle of female acquaintances. Louise Flint worked in the fund-raising office at the foundation where Jocelyn was employed. Louise was well aware that Jocelyn was out of town for an extended period of time. Why would she send Jocelyn a set of keys and a very odd note? It made no sense.

Charlotte glanced at the time. It was after five thirty, but there was a chance Louise might still be at her desk.

She called the familiar number and was startled when the receptionist answered.

"Elizabeth?" she said. "This is Charlotte Sawyer. You're working late this evening."

"Oh, hello, Charlotte."

Elizabeth sounded distracted.

"I'm calling to speak to Louise. Is she available?"

There was a long, alarming pause.

"You haven't heard the news, then," Elizabeth said.

"What news? What are you talking about?"

"I'm so sorry to be the one to tell you. Louise is . . . no longer with us."

"You mean she quit?"

"No, Charlotte, I'm afraid she died."

Charlotte clutched the phone. "What? When? How?"

"I'm not sure exactly when it happened. I understand her housekeeper found the body when she let herself in to do the weekly cleaning."

"This is awful. I can't believe it. What happened?"

"I don't know all the details, but there's a rumor going around that Louise may have . . . taken her own life."

"I'm stunned."

"We all are. The reason I'm working late is that I'm taking over some of Louise's work, at least until Jocelyn gets back. With both of them gone, we're a little overwhelmed, to put it mildly."

"I don't know what to say."

"There isn't much that can be said at times like this," Elizabeth said gently. "I know Jocelyn will be shocked when she finds out."

"Yes," Charlotte said.

51

Elizabeth lowered her voice. "There is another rumor circulating as well, but I don't believe it."

"What is it?" Charlotte asked.

"Someone said that Louise had a history of using drugs. Evidently the police suggested that she might have gone back to them."

"I'm sure that's not true. Good-bye, Elizabeth."

"Has Jocelyn called, by any chance?"

"No. She's off the grid at the retreat, remember?"

"Yes, but it's hard to imagine her being completely incommunicado."

"I know, but she was determined to do it."

"She won't have any way of knowing what happened to Louise until she leaves that island convent," Elizabeth said.

"No."

"She'll be absolutely devastated. She and Louise were so close."

"Yes, they were."

Charlotte ended the call. For a moment she stood in the center of the elegant room trying to decide what to do next.

Jocelyn had a small circle of female friends. They were all involved in an investment club. At one time or another, Charlotte had met the four other women in the group, but she did not know any of them well. Jocelyn had not encouraged a closer acquaintance nor had she invited Charlotte to put some of her own money into the club's investments. *You don't make enough to take the risk,* she had said on more than one occasion.

As stepsisters went, Jocelyn was great. But, like everyone else in the family, she was convinced that Charlotte was naïve, overly trusting and far too quick to assume that people would not actually lie to her — at least not to her face. The Brian Conroy fiasco had merely reinforced those opinions.

And, really, they had a point, she thought. She should have seen the telltale signs of impending disaster long before Brian dropped the bombshell. Instead she had made excuses for the small, subtle changes in his behavior. She had told herself that it was natural for the groom to get nervous before the wedding.

She looked at the packet of keys and tried to decide what to do next. After a moment she went to Jocelyn's desk and rummaged around in the files. It didn't take long to come up with a phone number for one of the four other women in the club. Emily Kelly worked in the human resources department of a local tech firm.

She keyed in the number, unaware that she was holding her breath until Emily answered.

"Who is this?" Emily asked.

Her voice was brittle with tension.

"It's Charlotte, Charlotte Sawyer. Jocelyn's stepsister. We've met a few times."

"Of course." Relief infused Emily's response. "Sorry, Charlotte. It's been a tough day."

"I'm calling because I just found out that something terrible happened to Louise."

"She's dead." Emily sounded shaken.

"Jocelyn will be devastated."

"We all are," Emily said.

"An accident?"

There was another long pause. When Emily spoke again, she lowered her voice.

"I heard she OD'd."

"The receptionist at the foundation said the same thing, but I find it very hard to believe."

"I know," Emily said. "Louise was always so careful about drugs because of her own history with them and also because she saw so many drug-related problems at the shelter where she volunteered."

"How did you find out about her death?" Charlotte asked.

"I got a call from Daniel Flint, Louise's cousin. He said he had a list of some of Louise's closest friends. He wanted to let us know what had happened."

"I remember Jocelyn mentioning that Louise had a cousin here in Seattle and that she was very fond of him. I think he's attending college somewhere in the area."

"Yes, it's just so tragic. Louise overcame so much — the abuse, the drugs, the streets — and now this."

"It's just awful," Charlotte said quietly.

There was another slight pause on the other end of the connection.

"Was there a particular reason why you were trying to get in touch with Louise?" Emily asked.

Charlotte looked at the packet containing the set of keys and thought about the urgent note inside. *In case it turns out that I've got a reason to be worried, I wanted to let you know that my copy of the file is in my condo storage locker.*

"I guess it doesn't matter now," she said.

"No, I suppose not."

"It's going to be a terrible shock for Jocelyn."

"Yes, it will." Emily hesitated. "Have you heard *anything* from her?"

"No. She's still at that island retreat."

"It's just so hard to imagine Jocelyn going totally off the grid like this."

"You know how she is. Once she makes up her mind to do something, nothing gets in the way."

"So true."

Charlotte ended the connection and slipped the phone back into her bag. She reread the note that had come with the keys.

"Crap," she whispered.

What would Jocelyn do if she were standing here with the packet of keys in front of her? she wondered. But she knew the answer to that question. She and Jocelyn were opposites in almost every way. That, of course, made it very easy to predict exactly how Jocelyn would react in any given situation.

Jocelyn would go straight to Louise's condo and try to find the file that had obviously been important to her.

But she wasn't Jocelyn. She was careful, cautious, risk-averse Charlotte. She drove the speed limit and followed the rules — most of them, at any rate. And she had no right to the file or anything else that belonged to Louise.

The bottom line, however, was that Louise had entrusted the file to Jocelyn and Jocelyn was not around to collect it.

It was ridiculous, but she could have

sworn she heard a clock ticking in some other dimension.

Maybe she watched too many crime dramas on television.

CHAPTER 5

The last light of the fall afternoon was gone and night had descended by the time Charlotte arrived at the lobby entrance of Louise's condo tower. The thought of walking home alone in the dark sent a chill through her. For some obscure reason, she suddenly remembered how that attractive man had watched her through the glass doors of the lobby at Rainy Creek Gardens.

She didn't like to think of herself as timid; just cautious and careful. Nevertheless, even though it was early in the evening and there were still a fair number of people on the downtown sidewalks, she promised herself that she would call a cab when she left Louise's building.

She looked through the lobby windows. There was no one sitting at the reception desk. Evidently the concierge was no longer on duty.

She had Louise's keys but she wasn't a

relative or even a close friend. She didn't feel right letting herself into the dead woman's personal space. It occurred to her that a member of the family might be in the condo. Unable to come up with a better idea, she used the entry system to call Louise's suite.

And nearly fainted from shock when a man answered.

"Louise Flint's condo," he said.

The voice was deep, masculine and anchored with a cool, rock-solid sense of control and command. It was not the voice of a college-aged young man.

Her pulse raced. Something was wrong. She could not think of any legitimate reason why a man would be in Louise's condo.

"Who is this?" she asked.

"Max Cutler. And you are?"

"A friend of Louise's. Or, rather, my stepsister is a friend of Louise's, but Jocelyn is out of town and I just heard what happened."

She broke off abruptly because the conversation was obviously not going well. It occurred to her that it might not be a good idea to mention the keys.

"I think we should talk," Max said.

"Why?" she asked.

"Because I'm a private investigator."

"A private investigator? What is going on?"

"Daniel Flint has asked me to look into Louise's death, and you're the first person to come around to her condo while I've been here. I'd like to ask you a few questions."

"Hang on, why has Daniel Flint asked you to get involved?"

"He has questions about the cause of death."

"Why aren't the police asking those questions?"

"They seem to be satisfied with the answers they found. Daniel Flint is not."

And neither am I, Charlotte thought.

She considered her options.

"All right," she said. "But I'm not going upstairs to talk to you. I'll meet you in the lobby."

"I'll be right down."

"I'll expect some serious identification."

"Understood."

CHAPTER 6

He walked out of the elevator a couple of minutes later, holding a leather wallet open in one hand. She could see something that looked like an official license behind a sheet of plastic.

"Max Cutler," he said.

She studied the license closely. She had never actually seen a private investigator's license in person, but the document appeared authentic. The photo certainly resembled the man standing in front of her, except that the picture was a little less intimidating than the reality.

Max Cutler looked as if he should have been wearing a law enforcement or military uniform. There was something solid and unyielding about him. Instead he was dressed in khakis, a plain white shirt unfastened at the collar and a slouchy jacket.

His dark hair was cut short with military-style precision. The style suited the rock-hard planes and angles of his face. It was impossible to read his gold-and-brown eyes.

Not the handsomest man in Seattle — not by a long stretch, she thought. But probably the one most likely to survive if he went into the gladiators' ring to confront the best-looking guy.

There was something cool and reserved about him. It was as if he deliberately kept an invisible barrier between himself and the world. She knew intuitively that this was a man who was not comfortable with the strong emotions of others. He would almost certainly fight to suppress his own passions. Definitely the no-drama type, she concluded.

She reminded herself that she was there to represent Jocelyn. It wasn't hard to decide how her stepsister would have handled the situation. Assertively.

"Licenses can be faked," she said.

"Right." He nodded, once, smiling just a little. "I don't have any particular reason to trust you, either."

"I knew Louise. My stepsister is — was — one of her best friends. Possibly her closest friend."

"Where is your stepsister?" Max asked.

The question sounded a little too casual.

"That's none of your business," she said,

going for cool and determined. "At least, not until I know more about you."

"I told you, I'm working for Daniel Flint, the cousin of the deceased." Max took a phone out of his pocket and keyed in a number. "I'll let you confirm that with him."

He spoke briefly into the phone and then handed it to Charlotte. Reluctantly she took it from him.

"Hello?" she said uneasily. "This is Charlotte Sawyer."

"You're Jocelyn's sister, right?"

"Stepsister, yes."

"I met Jocelyn once or twice, briefly. I know that she and Louise were very close. I'm Daniel Flint, by the way, and that guy who just handed you the phone is telling you the truth. He's working for me."

"I'm so sorry about Louise," Charlotte said. "I didn't know her well, but I liked her and I know that Jocelyn is going to miss her terribly. As you said, they were close. I don't intend to get in Mr. Cutler's way and I certainly don't want to intrude on your privacy. But the thing is, I've got some keys that belonged to Louise. What do you want me to do with them?"

"Keys to her condo?"

"And her storage locker."

Charlotte was aware that Max was watching her very intently with his sniper's eyes.

"I don't need another set," Daniel said. "You can give them to Mr. Cutler."

"There's a note with the keys," Charlotte added. She turned and walked a few steps away from Max and lowered her voice. "Something about a file that Louise wanted Jocelyn to have."

"What kind of file?"

"I've got no idea."

"Huh." Daniel thought about that for a moment. "Well, if Louise wanted Jocelyn to have it, that's fine with me. But make sure that Max Cutler has a chance to look at it first, okay?"

"All right." She glanced back over her shoulder and saw that Max was still watching her. "Mr. Cutler tells me you think Louise's death was suspicious. Do you believe she was murdered?"

"I'm sure of it," Daniel said. His voice was grim and resolute.

She cleared her throat. "Uh, the police — ?"

"They don't see it that way. I overheard a detective say, 'Once a junkie, always a junkie.' "

"Louise was not on drugs," Charlotte said. She did not realize how fierce she sounded until she saw Max's eyes narrow ever so

64

slightly. She immediately tried to steady her voice. "Jocelyn would have known if that was the case. She would have done something — maybe staged an intervention."

"I'm glad we agree that Louise was not using," Daniel said. "Talk to Cutler. Please. Maybe you know something that will help him prove that my cousin did not OD either accidentally or on purpose. And she wasn't hooking, either."

Charlotte was outraged. This time she made no attempt to moderate her tone. "The authorities implied that she was a prostitute, as well?"

"Yes."

"Obviously they didn't know much about Louise."

"No. Listen, I've got to go. My boss is yelling at me. Please, give Cutler any information you can."

"All right, Daniel. And — I am just so sorry."

"Thanks. So am I."

Charlotte ended the connection. She turned slowly and walked back to stand directly in front of Max. She held out the phone. He took it and dropped it into the pocket of his jacket.

"Satisfied?" he asked.

"I agree with Daniel. I can't believe that

Louise was on drugs and she certainly was not working as a prostitute. That's just not possible."

"How can you be so sure about the drugs or the prostitution?"

She moved one hand in an impatient, dismissing gesture. "I don't know how to prove it to you. But I'm quite sure my sister, Jocelyn, would have known if Louise was using or if she had become a call girl. Jocelyn would have been deeply concerned. She would have taken some sort of action."

"Probably not much she could have done about either the drugs or the prostitution."

"You don't know Jocelyn. She's a very determined person."

"I'll take your word for it for now."

"Gosh, thanks."

Max did not acknowledge the sarcasm. "According to my client, Louise wasn't having any money problems."

"No. Jocelyn would have stepped in to help her if that had been the case."

Max gave her a speculative look. "This seems to be all about Jocelyn's relationship with Louise. But you're the one who is here, not your stepsister."

"Jocelyn is on a monthlong retreat at a convent on a Caribbean island. She left her phone and computer behind. I have no way to reach her to give her the news."

"She didn't take any tech with her?"

Charlotte shook her head. "They call it a tech-free retreat for a reason."

"Interesting."

That simple comment stopped her cold.

"Why?" she asked.

"Louise's phone and laptop have gone missing. Both apparently disappeared the night she died."

"Stolen?"

"That's the prevailing theory," Max said.

Understanding dawned. "They were taken by the person who killed her?"

"Like I said, it's the prevailing theory."

"Whose prevailing theory?"

"My client's."

"What does that have to do with my sister's retreat?"

"I have no idea," Max said. "But here's what I've got so far: one woman dead — her tech stolen and ten grand missing — and the woman who may have been her best friend has gone off the grid."

Charlotte tightened her grip on the strap of her bag. "There is no connection. There can't be a connection."

"Then we're stuck with an amazing co-incidence."

Charlotte stared at him, unable to think

of a reasonable argument to counter his statement.

"What about the ten grand?" she finally asked.

"Louise Flint took it out of her account in cash on the morning of her death."

"Cash? Ten thousand dollars in *cash*?"

"You can see why I've got a few questions," Max said. "Why don't we take a look at that file you mentioned to my client?"

She thought about that for approximately three seconds and then decided there was no other obvious course of action except to hand him the keys and walk away from the problem. But she could not do that because Max Cutler was hinting that the problem might involve Jocelyn, who was not there to defend herself.

"All right," she said finally. "But keep in mind that in her note, Louise made it clear that she wanted Jocelyn to take charge of that file."

"Sure," Max said. "But your stepsister isn't here to do that, is she?"

She angled her chin. "That leaves me."

"You might want to see what's in that file before you stake your claim."

He had a point, she thought.

"Crap." She took the packet of keys out of her purse. "Let's go."

"Where are we going?"

"Louise's storage locker. I assume you know where it is?"

"Yes," Max said. "I know where it is. In fact, I was getting ready to take a look at it when you called."

CHAPTER 7

"Looks like whoever searched her condo also came down here to the locker," Max said. "He didn't take time to relock the padlock."

He opened the wooden door and did a quick inventory. The small space was filled with the kind of stuff that always seemed to end up in storage lockers. There was an outdoor table and a couple of folding chairs that had probably graced the small condo deck during the summer. One large cardboard box had been ripped open, revealing an assortment of holiday decorations. A bicycle hung on the wall. There was a neatly rolled-up sleeping bag, a tent, a camp stove and some ski gear.

There was also an assortment of suitcases.

"There's no way to tell if he found what he was looking for, is there?" Charlotte asked.

The quiet sadness in her voice made Max

take a closer look at her. He hoped she wasn't going to cry. He was not good with crying women.

"You okay?" he asked.

"Yes." She took a tissue out of the pocket of her jacket and dabbed at her eyes. "Well, as okay as I can be under the circumstances. The thing is, Louise was Jocelyn's best friend. It's just so depressing to think that she won't be around to use the things she stored here. Jocelyn is going to be devastated when she finds out what happened."

Damn. She was crying. He decided the best thing to do was to pretend he hadn't noticed.

"Your sister and Flint were that close?" he asked.

Charlotte sniffed a little, but when she spoke her voice was steadier.

"Yes," she said.

She had herself back under control, he thought. He breathed a small sigh of relief.

"Looks like he opened the cardboard boxes and probably the suitcases, too," he said. "But I don't think he found what he was looking for."

"How can you tell?"

"Just something about the recklessness of the search process," he said.

He had never been able to explain how he

worked. He looked for indications in patterns, and something about the hasty manner in which this person had gone through the locker hinted at rage and frustration.

He pulled out the suitcases and paused to examine the surroundings. The storage lockers occupied an entire floor of the building. They were arranged in such a manner that they effectively created row upon row of narrow floor-to-ceiling canyons with a lot of dead ends. At the moment he and Charlotte were the only people in the vicinity, but that situation was subject to change. A resident or some other individual could walk in at any time.

He told himself that he wanted to avoid unnecessary explanations to strangers, but that wasn't the whole truth. The reality was that he was deeply uncomfortable in confined spaces — especially spaces with limited exits. He could feel the old memories — and the old nightmares — stirring.

He needed to concentrate on the job at hand. He could not do that properly as long as some part of him was waiting for the monster to jump out from one of the storage locker doors.

He examined each of the suitcases in turn. All but one were empty. The small carry-on, however, contained a road map and three legal-sized envelopes.

"No drugs and no cash," he said. "But there are a few items inside." He closed the bag and picked it up. "We'll take a closer look upstairs in her condo."

For a beat or two he thought Charlotte was going to question the decision. She looked at him, her lips partly open, eyes widening. He knew she was intensely curious about the contents of the suitcase. But whatever she saw in his expression must have convinced her that there was no point arguing about such a small thing.

"Okay," she said.

She wasn't asking any questions, he thought. That was a good thing.

He let her lead the way back through the maze of lockers. She opened the door of the storage room. He followed her into the elevator and pressed the button for the tenth floor.

Neither of them spoke during the short ride, but he was very aware of her presence. She stood, tense and silent, and watched the floor numbers go past as though they conveyed a secret code. He wondered if she had any idea of what was inside the suitcase. All he could be sure of was that she was worried about what they might find. That was interesting.

No, he decided, *Charlotte* was interesting.

For a few seconds he tried to convince himself that his curiosity about her was of a professional nature. After all, he was investigating a possible murder and Charlotte was one of the first people to show up at the scene.

In his previous career he'd learned that there was some truth to the old saying that killers often revisited the scene of the crime. Sometimes they came back to savor their own handiwork. Sometimes they returned because they wanted to be sure they hadn't left any loose ends. And sometimes they were compelled to return because they were driven by an obsession too powerful to resist.

So, yes, he had professional reasons to be very curious about Charlotte Sawyer.

But he knew deep down that the curiosity was not just professional — it was personal.

Acknowledging that fact gave him a serious jolt. He tightened his grip on the handle of the carry-on.

He wasn't sure what he had been expecting earlier when he had taken the elevator down to meet her in the lobby. He always tried to keep an open mind at the start of a case because he had long since learned that first impressions were critical. He did not want to risk getting them wrong due to preconceptions.

But when the elevator doors opened, the only thing that had been shatteringly clear was that Charlotte Sawyer didn't fit any of the usual categories.

It was going to be hard to pin a label on her.

She wasn't the flashy, flirty, perky type. She wasn't the sultry type. She wasn't the cool, aloof, sophisticated type. She wasn't glamorous or bold or shy or nervous.

She had made no attempt to charm him. She hadn't tried to manipulate him, either, but he was pretty sure she would go toe-to-toe with anyone if she thought the battle was worth fighting.

And if she smiled at you, it would be a real smile, he thought. If her hazel green eyes warmed with humor or passion or any other emotion, that emotion would be the real deal.

She had unfastened the front of her anorak, revealing a dark green pullover and black trousers. The curves of the body beneath the clothes were not showy; rather, they appeared sleek and firm and feminine.

He could not point to any one feature that stood out, with the exception of her clear, watchful green eyes. But the various parts of her came together in a compelling way.

He followed her out of the elevator and walked beside her down the hall to Louise's suite. When he opened the door and stood back to allow her to enter first, she automatically started forward and then halted abruptly on the threshold. He thought he heard her catch her breath and he immediately understood.

"It's always like this when you know what happened in a room," he said quietly.

She glanced at him. "It's . . . weird."

"Yeah."

"Do you ever get used to the feeling?"

"I never have."

"Do you do this a lot?"

"Not anymore. I used to be a profiler, but now that I'm on my own, most of my work is corporate. Background checks. Insurance fraud. That kind of thing. That means I don't usually have to walk into places like this."

She nodded, took a breath and walked into the room with a firm, determined stride. He followed her and closed the door very gently.

It dawned on him that they'd just had a meaningful conversation without either of them needing to clarify the topic. They had both understood each other. He wasn't accustomed to conversations like that. He wasn't sure what to make of it.

He set the small suitcase on the rug, crouched beside it and opened it.

Charlotte went down on her knees beside the carry-on.

Together they looked at the road map of Washington State and the three envelopes.

"Okay, not quite what I expected," Charlotte said.

He looked at her. "What were you expecting?"

"I don't know," she admitted.

"That's the best way to go into a situation like this," he said.

"Is that a profiling thing?"

"It was my profiling thing. Everyone does it differently."

He removed the map of Washington and unfolded it slowly. "Not a lot of people use paper maps like this these days. They rely on GPS and the online mapping systems."

"I don't recall Jocelyn mentioning that Louise was planning a road trip. But, then, there wouldn't have been any reason to tell me about it."

He looked at her. "Your stepsister didn't bring you into her circle of friends?"

"Not really. Her closest friends are the other members of her investment club.

She's introduced me to them and I've seen them from time to time, but they are *her* friends. The truth is, I don't have a lot in common with them."

"Huh." He pondered that briefly. "So you weren't invited to invest with the group?"

"No." Charlotte wrinkled her nose. "Jocelyn said I didn't make enough money to take the risk. She said that her club's investments were basically a form of gambling. She and the others got together over drinks, did their research and then took flyers on a few stocks and start-ups they thought had the chance to go big."

"Did any of them go big?"

"Jocelyn said they made a little money on some, but for the most part the profits were offset by losses. However, she did tell me recently that they had high hopes for a local start-up that they invested in a few months ago. She said they think it's a good buyout candidate."

He spread the map on the carpet and examined it in more detail. "Five towns have been circled. I don't see any obvious connection between them. They're scattered all over the western side of the state."

"Louise used a yellow felt marker to circle three of them." Charlotte leaned over the map. "But the other two are marked in red.

I wonder if that's significant."

He reached into the carry-on and removed one of the envelopes. The initials on the outside were *J.K.* The flap was sealed. He opened it carefully and removed a couple of sheets of folded paper. Charlotte watched him intently.

"Well?" she prompted.

"First page is a computer printout," he said. He unfolded it. "It's a copy of an obituary notice for a woman named Jennifer Kingsley, age twenty-one. Date of death is about three months ago." He paused and glanced at the map. "According to this, she was living in one of those towns marked in red on the map."

Charlotte looked at the road map. "Does the notice list cause of death?"

"No. Which often means it was suicide or an overdose or some other cause that the family wanted to keep quiet."

"What's on the second sheet of paper?" Charlotte asked.

He unfolded it and studied it. "A note that says the victim worked nights and that the cause of death was a suspected drug overdose. Looks like Louise Flint's handwriting."

Charlotte plucked the next envelope out of the suitcase and opened it. There was only one page inside.

"Another obituary notice," she said. "A woman named Karen Ralston, age twenty. No cause of death listed, but Louise jotted down a note at the bottom of the page. It says, 'OD'd. Body found in apartment. Neighbors suspect it was suicide.' "

Max looked at her. "Two women dead, evidently because they overdosed on drugs. The bodies were found in the victims' homes. Now Louise is dead, apparently by a drug overdose. Body found in her own condo."

Charlotte looked at him, her eyes shadowed with anxiety. "What in the world is going on here?"

"I have no idea." He took out the third envelope. It contained several printouts. "These are newspaper clippings and police blotter reports."

"More mysterious drug overdoses?"

"No. These are reports of assaults. Suspected rapes." He read through the details, looking for similarities, searching for a pattern. "All of the victims were about the same age as the two dead women. The locations match the three towns on the map that are circled in yellow."

"Anyone arrested?"

"Not according to these reports. Louise

wrote another note: 'No descriptions of assailants. Drugs involved.' "

"What is that supposed to mean?"

"I'll do some research and see what I can find."

Charlotte sat back on her heels and looked at the items that had come out of the carry-on. "Louise was involved in something dangerous, wasn't she?"

"I think so, yes. The only thing that links these five women is drugs."

Charlotte shook her head. "I was so sure Louise wasn't involved with drugs. Well, I guess we can be certain of one thing: whatever the intruder was looking for, it wasn't the map and those obituaries and crime reports. He didn't even bother to open the envelopes."

"No."

"He was after something else, then. Drugs or cash, just like the police said."

"Probably."

He looked around the gloom-filled condo suite and then he refolded the map and tossed it into the suitcase. He stuffed the last of the printouts into the third envelope and put it on top of the map.

"I've had enough of this place for one day," he said. He closed the carry-on. "I need some time to process what we found.

Have you got your car?"

"No," she said. "I walked."

"I'm parked on the street. I'll take you home." It struck him that she might not want to be alone with him in a car. But night had fallen. He did not want her walking back through the rainy streets alone. "Unless you'd rather take a cab?"

She appeared to give that some close thought. He told himself not to take it personally. Then she gave him a small but very real smile.

"I appreciate the offer," she said. "Thanks."

It wasn't a huge leap forward in terms of establishing a level of trust, he thought, but it was definitely a step.

He immediately wondered why he was worried about trust levels. In his business, success was based on the assumption that everyone, including the client, usually lied. Everyone had secrets to protect.

Outside on the wet street Charlotte pulled up the hood of her anorak. He pulled up the collar of his windbreaker. It was all the protection he had. There was a baseball cap on the backseat of his car, but he hadn't thought to take it with him earlier when he met Daniel Flint at Louise's condo. He wondered if that made him look like a poorly prepared investigator. Image was everything in his new line, according to his family.

The vehicle he had used that afternoon was the nondescript gray compact that he kept for in-city work. It didn't stand out on the street, which, of course, was why he liked it. Then again, it didn't make much of an impression, either.

Not that he was trying to make an impression on Charlotte.

She didn't say anything when he opened the passenger-side door for her. She probably figured he wasn't doing all that well in the private investigation business. If so, she would be right.

He closed the door and hurried around the front of the car. By the time he got behind the wheel, his hair was plastered to his head and his jacket was soaked. He stripped it off and tossed it into the rear seat. The jacket would survive, but all in all he was not doing a good imitation of an ace detective.

And just why the hell did that seem important? he wondered.

He fired up the engine and pulled away from the curb.

"You're wondering if Louise had something to do with the deaths of those two women, aren't you?" he asked. "Maybe sold them the drugs?"

"No, I really can't see her as a dealer."

"You said yourself, you didn't know her that well."

Out of the corner of his eye he saw her tighten her grip on the strap of her bag.

"That's true, but I do know Jocelyn well," she said. "I can't imagine that she would have become close friends with a drug dealer."

"Take it easy. The trick to finding answers is not to get too far ahead of yourself. At this point all we've got are questions. Start making assumptions and we'll end up going down a blind alley."

Charlotte released her death grip on the strap of the bag and folded her arms very tightly beneath her breasts. She gazed straight ahead through the windshield.

"We?" she said.

He slowed for a stoplight and took the opportunity to get a closer look at her. She turned her head and met his eyes.

"You said at this point all *we've* got are questions," she said.

He flexed his hands on the wheel. The light changed. He eased his foot down on the throttle.

"Figure of speech," he said. "I'm working

for Daniel Flint. I have certain obligations to my client. There's the little matter of client confidentiality."

"Does that mean you can't work for me, too?"

He glanced at her again. "What, exactly, do you want me to do?"

"Isn't it obvious? I want you to find out if Jocelyn's sudden decision to go off the grid is in any way connected to Louise's death."

He thought about that for a minute. "I'll talk to my client about it. See if he has a problem with sharing information."

"Yes, please do that. Because if you don't want to take my case, I'll find someone who will."

"Wow. I sense blackmail."

"Leverage."

"You're tough."

She glanced at him, clearly surprised. "No. Jocelyn is the tough one."

"Not saying she isn't tough. Just saying you are."

Charlotte concentrated on the view of the wet street. "You've only known me for about an hour."

"Sometimes that's all it takes."

"I'm not tough," she said. "What I am is the one-foot-in-front-of-the-other type."

"You just keep on doing what you think

you have to do until you can't do it anymore."

"I suppose so. I'm definitely not the spontaneous type. Just ask my ex-fiancé."

He told himself not to get too excited just because she had labeled the fiancé an ex. Probably someone else in the picture by now, he thought.

"I've got a problem taking you on as a client," he said. "It could set up some conflicts of interest. But I'll talk to Daniel Flint this evening and explain that you and he both have a mutual interest in finding out what happened to his cousin. I'll see if he's on board with me using my judgment about sharing information with you."

"All right," she said. She hesitated a beat. "That one-foot-in-front-of-the-other thing?"

"What about it?"

"My therapist told me that it's not always a great strategy. She said I need to cultivate spontaneity and open myself up to new possibilities."

"You see a therapist?"

"I went to one for a while after my fiancé, aka the asshole, dumped me five days before the wedding. Not that I'm bitter."

"Of course not," he said, deadpan. "Holding a grudge against the guy who walked out just before the wedding would be way beneath you."

"Absolutely. Bad karma, too. But I will admit that there are times when I think about sticking little pins in a little doll."

"Totally understandable."

"Thank you."

He glanced at her. "So this therapist told you that you should learn to be more spontaneous?"

"Uh-huh."

"You still seeing her?"

"No."

"Why?"

"She insisted that in order to move on I had to accept the fact that I bore an equal share of the responsibility for the breakup."

He whistled softly. "That's cold. How the hell did she come up with that angle?"

"She said I had deliberately ignored the dysfunctional aspect of the relationship and the signs of incompatibility. I had allowed myself to indulge in magical thinking because I had convinced myself that Brian was Mr. Right. What can I say? I got tired of being told that it was my fault I got stood up at the altar — or, almost at the altar."

"So you fired the therapist."

"Yep." Charlotte paused. "Actually, that was the best part about the therapy. And I have absolutely no idea why I'm discussing my personal life with you."

"I'm no expert on creative spontaneity. I'm pretty much a one-foot-in-front-of-the-other type myself. But from what you've just told me, I'd say that dumping your therapist was a pretty good example of a spontaneous act."

There was a short silence.

"Yes, it was, wasn't it?" Charlotte said. "I hadn't thought of it that way."

She seemed pleased.

"Not to change the subject, but there is something I would like to point out," he said.

"What?"

"You said you didn't think your stepsister could possibly be close friends with a woman who was dealing drugs; one who might have been connected to the deaths of two women."

"Right."

"But I gotta tell you, whenever the cops arrest serial killers, child molesters and other assorted bad guys, the first thing all the friends and neighbors say is —"

" 'He seemed like such a nice, normal guy,' " Charlotte concluded. "Yes, that had occurred to me. But you have to admit that there is one thing here that argues in favor of Louise's innocence."

"What?"

"If she had been responsible in any way for the deaths of those two women or for selling drugs to the others, she certainly wouldn't have kept a record of her actions that might link her to the crimes."

"You don't know much about bad guys, do you?"

"Well, no."

"Take it from me, they like keeping score."

CHAPTER 8

Nothing.

There was nothing on Louise Flint's laptop or her cell phone that gave him even a hint about where she had hidden the package.

Thanks to the electronic keys the hacker had handed over, for a steep price, he had been able to open Flint's correspondence and files. But he had discovered absolutely nothing.

Now the one person who knew what Flint had done with the package — Flint herself — was dead.

Rage bubbled up like toxic waste. Trey Greenslade slammed the laptop closed and shoved himself up out of the chair. He started to prowl the narrow confines of the hotel room, trying to think. It wasn't easy because he was shivering a little. *Anxiety,* he thought. *Take a couple of deep breaths.*

Whatever you do, don't panic. You can handle this.

But he was on the edge of losing it and that was not good. Not good at all.

He yanked open the minibar and removed a small bottle of vodka. He unscrewed the cap and took a hefty swallow. The liquor burned, clearing his head in the process.

He went to the window, flattened one palm against the glass and looked out at the lights of the city while he tried to compose a new strategy. The problem was that he'd had to move too quickly, he thought. He hadn't had time to draw up a solid plan. But there had been no choice.

When he had discovered that Louise Flint had gone to Loring, Washington, there had been very little time to act. He'd had to move fast and he had done just that. Now Flint was dead, but he hadn't found the package in her condo, her storage locker or her vehicle.

Maybe she had stopped somewhere on the return trip to Seattle and hidden the damn package.

It was a two-hour drive to Loring. The route was dotted with small rural communities, farms and ranches. As far as he had been able to tell, she didn't have any friends or relatives in the area. She wouldn't have left something so valuable with a stranger.

He drank some more vodka and tried to concentrate.

It was possible that she had stopped off somewhere along the way and rented a commercial storage locker. But there were probably several of them scattered around the countryside between Seattle and Loring. Even if he identified the right facility, he would have to figure out which locker Flint had rented.

It was hopeless. He had to find another angle. The only good news was that, as far as he could tell from the list of recent calls on her phone and her e-mail files, it looked like Flint had not communicated the location of the package to Jocelyn Pruett or anyone else.

It made sense that she would have kept quiet, he thought. She must have known that the contents of the package were worth a fortune in blackmail.

Okay, so he could assume that Flint had taken her secret to the grave. He was safe. For now. But the thought of the package out there, waiting to be discovered and blow up his whole world, was terrifying.

All these years, he thought. All these years he'd never known that the package existed. He'd lived his life in blissful ignorance. But now that he was aware of it, he was never going to get another night of decent sleep until he found the damn package and neutralized the contents.

Shit. Just when everything had finally begun to go his way. Why had things started to spiral out of control at this point?

He drank the rest of the vodka and turned away from the window. It was all he could do not to hurl the bottle against the nearest wall. But the last thing he wanted was someone from the hotel security staff to come knocking on his door. He made himself put the empty bottle down very deliberately on the desk.

For a moment he just stood there staring at the damned laptop and cell phone.

All right, he thought. *Think this through carefully.*

Flint was out of the picture. She could not do any more damage. Furthermore, it appeared that she had not contacted anyone on the drive to or from Loring. That left only one realistic possibility — at some point she must have given the package to one of her friends in the club for safekeeping.

It was time to move on.

But first things first. He was a careful man and at the moment he was in possession of a computer and a phone that had belonged to a dead woman. It was highly unlikely that anyone would ever connect him to Flint, but it had long been his habit to take precautions. He had to get rid of the tech. That would be easy enough. He planned to run along the waterfront early in the morning. He'd go out to the end of one of the piers and toss the laptop and the phone into Elliott Bay.

His own phone rang, startling him. He glanced down at the screen and suppressed a groan. When he took the call, however, he made certain that there was no trace of impatience in his voice.

"Hi, Grandma," he said. "How are things at home?"

"I'm calling to make sure you haven't forgotten the special meeting of the board."

Marian Greenslade's voice never failed to grate on his nerves. She was nearly eighty, but she had been a formidable force in the Greenslade family for as long as he could remember — rigid, hypercritical, impossible to please. Age had not softened her — just the opposite. She saw herself as the keeper of the Greenslade family reputation. The death of her eldest son, Trey's father, a few months back had only hardened her resolve to ensure that the family business remained intact so that it could be handed down to the next generation.

Trey had no intention of letting that happen. He was not about to spend the rest of his life weighed down by the anchor of the company. He had his own plans for Loring-Greenslade. But first he had to get control.

"Don't worry, Grandma," he said. "I'll be at the meeting."

There was a short pause on the other end of the line.

"I assume you also plan to attend my birthday reception next week," Marian said.

"Wouldn't miss it for the world."

"It wouldn't look good if Charles showed up and you didn't," Marian said.

Marian was never subtle with her threats. But in this case there was no reason for her to worry, Trey thought.

In the weeks following his father's death, the board had appointed one of the vice presidents to act as interim CEO while it went through the formality of a search process. As everyone in Loring was well aware, however, Marian Greenslade would make the final decision. Trey knew that his cousin was his only real competition for the job.

Got to keep the old bitch happy.

If it became necessary, he would take care

of Charles. Accidents happened. Take the hunting accident that had killed his father, for instance.

No, Charles would not be a problem.

"I've got to go, Grandma. I'm having drinks with a potential client tonight."

"Good night," Marian said. "Remember, it's crucial that you attend the board meeting."

"Yes, Grandma."

He ended the connection, suppressing a shudder. He really did not like the sound of Marian's voice. It was even more annoying than his father's voice had been. The two shared other characteristics, as well. Gordon Greenslade had been just as rigid and critical; just as impossible to please. But at least he was gone now.

Trey went back to the window. What he was searching for was out there, somewhere. He had to find it.

At the start there had been five of them in the club. As far as he could tell, Louise Flint had no close friends outside the club. If she had entrusted the package to anyone, it would have been one of the other women in the group.

One down, one missing, three to go.

CHAPTER 9

"Yeah, sure, no problem," Daniel Flint said. "Use your own judgment, Mr. Cutler. I just want answers."

"Even if it turns out that those answers might affect Louise's reputation or your memories of her?" Max asked.

"Doesn't matter," Daniel said. "I'm sure she was murdered, but regardless, I just need to know the truth. If this woman — Charlotte Sawyer — is looking for answers, too, then as far as I'm concerned we're on the same team."

"All right. I'll keep you informed of my progress."

"Thanks," Daniel said. "Got to go. Chef is about to blow. We've got a full house here in the restaurant tonight."

The phone went dead in Max's hand. He set it on the old wooden table and looked out the kitchen window. A light Seattle drizzle was soaking the quiet neighborhood.

He could see the glow of a television set behind the curtains of the little Victorian down the street. Mr. and Mrs. Lund were addicted to PBS and a steady diet of British police dramas.

The windows in the house next to the Lunds' were still dark and probably would be for another hour or so. The two young men — newlyweds — had moved in recently, but they worked long hours and often met friends for dinner at one of the downtown restaurants.

The residents of the neighborhood were a mix of retirees obsessed with their gardens and cruise plans, and young families convinced they could double their money if they upgraded their starter houses and sold them in a couple of years.

He was too old to own a starter house, but after Whitney had walked out to "get on with her life," the fixer-upper was all he could afford. It was his own fault. He had compounded the financial disaster of the divorce by quitting his job as a profiler back in D.C. and moving to Seattle to go out on his own.

Everyone had warned him about the weather. Some said it wasn't the rain that got to some people, it was the long stretches of gray. But he had been living in the city for over six months and he was fine with the climate.

He had discovered that he liked being his own boss, too, even if he wasn't making a lot of money yet.

He probably should have rented when he arrived in Seattle, he thought. It would have made more sense financially. But he was an all-or-nothing kind of guy when it came to making commitments. The day he had walked off the plane he had made his decision. He would be staying in Seattle.

He opened a can of tuna and made a couple of sandwiches. There was one large dill pickle left in the jar. He added it to the plate. A well-rounded meal required a vegetable of some kind.

He took a beer out of the refrigerator, picked up the plate with the sandwiches and pickle on it and carried the meal to the kitchen table.

A light shifted in one of the windows across the street. The curtains were pulled aside. A familiar face appeared.

Anson Salinas raised a hand in greeting. Max returned the gesture. The curtain across the street dropped back into place.

Anson was also new to Seattle, having moved there some four months back. Prior to that, he'd spent over thirty years in law enforcement, much of the time as the chief of police of a small town on the rugged coast of northern California.

Max opened his laptop and contemplated the results of his latest search while he drank some beer and munched a sandwich. He was not entirely amazed to see that the two dead women and the three who had reported being raped had a few things in common. The circles on the map had indicated a pattern. The trick was to figure it out.

He studied the sparse details he had pulled up online for a few minutes. Then he looked at the time. It was not too late to call his new associate, he decided. He wondered if he should be worried about the fact that he was looking for an excuse — any excuse — to call her.

Charlotte answered on the first ring.

"What is it?" she said. "Did you find something?"

Urgency shivered in her voice.

"I just got off the phone with Daniel Flint," Max said. "He's okay with the three of us sharing information."

"Oh, good. I'm so glad. So now I'm a client, too?"

"No, you're a person with whom I will be sharing information," he said patiently. "I thought I made that clear."

He wasn't sure how to classify her, but he wanted it understood up front that she wasn't a client. It was bad policy to sleep with a client and he had been having fantasies of sleeping with Charlotte ever since he had walked out of the elevator and found her waiting for him in the lobby.

"I'm sort of a consultant, then?" she asked, dubious now.

"No, because then I'd have to pay you."

It probably wasn't smart to sleep with consultants, either, he thought.

"I see." She sounded almost amused. "Well, whatever you want to call it, we're working together, right? Colleagues."

Probably not a good idea to think of her as a colleague, but he was running out of descriptive labels.

"Colleague is good enough for now," he said. "I called to ask you some questions."

"Yes, of course."

Max looked at the carry-on sitting beside the kitchen table. "You said your stepsister is on a retreat in the Caribbean?"

"That's right. She's at a convent run by a cloistered order. They offer retreats to women several times a year. It's their primary source of income."

"What's the name of the island?"

"St. Adela. The convent is named after

101

the saint. Why?"

"How did your stepsister find it?"

"Jocelyn said she researched tech-free retreats online and chose St. Adela. Look, where are you going with this?"

"I don't know," he said. "I usually don't, not until I get there."

"Very philosophical."

He thought he heard a smile in her voice. Maybe it was just his imagination.

"Very philosophical for a PI, do you mean?" he asked.

"For anyone."

"I see." He tried to think of some way to extend the conversation. "Got plans for tonight?"

"Oh, yeah. Wild evening ahead. After dinner I'm going to do my nightly meditation and then I'm going to watch some television and then I'm going to go to bed and read. And during that entire time I will be worrying about Jocelyn and wondering why Louise Flint is dead."

"Sounds like a full evening. I'll be doing pretty much the same thing. Except for the meditation thing."

There was a long pause on the other end of the line. He waited for her to end the connection first. But she didn't make the move, at least not right away.

"Max?"

"Yeah?"

"Do you think my sister is okay?"

He hated questions like that.

"I have no idea," he said.

"I was afraid you were going to say that."

He was pretty sure she was going to hang up.

"I just remembered a question I wanted to ask you," he said.

"What is it?"

"I checked Louise Flint's GPS. It looks like the last trip she made was to Loring, Washington."

He heard a sharply indrawn breath.

"Loring?" she whispered. "Are you sure?"

"All I know for certain is that Loring was the last destination registered on the GPS. I can't find anything that tells me that Louise had any acquaintances there. Daniel Flint has no idea why she would have made the trip unless it was to see a foundation donor. But the receptionist at the foundation said there was no record of any big donors in Loring."

"When did Louise make the trip?" Charlotte asked quietly.

"The day she died."

"I have no idea what is going on, but if it is in any way connected to Loring, Washington, it can't be good."

"Tell me why."

"My stepsister went to college in Loring. She dropped out in her sophomore year and finished somewhere else."

"Why did she drop out?"

"She was attacked on the campus. Raped. They never caught the bastard. Jocelyn could not identify him because she didn't get a good look at him. He came up from behind with a knife and blindfolded her."

CHAPTER 10

"I don't know about the rest of you, but I'm damned scared," Victoria Mathis said. She tightened her grip around the stem of the martini glass. "First Jocelyn takes off on a monthlong retreat and now Louise is dead. I'm telling you, something has gone very, very wrong."

She was the one who had texted the others late that afternoon, summoning them to an unscheduled meeting of the club that night. Normally there would have been all five members present. But with Louise dead and Jocelyn in the Caribbean, there were only the three of them. And of the three, she and Emily Kelly appeared to be the only ones who were truly frightened. It was obvious that Madison Benson thought they were overreacting.

Maybe it was her background in marketing that was making her nervous. She was very good at spotting trends in the hothouse environment of the fashion world. She also knew just how fast a trending style could go south. She relied on her intuition for success and right now it was warning her that there was no way she could pretend that Louise's death and Jocelyn's disappearance didn't make for a disturbing trend. They all knew that they had been taking risks.

Madison Benson, seated on the other side of the table, gave her a disapproving look that was tinged with exasperation.

"There's no reason to panic," Madison said. "Louise died of an overdose. That's not the biggest shock in the world. We all know her history."

Victoria suspected that Madison was using the same tone of voice that she used to calm anxious investors. Smart and savvy, Madison had the whole package — glamorous good looks, a head for numbers, an eye for financial opportunities and an edgy, charismatic personality. Her business was still small compared to the big hedge fund managers, but she had a growing portfolio of satisfied clients.

Victoria was pretty sure that some of those clients — male and female — had fantasies about sleeping with Madison, who could have moonlighted as an exclusive dominatrix. But as far as the members of the club were aware, she was not particularly interested in sex. Jocelyn had suggested on more than one occasion that Madison was still looking for her true mate — a man or woman she considered to be her equal.

"Louise had been clean for years," Emily Kelly said. "I'm sure if she had gone back to drugs we would have had some indication. But I didn't notice anything different about her lately."

Victoria almost choked on her martini. "What are you talking about? You're in human resources. You're the one with the psych degree. You're supposed to be an expert when it comes to evaluating people. Of all of us, you should have been the one to notice that Louise was not herself lately. She was unusually quiet and withdrawn, almost secretive, for most of the past month. I thought she was sinking into depression."

"Maybe she was." Emily's mouth tightened.

Of all of them, Emily was the one who didn't really fit into the club, Victoria thought. She was sure that Emily was aware of that. It had become clear that Emily lacked the nerve for the kinds of risks they took.

It was Madison who had lobbied to make her a member, and admittedly Emily contributed a useful skill set. She had a talent for digging up background information and — the Louise issue aside — she was usually very insightful when it came to predicting the actions of their targets. But she lacked the assertive, risk-taking vibe that characterized the rest of them.

As far as they knew, Emily did not have anyone special — male or female — in her life. She rarely mentioned her family.

Emily was not exactly an introvert, but neither was she outgoing. She was the same age as the rest of them, but she seemed older. With a little makeup, a few blond highlights in her hair, some on-trend clothes and a big dose of self-confidence, she could have been attractive. The dorky-looking glasses didn't help matters. All in all, it seemed that she went out of her way not to draw attention to herself.

"I just assumed that Louise was seeing someone," she said. She sounded defensive. "I thought she was more quiet than usual because she wasn't ready to talk to the rest of us about the relationship, that's all."

"Why would she keep quiet about a new relationship?" Victoria asked.

"We all know that Louise was . . . complicated," Emily said. "Given her background, she would have been uneasy about becoming emotionally invested in a new relationship."

Madison's eyes narrowed. "Looks like the reason she seemed withdrawn and even secretive lately was because the new person in her life was her dealer, not a lover. Shit. She had to know we would have freaked if we thought that she was using again. That kind of behavior would have put all of us at risk. Everyone knows you can't trust a junkie."

Victoria sat back in the booth and looked at Emily. "You're the expert on people. Got any ideas about Jocelyn? Why do you think she suddenly decided to disappear?"

Madison frowned. "Don't say that. She didn't disappear. She went off on a retreat. Stop making it sound so mysterious. There is nothing odd about it."

Emily looked at her. "I'm not so sure. Victoria is right. It does seem a little strange that Jocelyn would suddenly head for a convent on some no-name island in the Caribbean for a month. It's not like she's seriously religious."

"It doesn't have anything to do with religion," Madison said. "A lot of people are going off on tech-free retreats these days. They're trying to unplug for a while. It's like doing yoga or meditation. Jocelyn has been complaining about feeling stressed out. She said the foundation was really pressuring her to bring in bigger donors."

"The thing is," Emily said, "Jocelyn is a planner. Sure, she takes risks, but she's not impulsive. She thinks things through. This idea of going on a retreat feels like it came out of left field. She never mentioned doing anything like that before she announced that she had booked a plane ticket."

Madison's delicate brows scrunched together. "Maybe she thought through the retreat idea for a while and just didn't bother to mention it to us."

"Maybe," Emily conceded.

But she didn't look convinced, Victoria thought. If anything, Emily looked more nervous than ever. And now Madison was finally starting to appear concerned, too.

There was a brief moment of silence around the table. Victoria drank some more of her martini and slowly lowered the glass.

"It seemed like a game at first," she said. "A real-life video game."

Emily shook her head. "It was never a game. We all knew we were taking chances. There was always the possibility that someone would realize what we were doing."

"But we were very careful," Madison insisted.

Victoria looked at her. "Maybe not careful enough."

CHAPTER 11

Max was rinsing off the dishes he had used for the tuna fish sandwiches and contemplating another beer when the doorbell chimed. He glanced at the clock. It was still early.

He wiped his hands on the dish towel and went to open the door. Anson Salinas stood there. He looked like the hard-core lawman he had been for most of his life. His hair had gone gunmetal gray and his lean, wiry frame had softened a little over the years, but his dark eyes were still cop eyes. His hard face, with its high cheekbones and grim jaw, was as intimidating as it had always been.

You had to know Anson awhile before you understood that appearances did not deceive. The man was as tough as he looked.

He was also lonely.

That makes two of us, Max thought.

"Come on in, Anson," he said. "Beer?"

"Won't say no."

Max headed for the kitchen. Anson closed the door and followed him. He lowered himself into one of the old chairs at the kitchen table.

"Well?" he asked. "Did you take the Flint case?"

"I did." Max carried two beers over to the table and sat down across from Anson. "Started out simple but it got interesting in a hurry."

"Yeah? How's that?"

Max gave him a brief rundown.

Anson drank some beer while he processed the details.

"Complicated," he said.

"At this point, yes. But sooner or later I'll find the trigger event. And when I do, everything will fall into place."

Anson snorted, amused. "You and your theories. That kind of thinking might have worked well when you were with that fancy profiling outfit, but out here in the real world you're gonna find out real fast that you don't always have time to find the trigger. Mostly you have to act on the information you've got."

"I know. I'm not ignoring the facts on the ground, believe me."

Anson's eyes glinted. "What's she like?"

113

"Louise Flint?"

"Not the dead woman. I'm talkin' about the one that turned up at the scene."

"Charlotte Sawyer."

"Yeah. Charlotte Sawyer."

"She's . . . interesting."

Anson nodded. "Pretty."

"I said interesting."

"Don't want to tell you how to do your job, but you know what they say about the first person who shows up at the scene."

"She wasn't the first person. Technically it was Louise Flint's housekeeper who was first on the scene."

"Still, from the sound of it, this Charlotte Sawyer showed up with a full set of keys. That raises questions."

"Yes, it does," Max said. "I'm looking for answers, trust me."

"I do. But you know me. I like to talk shop."

"I know. You need to find a job, Anson. You're going to drive yourself crazy if you don't. Probably drive me crazy, too."

"Got any suggestions? There's this thing called age discrimination. I'm too old for law enforcement. And I sure as hell don't plan to work nights as a minimum-wage security guard at some office building."

"We've talked about this. You should look

114

into volunteer work."

Anson shrugged and drank some more beer. "I'm thinking about it."

"Good." Max leaned back in his chair. "I was about to turn on the game," he said, lying through his teeth. "You want to watch?"

"Sure. Not like I've got anything better to do."

The game ended around ten thirty. Anson pushed himself up out of the recliner.

"That's that," he said. "Good game. Reckon I'll head back to my place. You'll be wanting to get some sleep tonight. Sounds like you've got a lot of interesting work ahead of you tomorrow. Let me know what you find out about that missing woman."

"Jocelyn Pruett," Max said. "I'll do that."

He got up and followed Anson to the door.

Outside Anson stopped and eyed the rain that was dripping onto the front porch.

"Porch roof leaks," he said.

"I know. I'll get to it. Got other priorities inside that need to be fixed first. Namely the plumbing. Speaking of which, you okay with supervising the plumber tomorrow?"

"Leave it to me," Anson said.

"Promise me you won't tell him how to do his job."

" 'Course not. But I'll keep an eye on him."

Anson went down the front steps and walked quickly through the light mist. At his front door he paused to raise a hand in a casual good night and then he disappeared into his house.

Max closed his door and went back into the kitchen. He thought about the day Anson Salinas had, quite literally, crashed into his life.

He had been a terrified ten-year-old kid and he had not been alone. There were seven other children with him. They had all been locked in the old barn for the night. Quinton Zane always locked them up for the night.

Zane said it was for their own protection. He said it was to help them overcome their fears. He said it was to make them strong.

But what they really feared was Quinton Zane. He was the real-life monster in their world; the young, charismatic, terrifying leader of the cult.

On the night that shattered Max's childhood forever, Zane told his followers that he'd had a vision in which he would soon disappear. And he did — but not before he had triggered a series of explosions that set fire to the buildings in the compound, including the barn where the kids slept.

Max and the others awakened to find themselves locked in a structure that was in flames. And then, as they huddled together in the middle of the barn, frozen in terror, aware that they were going to burn alive, a hero arrived to rescue them.

Anson Salinas, the chief of police of the nearby town, had used his vehicle to smash through the old barn door. He leaped out from behind the wheel, rounded up all eight kids, crammed them into the SUV and roared out of the blazing barn. Moments later the entire structure came crashing down.

Several of the adult members of the cult perished that night. Max's mother was one of them.

Ultimately the social workers were able to track down relatives for five of the eight kids. But three boys — Max, Cabot Sutter and Jack Lancaster — were all officially orphaned.

They had gone home with Anson Salinas the night of the fire because there was nowhere else for them to go. And in the end, they had stayed.

When it became clear that they were all headed for the foster care system, Anson had pulled some strings, twisted a few arms and completed the paperwork that made him a licensed foster parent.

Max cranked up the computer again and took another look at the data he had collected on the two murder victims and the three women who had been raped. Why had Louise Flint considered them so important she had hidden the file in a suitcase in a storage locker?

Now there was a connection to another rape victim — Jocelyn Pruett.

There was always a pattern. It was up to him to find it.

After a while he closed down the Louise Flint file and opened the one that he always checked before going to bed — the one labeled *Quinton Zane.*

He knew that each of his foster brothers also kept an open file on Zane. They rarely discussed the contents of the files with anyone outside the family. In the past, others, including his ex, had labeled the three of them obsessed and accused them of being paranoid. There were times when Max figured the critics were probably right.

He and his foster brothers had each paid a price for their pursuit of the ghost of Quinton Zane. In his case, the obsession had almost gotten him killed on his last case at the agency. It had destroyed his career, and his marriage had gone down in flames — collateral damage. He was well aware that as far as his former colleagues and his ex were concerned, he was no longer merely obsessed, he was burned out. They were convinced that he was at high risk of seeing patterns where none existed.

No one at the agency wanted to work with an obsessed, paranoid individual. No smart woman wanted to be married to one.

Over the years he and Cabot and Jack had pulled up occasional rumors, whispers and hints that indicated Zane was still alive. But they had never been able to nail down anything substantial. They had never found enough to reveal a pattern.

He closed the file and checked his e-mail before he powered off the computer. His in-box was empty except for the one e-mail that had come in a month back. He still could not decide whether to archive it or dump it into the trash, so he just let it sit in the in-box.

The message consisted of only two sentences and a signature.

Please be advised that you are not to contact me again. If you ignore this request, I will direct my attorney to take legal action against you.

It was signed *Davis Decatur.*
His biological father.

CHAPTER 12

Charlotte awoke to the ringing of her phone. For a few beats the reality of the gray light of dawn meshed with fragments of a dream in which she walked through a series of empty, fog-filled rooms searching for Jocelyn.

The phone rang again.

Jocelyn. Maybe she was calling to check in at last.

She pushed the covers aside, swung her legs over the side of the bed and grabbed the phone. The screen name read *Cutler.* For a split second she didn't recognize it. Then she remembered that Max had given her his card and she had entered his name and number into her contacts list.

"It's a little early," she said.

"We have another problem," Max said.

It occurred to her that he sounded as if he had been awake for some time. She tightened her grip on the phone.

"What?" she asked.

"Jocelyn Pruett is not at the convent on St. Adela."

Something inside her went very cold. She stood up quickly.

"How can you possibly know that?" she asked. "There's no phone at the convent. Jocelyn said her own phone would be off the whole time because there would be no cell service and no Wi-Fi available."

"Are you sure of that?"

"Yes. Look, last night I sent a text to Jocelyn on the off chance that she might have found a way to check her messages. I told her I had some bad news about Louise. There was no response."

"How did Jocelyn book the retreat?" Max asked.

"She used a travel agency that specializes in various kinds of exotic trips and retreats. They book vacations all over the world that focus on yoga and meditation experiences — that kind of thing."

"I just got off the phone with the chief of the St. Adela police department. He was very helpful. I told him we had an emergency on our hands and that we had to get in touch with Jocelyn Pruett immediately. He sent one of his officers out to the convent."

Charlotte closed her eyes. "I'm an idiot. I never even thought about contacting the local cops."

"You're not an idiot. You would have come up with the idea eventually. Yesterday you were still trying to wrap your head around Louise Flint's death."

Charlotte opened her eyes. "Thank you for making excuses for me. Are you certain Jocelyn isn't on the island?"

"As certain as I can be without getting on a plane to St. Adela."

Charlotte sank back down onto the edge of the bed. "Oh, my God."

"The sister in charge informed the officer that, yes, Jocelyn Pruett had booked a monthlong retreat and, yes, she had arrived and checked in on schedule."

"What?"

"But she checked out the following day."

"Crap."

"Evidently she could not tolerate the lifestyle."

"No kidding." Charlotte brightened. "Maybe she checked into a beachfront hotel instead."

"The sister didn't know where Jocelyn went, only that she was gone. And before you ask, no, Pruett is not staying at any of the local hotels. The police chief looked into

123

that possibility."

Charlotte breathed deeply, allowing the implications to sink in.

"Jocelyn never meant to stay there at the convent," she said. "She intended to disappear all along."

"That's how it looks," Max agreed. "Evidently she planned to remain invisible for at least a month, but she didn't want you, or anyone else, apparently, to worry about her."

Charlotte was tempted to take his crisp, impersonal tone of voice as a sign of heartlessness, but something told her that it was just evidence of business as usual for Max. Finding answers was what he did for a living. As far as he was concerned, he was simply updating her in the most efficient manner possible so that he could get on with his job.

"She bought the ticket to St. Adela and went so far as to actually check in to the convent so that anyone who tried to search for her online would be satisfied that she had traveled to the island," he said. "Most people would assume that she was where she was supposed to be."

Charlotte gripped the phone very tightly. "Most people like me, you mean. But you took matters a step further. You checked with the local police. Why didn't I think of that?"

"You didn't call the St. Adela police because, until yesterday, there was no reason for you to think that your stepsister wasn't where she said she would be," Max said.

So now he was reading her mind, too.

"But you automatically assumed that Jocelyn probably wasn't where she was supposed to be, is that it?" she asked.

"I didn't assume anything one way or the other. I just like to verify details whenever I can."

"So my stepsister really has gone off the grid."

"Looks like it. If she wants to get in touch with you without using her phone, there are ways. Burner phones. Public library computers. But she hasn't done that." Max paused very deliberately. "Right?"

The realization that he didn't entirely trust her hit her like a small electrical shock. Then she got mad.

"No, Jocelyn hasn't gotten in touch," she snapped. She paused. "Do you think she knows that Louise Flint is dead?"

"If she disappeared because she's running scared, it's logical that she would keep track of what's happening back here in Seattle. I think it's safe to say she is aware of Louise's death, yes. Whether or not Jocelyn suspects that her friend was murdered, I can't say."

"Trust me, Jocelyn will assume that Louise was murdered. She certainly won't believe that her best friend OD'd." Charlotte shot to her feet again, her hand clamped around the phone. "Oh, God, do you think that Jocelyn is . . ."

She couldn't bring herself to say the word, but Max evidently had no problem with harsh realities.

"It's possible she's dead," he said. "But I think it's unlikely. Dead bodies have a way of surfacing."

She flinched and then told herself that was probably Max's way of trying to sound reassuring.

"The way Louise's body showed up, you mean?"

"Yes." Max paused briefly. "At this point it looks like Jocelyn has gone into hiding. The fact that I haven't been able to find her yet is a good indication that she knows what she's doing."

"She's very tech savvy."

"That's obvious. What about the other members of her family? Is there anyone else she might have contacted?"

"There is no one else," Charlotte said.

"Her father died years ago. She has no brothers or sisters. Her father married my mother when Jocelyn and I were in our teens. The question is, who is she hiding from?"

"Maybe from the person who murdered Louise Flint," Max said.

"I was afraid you were going to say that."

Charlotte gazed blankly out the window.

"Are you still there?" Max asked after a while.

She swallowed hard. "Yes. Yes, I'm here. I'm just having trouble trying to process all this. If you're right, it means Jocelyn was keeping some huge secrets from me."

"Yes."

"She was trying to protect me."

"Think so?"

"She's always been that way. Almost from the start."

"I don't want to be the one to spoil your image of your stepsister," Max said, "but there are other reasons why she might have kept you in the dark. It might be herself she's protecting."

"No," Charlotte said. "If she's keeping secrets, it's because she doesn't want to drag me into whatever is going on."

"I'll find out what happened to your sister," Max said. "It's what I do."

"Well, you're not doing it alone, remember? I'm part of this thing."

"Got some idea of where you want to start?" Max asked.

He didn't sound sarcastic or arrogant. He sounded curious and interested, as if he was paying close attention.

"During the night I suddenly remembered that note that Louise put into the envelope with the keys that she mailed to Jocelyn."

"What about it?"

"Louise said that *her* hard copy of the file was in the storage locker and that it wasn't online."

"Which implies that your stepsister has a hard copy, as well," Max concluded. "Is that what you're saying?"

"Exactly."

Max was quiet for a few seconds. "Any idea where she might have stashed it?"

"Jocelyn keeps most of her important records and files online. But she also maintains one very old-fashioned storage system — a safe-deposit box."

There was a short silence from Max's end of the connection.

"We'd need a key," he said finally.

"I've got one," Charlotte said. "I'm the only person she trusted completely." She realized with a shock of horror that she had used the past tense. "I mean, I'm the only one she trusts. Okay, she obviously doesn't tell me everything, but she trusts me."

"I understand," Max said. "We'll find her."

She was surprised by the oddly gentle current in the dark tide of his voice. He made the statement sound like a vow. But she also noticed that he didn't go beyond that. He didn't offer hope that Jocelyn was alive. He just promised to find her.

Max Cutler was not the type to make a promise he was not sure he could keep, she decided. On the other hand, something told her that if he did make a promise, you could depend upon him to walk into hell to fulfill it.

Then again, she had been wrong about men before. Brian Conroy was Exhibit A.

"I'll call my boss and tell her that I'll be late getting in to the office," she said.

CHAPTER 13

Charlotte emptied the contents of the grocery sack on top of the dining bar that divided the kitchen and living room areas of her apartment. Together she and Max studied the items — a road map of the state of Washington, three legal-sized envelopes marked with initials and a larger envelope that appeared to be stuffed with papers or documents.

The contents of Jocelyn's safe-deposit box.

Neither of them had wanted to go through the box in the vault room at the bank, so they had dumped the items into the grocery sack. Charlotte had clutched the sack with both hands during the short drive across town to her apartment. She had felt as if she was holding a bag of snakes — afraid to open it and at the same time knowing she could not throw it away.

Max flattened both palms on the table and

studied the materials scattered across the surface.

"Another road map of Washington," he said. "Let's start with that."

He unfolded the map. Charlotte looked at the red and yellow circles.

"Same towns," she said. "Including the two towns in which the two women supposedly OD'd."

Max picked up the envelopes and opened them.

"Same data that we found in the envelopes in Louise's carry-on," he said. "Duplicates of the obituary notices and the rape reports. Also some handwritten notes indicating that drugs were involved in all five cases."

Charlotte studied the notes. "These were written by Jocelyn, not Louise."

"So they were keeping duplicate files, just as Louise indicated."

Charlotte looked up. "They obviously did some of the research online, but when it came to creating a file that included their notes, they kept everything in hard copy. Why?"

"In the modern age, the only safe way to hide something is to do it the old-fashioned way — keep the data in hard copy only. The three rapes occurred over the course of several months within the past year. The two drug-related deaths are more recent. One was mid-August. The other was late September."

He picked up the large envelope and let the contents spill out onto the table. A number of newspaper clippings, documents and notes landed in a pile.

Charlotte selected one of the clippings and picked it up. For a split second the significance of the headline did not register. When it did, she sank down on the nearest chair.

"I knew Jocelyn had kept the important documents, but I hadn't realized she kept so much material."

She handed the clipping to Max. He read it quickly, frowning in concentration.

" 'Local college student reports assault,' " he read. " 'Unidentified assailant escapes.' " He set the clipping aside and picked up one of the documents. "It's a copy of a police report of your stepsister's rape. It says that she could not provide a description because the assailant blindfolded her and held a knife to her throat."

"Yes." Charlotte picked up another sheaf of papers. "It's a list of names. There must be two or three hundred of them."

Max took the pages from her. "These are all male names. A few have been crossed out. Some look like they were added to the list at different times."

"I think it must be Jocelyn's list of all the possible suspects," Charlotte said. "I wonder how she compiled it."

"The rape occurred on the Loring College campus. Maybe she used the college yearbooks to assemble a list of suspects."

"Yes, of course. I never thought about that. She was convinced from the start that her attacker was a student. It's a small college and it was even smaller at the time." Charlotte contemplated the contents of the envelope. "All these years we thought Jocelyn had moved on. And she let us believe it."

Max's eyes tightened a little. "We?"

"Our family. Me. She let us think that she had put it all behind her because she knew we were worried about how the attack had affected her emotionally. But all this time she was keeping the horrible newspaper clippings and that list of names in her safe-deposit box. It wasn't like any of those things would ever do her any good."

"Why do you say that?"

She looked up at him, fighting tears. "Because those assholes in the Loring Police Department lost the evidence box, that's why. We don't even know when it disappeared from the locker. No one took responsibility. But when it vanished, any hope of identifying the attacker vanished with it."

"I see."

Max sat down and considered the items scattered across the table. He pulled a couple of computer printouts from the pile.

"Evidently she was trying to collect reports of rapes with similar MOs," he said. "At least back at the start. These two are dated that same year. Both victims said that their attacker blindfolded them using a cloth sack and threatened them with a knife."

"Jocelyn was obsessed with following the news on those two crimes. They occurred on other campuses, not at Loring, so it wasn't easy getting information."

"Could have been a copycat situation."

"Jocelyn didn't think so. She actually tracked down the two victims and talked to them. She returned convinced that the assailant was the same man who had attacked her. She said she was going to try to find a pattern. But then the reports just stopped."

"Guys like that don't usually change the way they do things," Max said. "But sometimes they modify their methods or try to make them more efficient."

A little shock of unease whispered through Charlotte. Max sounded disturbingly cold-blooded, as if Jocelyn's case were nothing more than an interesting puzzle.

But when she took a closer look at him, she realized that there was an aura of quiet intensity about him.

"Jocelyn wondered from time to time if her attacker had left the state," she said. "Or maybe been arrested for crimes she hadn't heard about."

"Both possibilities." Max flipped through some of the other printouts and clippings. "The thing we have to ask ourselves is, what does her story have to do with those two dead women, the three rape victims and the death of Louise Flint?"

"Maybe it's all unrelated," Charlotte said.

"I don't think so. Coincidences do happen, but they rarely look like this." He picked up the police report for Jocelyn's case. "We may have another angle into this thing."

"What?"

"Not what, who. Detective Egan Briggs of the Loring Police Department. Looks like he was in charge of the investigation."

"Jocelyn was assaulted over a decade ago. Briggs looked like he was in his fifties at the time. He's probably retired by now. Even if he's still around, I doubt that he'll be helpful. He never got anywhere with the case.

No one was ever charged."

"If Briggs is still alive, I'll find him."

She almost smiled. "Yes, I believe you will."

He shrugged. "It's what I do."

"I understand."

"Meanwhile, you and I are going to act like we think that Jocelyn is at that retreat on St. Adela."

She tapped one finger on the list of names. "Because if she thinks she needs to disappear, she must have a very good reason."

"And because one woman is already dead."

CHAPTER 14

Louise was dead.

Jocelyn stared at the computer screen, reading and rereading the terse newspaper reports.

Victim declared dead at the scene . . . Illicit drugs and syringe found on bedside table . . . Suspected overdose . . . Toxicology tests ordered . . . Victim had a history of drug use . . . Volunteered at a local women's shelter . . .

Murder, Jocelyn thought, not an overdose. She and Louise had been right. Somewhere along the line, one of them had made a terrible mistake. The bastard they were hunting had been alerted.

He'd always had one huge advantage, she thought. He had known her identity all along. But she had never known his.

Still, why had he murdered Louise?

Because he couldn't find me?

The terrible weight of guilt stole her

breath. It was her fault Louise was dead.

She forced herself to breathe through the ghastly pressure. When her head cleared a little, she tried to follow the logic of her conclusion. She and Louise had known that the monster was escalating. If they were right, he had murdered his last two victims. But what had made him realize that someone was tracking him? They had been so damned careful.

So damned careful, but now Louise was dead.

If he had murdered Louise, there was no reason to think he would stop there. She had to assume that he knew the true purpose of the investment club. If so, he might conclude that he had to get rid of all of them.

She had to warn the others. But she had so little to tell them. No name. No hard evidence, just a conviction that they might be targets of a serial rapist turned killer.

There was an annoying hum of activity around her, making it difficult to concentrate. It was late afternoon and the library was crowded. Much of the noise was coming from the children's department. Story hour was in progress. The librarian in charge was encouraging audience participation, and the kids were cooperating with enthusiasm. In addition, there was a group of raucous teenagers in the video room and a constant stream of patrons coming and going from the checkout desk.

But the busiest section was the large room that provided online access. Every computer terminal was busy. She'd had to reserve one and then wait for her turn.

Due to demand, she had been allowed a mere half hour. She had intended to use the time to continue searching for information on the man she and Louise were hunting, but she had taken a moment to check the office e-mail at the foundation. That was how she had discovered that Louise had died.

The killer had managed to murder her with drugs. That could not have been easy. Louise hated drugs. She must have been overpowered, but according to the police reports there had been no sign of a struggle. That didn't make sense, either. Louise would have fought.

Jocelyn shut down the computer and sat quietly for a moment, trying to think. Until she had discovered that Louise was dead, she had allowed herself to believe that the two of them were still in control of the situation. They had assured each other that the bastard could not possibly know that they were closing in on him.

But now she had to accept the fact that he was hunting them.

She wished she could talk to Charlotte. Charlotte was the calm, levelheaded one. She thought of herself as unexciting. Having her fiancé dump her shortly before the wedding had certainly not enhanced her self-esteem. But her real problem was that she was too trusting. She tended to take people at face value.

Charlotte never lied to others, so she made the classic mistake of the habitually honest — she assumed that other people did not lie to her, at least not to her face. In her world, people were innocent of deliberate deceit until proven otherwise, which was, of course, way too late.

Even when Charlotte discovered that some people could not be trusted, her reaction tended to be disappointment, not anger and cynicism. And to top it off, she usually blamed herself for failing to perceive the truth about the other person's character flaws.

When Brian Conroy had announced that he could not go through with the marriage, she had concluded that it was her own fault because she had allowed herself to be deceived into thinking he was Mr. Perfect.

The dumbass therapist she had seen for a few weeks had reinforced that notion.

It was wrongheaded, but that was Charlotte.

Jocelyn closed her eyes for a moment, trying to steady her breathing. The thing was, Charlotte was the only person she really trusted now that Louise was gone. But she didn't dare contact her for fear of putting her in jeopardy.

"Hey, lady, if you're finished with the computer, I'm next."

Startled, Jocelyn looked up and saw a scruffy-looking teenage male in running shoes, jeans and a hoodie.

"It's all yours," she said.

She got to her feet, took her pack off the back of the chair and moved out of the way.

"Thanks. Got homework to research."

Yeah, right, Jocelyn thought. Kids his age all had enough tech to stock a big-box store. They didn't need to hog the public library's computers to do their homework.

The kid sat down in the booth and cranked up the computer with quick, skillful movements. He had obviously done it many times before.

She slung her backpack over one shoulder and prepared to head for the front door of the library. She glanced casually at the computer screen before she turned away.

The kid was already on a porn site watching naked, unnaturally endowed people have sweaty sex.

"Interesting homework you've got," Jocelyn said.

The kid looked up long enough to mouth a reply. "Fuck off, lady. I got my First Amendment rights."

So the kid liked to view porn on a public computer to make sure his parents didn't find out how he spent his study time. So what? She had just finished using the library's computer to research the murder of a good friend because she didn't want to let a killer know her location. Each to his or her own. The public library was the great equalizer.

She headed for the door. It was not her job to correct the manners of the younger generation. She had more pressing issues — like staying alive.

She pushed through the glass doors and went out into the chilly afternoon. She had chosen Portland, Oregon, as her bolt-hole. She hadn't dared stay in Seattle. Too many people knew her and, although the city had boomed in recent years, it was still a small town in many ways.

She would have given anything to buy a

throwaway phone and call Charlotte, but she didn't dare. Charlotte was safe only as long as she was not involved. Besides, she was pretty sure that Charlotte would tell her to go straight to the police. But that wasn't an option. She had nothing concrete to take to the cops. Zero.

If there was one lesson she had learned after being attacked all those years ago, it was that there was no use going to the authorities if you couldn't positively identify the bastard and provide absolute proof of what he had done. The cops hadn't believed her when she had been a sophomore at Loring College. They wouldn't believe her now.

The question was what to do next. Anxiety pulsed through her. The old fear that she had worked so hard to master gnawed at her guts. She sensed the oppressive night-mare closing in around her. Memories of the knife against her throat and the cloth sack over her head threatened to overwhelm her. She could not breathe. She wanted to jump out of her own skin.

She opened the pack with shaking fingers and took out the little bottle of anxiety meds. She swallowed one tablet dry. Predict-ably, it got caught in her throat. Probably just her imagination. She swallowed hard again and again. But she could still feel it lodged there in her throat.

In a full-blown panic now, she leaped to her feet and rushed back into the library. She managed to make it to the drinking fountain. She gulped water until the choking sensation eased.

She went back outside, sat down on a bench and waited for the medication to kick in. Streams of people came and went from the library.

After a while she grew calmer and began to ponder her next move. The problem was that it was impossible to know if the other members of the club were in danger. She had to assume that the bastard who had murdered Louise was after her, as well. But if he was thinking logically, he would realize that he did not have to be concerned with Madison, Victoria and Emily. She and Louise had never told any of the three about the hunt for the killer.

But there was no reason to assume that he was thinking logically. He was a rapist and a killer, after all. That meant he was obsessed, violent; maybe flat-out crazy. At the very least he was a full-on psychopath.

The only real question was why he had started to escalate a few months back. As far as she could tell, until that point he had continued to rape and terrify victims, but he had not murdered them. Something must have happened to alter his pattern.

Whatever the case, this was no longer about just her past. She had an obligation to warn the others, she decided. Back at the beginning they'd prepared a contingency plan in case things went wrong. It had been Madison's idea. Madison was the founder of the club. One by one she had brought each of them into her exciting, secret world.

After a while Jocelyn got up and went back inside the library. She stood in line again to put a fake name down on the list of those waiting for computer access.

She hoped the clerk would not assign her the same booth that the porn-obsessed kid had used.

CHAPTER 15

The birthday party was in full swing when Max arrived. He stood in the doorway and watched Charlotte hand out slices of cake and glasses of pink punch to a crowd of seniors.

The partygoers appeared to range in age from early seventies to late nineties. One or two might have been pushing a hundred. The banner strung across the room read *Happy Birthday.* Balloons bobbed and colorful streamers hung from the ceiling.

An elderly woman with a helmet of white curls wheeled her walker forward and stopped directly in front of him.

"Come on in," she said. "Join the party. I'm Ethel Deeping, by the way."

"Pleased to meet you, Ms. Deeping," he said.

"Call me Ethel. The party is for everyone here at Rainy Creek Gardens who has a birthday this month. Plenty of cake and punch."

"Thanks," he said. "But I just came by to speak with Ms. Sawyer."

"Charlotte?" Ethel glanced toward the cake table. "She's right over there." Ethel raised her voice. "*Charlotte.* There's a gentleman here to see you."

Charlotte glanced up at the sound of her name. Max thought he glimpsed a little spark of welcome in her eyes when she saw him. But maybe that was just his imagination. Or wishful thinking.

"Thank you, Ethel," she said. She smiled at Max and held out a paper plate with a slice of cake on it. "Would you like a piece?"

He realized that every eye in the room was on him. There was open curiosity and speculation on every well-lined face. He was aware that a few of the celebrants were watching him with something that looked a lot like suspicion.

"Sure," he said.

He walked to the cake table and took the paper plate. Charlotte handed him a plastic fork. He took a bite.

The buzz of conversation immediately got louder.

He moved a little closer to Charlotte and lowered his voice.

"Why is everyone staring at me?" he asked.

"They're just curious about you," she whispered.

"Because I'm a stranger?"

"Well, not entirely. I'm afraid it's more about me than it is about you. The last man who dropped by to see me here at Rainy Creek Gardens was my fiancé. He came to tell me that he couldn't go through with the marriage."

"He did it here? In public? With all your coworkers and the residents around?"

"Brian said he thought it would be easier for me that way."

Dumbfounded, Max stared at her. "Easier? For you?"

"You know, so I wouldn't be alone afterward. He said he knew that I would be among friends who could comfort me."

"That's complete bullshit."

He didn't realize that he had spoken into one of those strange silences that can fall over a room without warning until the words were out of his mouth. By then it was too late.

The birthday crowd froze. He was suddenly the focal point of a variety of expressions that ranged across the spectrum from stern disapproval to acute interest. He was sure he heard a couple of snorts of muffled laughter.

At the back of the room a tall woman with thinning gray hair rammed her cane against the floor a couple of times.

"What did he say?" she demanded in a voice that carried the weight of authority.

Max figured her for a retired professor or maybe a doctor.

"He said *bullshit,*" Ethel responded, raising her own voice to make sure the questioner heard her.

"For pity's sake," Charlotte muttered.

"Why'd he say *bullshit*?" the woman with the cane asked.

"Good question," someone else said.

"This is your problem," Charlotte said out of the side of her mouth. "You solve it."

There was another sudden silence. Max swallowed a bite of cake and faced the crowd.

"Ms. Sawyer just told me that her former fiancé, who evidently was an asshole, came here to Rainy Creek Gardens to tell her that he was calling off the wedding. She said she thought he chose to drop the bomb on her here for her sake. She thinks the s.o.b. was trying to be thoughtful. He didn't want her to be alone afterward. He wanted her to have friends around who could comfort her. I said that was bullshit. He did it here because he knew she wouldn't make a scene in front of all of you."

"Damn right," a man declared.

"Bullshit, for sure," another man said.

"Yep, he did it here to save his own hide," Ethel announced. "That jerk was a coward if ever there was one. You're better off without him, Charlotte."

A chorus of voices chimed in, agreeing with Ethel's conclusion.

Max looked at Charlotte.

"They're right," he said. "You're better off without him."

Charlotte gave him a steely look. "Why, exactly, did you come here, Mr. Cutler?"

"I wanted to see if we could meet after you get off work. Maybe have drinks. I have a few things to discuss with you."

A ripple of approval swept across the room.

Ethel beamed. "Say yes, Charlotte. This one looks like a much better catch than the jerk."

"Thank you," Max said. "But it doesn't sound like the jerk set the bar very high."

There was another wave of laughter.

Charlotte's jaw tensed.

Max lowered his voice and leaned in close to whisper in her ear.

"I tracked down the Loring detective who

handled your stepsister's case. He's willing to answer a few questions."

Charlotte caught her breath. Her eyes widened with excitement. "I leave here at five. Would it be convenient for you to come to my apartment around six? We would have some privacy there."

"I can do that," he said.

CHAPTER 16

Madison waited until she was certain that her administrative assistant had left the office. When she was satisfied that she was alone, she took out her phone.

Victoria answered immediately, her voice terse with dread.

"Did you get the warning, too?" she asked.

"Yes." Madison walked to the wall of windows. Her office was on the thirty-seventh floor of the office tower. She had a sweeping view of Elliott Bay and the Olympics beyond. "I just heard from Emily. She said she received the same message."

"At least that means that Jocelyn's alive. She's gone into hiding."

"Not necessarily. That message was sent from an anonymous e-mail address. There's no way to know if Jocelyn was the sender."

"What are you talking about?" Victoria asked, clearly startled. "Who else could have sent it? Only the five of us knew the emergency code."

"Exactly. Now Louise is dead and Jocelyn is off the grid — supposedly."

"Where are you going with this?" Victoria demanded.

"It occurs to me that Emily might have sent the code. She's very, very good with computers. She would know how to make the message look like it came from an anonymous e-mail address."

There was a short, startled silence before Victoria responded.

"But why would she do that?"

"I don't know for sure, but I can think of one possible scenario and, frankly, it scares the shit out of me."

"What?"

"The Keyworth Investment."

"What about it?" But Victoria sounded wary now.

"The buyout looks like a sure thing. There's a lot of money at stake."

"Oh, shit, Madison. You can't be serious."

"Originally we were going to split it five ways. But with one member of the club dead, that becomes a four-way split. And if two members of the club are gone, we're down to a three-way split. What if it doesn't stop there? What if another member of the club suffers an unfortunate accident or an overdose? You or me, for instance?"

"You're saying that Emily is deliberately getting rid of the members of the club? But you're the one who brought her into the group."

"She seemed like a good fit at the time. And she had the skill set we needed. I think she saw it as a game at first. But maybe now she sees the opportunity of a lifetime — a chance to make a fortune off the Keyworth deal."

"Are you sure about any of this?"

"No," Madison admitted. "But in my world, the first rule is to follow the money."

"Emily is as nervous as the rest of us. You saw her."

"Maybe it's an act."

"If Emily really did murder Louise, it means she had access to some exotic street drugs and knew how to use them to kill someone."

"It's not rocket science," Madison said. "Emily volunteers at the shelter. A lot of the people who come and go from that place are dealing with drug issues. It wouldn't have been difficult to hook up with a dealer. All Emily would have needed was a date rape drug to render Louise unconscious. After she was out, Emily could have injected her with the lethal stuff."

"You've got this all figured out, don't you?"

"I've had time to think about it."

"So, are you going to run, too?"

"It's not that easy," Madison said. "I've got to stay on top of the Keyworth deal. I can't afford to disappear while it's brewing. Too many things can derail the buyout at the last minute."

"Can't you keep an eye on it online? You don't have to be here in Seattle, do you?"

Madison tightened her grip on the phone. Her stomach clenched. *So much money at stake.*

"I can't just vanish like Jocelyn did," she said.

"Suit yourself. I could really use my share of the profits, but I'm not going to risk my life for them."

"You can't stay lost forever," Madison said.

"No, but I can stay gone until we find out what is going on. If you're right, then this thing will end after the buyout takes place. I'm leaving tonight."

"Vicky, wait, where will you go?"

"My aunt's place on the coast, at least for now." Victoria paused. "By the way, since you're weaving conspiracy theories, I've got one for you."

"What?"

"Maybe Emily isn't the one we should be worrying about."

Madison almost stopped breathing. "You think maybe *Jocelyn* is the problem?"

"She's the one who disappeared first," Victoria said. "And she's almost as good with computers as Emily. Good-bye, Madison."

The connection went dead.

CHAPTER 17

Charlotte sliced the very expensive cheese that she had picked up in the Pike Place Market on the way home and reminded herself again that the appointment with Max was not a date.

He was coming to her apartment to tell her about his conversation with the retired Loring police detective.

It was definitely not a date.

But the knowledge that he would soon be at her front door sent another little rush of anticipation through her. It was a weird sensation. She hadn't invited any man up to her apartment since the disaster with Brian Conroy.

Jocelyn had begun to lose patience with her and had accused her of hiding from the world. But it hadn't felt like she was hiding out, she thought. Instead it was as if she had simply lost interest in that aspect of life.

She wondered what Max expected from their meeting. He probably saw it as a business appointment, too. After all, he was a professional.

She studied the neatly arranged slices of cheese on the plate. Max looked very fit and quite healthy. He probably had a good appetite.

She added the remainder of the cheese and a few more crackers to the plate. She wouldn't produce the wine and the cheese unless the situation felt comfortable. If it didn't feel right, she would let Max deliver his report and then see him out the door. She would drink the wine and eat the cheese all by herself.

The muffled ring of her phone sent a jolt of alarm through her.

Max. He was calling to cancel the appointment.

She could almost hear Jocelyn mocking her. *That's it, think positive.*

It dawned on her that the reason her phone sounded muffled was because she had forgotten to take it out of her shoulder bag. She hurried into the living room and retrieved the device.

She glanced at the screen. And froze. She had removed Brian Conroy from her list of contacts just hours after he had told her that he could not bring himself to go through with the marriage, but she recognized his number.

She really, really did not want to talk to him. On the other hand, she had once been convinced that she was in love with him and she wanted to believe that his feelings for her had been real, too, at least for a while. He was not a bad person, she thought. In hindsight she realized that she had reason to be grateful to him. After all, he had changed his mind before the wedding rather than afterward.

She also knew what Jocelyn would have said if she were standing there: *Dump the bastard's call.*

She took the call, telling herself it was pure curiosity that made her do it.

"Hello," she said, going for casual.

"Charlotte, sweetie, it's so good to hear your voice. I've been worrying about you. I wanted to check in and make sure you were okay."

He sounded sincere. It was the *sweetie* that rankled. She tried to analyze her reaction and was vaguely surprised to discover that she was mostly impatient and annoyed. She glanced at the clock. She had a guest due any minute now.

"I'm fine, Brian, but I'm a little busy at

the moment," she said. "Thanks for checking up on me. Got to go now —"

"Wait, don't hang up. I really need to talk to you."

"I can't imagine why. Look, I've got someone coming by soon and —"

"Taylor is no longer in the picture."

He sounded as if he were announcing the end of the world. Film at eleven.

She went back into the kitchen and opened the refrigerator to see if the bottle of white wine she had stuck inside earlier was getting properly chilled.

"Who in the world is Taylor?" she said. "Oh, right. Taylor. The woman you said was in a bad relationship. You were going to rescue her, as I recall."

"She used me."

"No shit. Sorry, got to run."

Now she sounded downright vengeful. *So what? I'm entitled.*

"Sweetie, I know you've probably got some issues because of what happened, but deep down you and I are friends."

"Got news for you. Friends don't leave friends with the bills for a canceled wedding. I just finished paying off the damn dress and the flowers."

"That's not right. You should have gotten refunds on everything."

160

The outrage in his words would have been laughable under other circumstances.

"There are these little paragraphs called cancellation clauses in all the contracts," she said. "If you had given me a couple of months' notice instead of a few days, I could have gotten most of the money back, but that's not what happened, is it? Good-bye, Brian."

"Sweetie, please, I really need to talk to you."

"You want my advice?"

"Of course. You always see things so clearly."

"Here are my words of wisdom. *Do not call me sweetie.*"

"You sound bitter and angry. That's not like you, Charlotte."

"Turns out I can hold a grudge. Who knew?"

She zapped the call and dropped the phone on the counter. For a moment she stood very still, aware that she was buzzed on a shot of pure adrenaline. Okay, refusing to let Brian cry on her shoulder was probably a very mean and petty sort of revenge, but damn, it was exhilarating.

Jocelyn would have cheered, she thought.

The rush faded, but her mood did not. She hurried down the short hall to check her hair and makeup. She had a feeling Max would be right on time.

It was not a date, she reminded herself one last time. They were going to discuss some very serious matters. But, as Jocelyn would say, a little lipstick never hurt. It gave a woman confidence.

CHAPTER 18

Victoria threw the last two items — a nightgown and a robe — into the over-stuffed suitcase and closed the lid.

It had been a righteous game back at the start, an opportunity to play the role of an avenging goddess. Sure, there had been some risk involved, but none of them could have foreseen the disaster that was unfolding. They had convinced themselves that they were safe behind the seemingly impenetrable wall of anonymity provided by the online world.

It was a struggle to get the bag zipped. Under other circumstances she would have packed a second suitcase, but there wasn't much point in taking a lot of stuff. She was not going on vacation. She was going into hiding. She certainly didn't require an extensive wardrobe. She wouldn't need any of her professional suits and there would be no call for her prized collection of high-heeled shoes.

She hauled the suitcase off the bed, set it on the floor, gripped the handle and rolled it out of the bedroom. She went down the hall, turning off lights along the way. Tears burned in her eyes. She loved her precious little condo. Leaving it was one of the most painful things she had ever done.

At the front door she paused to take one last look around the home she had worked so hard to create. Until now it had embodied all the things she had longed for as a young girl trapped in a nightmare — a safe and serene refuge.

It was the home she had fantasized about when she had hidden in the closet in a desperate effort to shut out the terrible sound of her drunken stepfather beating her mother. It was the place she had dreamed of when her mother had awakened her in the middle of the night and told her they were leaving. She had stuffed her most valuable treasures into her school backpack.

She'd had only one brief glimpse of her stepfather as she and her mother had rushed across the living room. He was passed out in front of the television, an unfinished bottle of booze on the floor beside the chair.

Her mother had driven them straight to her aunt's home out on the coast.

They had lived with the threat of the bastard hanging over their heads for months until he had done everyone a favor and killed himself in a single-car accident. He had been driving drunk at the time.

Victoria was fiercely proud of the fact that she had triumphed against long odds. She had earned a degree in arts and communications at a small college and wound up in a field she loved — marketing. She was good at what she did.

The future she had been crafting for herself had been full of promise — right up until the fateful moment when Madison Benson had introduced her to the other members of the investment club. Madison had seemed like the very embodiment of the avenging warrior queen that the terrified little girl inside Victoria longed to emulate.

The members of the club had told themselves that they were all strong, powerful women; women on a mission.

But somewhere along the line they had taken one risk too many and now they were being hunted.

She locked up her condo and went down the hall to the elevator. It dawned on her that what troubled her the most was that once again she was running, just as she and her mother had run all those years ago.

Walking through the concrete garage unnerved her. The shadows were long and her footsteps echoed loudly in the gloom. She moved more quickly. By the time she reached her car, she was sprinting.

She checked the backseat before she opened the door. There was no one hiding there. No one leaped out from behind a pillar.

She got behind the wheel and locked the doors, reversed out of the parking stall and drove toward the exit. The steel gate seemed to take forever to operate. She had visions of being trapped in the garage with the killer.

Who are you? she wondered. *Are you one of us?*

Madison was right. Money was a huge temptation and there would be a fortune at stake if the Keyworth buyout went through.

Or are you one of our targets?

Revenge was an equally powerful incentive. She knew that all too well.

When the gate finally opened, freeing her vehicle, the relief was nearly overwhelming.

A short time later she was out of the city center, driving fast toward the one place she was certain the killer would never think to look for her.

CHAPTER 19

"I'm surprised Detective Briggs even re-membered my stepsister's case," Charlotte said. "At the time Jocelyn was convinced that he didn't believe her or, if he did believe her, he considered it her fault that she was attacked. She said that the cops took the blame-the-victim approach to the investigation. The campus security guards were even more obnoxious."

"Briggs said he believed Jocelyn's story but he was never able to identify a solid suspect," Max said. "He also implied that he didn't get much cooperation from the campus security people."

"I can believe that," Charlotte said. "I'm sure they were told to make the problem go away."

"Briggs did say that the school authorities exerted pressure on the chief to keep things quiet. The college was new and trying to establish a reputation. The people at the top were afraid the bad publicity would hurt when it came to recruiting staff and students."

He was sitting in the biggest chair in the small living room. The chair was not all that large, however. It was small and sleek, almost dainty. He just hoped it would not collapse under his weight. He was trying to make a good impression.

Charlotte was perched on the edge of a delicate sofa that looked like it had come from the same store as the chair, a store that evidently specialized in miniature furniture for small apartments. There was a classy little glass-topped coffee table between the sofa and the recliner.

The entire apartment probably would have fit into the front room of his new house, but it was warm and cozy and oddly lush. There were plants everywhere — big ones framed the windows, small ones decorated the dining bar that separated the kitchen and living room area and still more pots of greenery sat on various end tables.

The space was also colorful. *Very* colorful. It looked like a spice factory had exploded in the small space. Saffron walls were set off with cinnamon trim work. The area rug was the color of crushed red peppers and accented with splashes of turmeric. Anson would approve, he thought. Anson had learned to cook after he found himself with three young boys to feed. He had gotten very good at it.

Max wasn't sure what he had expected when he walked through the front door of the apartment a short time earlier. But now it occurred to him that he liked the sunny, vibrant palette. He liked it a lot. He wondered if Charlotte would be willing to advise him on paint colors when he finally got around to painting his house.

"The problem was that there was so little to go on," Charlotte said. "Jocelyn never saw her attacker."

"For what it's worth, Briggs said that may have been what saved her life."

Charlotte set her wineglass down very carefully. "That did occur to us later, believe me."

Max reached for another cracker and another slice of cheese. "Briggs said that he did develop a few theories. He's willing to discuss them with us."

"When?"

"I told him that we would drive to Loring tomorrow. Will that work for you? Sorry I didn't check first. I didn't want to waste any time or give Briggs an opportunity to change his mind."

"Yes, tomorrow is Saturday. No problem." Charlotte paused, brows scrunching together a little. "You said that Louise Flint drove all the way to Loring and back shortly before she died."

"According to her car's GPS, yes."

"Did you ask Briggs if Louise had contacted him recently?"

"No. I thought I'd save that for our interview with him."

Charlotte looked first surprised and then curious. "Why?"

"Hell if I know. Just the way I work. In my experience, it's easier to judge a person's reactions when you're face-to-face."

"That makes sense." Charlotte sat very straight on the sofa, determination radiating from her. "What time do you want to leave?"

"Briggs said he was going fishing in the morning and that he had some chores to do after that. He asked us to show up in mid-afternoon. So what do you say I pick you up a little after noon?"

"I'll be ready."

He looked at the plate on the glass coffee table. He had eaten the last of the cheese and crackers.

Crunch time, he thought. *Make it look casual. Just business.*

"Want to grab a bite to eat?" he said, going for an offhand vibe so that it wouldn't sting too much if she turned him down.

She appeared surprised, as if she hadn't given dinner any thought.

"All right," she said. "There's a nice little place on the corner. Gluten free, vegan, paleo and vegetarian friendly."

He felt as if he had just taken a very strong tonic. He felt good. Thrilled.

Just business, he told himself.

"So long as there is actual food," he said.

She smiled. "Don't worry, there will be crab cakes. With actual Dungeness crab. And French fries. The traditional Pacific Northwest comfort food."

Suddenly the spicy hot room got even brighter. He had been right, he thought. Charlotte's smile was the real thing.

CHAPTER 20

"How did you end up in the private investigation business?" Charlotte asked.

Max thought about the question while he munched a bite of the very good crab cakes he had ordered.

The restaurant was one of those casual, comfortable places that were scattered around Seattle and its neighborhoods. It featured an extensive list of craft beers and regional wines. There were also a lot of "small plates" on the menu. He had ordered a full entrée, but Charlotte had opted for two little dishes — roasted Brussels sprouts and a tiny dish of deviled eggs. Evidently in addition to buying miniature furniture she ate miniature food. No wonder she looked a little thin.

"My ex-wife asked me the same question," he said.

Belatedly he remembered having read somewhere that one of the rules of successful dating after a divorce was that you weren't supposed to bring up the ex. On the other hand, this was not a date. This was business. But there were rules about discussing your personal life with a business associate, too.

Charlotte winced. "Sorry. Didn't mean to dredge up old history."

"My fault." He drank some beer. "I'm the one who mentioned my ex."

"Yes, well, it's not like I haven't got one of my own. Sort of."

"How long has it been since the jerk told you that he wasn't planning to show up at the wedding?"

"Two months, one week and three days." Charlotte smiled a very bright, shiny smile. "Not that I'm counting."

He grinned. "Of course not."

"But on the plus side, I managed to pay off the dress and the florist's cancellation fees last month. That was a very good day in Charlotte-land. Unfortunately I got stuck with the full price of the dress because it had already been altered."

"What did you do with it?"

"Sold it for pennies on the dollar to a rental shop. It wasn't like I was ever going to wear it."

"What if you decide to get married again?"

She looked at him as if he had said something extremely foolish and/or incredibly dumb.

"Obviously, if that happens, I'll get a new dress," she said patiently.

"Right," he said. Feeling like a complete idiot, he made a stab at getting the conversation back on track. "Financially, I'm free and clear, too. She got the house outside of D.C. and I cashed in my retirement account to come up with the settlement, but it was worth it. I wanted a clean break."

Charlotte nodded and took a bite of her roasted Brussels sprouts. "Sounds like we're both in the process of reinventing ourselves."

He almost choked on his beer. "That's putting a positive spin on things."

"You don't believe in the possibility of reinventing yourself?"

He reflected briefly. "People are what they are. Mostly they don't change. Not much, at any rate."

"That's a rather negative view of human nature."

He smiled slowly. "It has an upside. I make my living by identifying patterns of behavior and predicting people's actions. The fact that most folks don't change much over time is very good for my business."

"I take your point. And I do see plenty of real-world examples of your theory at Rainy Creek Gardens. People don't change much. They just become more concentrated versions of what they always were."

"Uh-huh." He ate a French fry. "Like I said, it's one of the cornerstones of my business model."

"You said you used to be a profiler," she said after a moment.

"We had a fancier name for the job — forensic behavioral analysis — but, yeah, I was a profiler. I worked for a consulting firm that took contracts with various police departments around the nation and the occasional government agency."

Charlotte put down her fork and studied him with a somber expression.

"How did you stand it?" she asked.

He had been about to eat another bite of his crab cakes. Slowly he lowered the fork.

"I don't think anyone has ever asked me that," he said. "When people find out what I used to do for a living, they ask me all sorts of questions. They want to know if real-world profiling works the same way it does on television. They ask me to tell them about the worst case I ever worked. They ask if I ever caught any famous killers. All kinds of questions. But not that one."

"Sorry. Didn't mean to get so personal. It's none of my business."

"It's okay," he said. "The answer is that there were a lot of times when I didn't think I would be able to go to one more murder scene. Times when I got sick to my stomach. Times when I woke up sweating from the nightmares. Times when I had to use booze or meds to get some sleep."

"But still you did the work."

He shrugged. "Yeah. What can I say? It paid well."

"That's not why you did it."

He raised his brows. "No?"

"No. I think you did the work because you were good at it and because someone has to do it. Sounds like it was a calling for you."

He considered that briefly. "Don't know about a calling. In the end I had to leave."

"You burned out on the profiling?"

It was a simple question — with a devastating answer. He should never have allowed the conversation to get this deep into the weeds of his personal problems.

He met her eyes. "There was a case. It ended badly. Afterward my issues — the night sweats and the insomnia — got worse. The company shrink concluded that I was no longer a useful member of the team. My colleagues thought I had become a full-blown paranoid. My wife announced she wanted a divorce. I was asked to resign. It was either that or be fired. So I resigned."

He braced himself for the fallout. He hadn't meant to tell her that much; he shouldn't have told her that much. But for some inexplicable reason, he wanted her to know the truth. He was not sure what to expect. Shock, maybe. Alarm, for sure. After all, she now knew that she was working with an investigator who had been forced out of his last job because he'd lost his nerve.

But Charlotte simply nodded in an understanding way, accepting the news in a manner that indicated she had sensed it before he told her — sensed it and wasn't concerned about it.

"So you moved out west to Seattle to find another way to use your talents," she said.

He wasn't sure where to go with that.

"Yes," he said.

"Why Seattle?"

Again he found himself surprised by her question.

"I was born here," he said.

"Did you grow up here?"

"No."

"But you feel a connection to Seattle because this is where you were born. I understand."

"My turn to ask the questions," he said. "How did you and Jocelyn come to be stepsisters?"

"My father died when I was a kid. Jocelyn lost her mother when she was in her teens. My mom and Jocelyn's dad got together when they each made the decision to go to their high school reunion. It turned out they had dated in their senior year, but they went off to different colleges and their lives took different directions."

"I take it that the old spark was reignited when they got together at the reunion?"

"Yes. They were quite happy together, but we lost both of them two years ago."

"What happened?"

"Jocelyn's father was a pilot. Owned his own plane. He and Mom were on their way to a resort in Colorado. They ran into bad weather over the mountains. The plane went down. They were both killed."

"I'm sorry," Max said.

"Thank you."

"So now it's just you and Jocelyn?"

Charlotte nodded and drank some of her wine.

"I take it you and Jocelyn got along after your parents married?"

"Are you kidding? We hated each other at first."

"When did the two of you become close?" Max asked.

"I told myself I didn't want to be friends with Jocelyn, but the truth was, she was everything I wanted to be — what every teenage girl wants to be — savvy, gorgeous, confident, bold. She had a sense of style and she always had a boyfriend or three on the line. Plus she got good grades."

"An A-list girl."

"Definitely." Charlotte wrinkled her nose. "I was B list, believe me."

"All good reasons for you to resent her."

"Sure. But she had one other quality that changed everything. Jocelyn was kind to me."

"Kind?"

"Somewhere along the line she started to feel sorry for me. She kept an eye on me. For example, I got asked out by a senior. He was one of the A-list boys. Played on the football team. Dated the prettiest girls. Got accepted into a fine university. Needless to say, I was thrilled when he asked for a date. I'd never had a real date and now I'd been asked out by one of the most popular boys in school."

"Something tells me this story doesn't end well."

Charlotte raised her wineglass and looked

at him across the top. "What's wrong with this picture, hm? You're right. It didn't end well. At least, that was what I thought at the time. But the truth was, Jocelyn rescued me. When I told her who had asked me out, she was furious. At first I thought it was because she was jealous. But she knew that the creep was involved in a nasty competition with some of the other boys on the team. They racked up points by having sex with as many girls as possible in their senior year. The guy who asked me out saw me as an easy target."

"You took Jocelyn's advice, I hope?"

"After a lot of heavy drama, yes, I took it. I was crushed, of course. But even then I knew that Jocelyn was a lot smarter than me when it came to the dangerous games played in high school. And she had one very important thing going for her when she made her pitch."

"What was that?"

"I'm risk averse, according to my therapist," Charlotte said. "I didn't know that back in those days, I just knew I wasn't terribly brave."

"The cautious type, huh?"

"Yep. Jocelyn, on the other hand, is an adrenaline junkie. I always leave the bungee jumping to her. At any rate she gave me enough details about what would happen on my big date with the football hero to scare the hell out of me. I canceled."

"So what went wrong with the fiancé? Why didn't Jocelyn save you from that mistake?"

"Good question. Brian Conroy seemed perfect. Jocelyn agreed. When we did the postmortem, we decided that we had both overlooked the obvious red flag."

"Which was?"

"Brian was just too good to be true."

Max picked up his beer glass. "So Jocelyn isn't always right when it comes to her judgments of other people?"

"Nope. But, then, nobody is."

"Yeah, the sociopaths are out there and they can fool anyone, at least for a while."

Charlotte frowned. "I'm very sure that Brian isn't a sociopath."

"I'll take your word for it."

"He's just . . . commitment-phobic. I don't think he realized it himself, until he got to the edge of the abyss and looked down."

"Speaking of ex-boyfriends, was your stepsister seeing anyone before she disappeared?"

Charlotte looked startled. "Wow. Slick way to change the subject."

He could feel himself turning red. Luckily the restaurant was heavily shadowed.

"Sorry," he said. "I do that sometimes when I'm working a case."

"Jump from one topic to another?"

"Yeah."

"Well, the answer is that Jocelyn wasn't seeing anyone in particular recently. There is no stalker lurking in the background, if that's what you're wondering, at least not that I know of."

"That would have been too easy."

Charlotte hesitated. "But there is one thing you should know."

"What?"

"If Jocelyn had attracted a stalker, there's a very real possibility that she would not have told me. She wouldn't have wanted me to worry about her."

"We need more data. With luck, we'll get something useful from Briggs."

CHAPTER 21

Egan Briggs had described the location of his cabin in considerable detail, and Max had taken careful notes. But there were no street signs this deep into the Cascades, and GPS hadn't functioned reliably since they had left the town of Loring some forty-five minutes earlier.

The trees grew thick and close on either side of the narrow strip of winding pavement. The heavy foliage formed a nearly impenetrable screen, making it difficult to spot the occasional cabin or lodge tucked away in the woods. The rain wasn't helping matters, Max thought. It fell in a steady sheet on the windshield of the SUV.

He had used the heavy vehicle for the trip not because it was more impressive than his city car but because they were heading into the mountains and the weather was bad. Anson Salinas hadn't raised his sons with a lot of rules, but he had enforced the few that he set down. One of those rules was that you never went into unforgiving territory without taking a few precautions. The SUV had four-wheel drive. There was an emergency kit, some bottled water, a flashlight and some energy bars.

His gun was in the console between the two front seats.

Charlotte looked up from the directions that he had jotted down on a piece of paper.

"I think we just passed the cutoff to the bridge," she said, peering out the side window.

"You think?" He did not take his eyes off the winding road. "You're the one in charge of directions."

"You're the one who wrote them down. What does 'HR after cross 1 ln br then HL on gr rd' mean?"

"It means hard right after we cross the one-lane bridge followed by a hard left on a graveled road. Seems clear to me."

"Of course. I don't know what I was thinking. Okay. We have definitely gone too far. We need to turn around and head back."

"What makes you so sure of that?"

"Because we just passed another lookout. In your notes you wrote down something that I think says that if we pass Ribbon Falls Lookout, we've overshot the turnoff to the bridge."

"How do you know if that was Ribbon Falls Lookout?"

"I think I saw a waterfall."

"Okay, I'll take your word for it."

The road was too narrow to allow a U-turn and the shoulders on either side had been rendered into mud by the rain. He executed a cautious three-point turn on the pavement.

"Nice work," Charlotte said. "I tried that maneuver once. It didn't go well."

"We all have a talent," he muttered.

He was startled when she laughed.

The drive from Seattle had been a slog because of the rain and the limited visibility, but he had found himself savoring the enforced intimacy of the road trip. He did not think of himself as a good conversationalist, but Charlotte was surprisingly easy to talk to. And the silences, when they fell, were comfortable. At least, he was comfortable with them. He wasn't sure how she felt.

He drove slowly back down the twisting road.

Charlotte leaned forward in her seat, studying the scene through the windshield with an intent expression.

"This is it," she announced. "There's the turnoff. I can see the little bridge."

Max made the turn and cat-footed the big vehicle cautiously over the old logging bridge. It was a single lane with no guard-rails. The water was not far below.

"I don't like the look of the river," he said. "It's running high. If this downpour doesn't let up, the water could be over the top of the bridge in a few more hours. We aren't going to stay very long at the Briggses'. We don't want to get caught up here in the mountains tonight."

"If Detective Briggs has any hard information for us, I doubt it will take him long to provide it."

On the far side of the bridge, Max turned off onto a steep graveled road that was gouged with potholes.

"You get the feeling that maybe Briggs's career in law enforcement made him a tad paranoid?" Charlotte asked. "I mean, he couldn't have chosen a more out-of-the-way location for his retirement home."

"One thing's for sure, no one is going to sneak up on him — not using this road," Max said. "He'd hear a vehicle coming long before it arrived."

A few more twists in the old logging road brought them to a small clearing. There was a large cabin with a front porch set in the center. Two vehicles — a relatively new pickup and an equally new, mud-spattered SUV — were parked near the cabin.

The front door opened just as Max brought his vehicle to a halt in the clearing. A big, burly, bearded man appeared on the front porch. His thinning gray hair was pulled back in a low ponytail. He was dressed in a faded plaid flannel shirt, baggy jeans and scuffed work boots.

Max opened the console, removed the holstered gun and strapped it around his waist. He pulled on his slouchy sports coat to cover the weapon.

Charlotte looked startled.

"You brought a gun?" she said.

"Just a precaution. By all accounts, Briggs has been living off the grid for a while now. That can do things to the mind."

"Oh. I never considered that he might be a little crazy."

"Don't know that he is."

He reached into the backseat for his waterproof windbreaker and then angled the baseball cap down over his eyes.

"Ready?" he said.

"Yes."

"One more thing. Be polite, but don't eat or drink anything that's offered."

"What?"

"This case involves drugs. We're not taking any chances."

Charlotte gave him a strange look. *Probably thinks I'm borderline paranoid.* Hell, maybe he was.

But Charlotte merely nodded. "Okay."

She pulled up the hood of her anorak and opened her door.

He climbed out from behind the wheel and jogged around the front of the SUV. Together he and Charlotte hurried toward the shelter of the porch.

"Detective Briggs?" Max said.

"Retired. Call me Egan. You must be Cutler. Sorry about the weather. Hell of a day for a drive up into these mountains. Didn't know the storm was going to turn bad like this. It's gonna catch a lot of folks by surprise."

The voice matched the man: deep, booming and infused with an authority that, in Max's experience, was common to those who'd had a long career in law enforcement.

"Max Cutler," Max said. "This is Charlotte Sawyer."

"I'm Jocelyn Pruett's stepsister," Charlotte said. She lowered the hood of her jacket. "We appreciate your taking the time to talk with us today, sir."

"Yeah, well, not like I had anything else planned this afternoon," Egan said. "Not with this weather. Figured you two were damn serious about talking to me if you were willing to drive all the way up here. Come on inside. My wife is making coffee."

CHAPTER 22

"Let me get this straight," Egan said. "You think that the death of this Louise Flint might be connected to that old rape case at Loring College?"

"At this point it's just one more angle I'm trying to check out," Max said. "Ms. Sawyer is assisting me because her stepsister is unavailable."

Egan frowned. "Something happened to Ms. Pruett?"

Thank goodness she had prepared for this question, Charlotte thought. Max had been very clear right from the start that they were not going to give away any more information than was absolutely necessary in the course of the interview. But he hadn't been convinced that she would be able to lie well enough to fool a former cop, so he had made her practice a few things on the drive from Seattle.

"No, she's fine," Charlotte said. She was

proud of the cool, calm manner in which the words came out. "But she's away on an extended retreat for a month. I can't get in touch with her, so I'm here in her stead. I know she'll want to be informed about any developments."

"Yeah, well, just to clarify, I never really doubted your stepsister's story of the rape," Egan said. He leaned back in the big easy chair and propped his booted ankles on a needlepoint hassock that looked handmade. "I could see that she'd been terrified and there was definitely a bloody nick on the side of her throat. She said that was where the assailant had held the tip of the knife."

Charlotte was very careful not to look at Max. She was afraid that if she did, she would reveal her rage. She remembered all too well Jocelyn's furious, anguished description of how the detective in charge of the case had insinuated again and again that the rape had been consensual — just some adventurous sex that had gotten out of hand.

"Did the Loring Police Department's investigation produce any leads?" Max asked.

He sounded so easygoing and professional, Charlotte thought. Like he believed everything Briggs said.

Her damp anorak was hanging from a wall hook near the front door. Max's windbreaker was next to it. He was still wearing his ill-fitting sports coat. He kept it fastened to conceal his gun.

The interior of the cabin was a real-life version of what designers liked to call rustic. The sturdy wooden dining table looked handmade. So did the drapes and the area rug. Genuine logs, not gas, burned in the fireplace. Lanterns were scattered around the room, an indication that the occupants of the cabin were accustomed to losing their power during storms.

There was a television that was hooked up to a satellite dish, and a landline phone, but Charlotte did not see any signs of cell phones or computers. The Briggses were doing their best to live off the grid without cutting all ties to the outside world.

The only indications that the Briggses had once lived a more conventional life were the framed photos on the mantel. One showed a much younger Egan Briggs dressed in a policeman's uniform. He was smiling proudly and he had his arm draped possessively around his wife, Roxanne. Her long blond hair was blowing in the wind and she looked very pretty. She also looked a lot younger than her husband.

The other two photos were pictures of a handsome youth — a son, Charlotte decided. The first picture showed him dressed in a high school graduation gown. He was smiling a big, can't-wait-to-take-on-the-future grin.

The second picture was a snapshot that showed the same young man a few years later. He lounged against the railing on the porch of the cabin and he was no longer smiling. There was something sullen about the way his shoulders were hunched. He looked as if he was angry at having been forced to pose for the picture. Or maybe just angry at the world, Charlotte thought.

"Nothing solid," Egan said in response to Max's question. "Seem to recall that there were a couple of popular theories at the time. No offense, Ms. Sawyer, but one of those notions was that Jocelyn Pruett was involved in some nasty sex games that had gotten too rough for her."

Charlotte gripped the arm of her chair. "My stepsister has never been into bondage games."

She was aware that Max was sending her a warning look, but she couldn't help it. Someone had to stand up for Jocelyn, who was not there to defend herself.

Egan exhaled a heavy sigh. "Like I said, I

believed Ms. Pruett. But no one else did. According to the people we talked to at the time, she had a reputation for being what you might call high-spirited. Adventurous."

Charlotte shook her head. "She wasn't into that kind of adventure."

Roxanne Briggs appeared from the small kitchen. She was still tall, but the lushly rounded figure she'd possessed when she posed for the photo on the mantel had thickened over time. Somewhere along the line she had adopted an earth mother vibe. She wore a long, flowing caftan-style dress that was decorated with brilliant splashes of color. Her blond hair was just starting to turn gray. It hung in a single heavy braid down her back.

She watched Charlotte with somber, unreadable eyes and extended a wooden tray that held two steaming mugs.

"Coffee?" she asked in a whispery voice that did not seem to go with her size and stature.

It was, Charlotte reflected, the first word Roxanne had spoken since acknowledging the introductions with a nod of her head a short time earlier.

"Yes, thank you," Charlotte said.

She took one of the mugs.

"Cream and sugar?" Roxanne asked.

"No, thanks," Charlotte said.

Roxanne offered the other mug to Max.

"Thanks," he said. He took the coffee. "No cream or sugar."

Roxanne put the empty tray on the hand-carved chunk of polished wood that served as a coffee table. She sank down onto an overstuffed sofa.

Max turned back to Egan. "You said there were two major theories of the crime. What was the second one?"

"I ruled out the BDSM angle because I figured that if Ms. Pruett was into that scene she probably would have known her attacker."

"He blindfolded her," Charlotte said. "He put a bag over her head and threatened to choke her."

"I know, but still, if she'd been having regular sex with him, it seemed like there would have been something about him that she would have recognized. Also, if there had been a sex club like that operating on the campus, I'm pretty sure I would have turned up someone who knew something about it. Loring College was small at the time and the town was not exactly a big city. Still isn't, come to that."

"You're right," Max said. "It would have

been hard to keep a BDSM club completely secret."

Egan nodded. "That's why, in the end, I went with the second theory — that Ms. Pruett was the victim of a serial rapist who protected himself by moving from campus to campus."

Charlotte started to open her mouth to tell him that Jocelyn had always been sure that her attacker was someone who knew the campus well. But Max flashed her a quick, silencing look. This time she heeded the order.

He looked down into his coffee for a few beats, as if he was mulling over the information that Egan had provided. When he raised his eyes, his expression was unreadable.

"You're sure it couldn't have been someone local?" he asked.

"Trust me, we looked into that possibility very thoroughly," Egan said. "Talked to a lot of students, male and female. Also talked to several members of the faculty and staff. To this day I'm convinced that whoever attacked Jocelyn Pruett moved on. If he hasn't been picked up on some other charge by now, he's probably still at it."

"Guys like that don't quit," Max said.

Egan shook his head. "Nope."

Charlotte tightened her grip on the mug. "My sister believes that she was stalked before she was assaulted. The rapist seemed to know her routine. He struck at the one place on the path where she would be most vulnerable. Doesn't that indicate that it was someone who knew the campus well?"

Egan gave her a sorrowful look. "It indicates that someone studied the campus, but it doesn't indicate that he stalked your sister. It's more likely he simply chose his victim at random. Any girl who came down that path that night was a potential target. Jocelyn Pruett was in the wrong place at the wrong time."

Charlotte started to argue, but Max set his coffee mug aside with just enough force to get her attention. She closed her mouth. This was his area of expertise, she thought. Let the man do his job.

"There are some distinctive elements in the case," he said. "Getting a feel for the territory, the attack from behind, the bag over the head and the use of a knife suggest a carefully thought-out plan. This guy is into strategy."

Egan grunted. "Assuming that's the way it happened."

"What's that supposed to mean?" Charlotte demanded.

He gave her a sympathetic look. "The thing is that people who are subject to serious violence and trauma often have difficulty remembering the details of the events exactly as they occurred."

Charlotte kept her mouth shut, but it wasn't easy.

Egan turned back to Max. "I agree with you. Assuming Ms. Pruett did remember the details correctly, the attacker had a plan. And he would have used it again and again because it worked. But there were no more reports like that on the campus or in the town of Loring. Believe me, I kept an eye out for any assault that was even remotely similar. Nothing came to my attention. That's why I think he moved on."

"What about assaults elsewhere in the region?" Max asked.

"I examined the rape reports from campuses around the Pacific Northwest for a while," Egan said. He propped his elbows on the arms of the chair and put his fingertips together. "There were two more that year that could have been a match. Both took place on other college campuses. Both involved blindfolds and knives."

"Was anyone caught?" Charlotte asked.

"No, unfortunately." Egan's jaw tensed. "I followed up, but no one was ever arrested.

There were never any viable suspects. Like I said, if the person who attacked those other two women was the same man who assaulted Jocelyn Pruett, then he was smart enough to move from campus to campus. For a time I even thought I might be able to track him, but the trail went ice-cold after the second report. There were no more assaults using the same MO."

"But you don't think he quit, do you?" Max said.

Egan shook his head. "No. But like I said, it's possible he was arrested on some other charge and is doing time. Hell, it's also possible that he moved out of the state. He could be clear across the country by now. There's no good way to track those kinds of crimes when large distances are involved."

"No," Max said, "there isn't."

A strange hush settled on the interior of the cabin. Charlotte was suddenly aware of the muffled clash of the wind chimes on the front porch. The wind was picking up again. She looked at Roxanne Briggs. The woman seemed frozen in place, staring at Max.

It was Egan who broke the spell. He peered out the window.

"Weather's taking another turn," he said. "You might want to think about getting down off this mountain before things get too bad."

Roxanne stirred. "They haven't even finished their coffee, Egan."

Egan frowned and looked as if he was about to say something, but, as if on cue, the lights flickered and went out. The cabin was plunged into an early twilight.

Roxanne flinched and then got to her feet. "There goes the electricity."

Egan groaned and heaved himself up out of the chair. "Business as usual during a storm, I'm afraid. We always lose power. Well, that's why they invented generators."

"I'll light the lanterns," Roxanne said.

She moved across the small space to the dining room table and struck a match. Light flared in a glass storm lantern.

"I'll go crank up the generator." Egan looked at Max again. "Take it easy driving back down the mountain. The rains have been heavy all week. Rivers and streams are running high. We frequently get a few landslides and downed trees in a storm like this. Once in a while a bridge washes out."

"Right." Max was on his feet. "Thanks for the information. We'll be on our way."

Charlotte set her untouched coffee aside and stood. Roxanne handed her jacket to her without a word. Max shrugged into his windbreaker and yanked his cap down over his eyes.

"One more thing before we take off," he said to Egan. "Has anyone else contacted you recently about that old rape case?"

"No," Egan said. "You two are the first people to ask about it in years. Why?"

"Just curious," Max said. He handed Egan a card. "If you think of anything else, I'd appreciate it if you would give me a call."

"Will do," Egan said. He opened the front door. "Do me a favor, keep me in the loop. I'd really like to know if your investigation goes anywhere. After all these years it would be nice to get some answers."

"I'll be in touch," Max said. He looked at Charlotte. "Ready?"

"Ready."

She moved out onto the sheltered porch. Max followed.

She hurried down the steps. The wind chimes crashed and clanged, creating a dark, unnerving music. The rain was letting up, but the wind was growing stronger. The atmosphere was stirring with a violent energy. She was very glad they were leaving.

She went quickly toward the SUV. Max moved ahead of her. She knew he was going to open the passenger-side door for her.

"I'll get it," she said.

She waved him off, got the door open and

jumped up into the seat.

Max loped around the front of the vehicle, climbed in behind the wheel and fired up the engine. He paused long enough to shrug out of his windbreaker and sports coat. She noticed that he did not unbuckle the gun belt.

She removed her anorak and put it neatly on the floor of the rear compartment to dry.

Max put the SUV in gear and drove cautiously down the steep, graveled driveway.

Charlotte looked back at the darkened cabin.

Roxanne Briggs, illuminated by the glow of the lantern, was at the window, watching them drive away.

"That is one unhappy woman," Charlotte said.

CHAPTER 23

Charlotte turned back around in her seat and studied the scene through the windshield. The rain was still coming down. It was going to be a long drive back to Seattle.

She realized that the uneasy sensation that had been icing her nerves for the past couple of days had grown more intense during the interview with Egan Briggs.

"Briggs didn't seem to know anything about Louise Flint," she said after a while.

"No," Max said. "He didn't."

"He didn't even recognize her name, so obviously she didn't travel to Loring to speak to him."

"Evidently."

"I guess that's not very surprising. Briggs is retired, after all. Louise had no reason to look him up."

"Not unless she thought she had a lead on the man who attacked Jocelyn. In which case it seems likely that she would have wanted to talk to the cop who handled the case."

"Just like you wanted to talk to him," Charlotte said.

"Right." Max reduced his speed to drive around a fallen tree branch. "But maybe Louise Flint had another reason for making the trip to Loring."

"Any idea what that reason might be?"

"Not yet."

"Maybe she came across some information that convinced her that Jocelyn's attacker was still living in the area." Charlotte paused. "But why would she try to investigate on her own?"

Max glanced at her. "You don't think Louise was the type to try to conduct her own investigation?"

Charlotte considered that for a moment. "To be honest, I didn't know Louise well enough to be able to predict her actions. But I can tell you that Jocelyn would not have wanted Louise to take any risks on her behalf."

Max changed gears, slowing the SUV a little more to deal with the bad road.

"Maybe Louise didn't realize that she was taking a risk," he said.

"Or maybe she really did drive all the way to Loring for some reason that had nothing to do with Jocelyn."

"Then we're back to coincidence, and I'm not buying that," Max said.

"Not to change the subject, but did Mr. and Mrs. Briggs strike you as a bit eccentric?"

"A lot of retired cops are a bit eccentric. Some get downright paranoid. Hazard of the job."

"I suppose I can understand that."

"I've got no problem with eccentricities," Max said. "Got a few of my own. What bothers me is that Briggs showed almost zero interest in Louise Flint."

Startled, Charlotte turned partway around in the seat. "What do you mean? He said she hadn't contacted him. Why would he be interested in a woman he never met?"

"Because we drove all this way to ask him about her. Because we brought up Jocelyn's assault case. And most of all because Louise Flint is dead. In my experience, cops don't blow off that kind of data."

"You think he should have been more curious about Louise?"

"Yeah, I do. And there's something else I didn't like."

"What?" Charlotte demanded.

"Briggs claimed that he watched for reports of attacks against women that exhibited an MO similar to the one Jocelyn's assailant used."

"Right. He said there were only two more that year and then they stopped. You were the one who told me that criminals don't change their methods very much."

Max checked his rearview mirror, frowning a little. Then he returned his attention to the rough road.

"No," he said. "But sometimes the smart ones refine their techniques."

"Where are you going with this?"

"It's possible that the blindfold was part of the attacker's fantasy. But what if it was just a means to an end — part of his strategy? What if the purpose was simply to make certain the victim was helpless and to ensure that she couldn't describe her assailant?"

"Meaning?"

"Meaning there are other ways to achieve those objectives. Drugs, for example."

Charlotte caught her breath. "That theory opens up some very scary possibilities."

"Yes, it does. You said that the reason your sister's case wound up in the deep-freeze file was because the evidence box disappeared."

"Right."

"What if someone made certain it got lost?"

Understanding slammed through Charlotte. "Are you suggesting that Briggs may have destroyed the evidence box?"

"I'm just juggling chain saws at the moment. But according to what I found online, Egan Briggs retired less than a year after your sister's case went nowhere."

Charlotte exhaled slowly. "Briggs kept telling us that he believed Jocelyn's account of the assault. But Jocelyn was convinced that he didn't believe her. Still, why would he go so far as to make the evidence box disappear?"

"You told me that the college authorities applied a lot of pressure on the local cops."

"Yes, but to deliberately destroy evidence? That is . . . breathtaking."

"Wouldn't be the first time that people in power have leaned on the local police to make a crime go away. Briggs might not have liked it, but if he didn't have the support of his superiors, there wouldn't have been much he could do about it. Maybe he had nothing to do with losing the evidence box. But the fact remains, it vanished."

"And any way you slice it, he should have shown more interest in Louise Flint's death."

"Right."

"So why would he invite us up here and pretend to be helpful?" Charlotte asked.

"I can think of a couple of reasons. He may have hoped to persuade us to discontinue the Loring angle in our investigation."

"And reason number two?"

"He wanted to see how much we already knew and find out where we were headed."

"So, while we were trying to extract information from him, he was doing the same thing to us."

"Just a theory." Max glanced in the rearview mirror again. "Looks like we're not the only ones trying to get off this mountain before the worst of the storm hits."

It was late afternoon, but twilight descended early in the mountains. When Charlotte checked the side mirror, she saw the laser-bright headlights of another vehicle flash briefly.

The twin beams disappeared when Max drove around another tight curve. She turned in her seat and looked back through the rear window.

The headlights of the other car appeared again, closer this time.

"It looks like the same SUV we saw parked at the Briggses' cabin," she said. "Whoever it is, he's driving awfully fast for these conditions."

"Yes." Max gave the rearview mirror another swift, assessing look and then he concentrated on his driving. "He is."

"Maybe Briggs is trying to catch up with us because he remembered something about the case."

"You really believe that?"

"Well, no." She studied Max's hard face. "You think we might have a serious problem, don't you?"

"Yes, I think we've got a serious problem." He took one more look in the mirror. "Whoever it is, I'm not going to risk trying to outrun him. I don't know the road as well as he does and the visibility is too low. So we're going to bail."

She took a deep breath. "Okay," she said.

"Okay?"

"It's not like I've got a better plan. So, yeah, okay."

"The bridge is coming up soon. There's no cover on this side, but the woods are pretty thick on the other side. As soon as we're across, I'm going to pull over. Get ready to jump out when I give the word. Head into the trees. Understand?"

"Yes," she said.

"I'll be right behind you. If he gets out of the vehicle to pursue us, we'll have the advantage of plenty of cover."

There didn't seem to be anything else to say, so she said nothing.

Max went into a close turn, accelerating hard on the far side. She realized he was trying to buy them a little time to get over the bridge and into the shelter of the trees.

The narrow bridge suddenly appeared. The river looked even higher now. Just another sixty seconds, Charlotte thought. That was all the time they needed.

"Shit," Max said very softly.

He started to brake.

Charlotte opened her mouth to ask him why he was changing his mind. Then she saw the massive tree that had fallen across the road at the far end of the bridge. It blocked the narrow strip of pavement as effectively as a brick wall.

The front wheels of the SUV were already on the bridge.

"Hang on," Max ordered.

He slammed the vehicle into reverse and managed to back up a few feet, angling the SUV to the left side of the road.

Briggs's vehicle shot out of the last turn before the bridge. The driver must have taken in the situation in an instant. He slowed but not much. Charlotte realized he was taking aim at Max's SUV.

Max hit the switch to lower the windows.

"He's going to push us into the river," Max said. "Grab the handhold and brace yourself. The air bags will probably blow. Don't unfasten your seat belt until we're in the water."

There was no time to think about what was happening. Charlotte reached up and took what she hoped would not prove to be a death grip on the handhold. Before she could ask any questions, Briggs sideswiped the SUV with enough force to send it hurtling forward off the muddy riverbank into the water.

The explosion of the air bags was followed immediately by the impact of the landing. For a few seconds Charlotte could not focus. She heard Max giving orders and followed them blindly.

"Seat belt," he snapped.

She fumbled with her seat belt and got it undone.

"Window," he said. "You won't be able to open the door. Whatever you do, don't lose contact with the car."

She managed to scramble halfway through the open window.

"Grab the door handle," Max ordered. "Don't let go."

She reached down, groping wildly for the

outside door handle. Miraculously she found it.

"Got it," she shouted.

Max pushed her all the way through the opening. The shock of the cold water hit her with such paralyzing force she could not catch her breath.

"Don't let go of the door handle," Max said again.

"I won't."

She realized he was not following her. Instead he was scrambling into the rear seat, reaching for something in the cargo area.

Water was filling up the interior of the SUV very quickly.

"Max," she shouted. "What are you doing?"

"I'm here," he said.

He emerged through the rear window behind her.

The SUV was now firmly in the grip of the river. The water was carrying it swiftly downstream, away from the bridge.

She looked back one last time and caught a glimpse of Egan Briggs. He was out of his vehicle, standing on the bridge. He had a gun in his hand. She saw him take aim.

She thought she heard the crack of a shot being fired, but in the next instant the river

took them around a bend and out of sight
of the bridge.

CHAPTER 24

"We're going to get on top of the car," Max said. "Just do as I tell you. Got that?"

"Yes."

He thought her voice sounded steadier. He took a closer look, doing a fast assessment. He needed to know if she was in a state of panic. That would complicate matters even more.

She seemed to realize what he was doing.

"I'm okay," she said. "I'll panic later."

"Good plan," he said.

Adrenaline had kicked in, he decided. Like him, she was wholly focused on survival now.

"I'll go first," he said.

The water was up to the edge of the front windows because the weight of the heavy engine was dragging down the front end of the SUV. There was still enough air left in the interior of the vehicle to keep the SUV afloat for another couple of minutes but no more.

He gripped the window frame with one hand and reached up to grasp the luggage rack with his other hand. Bracing one foot on the bottom edge of the window frame, he hauled himself up on top of the vehicle. It wasn't easy because his soaked clothes and his boots might as well have been lead weights.

When he was sure his grip was secure, he crouched, leaned over the edge and reached down.

"Give me your left hand," he said. "But don't let go of the door handle until I tell you."

She reached up. He locked his fingers around her wrist.

"Got you," he said. "Let go of the door handle. Try to get one foot on the bottom of the window for leverage."

She was already in motion. She managed to brace one foot on the lower edge of the window frame just as he had done.

He hauled her up out of the water and onto the top of the SUV. She was breathless from the exertion and thoroughly soaked, but she crouched on the luggage rack and looked at him.

"Now we hope for an eddy, right?" she said.

"You've done this before?"

"No. But I took some kayak lessons a few weeks ago. I know how eddies work."

"Okay, that is very good news."

He allowed himself a small sigh of relief. He wasn't going to have to explain the principles of fluid dynamics. Anyone who had spent time on a river understood eddies. They formed when water hit an object like a boulder. A whirlpool effect was created on the far side of the obstruction, producing a reverse current. If they could get into an eddy near the edge of the river, there was a good chance that the countercurrent would wash them up onto the bank.

He took off his belt and looped it loosely around Charlotte's waist.

"When I say jump, we'll go together," he said. "I'll hang on to the belt to make sure we don't get separated."

She nodded.

Driven by the strong current, the SUV swung in a slow arc, pivoting around the heavy front end. Max studied the river. Eddies frequently formed immediately after a bend or a natural obstruction.

"There's a bunch of boulders coming up," he said. "There should be an eddy right after them. Get ready to jump."

The SUV bumped along, scraping the river bottom in places, swinging lazily from side to side. The vehicle was almost completely submerged now.

The SUV was dragged past the boulders seemingly in slow motion. He saw the change in the surface of the water that indicated the eddy and tightened his grip on the leather belt.

The boulders slipped past.

"Now," he said.

Charlotte didn't hesitate. They went into the slack water on the far side of the rocks. For a few seconds he worried that he'd miscalculated. But he got his feet under him. He felt Charlotte catch her balance, too.

They were close to the edge of the river. The water was fairly shallow and the eddy formed by the boulders protected them from the heavy current.

They staggered up the muddy bank and onto the road. The chill of the air felt like a blast from a freezer. Charlotte was shivering. So was he. It was time to stop worrying about drowning and start thinking about the dangers of hypothermia.

"We need shelter," he said. "The rain is easing up, but the wind is getting worse."

Charlotte looked around. "We passed several cabins and a couple of closed lodges on the way to Briggs's place."

"Right. Let's move." He pulled the two small plastic packets out from under his shirt. "Here, take one of these."

She accepted one of the packets. "Emergency thermal blankets?"

"I keep a stash of them in the emergency kit. Couldn't bring the whole damn kit, but the blankets will help us ward off hypothermia until we find shelter."

They unfolded the paper-thin reflective blankets and wrapped them around their shoulders. They started walking down the road.

"Out of sheer curiosity," he said, "what made you sign up for that course in kayaking?"

"My therapist told me I needed to learn to be more spontaneous. One of the residents at Rainy Creek Gardens suggested kayaking. Mildred said she'd done it for years. She told me it was a great way to meet outdoorsy-type men."

"How'd that work out for you?"

"Quite well, actually. Here I am in the great outdoors — with a man."

CHAPTER 25

The road followed the river, more or less. It would have been an easy, pleasant hike on a warm summer day. But with the wind and the rain, the trek was dangerous and exhausting. The thin thermal blankets trapped some of their body heat, but they offered only minimal protection.

The wind was whipping the heavy branches of the trees. There was a real risk that some of the limbs would snap and come crashing down. They were potentially lethal in their own right, but there was an added problem. Some of the falling branches would almost certainly take down power lines, which, in turn, were another serious hazard.

At one point they had to detour through the woods to avoid a landslide that blocked the road.

"Do you think Briggs will come after us to see if we made it out of the river?" Charlotte asked.

"Damned if I know. He'd have to move the tree that's blocking the bridge before he could follow us in a vehicle. That won't be easy. I doubt if he'll try to pursue us on foot because the river was moving too quickly. My SUV is long gone. Even if he thinks we might have made it out, he'd have no idea where to start searching for us. I'm guessing that he is probably back at his cabin by now, telling himself that we both drowned in the river. In his eyes, we're just a couple of city slickers who wouldn't know how to survive in his world."

"Probably."

"No way to be sure, though."

"Y'know, that's one of the things I admire about you, Cutler. No excess optimism."

"Excess optimism is the kind of thinking that can get you killed."

"Don't remind me." She looked at him. "Do you think Briggs is flat-out crazy?"

"No. I think he's a dirty cop who took a payoff a long time ago to make an evidence box disappear."

"Bastard."

"A bastard who is now linked to a couple of attempted murders."

"Us."

"He's also connected to the death of Louise Flint."

"Think he killed her?"

"I think it's a possibility."

"So, there was a third possible reason he invited us up here to chat."

"What?" Max asked.

"You said there were two reasons why Briggs may have been so helpful. He wanted to see how much we knew and where we were headed with our investigation. But it seems there was a third reason — he planned to kill us if he concluded that we knew too much or that we were going to make things difficult for him."

"No." Max helped her scramble over a downed tree. "I don't think he planned to kill us. I think the decision to try to get rid of us was a last-minute thing. He panicked because he realized that we were going to open up your stepsister's cold case."

"Why didn't he just try to shoot us?"

"Two reasons. The first is that it would have been tough to explain the bodies."

"And reason number two?"

"He knew I had a gun on me."

"How?"

"He was a cop. He knew why I didn't take off my jacket."

In the end they found the cabin almost by accident. It was veiled by a heavy stand of trees. The road that led to it had been washed out by the rain. Max caught a glimpse of the small structure when some wind-tossed branches parted briefly.

It was a small, one-bedroom structure with a stone fireplace and a tiny kitchenette. It wasn't hard to snap the lock on the back door. He set about building a fire while Charlotte went into the bedroom to see what she could find in the way of blankets. First things first. They had to get warm.

One thing had become clear in the course of the afternoon, he thought. Charlotte was not the kind of person who wasted a lot of energy whining about a situation that could not be effectively altered. She knew how to prioritize. He liked that about her; liked it a lot.

They had both declared themselves to be the one-foot-in-front-of-the-other type. But there were times in life when the ability to put one foot in front of the other and just keep going was a very handy character trait. It was, he decided, the one thing that might get them safely through the night and off the damned mountain.

By the time Charlotte returned to the small living room, he had the fire going.

"It's not the Ritz," he said, "but it will do."

"Home sweet home," Charlotte said.

CHAPTER 26

"No one has ever tried to kill me before," Charlotte said. "It's sort of a life-changing experience."

"Definitely, assuming you survive the attempt."

"Yes, well, we did, thanks to you."

"We're not home yet," Max said.

He cradled a mug of lukewarm coffee in his hands and contemplated a strategy for getting safely through the night and back to civilization in the morning.

He and Charlotte were sitting on chairs that they had pulled up close to the big stone fireplace. They were wrapped in comforters they had found in the bedroom. Their clothes were draped over various items of furniture arranged around the hearth. He had done his best to dry and clean his gun. It was now close at hand on the floor beside his chair.

His cell phone, clipped to his belt in its

waterproof case, had miraculously survived, although there wasn't any service available. Charlotte's phone had been inside her handbag, which had gone down with the SUV.

The fire was a risk, but it wasn't as if there had been an alternative, he thought. They had both been dangerously cold and wet. He had drawn the heavy drapes across the windows to ensure that the flames were not readily visible from outside the cabin, but other than that simple precaution there wasn't much he could do to conceal their presence. He just hoped that he was right about Briggs having given up and gone home.

The cabin's amenities were minimal. The best news, at least as far as Charlotte was concerned, was that it was still fall, so the owners had not yet turned off the water to protect the pipes during the cold winter months. When she discovered that the toilet flushed, she acted as if she had just won the lottery. He had to admit to having been quietly thrilled at the thought of a hot cup of coffee. Sometimes it's the small things, he thought.

In addition to some instant coffee, they had found several cans of stew and soup. The electricity was still off, but they had been able to warm some food as well as the coffee by the fire.

Charlotte gazed into the flames, her eyes deeply shadowed.

"I just had a thought," she said. "Maybe it was Briggs himself who raped Jocelyn."

Max considered that for a moment.

"It's possible," he said. "But I think it's more likely that he was the one who made sure the case went nowhere."

"Jocelyn did notice a few details about her attacker. His voice. His shoes. Those kinds of things. Enough to convince her that he was about her own age. That lets Briggs off the hook, I guess."

"He was the detective in charge of the case. He had the power to lose the evidence box."

"In other words, he was complicit in a cover-up."

"Wouldn't be the first time a cop has made a case go away because someone applied pressure and, very likely, a financial incentive."

Charlotte drank some coffee and lowered the cup. "You mean he was probably paid to shut down the case."

"At the moment, that appears to be a likely scenario."

"We now know that Briggs is capable of

attempted murder. That means we can't believe anything he told us."

"Well, practiced liars usually sprinkle some truth into their stories. But, yes, everything he said is suspect."

"So maybe Louise Flint really did drive to Loring to speak with him the day she died," Charlotte said. "And whatever she said made him decide he had to get rid of her."

"Maybe. What is clear is that what we told him was enough to make him panic. Hard to make a tough cop panic."

"When you think about it, all we really told him was that you were investigating the murder of a woman with a close connection to my stepsister."

"No, we indicated we were looking for a connection to Jocelyn Pruett's cold case. That's what scared the hell out of him."

"Briggs must have been the one who murdered Louise. It's the only thing that makes sense."

"I'm not so sure of that," Max said. "The thing is, Louise was murdered by someone who got close enough to her to use drugs. That suggests she knew her killer."

"Not necessarily. In fact, if you hadn't warned me off, I would have had some of the coffee that Mrs. Briggs made and thought nothing of it."

"When drugs are involved in a case, I tend to err on the side of caution. But that said, I think Briggs would have been more likely to use a gun or maybe brute force to get rid of someone."

"Like he did when he tried to kill us."

"Yeah."

Charlotte closed her eyes briefly. When she opened them, her expression was stark but determined.

"We're stirring up a hornet's nest, aren't we?" she said.

"Uh-huh."

He drank some more coffee.

She surprised him with a faint, wry smile. "You really know how to reassure a client. Yes, sir, I feel a lot more confident now."

He suppressed a sigh. "You're not a client, remember?"

She tilted her head slightly to the side. "Do you talk to your actual clients any differently?"

"In my experience, it's usually best not to raise false expectations."

She nodded and gazed into the fire for a long time.

"Mind if I ask you a personal question?" she said eventually.

"Depends," he said.

"Always the cautious type," she said.

He didn't have an answer for that, so he drank some more coffee.

"How did you end up in Seattle?" she asked.

"I told you. I burned out on the profiling job. Got divorced. I needed a change of scene."

"Yes, I know the short version. I just wondered about the rest of the story. You said your last case went bad. Will you tell me what happened?"

"You sure you want to know?"

"Only if you feel comfortable telling me. I'm well aware that I have no right to pry. You don't owe me any explanations."

He watched the ghost of the nightmares shiver in the flames on the hearth for a moment. And then, somewhat to his own surprise, he started talking.

"By definition, all of the cases we handled at the profiling agency were bad. But the last one got to me in ways the others hadn't because, among other things, it involved fire."

Charlotte looked at him. "Fire?"

"I have a thing about fire. When I was a kid, I and some other kids were trapped in an old barn that was deliberately torched by a psycho named Quinton Zane."

Charlotte's eyes widened. "Oh, Max. How

did you get out?"

"We were rescued by the local chief of police. It's a long story. My mother was a single mom. She was an artist and what people like to call a free spirit. She was really into the metaphysical thing."

"The metaphysical thing?"

"She was always looking for enlightenment. We moved around a lot — going from one guru type to another. Trust me, there are an astonishing number of con artists out there posing as gurus and cult leaders. And an even greater number of people like my mom who desperately want to believe the pitch."

"Yes, I know. It's very sad."

"The year I was ten, we ended up on a commune run by Zane. One of his followers had provided some land, an old ranch located just outside a small town on the California coast. There were several buildings on the grounds. The women lived in one of them. The men in another. And the kids were all required to sleep in an old barn."

"What about Zane?"

"He took over the original ranch house. And every night he sent for one of the women. It was supposed to be an honor for the chosen wife of the night."

"How ghastly."

"Like most cult leaders, Zane was focused on two things — money and power. But Zane was young — in his midtwenties — and he was also a very modern kind of cult leader. He took his business model online. The adults in the commune brought in the cash in a variety of different ways. They surrendered all of their worldly possessions, including money and stocks and properties, when they joined the group. After that, they continued to have to pay their way — mostly by operating a variety of online cons devised by Zane."

"What about the children?"

"We were required to do most of the physical labor around the ranch, but mostly we were groomed to work the online scams. I will admit that we liked that part. It was like playing real live video games. You won, you made some money."

"But you didn't get to keep the money."

"Of course not. It all went into Zane's offshore account."

"What happened?"

"The sex factor kicked in. Historically that's usually what destroys a cult from the inside. Eventually some of the men got pissed off because their wives and girlfriends were sleeping with Quinton Zane. Several of the women got upset because they weren't allowed to refuse Zane for fear of being tossed out of the compound. For those who had children, it would have meant losing access to their kids."

"Who were locked up every night so that their parents couldn't decide to take them and leave," Charlotte said. "In other words, they were hostages."

"Right. Predictably, the situation at the compound deteriorated. Looking back, I'm sure the cult was about to fall apart. Zane must have known that. He didn't want to deal with the fallout and he didn't want to risk losing all the money he had stashed offshore. One night he set off several explosions designed to destroy the compound, all the computers and the evidence of the scam. It's unclear whether he meant to kill a lot of people in the process or if the fires just got out of control."

"You and the other children were trapped in that barn?" Charlotte asked, horrified.

"Yes. And we would have died there if Chief Anson Salinas hadn't crashed his vehicle through the front of the barn, shoved eight terrified children into his SUV and reversed like hell out of that damn inferno."

"I've got cold chills just listening to you tell the story. He saved you and the others.

What an incredible thing to do."

Max smiled faintly. "Especially when you consider that everyone outside was warning him that the entire structure was about to collapse."

Charlotte hesitated. "What about your mother?"

Max turned his attention back to the fire. "She and several other women didn't make it out of their quarters. Zane had locked them in for the night, as well."

Without a word Charlotte put out her hand and touched his bare arm.

For a moment he let himself absorb the warmth and tenderness of her touch.

"What happened to Zane?" she asked after a while.

"In the chaos and confusion of the fire, he got away."

"Was he ever caught?"

Max met her eyes. "No. But a few months later a man matching his description, and carrying identification that was the same as one of the identities Zane was known to have used, rented a yacht at a marina near L.A. He took the boat out alone. There was a fire on board. The boat sank. Zane's body was never recovered. Officially he is presumed dead. But my brothers and I don't buy that version of the story. We've been searching for him ever since."

"Your brothers? They were there at the compound?"

"Of the eight kids in the barn that night, three of us lost our mothers in the fire. None of us had any other family, at least no other family that was willing to come forward and take responsibility for us. We were headed for the foster care system. Anson Salinas came to the rescue again. He took us in. Got himself licensed as a foster parent. Raised us. So, yes, I've got a couple of brothers, Cabot Sutter and Jack Lancaster."

Charlotte gave him a searching look. "And you've got a father, too, from the sound of it."

Max smiled. "Oh, yeah. I definitely have a dad."

"So what went wrong on your last job with the profiling agency?"

"Everything. My colleagues, my friends and my wife were all convinced that I was obsessed. Maybe paranoid. Maybe flat-out crazy."

"Why?"

"Because, for a while, at least, I was convinced that Quinton Zane had somehow come back from the grave."

CHAPTER 27

It was the haunted look in Max's eyes that chilled Charlotte to the very core of her being.

"We knew we were dealing with a serial arsonist," Max said. "He targeted lonely people he identified at online dating sites. He made them believe that they were connecting with their soul mates. Sooner or later he suggested that they meet."

"And then he killed them?"

"Yes. The pattern seemed straightforward. He had sex with his victims, murdered them in a location where he felt safe and then dumped the bodies. He always tried to destroy the evidence by setting a fire. Sometimes he torched the victim's car. Sometimes he set fire to the house where the victim lived. Sometimes he left the body in a trash bin and poured accelerant on the contents. Sometimes he used an old, abandoned building. But there was always fire."

Charlotte studied Max's grim face. "Did you catch him?"

"We put together a special team. We created a fake online identity that matched the profiles of the victims the killer targeted online. When the killer went for the bait, Beth, one of the women on the team, posed as the date. But something went wrong. Turned out the killer was onto her almost from the start. Beth was wired and we were tracking her, but the bastard found the devices. He destroyed them."

"What happened?"

"My only hope was that he hadn't killed her. I figured he might want to keep her alive for a while because he wanted to taunt those of us who were looking for him. I took another look at the pattern."

"What pattern?"

"The bodies were found in different locations, but when I looked hard I could see that those locations formed a pattern. And at the heart of that pattern was an old, abandoned hospital. I wondered if he was using it as the killing ground. I tried to convince the team that it was worth a look. But there was a new guy who was supposed to be some kind of wonder boy. He was always carrying on about his algorithms and his computer models. He was sure that the perp was using another location as his base. The cops focused on it. In the end I went out to the hospital on my own."

"No backup?"

"I was afraid that if the killer saw cops, he would kill Beth — assuming he hadn't done so already. I pulled up a floor plan of the hospital and discovered that there was an underground tunnel that connected two of the wings and the morgue. I took a chance and went in that way."

"The tunnel was open?"

"Yes. The electricity was off, of course. Every hallway, every closet, every storage compartment was a potential trap. I found Beth in an old operating theater. She was bound and gagged. I freed her and we started to leave. But the killer was watching. And waiting. I got off a shot — managed to hit him in the thigh. He was bleeding out, but he had splashed accelerant around the floor. He ignited the fire just as Beth and I emerged from the operating theater."

"You were trapped in what must have been your worst nightmare — a building burning down around you."

"Yeah, that pretty much describes the experience." Max's forehead was damp with sweat. He used the end of the comforter to swipe off the perspiration. He never took his eyes off the flames on the hearth. "Beth and I got out because I had studied the hospital's floor plan. We made it to the emergency stairs and out through the morgue tunnel."

"Thank heavens. So the killer died in the blaze?"

Max finally looked away from the fire. "Yes."

"Was it Quinton Zane?"

"No." He exhaled slowly. "There were a couple of other casualties, as well — my career and my marriage."

"Why? You saved Beth. You got the bad guy. You were a hero."

"No, I just got damn lucky. But I wasn't asked to resign because of what happened at the old hospital. It was because of what happened afterward."

"What?"

"I became obsessed with the case. There's no other word for it. I couldn't let go of it."

"Because you weren't positive the killer was dead?"

"I knew that the killer was dead, but I couldn't get past the idea that there was a link to Zane. My wife, my boss, my colleagues, all concluded that I had gone over the edge. I was told to take some vacation time. See a therapist. I did both, but neither helped. I started having nightmares again. Cold sweats. Insomnia. Started seeing patterns where none existed. The works. Eventually the agency decided that I was no longer an asset. My wife concluded that I was on a downward spiral and refusing to get help. She left to move on with her life. I don't blame her."

Charlotte did not take her hand off his arm. She wasn't sure if he was aware of it, but she had the feeling that she shouldn't stop touching him. Not yet.

"It's been several months now," she said. "Are you still convinced there was some connection between it and Quinton Zane?"

For a moment she didn't think he was going to respond. But in the end he did, his eyes stark.

"Yes," he said.

"Are you still experiencing the nightmares and the cold sweats and the insomnia?" she asked.

"Not every night — but, yes. There are . . . a lot of bad nights. The therapist said I should fight the obsession. Learn to distract myself with other tasks. Practice shifting my focus, et cetera, et cetera. She said my real issues were abandonment issues left over from my past. Maybe a form of attachment disorder complicated by some PTSD. She gave me some meds. I took them for a while. They didn't make the questions go away. So, yes, on the really bad nights I crank up the computer and I go looking for Quinton Zane."

She studied him. "You're afraid your ex-boss and your ex-wife and the therapist might be right, aren't you? You're afraid you might have gone off the deep end; that maybe you really are in the grip of an obsession, trying to find patterns and connections where none exist."

"It's crossed my mind."

"For what it's worth, I don't think you should ignore what your intuition told you all those months ago. You found that old hospital. You rescued Beth. You obviously have a gift for seeing connections, and that gift is trying to tell you something."

"My gift, as you call it, is a form of obsession. Just so you know, it is not considered to be a sign of sound mental health."

She looked at him. "The man I am getting to know, the one who is hunting for Louise Flint's killer and who just rescued us from a car that had been pushed into a flooding river, is not crazy."

He exhaled deeply. "Sorry. I shouldn't have growled at you."

"Look, you tried therapy. You tried meds. And now, as a PI, you're trying to distract yourself with other people's questions."

He frowned. "You think that's why I opened my business?"

"Probably. But here's the thing — you've got questions of your own. The questions won't go away just because you try to ignore them. I think you need to acknowledge them. You may never get answers, but you need to accept that the questions are real and that you have reasons for asking them."

His mouth kicked up a little at one corner.

"And you know this, how?" he asked.

"Because I've seen what unanswered questions can do to a person if she tries to suppress them. Take my stepsister, Jocelyn, for example. And it's not just her. I've met a lot of people at Rainy Creek Gardens who never got the answers they needed. The questions don't just go away, Max. Somehow, you have to learn to allow them a place in your mind. Give them some space. Contain them, set boundaries, but don't try to pretend they don't exist. Questions fester in darkness. If you want to put them into a rational context, you need to examine them in sunlight."

He smiled. And this time the smile was real.

"Where'd you learn to talk like that?"

"After the kayaking class and a few others that were designed to make me more spontaneous, I gave up and took a class in meditation. What can I say? It changed my life."

CHAPTER 28

She did not expect to be able to sleep, so she was startled when she woke up from a dream in which she was searching for Jocelyn. For a moment she lay very still, trying to orient herself.

Memories flooded back. She was curled on the floor in front of the fireplace, wrapped in a well-worn down comforter.

She opened her eyes and saw Max. He was crouched at the hearth, feeding a few more sticks to the low-burning fire. He, too, was still draped in a comforter. His holstered pistol was on the floor beside him.

She sat up slowly. "Is something wrong?"

"No." He looked at her over his shoulder. "Everything's fine. Just keeping the fire going. Didn't mean to wake you."

"What time is it?"

"A little after two o'clock."

"I've had a few hours' sleep," she said. "Your turn."

"I'm all right. Not the first time I've pulled an all-nighter."

"I'm sure it isn't, but that's not the point. I realize that one of us needs to keep watch. I'm perfectly capable of taking over for a few hours while you get some rest."

For a moment she thought he would refuse the offer.

Then, to her surprise, he nodded once. "Wake me if you hear even the smallest sound or think you see a shadow. Don't tell yourself it's your imagination. Wake me."

"I will."

She got to her feet, careful to keep the comforter tightly closed, and lowered herself into a chair. The wind had died down. She could not hear any rain. The storm had blown through. The deep silence of the woods was a little unnerving, but at least it increased the chances of hearing someone trying to make a stealthy approach.

Max adjusted the quilt, wrapping it more securely around himself, and stretched out next to the gun. He turned on his side, rested his head on a throw pillow and closed his eyes.

It was oddly gratifying to know that he trusted her to keep watch. There was a bond between them now, she thought.

Don't go there. Two people who had faced

danger together were bound to develop a sense of connection. It was a superficial and no doubt temporary state of affairs. It would fade when they were once again safe.

Still, she had never felt such an intimate connection with any other man, not even Brian. Regardless of what happened in the future, she was pretty sure she would never forget the sensation.

She rose after a while and made some more lukewarm instant coffee. She sipped it slowly, thinking about Jocelyn, wondering where she might have gone to ground.

When those thoughts began to chase each other in ever-tightening circles, she thought about Louise Flint and the other members of the investment club.

What the hell were you and your friends doing, Jocelyn? What devil did you awaken?

CHAPTER 29

Max drifted in and out of a strange, twilight sleep. Every so often he came fully awake for a moment, automatically checking all of his senses for any indication that something had changed in the environment — new sounds, movement in the shadows, a draft of air.

Each time he was satisfied that all was well. Each time he saw that Charlotte was awake and attentive. Each time she smiled at him and he closed his eyes and drifted back into the weird state between sleep and wakefulness.

It was still dark outside when he emerged once again from the in-between place. This time it was the scent of warming stew that roused him.

He opened his eyes and saw Charlotte crouched in front of the small fire. She was stirring the contents of a battered pot. The first thing he noticed was that she was no longer draped in the comforter. She was dressed in the clothes she had been wearing when they went into the river.

She looked at him.

"Good morning," she said.

" 'Morning."

He started to unwind the comforter. Belatedly he remembered that he was not dressed. He sat up cautiously.

"I assumed you'd want to get an early start," she said. "If we don't get a ride, it's going to be a long hike to Loring."

He managed to keep the comforter around his midsection as he got to his feet. He reached down to collect the holster and gun.

"We'll get a ride," he said. "Bound to be a lot of repair crews out first thing this morning. They'll be checking for downed power lines and trees, damaged bridges, landslides."

She ladled the stew into a bowl and handed it to him.

"I assume we will be stopping at the Loring Police Department," she said.

"Yes." He spooned up some of the stew, surprised at how good it tasted. "I'll call Anson as soon as I can get some service. He'll be wondering what the hell happened."

"What if the cops we run into at the

Loring Police Department were involved in the cover-up with Briggs?"

"It's a possibility, but I don't think that's too likely. I did some checking when I went looking for Briggs. There's been a lot of turnover in the department since he left. The current police chief has only been on the job for a couple of years."

"It will be interesting to see if they pretend to believe us when we tell them that Briggs tried to murder us."

"I'm getting the impression that you don't have a lot of faith in the forces of law and order."

"Generally speaking, I do — I just don't trust the forces of law and order in Loring, Washington."

"Things change."

Charlotte sniffed. "Look who has suddenly metamorphosed into Mr. Positive Thinker."

"Must be the company I'm keeping."

She smiled a small, mischievous smile. "Ah, so now I'm a bad influence? That is so cool. I've always wanted to be a bad influence."

He leaned in very close. She did not retreat. For a moment it seemed as if the world around them had stopped.

He kissed her. It was just a quick kiss. He

told himself it was an experiment. But she did not pull back. Instead she put one hand on his bare shoulder. Her fingers were incredibly warm and soft on his skin. Her mouth softened under his.

When he raised his head, she did not speak. She just watched him as though fascinated.

"For the record, you are a very, very good bad influence," he said.

She took a deep breath. "Thanks."

He turned away, grabbed his dried trousers and headed for the bedroom to get dressed before he did something really dumb — like tell her that he had been wanting to kiss her since he had met her. Like tell her that he wanted to go on kissing her now.

Priorities, he thought. *You've got a few.* One foot in front of the other.

CHAPTER 30

Roxanne Briggs stirred the simmering pot of oatmeal with a wooden spoon and reflected on the past. It occurred to her that that was all she ever thought about these days — the past.

It was early — not yet five thirty. It would be a while before the first light of dawn, but the storm had passed. She had not slept at all during the night. Egan had said very little when he had returned from going after Max Cutler and Charlotte Sawyer. He had been in an adrenaline-fueled rage. He'd headed straight for the whiskey bottle.

When she'd asked him what he'd done, he'd said only that Cutler and Sawyer wouldn't be a problem now. She had demanded an explanation. He'd told her that there had been an accident. Cutler's vehicle had gone into the river. He and the Sawyer woman could not possibly have survived.

She had known then that he had attempted to murder Cutler and Sawyer. But she was not so certain that he had been successful. There had been something very competent-looking about Cutler. Her intuition told her that he would not panic in a crisis. Charlotte Sawyer had also seemed very formidable in her own right.

Still, they were just a couple of city people who had wound up in a flooding river. Odds were, they hadn't made it out. But even if they were both gone, it was clear now that the world was falling apart. The secrets that she and Egan had kept for so long were coming back to haunt them.

Karma was a bitch goddess.

Eventually Egan had passed out in his big leather chair. She had undressed and gone to bed, but she had not slept at all. How could a woman sleep when she knew she was coming to the end of a very dark road?

Until now she had been able to endure the misery of her marriage because of Nolan. She had sacrificed everything for him. She was a mother, after all. But on this bleak morning she was no longer sure she could keep going, not even for the sake of her son.

Egan loomed in the doorway. "Pack your things. We're leaving."

She turned toward him. "What?"

"Did some thinking last night. Cutler and Sawyer are probably dead, but there's a chance they made it out of the river. Doesn't much matter. Alive or dead, they're a problem. They've been poking around in the past, and sooner or later the shit is gonna hit the fan. We need to get the hell off this mountain. Find a new place. Idaho, maybe. Or Wyoming."

Roxanne looked down at the simmering oatmeal and made her decision. "No," she said.

"Don't be a fool. We can't risk hanging around here. If Cutler and Sawyer survived, they'll go straight to the cops. If they're dead, the cops are gonna come around asking questions. Forget the oatmeal and start packing."

"No," she said again, her voice very steady now.

"Suit yourself. I'm getting out. Up to you if you want to come with me or not."

She tightened her grip on the spoon. Only one thing was clear — she had never hated Egan more than she did in that moment.

"I told you years ago it would blow up in our faces," she said.

"Bullshit. You were as happy to take the money as I was."

She did not answer that. There was nothing to say. She had agreed to keep the secret and take the money. *For Nolan's sake.*

"When are you leaving?" she asked, trying to sound matter-of-fact.

"Today. I'll take the SUV. Got to make a phone call first. Get one last payment out of the bastard."

"Under the circumstances, that might not be smart," she said. "You told me yourself that Trey Greenslade has become a lot more dangerous in the last few months."

"The death of his old man set him off, no question about it. At least two women are dead. Cutler was right about one thing — the murders aren't going to stop. Trey is escalating. But he's smart. He knows he's got a hell of a lot to protect — he's first in line to take control of Loring-Greenslade. Trust me, he'll make one more payoff, especially if he knows he's going to get what he wants."

The oatmeal was starting to scorch. Automatically Roxanne moved it off the heat.

Egan was right. Trey had inherited everything — the Greenslade name, the Greenslade pharmaceutical company, the Greenslade position in Loring. The only thing that stood in his way was Egan.

"Well?" Egan asked. "You sure you want to stay here?"

She had made her decision. She and Egan were bonded by the secrets they kept, but that was the only thing that connected them.

"I told you," she said. "I'm not going with you."

For a moment she thought he might try to talk her into leaving with him — not because he loved her but because she knew his secrets and had kept them faithfully for so long. She was the only person on the face of the earth that he could trust and they both knew it.

And then she wondered if he would kill her to make sure she didn't tell anyone the truth about the past.

Surreptitiously she moved her hand to the kitchen towel crumpled on the counter.

But in the end, Egan merely shrugged and walked away into the other room.

"Suit yourself," he said.

She stood quietly in the kitchen, her hand resting on the counter near the towel.

She could hear Egan in the bedroom, tossing clothes into a suitcase. After a time she heard him go down into the basement. When he returned, he had the old cardboard file box in his arms. She held her breath.

"I'm taking this with me," he said, daring her to argue.

"You're welcome to it," she said. She

looked at the picture of her son on the mantel.

"What should I tell Nolan?" she asked.

"Tell him whatever the hell you want to tell him." Egan headed for the door with the file box. "He won't give a damn. All he cares about is his next fix. He's a junkie, Roxanne. Junkies don't change. One of these days he'll OD and that will be the end of it. The only one who's going to shed any tears will be you."

She stayed in the kitchen while Egan finished packing up the SUV. Only when he finally climbed behind the wheel and drove off down the graveled road did she finally take a deep breath.

Heart pounding, she picked up the towel and looked at the gun on the counter. The previous night she'd toyed with thoughts of using it on herself. But that morning her maternal instincts had kicked in. She had been prepared to kill Egan if he had made a move to get rid of her.

She had to survive to take care of Nolan.

CHAPTER 31

"What the hell made you go up that damn mountain to meet with Egan Briggs? Everyone knows he and his wife are both batshit crazy. They're a couple of world-class preppers. You're lucky all you lost was your vehicle. You could just as easily have gotten your heads blown off."

"Trust me, that thought has occurred to us," Max said. "And the reason we went to see Briggs is because I'm investigating the death of Louise Flint."

The detective's name was Tucker Walsh. He was in his midthirties. He had explained that he had joined the Loring department two years earlier because he and his wife had wanted a nice, safe, small-town environment in which to raise their kids.

Walsh came across as both intelligent and professional, but, like Charlotte, Max was withholding judgment on anyone who was even remotely connected to the Loring

Police Department. Maybe we're both a little paranoid, he thought. Nearly getting murdered sometimes has that effect on a person. So sue us.

The trek out of the mountains had gone smoothly, all things considered. There were a lot of repair crews out, as he had predicted. In the end he and Charlotte had been chauffeured into Loring by the friendly owner of a tree removal service.

By prior agreement, they had been careful not to mention Egan and Roxanne Briggs to the driver. Instead they had explained the loss of their vehicle as an accident. Just a couple of tourists who'd had no business trying to navigate the treacherous mountain roads in bad weather.

The first stop in Loring had been a rental car agency, not the police station. Charlotte had lost her handbag and with it her credit cards, cell phone and identification. But his wallet and the plastic in it had survived in his hip pocket. He'd had no trouble renting a vehicle.

Satisfied that he now had a way to get Charlotte and himself back to Seattle, he had made the Loring PD their next stop.

The department's headquarters was housed in a gleaming new building in the center of town. There was a shiny new library across the street. The nearby shops and stores appeared prosperous. The coffeehouses and eateries were filled with students and various academic types.

The campus dominated the north end of town. It consisted of a collection of handsome, brick-fronted buildings scattered across a serene, heavily wooded landscape.

From what Max had seen, the college was one of the community's two major economic engines. The second was a large, prosperous-looking pharmaceutical company named Loring-Greenslade Biotech.

Walsh eyed Max with a speculative expression. "This Louise Flint woman isn't local, is she? Because I don't recall any reports —"

"No," Max said. "She lived in Seattle. But she made a trip to Loring on the day she died."

Walsh narrowed his eyes. "To see Briggs?"

"He says no," Max said. "But there's a possibility that the Flint case is connected to an assault that took place here on the college campus a little over ten years ago. Briggs was the detective in charge."

"What happened to the assault charge?" Walsh asked.

He looked wary now, Max thought. Maybe the detective had a bad feeling about where the chat was going.

"It was a rape case," Charlotte said coolly. "My stepsister was the victim. And what happened was that the case went nowhere because the evidence box disappeared."

Walsh's mouth tightened into a grim line. "I see. Sorry to hear that. I wasn't working here at the time."

"Yes, we know that." Charlotte frowned. "You said the Briggses are preppers?"

"You know — folks who are convinced that there will be a major natural catastrophe any day now or that the country is going to implode," Walsh said. "They stockpile food and ammo and probably a hell of a lot of toilet paper."

"I know what the word means," Charlotte said. "I was just interested to hear that that's how the local community views the Briggses."

Walsh sighed. "Look, they're reclusive and eccentric, but they don't make trouble — unlike their junkie son. He's been in and out of rehab like clockwork for the past few years."

"I saw the photo of a young man on the mantel at the Briggses' house," Charlotte said. "I assumed it was a picture of their son. He looked okay."

"Trust me, Nolan Briggs is not okay,"

Walsh said. "I think I speak for the entire department when I say that any day he shows up in Loring is a bad day. Luckily he doesn't spend much time here. He just comes to see his folks when he needs money. But getting back to Egan Briggs, you said you went to see him about that cold case you mentioned?"

"That's right," Max said. "He seemed willing to discuss it. Gave the impression that the failure to close the case had really bothered him all these years. But in hindsight, it's obvious he just wanted to know how much we knew or suspected. When he realized that we were going to keep looking into the death of Louise Flint and the old rape case, he panicked. That's why he came after us."

Walsh exhaled heavily and sank back in his chair. "And you figure there's only one reason he would be so accommodating and then dump you into the river. Someone paid him off years ago to make that evidence box disappear. Is that what you're thinking?"

"That seems like the most likely scenario," Max said, going for polite. "It's also possible that he knew more about Louise Flint's death than he let on."

"Keep in mind that Briggs is probably borderline crazy," Walsh said. "Crazy people do things that don't make any sense. It's sort of the working definition of crazy."

"Actually, crazy people do things that make sense in their own worlds," Max said.

Charlotte leaned forward. Her hands were clenched very tightly in her lap.

"Detective Walsh, you don't seem to be grasping the gravity of the situation here. My stepsister is missing. The detective who may have been bribed to make her case disappear over a decade ago has just tried to murder us. And a woman named Louise Flint, who happened to be my stepsister's best friend, is dead, supposedly of an overdose. The one common link between all of those things is this town."

Walsh was starting to look annoyed.

"I'll talk to Briggs," he said. "That's about all I can do until we locate your vehicle and pull it out of the river. But even then, I can't promise much. The water will have washed away a lot of evidence."

Charlotte was seething. Max decided to intervene before she went for Walsh's throat.

"Is there anyone left on the force who was here when Jocelyn Pruett reported the rape?" he asked.

Walsh had been watching Charlotte with a wary expression. Reluctantly he switched his attention back to Max.

"There has been a lot of turnover, but I think Atkins might have been around a decade ago. He's set to retire this year."

"We would like to talk to him," Max said.

"Hang on, I just saw him go down the hall." Walsh got out of his chair, crossed the cluttered office and opened the door. "Atkins? Got a minute? Some people here would like to ask you a few questions."

A big, middle-aged, florid-faced man with thinning blond hair and a beer belly appeared in the doorway. He gave Charlotte and Max a quick survey.

"This is Charlotte Sawyer and Max Cutler," Walsh said. "Cutler is a PI from Seattle. He's investigating a death."

Atkins grunted acknowledgment of the introductions.

"What can I do for you?" he asked.

"Were you with the department a little more than a decade ago when Jocelyn Pruett filed a rape report?" Max asked. "You may remember it because at some point the evidence box disappeared."

Atkins's brows scrunched together. "I was an officer at the time. Always wondered what happened to the evidence. The investigation never got off the ground because it was lost."

"I'm surprised you remember the case so

clearly," Charlotte said.

"I was the first officer on the scene. I took the initial report. I could tell the victim was traumatized, but she insisted on being taken directly to the hospital so that evidence could be collected. She was very focused. Very determined."

"The victim's name was Jocelyn Pruett," Charlotte said. "She's my stepsister. She has disappeared and Egan Briggs just tried to murder us. Do you see a pattern here?"

Atkins scowled, startled by her vehemence. He looked at Walsh for guidance.

"What the hell is this?" he asked.

"Mr. Cutler and Ms. Sawyer tell me that Egan Briggs deliberately forced their vehicle off the road and into the river. They were fortunate to survive."

"Shit." Atkins looked disgusted. "Sounds like the rumors are true. Briggs really has gone crazy. Can't believe his wife is still with him after all these years. I guess she's just as nuts. What a waste."

Charlotte looked at him. "What do you mean?"

"Roxanne Briggs was a fine-looking woman in her day," Atkins said. "But she got pregnant the year after she graduated from high school. Never could figure out why she slept with Briggs. He was too old for her and with her looks, she could have done better. But, like I said, she was pregnant and this was a real small town back then. Guess she figured she had to marry the father. Surprised she stayed with him, though. Always thought she'd ditch him and head for the city. What's all this got to do with that old rape case?"

"That's what we're trying to find out," Max said before Walsh could reply.

"Did a woman named Louise Flint talk to you a few days ago?" Charlotte asked.

"No, I don't know any Louise Flint," Atkins said. "And there's not much I can tell you about your stepsister's case except that it went nowhere."

"Here's what I think happened all those years ago," Charlotte said. "I think someone decided to make the case go away and someone paid off at least one cop — Briggs — to make sure that happened. What about you, Detective Atkins? Did you take a bribe, as well?"

And people think I'm the one who lacks social skills, Max thought. It occurred to him that he was seeing yet another side of Charlotte. The woman had a temper.

Atkins's face flushed a dark shade of red. "I've been with this department for twenty years and I've got a clean record. You've got

264

no right to ask me a question like that."

"You lost the evidence box," Charlotte said. "But you must still have a file. I want to see it."

"I didn't lose the damned box," Atkins snarled. He pulled himself together with a visible effort. "As for the file, I'm sorry. It's not available."

"Do we need to file a Freedom of Information Act request?" Max asked.

"No point." Atkins grunted. "The files in those days were all on paper. When the department finally got around to digitalizing them a few years ago, we discovered that some of them had gotten lost."

"Let me take a flying leap here," Charlotte said. "My stepsister's file just happened to be one of those that vanished, right?"

Atkins was almost purple now. Max wondered if he was going to stroke out. But Walsh gave the big man a warning look. Atkins calmed down a little.

"Yes, that's what I'm saying." Atkins shook his head. "I'm sorry, but there is nothing I can do for you. I'd like to know why you think your stepsister's disappearance now might be connected to that old case, though. Hell, it's been — what — eleven, twelve years?"

"If we knew the answer to that question, we would not be here in your office," Max said. He got to his feet. "Are you sure there's nothing else you can tell us?"

Atkins grimaced. "Maybe one other thing."

"What?" Charlotte asked quickly.

"Like I said, I was an officer back in the day. Briggs was in charge of the case. But at the outset, I was pretty sure the perp was a local guy, maybe a student or a teacher on the campus."

"What made you think that?" Max asked.

"Because from the way Pruett described the attack, it seemed likely that he knew the layout of the campus very well. Knew exactly where to wait for her. Briggs assigned me to start talking to some of the male students who might have followed her from the library that night. I was taking statements when Briggs told me to stop. He said the rape kit had been contaminated and that there was nothing left of the case. The whole damn evidence box disappeared shortly after that."

"Do you think someone paid Briggs to dump the case?" Max asked.

Atkins shook his head. "I don't know about that. I can tell you that Briggs retired less than a year later. Said he'd come into a little money from an inheritance. That's when he and his wife moved up into the mountains and got weird. At the same time it was no secret that the college authorities were leaning hard on the chief. They didn't want the bad publicity. That's all I can tell you. I'll let you come up with your own conspiracy theory."

"I'm good at that," Max said.

CHAPTER 32

Max opened the passenger-side door of the rental car. Charlotte got in and buckled her seat belt. He rounded the front of the vehicle and got behind the wheel.

For a moment they both sat quietly, looking at the modern headquarters of the Loring Police Department.

"I wonder if Louise Flint did drive up that mountain to talk to Briggs," Max said after a while.

"We know she didn't die there. She died in her condo in Seattle."

"Doesn't mean there isn't a connection." Max fired up the rental and eased it out of the parking stall. "I'm sure now that whatever happened when Louise made the trip to Loring, it's what got her killed."

"Damn."

"Yeah. One thing we need to talk about before we get back to Seattle."

"What's that?"

"Given what has happened, I don't want you to be alone," Max said. "Not until we figure out what's going on here."

"You think I need a bodyguard."

"Yeah."

"But I've got a job. I can't just go into hiding."

"I think you'll be okay at Rainy Creek Gardens. From what I saw, they've got good security. Strangers aren't allowed to wander in and out. The front desk staff pays attention. There are a lot of cameras."

"Security is one of the amenities that Rainy Creek Gardens offers," she said. "Also, everyone knows everyone else, which is an added bonus. But I've got decent security at my apartment building, too. Jocelyn insisted on it when I first moved to Seattle. There is someone at the front desk during the day. You can't get in or out without a key. There are cameras in the garage and elevators. What more do I need?"

"I don't know. That's why we're going to stick together until this is finished. My house or your apartment. Either one works for me."

She gave him a quick, searching look. "You're serious about this, aren't you?"

"The more you get to know me, the more you'll realize that I'm serious about most

things. It's one of my more boring qualities."

"I see." She smiled faintly. "Well, in situations like this, it's good to have a serious
person around. All right, let's go with my
apartment, at least for now. The sofa pulls
out into a bed and I've got a powder room
you can use."

"A powder room?"

"No shower in it. You'll have to use mine."

He thought about the security features her
building offered. Then he thought about the
warm, sunny colors of her little apartment
and how he would have to make do with
her shower.

"Your place works for me," he said.

CHAPTER 33

Trey Greenslade parked the old, battered pickup behind the row of closed-up cabins. He got out, careful to keep the bulk of the truck between himself and the lodge buildings. He kept the driver's-side door open and positioned himself behind it.

He had bought the pickup at a used car lot shortly after he had discovered the truth about the past. He had known then that the time would probably come when he would need a vehicle that would not draw attention on the mountain roads.

He had a talent for planning ahead; for strategy. It was why he would be the one to take control of Loring-Greenslade.

When he had come across the mysterious cash withdrawals in his father's financial records — withdrawals that had occurred like clockwork every few months for over a decade — he had assumed that the old man had kept a mistress on the side. It had amused him to think that the domineering, self-righteous bastard had been such a hypocrite.

True, an illicit love affair that had lasted well over a decade didn't amount to much of a character flaw. But to the people of Loring, who had long since put Gordon Greenslade on a pedestal, it would have come as a shock to know that he had cheated on his wife and lived a secret life for years.

Trey had pondered whether or not to tell his grandmother what he had discovered. It would have been amusing to see the expression on the old bitch's face when she learned that her firstborn son had kept a secret lover. But he had concluded it would be more interesting to figure out the identity of the girlfriend first.

It was only when he had taken a closer look at the timing of the withdrawals that he had realized just what he had uncovered. The shock had hit him with the force of a backcountry avalanche.

The payments had started less than a month after the Pruett case had been dropped by the detective in charge. That could not be a coincidence. His father had been paying blackmail for years to keep him from being identified as a suspect.

But the real fright had set in when it dawned on him that he had no idea of the identity of the extortionist. It could have been almost anyone in town — another student or a member of his old fraternity, maybe — someone who had seen something that night. It could have been a janitor or a professor who was able to place him at the scene. Maybe there were *photos.*

He had been very careful that night, but Pruett had been his first. He hadn't yet gotten the strategy down perfectly. There had been problems. The stupid woman had fought him. She'd scratched his arms. He'd had to wear long sleeves for days afterward. He'd worn a condom, but in his rush to escape the scene afterward, he'd lost it. What if there was a surveillance camera that he hadn't noticed somewhere on the path or in the parking lot where he had left the car? He'd heard that Pruett had insisted on an examination at the hospital. A rape kit had been prepared.

So many things hadn't gone right that first time. The memory of his close call still gave him chills. But when no one had so much as even questioned him, he'd assumed he'd dodged all the bullets. It was only when he'd settled his father's financial affairs after the funeral and understood what the cash withdrawals meant that he'd realized he hadn't been so lucky after all.

Once he was no longer in the grip of the initial panic, he had calmed down and started to think more clearly. That was when it had occurred to him that all he had to do was wait. The blackmailer had grown accustomed to the regular cash payments. He or she would want to keep the money coming in.

And sure enough, the first demand had arrived less than a month after his father's funeral. There had been nothing high-tech about it. No mysterious text. No anonymous e-mail. No phone call. He had found a note on the front seat of his car.

The instructions had been simple and straightforward. He had followed them precisely and left the briefcase filled with cash in the designated place on a hiking trail. And then he'd used a pair of binoculars to keep watch from a distance.

He'd had no luck the first time. It was late summer and there had been a steady stream of tourists, hikers and vacationers trekking up and down the trail. He hadn't spotted the person who had retrieved the briefcase.

A month later, however, he'd gotten another demand. It was early fall in the mountains. The day-trippers were gone. He had been instructed to leave the money under a bridge.

Once again he had watched from a distance and that time he had gotten lucky. An SUV — the license plates obscured with mud — had pulled into the lay-by at one end of the bridge. Egan Briggs had climbed out of the front seat to retrieve the cash.

For a time he had been content to let Briggs continue to think that he was safe. There was no reason to believe that a confirmed blackmailer would want to cut off the flow of money. Besides, taking out Briggs wouldn't be easy. The man was not only an ex-cop, he was, by all accounts, a skilled hunter. He was also said to be dangerously paranoid, maybe flat-out crazy.

Trey had told himself that he needed a foolproof strategy and he'd been working on it when Louise Flint had seen fit to further complicate his already very complicated life.

Now, in the midst of dealing with the members of the investment club and trying to find Jocelyn Pruett, he had received a new demand from Briggs. It had come in well ahead of schedule; and, with it, a promise to make a final trade.

He studied the big SUV parked near cabin number 6. The tinted glass made it difficult to see into the interior, but as far as he could tell there was no one in the driver's seat. Something about the shadows in the rear cargo area suggested a pile of boxes and suitcases.

It would take a lot to make Egan Briggs run, he thought.

A curtain twitched in the window of cabin number 6.

"I'm here, Briggs. I've got the money. Where is the evidence box?"

The rear door of the cabin opened. Egan Briggs emerged. He had a gun in his hand.

"Figured you knew it was me your old man had been paying off," Briggs said.

"You were the only one in a position to make the Pruett case go away," Trey said. "I just hadn't realized until recently that the old bastard had been making blackmail payments to you."

"Came as a shock, huh? It wasn't you he was protecting, you know."

"I'm well aware of that. It was the Greenslade name and the reputation of the company that he worried about. It was pretty much all he cared about."

"Yep. If the truth about what you'd done all those years ago had come out, it would have destroyed some kind of acquisition deal that was in the works at the time. Might have taken down the whole company. It sure as hell would have pissed off your grandmother. And everyone knows she controls Loring-Greenslade."

"That's what she keeps telling me."

"You kept at it, didn't you? Pruett was just the first. I reminded your pa of that from time to time."

"So you know that, too?"

"I used to be a damn good cop."

"A damn dirty cop. Where's the evidence box?"

Briggs jerked his head toward the doorway of the cabin. "In there."

"I'm sure you can understand that I want to see it before I turn over the cash."

"You'll see it when I'm gone. Put the briefcase in the front seat of my vehicle."

"Here's the thing, Briggs, I'd like to keep the truck between us."

Briggs snorted. "You think I'm gonna kill you?"

"Isn't that the plan? I give you the money and you get rid of me?"

"No need to do that. I'm the one who's going to disappear. Been planning to do it for a while now. After I found out that the Sawyer woman and that damned PI from Seattle were poking around in the Pruett case, I figured it was time to get into the wind."

"Still, I'd rather not take any chances," Trey said. He raised his right hand, showing Briggs the pistol he had brought with him. "Just so you know you're not the only one with a weapon. I didn't much like my old man, but I gotta tell you, I learned a couple of things from him. One of those things was how to run Loring-Greenslade. The other was how to shoot."

Briggs spit on the ground. "So we got us a standoff. No reason we can't do a little more business. Tell you what. I'll bring out the box and put it right here on the step. Then you toss the briefcase to me. I'll get into the van and leave. That suit you?"

"All right. You go first. I want to see that box."

Briggs backed into the cabin, never lowering the gun. A moment later he reappeared with a cardboard file box bearing the faded logo of the Loring Police Department. A series of numbers and the word *Evidence* had been scrawled by hand on the front.

Trey's heart pounded. He would soon be able to breathe freely again.

"Here's your box," Briggs said. "Wait until you see what's inside it. Had you dead to rights, you fool. You made a couple of serious mistakes that night. I knew what I had straight off. Called your pa the next day. He didn't hesitate for a second. Offered me half a year's salary right then and there. And that was only the beginning."

"Shut up and put down the box."

Briggs crouched to set the box on the front step. He kept the gun leveled. "Put the case on the hood of your truck," he said.

"You're making me nervous, Briggs."

"Put the goddamned case on the hood."

Trey set the briefcase on the front end of the pickup and gave it a shove. It slid a short distance across the hood.

Briggs moved out of the doorway of the cabin. He edged toward the pickup, keeping the gun aimed at Trey.

When he reached the truck, he seized the handle of the briefcase and backed swiftly to the SUV. He made his way around the front to the driver's side.

The bulk of the SUV now formed a barricade. Briggs opened the driver's-side door and put the briefcase on the front seat. Trey waited while he opened it and verified that the cash was inside.

"Satisfied?" Trey asked.

"Yep, looks good. Been nice doin' business with the Greenslade family."

Briggs got into the van, cranked up the

engine and put it in gear. He drove off down the old logging road, mud and gravel spitting from under the wheels.

Trey counted to three and decided the van was far enough away. He took the remote out of the pocket of his jacket and pressed the button.

The small device hidden under the cash in the briefcase exploded. The big vehicle swerved violently; it slammed into a tree and bounced back onto the dirt road. The vehicle burst into flames.

Given the rain-drenched landscape and the fact that the van was in the center of the muddy road, there wasn't much danger of a forest fire that would attract attention, Trey thought.

Dazed with the intoxicating adrenaline rush of what he had just done, he walked slowly toward the burning SUV.

The explosion had ripped off the driver's-side door. Egan Briggs had been thrown from the vehicle. He was a bloodied mess, but he was still alive — barely.

His eyelids flickered. He squinted up at Trey.

"Told your dad there wasn't much point giving you a second chance," Egan whispered. His voice was almost gone. "You're broken. But he said he didn't have a choice."

Briggs closed his eyes. He was dying.

Trey shot him in the head, just to make certain. Then he tossed several plastic packets of drugs into and around the SUV. When the police finally got around to investigating, they would conclude crazy Egan Briggs had been dealing and had been taken out by his competitors.

One of the useful things about having grown up in a family that had made its fortune in pharmaceuticals was that you had access to a lot of interesting chemicals and meds, Trey thought. He'd been twelve years old when he created his first exotic street drugs and sold them to some out-of-town kids whose families were vacationing in the mountains outside of Loring.

Satisfied with the scene, he hurried back to cabin 6. With the blackmailer out of the way he could return to the hunt for Pruett. For years he had told himself that she would never be a problem. He had liked knowing she was out there. He was sure she thought about him every single day. But he hadn't realized that she was actively searching for him until recently. That news had come as a shock. She had gotten too close. The time had come to get rid of her.

But the evidence box was the more immediate threat. Once the contents had been destroyed, he could relax and take his time with Pruett.

He reached the step and bent down to examine the evidence box. The contents chained him to the past. He would not be free until everything inside had been destroyed.

He tore off the tape and raised the lid of the box.

For a few seconds he did not comprehend what he was looking at. Then it hit him. There was nothing inside the evidence box except some yellowed paperbacks and a handful of old magazines.

Egan Briggs had cheated him.

CHAPTER 34

It was afternoon by the time they got back to Seattle. Max drove straight to his house to pack a bag.

His phone rang just as he shut down the car engine. He glanced at the screen. *Loring Police Department.*

"Cutler," he said.

"Detective Walsh. Thought you might be interested in knowing that a road repair crew just found the body of Egan Briggs."

"Briggs is dead?"

"The investigation is still ongoing, but it looks like Briggs was running. Unfortunately for him it appears he tried to do a drug deal before he pulled his disappearing act. Whoever he met got rid of him with a small explosive device. There was charred money and drugs at the scene. Briggs was shot once in the head, execution style. The killer wanted to be sure."

"You think Briggs was dealing?"

"Might explain how he was able to take early retirement."

Charlotte was listening intently.

"What about Roxanne Briggs?" she asked.

"Charlotte's asking about Mrs. Briggs," Max said.

"I went to see Roxanne Briggs personally to deliver the bad news," Walsh said. "She didn't seem particularly surprised. Not exactly grief-stricken, either. It was more like she had been expecting to hear that her husband was dead."

"In other words, she probably knew that Briggs was going to meet someone and that things might end badly."

"Yeah, but she denied it. She said Egan told her he was headed for Idaho or Wyoming."

"Have you got anything else from the scene?"

"Not much," Walsh said. "It started raining again about an hour after you left Loring. You know what water does to evidence."

"Yeah."

"One more thing. A road crew spotted your vehicle washed up on the side of the river. They hauled it out. Good luck dealing with the insurance company, by the way. But Ms. Sawyer's handbag was still inside, all zipped up. Her phone probably didn't survive, but her plastic is all intact — she won't have to cancel her credit cards or get a new driver's license. I've got her address. You can tell her I'll overnight the bag and everything in it to her today. She should have it tomorrow."

"Thanks," Max said.

"If you come across anything I ought to know, you'll give me a call, right?"

"Right."

Max ended the connection and looked at Charlotte. "You heard all that?"

"Yes. They found my bag and Briggs is dead."

"At this point the cops think Briggs tried to pull off one last drug deal before disappearing. Things did not go well."

"Well, it makes sense that he would want to vanish after failing to get rid of us. He had to know we'd go straight to the police and that he would be questioned. He probably needed cash to live on for a while, so I suppose the drug deal makes sense."

"Maybe. But if we're right about his past, he might have had something else to sell."

Charlotte's eyes widened in shocked comprehension. "The evidence box from Jocelyn's case?"

"If Briggs was paid off to make it dis-

285

appear, it doesn't automatically follow that he destroyed the contents. Maybe he hung on to it because he knew it might be worth a lot of money to someone."

"Jocelyn would have given anything to get her hands on that box."

"Yes, but there's someone else who would have wanted it just as badly."

Charlotte's expression sharpened. "The man who raped her."

"Yes."

"If Briggs tried to sell the evidence box to the person who attacked Jocelyn all those years ago, it means the bastard is still around. He isn't on the other side of the country. He's right here — in Washington."

"Until we know more, we can't draw any conclusions." Max thought about that for a moment. "Although there is one thing that links the Briggs hit to Louise Flint's death."

"What's that?"

"Drugs were found at both scenes."

He opened the door and climbed out from behind the wheel. Charlotte emerged from the passenger side.

The front door of the house across the street popped open. Anson appeared. He walked toward them and inclined his head politely to Charlotte.

"Ma'am," he said.

Max remembered his manners.

"This is Charlotte Sawyer," he said. "Charlotte, Anson Salinas, my dad."

"A pleasure, Ms. Sawyer," Anson said.

Charlotte smiled, clearly charmed by the old-fashioned formality.

"Glad to meet you, sir," she said. "Please call me Charlotte."

Anson chuckled. "I'll do that so long as you don't call me sir."

"It's a deal," Charlotte said.

Anson turned to Max. "They find your car?"

"Yeah. Probably totaled. I'll take care of it later. I don't have time to deal with it or the insurance company at the moment. This case is getting very hot."

"I could drive to Loring and take a look at it for you. Figure out what to do with it."

Max was heading for the porch steps. He paused and glanced back over his shoulder. "Thanks. I'd appreciate it. I'll call Detective Walsh and tell him that you'll pick up Charlotte's handbag, too, if that's okay. That way he won't have to bother with overnighting it."

"No problem," Anson said.

Max took a closer look at him. Anson sounded downright enthusiastic. *Because he's got a job,* Max realized. Every man needs a job.

"Thanks," Charlotte said. "I would be very grateful to you, Anson."

She was practically glowing, Max thought. And he could have sworn that Anson was blushing.

"Not like I've got anything else to do," Anson said. "You two are both okay?"

"Yeah." Max unlocked the front door. "They found the body of that retired detective who dumped us into the river. Looks like he tried to do a drug deal before leaving the area. Got killed for his trouble."

Anson squinted a little. "Drugs, huh?"

"They keep showing up in this case."

Max got the door open, deactivated the alarm system and then stood aside. He summoned up a mental image of the extensive list of remodeling projects that he had made and his gut tightened. Compared to Charlotte's neat, cozy little apartment, his place was a train wreck.

"Got a deal on the house," he said to her, trying not to sound desperate or embarrassed. "Lot of work to be done. Haven't had a chance to really get going on it, though."

"Looks like a good neighborhood," Charlotte said. "That's the most important thing."

"Right," he said.

He wondered if *Looks like a good neighborhood* was a polite euphemism for *Too bad it's the ugliest house on the street.*

She went past him into the house. Anson followed. Max closed the door. Together he and Anson watched Charlotte walk through the little foyer and stop at the end to survey the living room.

Then she disappeared around a corner into the kitchen. He thought about the ancient appliances and the old, stained flooring. He did not move. He wasn't sure what he was waiting for, but he figured he'd know it when it happened.

Anson frowned. "You sure you're okay?"

"I'm fine," he said. "I'm going to stay with Charlotte for a while, just until this case gets resolved."

Anson cocked a brow. "You think she needs a bodyguard, huh?"

"This thing is getting complicated and she's right in the middle of it."

Anson nodded.

Max made himself release the doorknob and walk through the foyer into the front room.

Charlotte appeared from the kitchen.

"You were right," she said, enthusiasm warming her eyes. "You did get a good deal.

This house has great bones, as they say. You've got a lot of work ahead of you, but when it's finished it will be wonderful."

Out of the corner of his eye Max noticed that Anson was smiling a small, secret, satisfied smile. He wasn't sure what that was about, but one thing was certain — he suddenly felt as if a great weight had been lifted from his shoulders.

"I'll go get my stuff," he said.

CHAPTER 35

Roxanne Briggs went into the kitchen to make a cup of herbal tea.

The news that Egan was dead should not have come as a shock, but for some reason, it had. You lived for years with a man you had never really loved because the two of you were bound by secrets, you got used to each other, she thought.

She could have told Walsh that Egan had gone to meet Trey Greenslade in an effort to exact one last blackmail payment and that Trey had no doubt been the person who had killed Egan. But who would have believed her? She had no proof to offer. This was Trey Greenslade, after all, the heir to Loring-Greenslade.

It was so much simpler to let the police assume that Egan had been murdered in a drug deal gone bad.

When the tea was ready, she sat at the table and tried to decide exactly what she was feeling. After a while it dawned on her that mostly she felt relieved.

By the time she finished the tea, she was starting to wonder if she ought to be feeling afraid. Trey Greenslade might conclude that she was aware of the secret that Egan had kept. He might decide that he should get rid of her, too.

She should run, she thought.

She set down the mug, pushed herself to her feet and walked toward the bedroom to pack. When she went past the mantel, she paused to take down the framed pictures of Nolan. They were the only things in the house that were important enough to take with her.

A short time later she put two bags into the back of the pickup. She tucked the pistol under the front seat and got behind the wheel. She drove down the long, graveled drive, across the bridge and onto the old mountain highway.

She never once looked back.

Egan had not given her a lot over the years, she thought. There had been some affection at first, when he had liked having sex with her, but that hadn't lasted long. He had never shown her any true kindness. No true companionship. But he had provided her with something.

Thanks to Egan she had the survival skills she needed to disappear.

CHAPTER 36

Anson had time to think on the long drive to Loring. He spent some of that time thinking about Charlotte Sawyer. When he wasn't thinking about Charlotte, he thought about Max and Cabot and Jack. And he thought about the past.

He was damn proud of the three men he had raised. One way or another each of them had followed in his footsteps: each had pursued a career in law enforcement. True, they had taken very different routes — Max had become a profiler and was now trying to set up shop on his own. Cabot was the chief of police of a small town in Oregon. Jack had taken the academic path. He taught highly specialized classes that focused on obscure and exotic forms of criminal behavior. He had even written a book on the subject — *Warped Visions.*

But Anson also knew that all three of his sons had been scarred by their time in

Quinton Zane's compound and by the fire that had left them orphaned. It was no accident that each of them had wound up chasing criminals for a living. The events of the past haunted them and at the same time fueled them, providing the fire that made each of them so good at what they did.

But the fallout from the past also had a way of wreaking havoc with their most intimate relationships.

He had done what he could to give Max, Cabot and Jack the tools they needed to cope with their past. But he had not been able to provide them with the answers they craved. He was well aware that each man was doomed to find his own path when it came to dealing with the ghost of Quinton Zane.

Anson went back to thinking about Charlotte. Something told him that she just might be the woman who could accept the part of Max that could not let go of the past.

CHAPTER 37

Charlotte awoke, breathless, on the jagged fragments of a dream in which she was trying desperately to reach Jocelyn, who was being swept away by a river.

Okay, not hard to figure out where that imagery came from, she thought.

She sat up quickly. Moonlight and the sparkling lights of the city spilled through the uncovered window, illuminating the bedroom.

She pushed aside the bedding, intending to go out into the living room and walk off some of the dark energy of the nightmare. She took two steps toward the closed door of her bedroom before she remembered her houseguest.

She stopped, listening intently. There was no sound from the living room. Max was most likely asleep. He needed his rest. The last thing she wanted to do was wake him.

On the other hand, the bedroom was too

small for her purposes. She needed to *move.* She certainly wasn't going to be able to go back to sleep for a while.

She regarded the door with a deep sense of dread. In the shadows of the bedroom it seemed to have been transformed into a solid wall — the one thing that was keeping her from escaping to the freedom of the living room.

She knew it was ridiculous, but she was suddenly convinced that if she didn't get out of the bedroom she was going to have a full-blown anxiety attack.

The hallway that connected her room to the living room and kitchen would be a reasonable compromise, she decided. She could pace up and down that narrow corridor until her nerves settled.

She opened the door and stepped, barefooted, out into the hall. She stood quietly, listening. There was still no sound emanating from the living room.

Cautiously she began to pace the short hallway, focusing on her breathing, as she had learned to do in the meditation classes she had taken. Gradually the last traces of the nightmare faded. Her pulse slowed.

She was considering a glass of water when she heard the squeak of springs. There followed a faint rustling in the living room.

She thought about rushing back to the bedroom, but she told herself there was no point. Max was awake.

He appeared silhouetted in the entrance of the living room.

"Bad dream?" he asked. "Or just couldn't sleep?"

His low voice, a little roughened from sleep and edged with a darkly sensual vibe, made her catch her breath. A thrill of excitement swept through her.

He was wearing a dark T-shirt and she saw that he had taken the time to put on his trousers. That explained the rustling sounds, she thought. She was suddenly very conscious of her robe and bare feet.

"Sorry," she said. She was surprised at the husky note in her own voice. "Didn't mean to wake you."

"Not a problem. I'm a light sleeper."

She cleared her throat. "Right."

"You didn't answer my question. Bad dream or insomnia?"

"A little of both."

He folded his arms and propped one shoulder against the doorjamb. "No need to explain. I'm having the same kind of night."

"We both need sleep," she said. "We didn't get much last night. Maybe we should try some brandy or hot cocoa."

"Either one sounds good."

"The brandy will be quicker. I've got some in the kitchen."

"Okay."

The kitchen doorway was just before the living room entrance where Max waited in the shadows. She padded down the hall toward him. He did not move, but he watched her with an intensity that stirred her senses. She could not recall ever having felt so aware of a man. There was something deeply primal about the sensation.

She told herself to calm down and remember that the attraction between them — assuming it went both ways — was based on the connection created by the harrowing experience they had gone through together. The reality was that they barely knew each other. Their relationship was not founded on stable ground.

Relationship.

That was probably not the right word to describe their association. Partnership was more accurate. And it was a short-term partnership at that. A business partnership.

And if she tried to define their situation any more clearly tonight, while they were standing only a few feet apart in the darkened apartment, she really would bring on a panic attack.

She made it to the kitchen doorway and stopped. Max was so close now that she could reach out and touch him. To keep herself from doing just that she locked her arms together beneath her breasts.

"Do you mind if I ask you a personal question?" she said.

"How personal?"

"I was just wondering if you ever have a problem with female clients."

"In the six months I have been in the investigation business, I have discovered that I have problems with every client. Goes with the territory. What sort of problems did you have in mind?"

"It just occurred to me that there's a certain intimacy factor involved in your work."

"Intimacy." He said the word as if he wasn't sure what it meant.

"I mean, your clients probably share some of their most closely held secrets. They trust you to get answers to questions they're often afraid to ask."

"It's not like the kind of relationship you have with a doctor or a lawyer, if that's what you're thinking."

"Maybe not," she said. "But you've probably dealt with a lot of clients who are in a highly emotional state. You must have had some who are angry or fearful or desperate. They see you as the one person who might be able to solve their problems. They probably project some of their strong feelings onto you."

"I'm kind of new at the PI business, remember? I told you, until I went out on my own six months ago I worked for a consulting firm. Our clients were usually members of law enforcement or government agencies — not private individuals."

"Yes, right, sorry. Just wondered."

"I interviewed people from time to time — suspects and victims and witnesses. And sometimes it was bad. Real bad. But it was usually someone else who had to deal with the emotional fallout of a case. My job was to identify the patterns and figure out how to predict what the bad guy was going to do next."

"I see."

"Mind if I ask where you're going with this?"

She felt the heat rise in her cheeks. "I have absolutely no idea. Sorry." *Stop apologizing, you dork.* "Nervous chatter. Blame the bad dream and the insomnia. I'll get the brandy."

She escaped into the kitchen and opened a cupboard door to take down the brandy bottle. She sensed rather than heard Max move into the doorway behind her.

"Were you wondering if I've ever slept with a client?" he asked.

"No, no, no. Nothing like that." Horrified, she yanked the cork out of the bottle. "It's none of my business. I wouldn't dream of asking such a personal question."

"No."

She froze. "No?"

"No, I have never slept with a client."

She took a deep breath. "Of course not. I never thought you had. I was speaking in more general terms about your emotional involvement. You know — how do you handle an angry client who takes his anger out on you when he gets an answer he doesn't want — that kind of thing."

"It happens. That's why I always get a retainer up front. But a lot of my work is business and corporate stuff. Not much emotion involved in those cases, but they're the kind that pay the rent."

"I see." Why in the world had she started this ridiculous conversation? Her hand shook a little as she tried to splash brandy into two glasses. "Forget I asked. Just idle curiosity."

"And maybe the fact that you've got a strange man sleeping in your living room is giving you an anxiety attack?" he asked a little gruffly. "Sorry about that."

"No." She set the bottle down hard on the counter and gulped some of the brandy from one of the glasses. The stuff burned all the way to her stomach, robbing her of breath for a few seconds. She coughed and managed to gasp, "You're not a stranger."

"And you're not a client." He took a couple of steps into the kitchen and stopped. "You're assisting me in exchange for my services as an investigator."

She looked at him. "What does that mean?"

"I don't know about you, but as far as I'm concerned the usual rules don't apply here."

She handed him the other glass of brandy. He took it and swallowed some.

"So?" she prompted.

He lowered the glass. In the shadows his eyes seemed to heat.

"So we get to make up the rules as we go along," he said.

She drank a little more brandy to fortify herself and lowered the glass slowly, proud of her control.

"Okay," she said.

He closed the distance between them, halting less than a foot away. His eyes never left her face.

"Got any?" he asked.

"Any what?"

"Any rules I should know about."

She was suddenly standing on the edge of a very high cliff. She really ought to think long and hard before she jumped. *Screw thinking.* She'd done a lot of thinking before she agreed to marry Brian Conroy. What good had it done?

"No," she said. "No, I can't think of any rules that apply. At least not tonight."

He set his glass down on the counter. "I want to be very sure of what's going on here."

"In all honesty? I haven't got a frickin' clue."

"Do you want me?"

She took a breath. "So much for the subtle approach."

He caught her chin on the edge of his hand. "I'm not good with the subtle approach. I need to be sure. I need a yes or no."

She was still in free fall, she realized, about to spread wings she didn't know she possessed.

"Yes," she whispered. "But only if you want me, too."

He smiled a slow, intimate smile that left her breathless. She could have sworn his eyes got a little hotter.

"That's important to you?" he asked.

"It would be a disaster otherwise."

"Good to know." He took her glass from her unresisting hand and set it down on the counter. Then he cupped her face between his palms. "Just to be clear, I want you, too."

"You're sure?"

"Positive."

He leaned in close, pinning her slowly, relentlessly against the kitchen counter with the weight of his body. The kiss started out as a slow burn. His mouth moved deliberately on hers, as though he was issuing an invitation. Or making an exploratory foray. Or trying to seduce her.

But she didn't need to be seduced. She was shivering with anticipation, intoxicated by an incendiary brew composed of equal parts reckless abandon and absolute certainty. She acknowledged the risks and simultaneously concluded that she could handle them. Hell, someone had tried to murder her. She could have died trapped in a car that had plunged into the cold waters of a raging river. She could have perished of hypothermia on a merciless mountain. On top of all that, she was helping a professional PI — a former profiler, no less — look for her missing stepsister.

Compared to all that, the potential drawbacks of having sex with the man who was sharing the danger with her just didn't seem very worrisome. Tonight she was going to do what she wanted to do and let tomorrow take care of itself.

The decision set her free — gloriously free — in ways she could not possibly have imagined. For once she was not trying to think through to the logical conclusion; not trying to play it safe. For once she simply did not give a damn about the risks involved.

She reached up to grasp Max's shoulders. Everything about him was hard, honed and heated. She knew then that in setting herself free, she had freed him, as well.

Lightning struck. The slow-burn kiss flashed into a firestorm. Max gripped her around the waist and lifted her up onto the counter. Her robe fell away. He pushed her knees apart. She wrapped her legs around his waist and wound her arms around his neck.

He groaned, swept her off the counter and started toward the bedroom. She clung to him, her thighs snugged tight as though he were a wild stallion she could ride.

There was something very focused about the way he carried her down the hall. She had the sense that he would have walked through hell to get to his destination. She liked knowing that, she discovered. She liked it a lot.

He fell with her onto the tumbled bed. She came down on top of him. He got the robe off her shoulders, yanked the sleeves down her arms and tossed the garment aside. A moment later he hauled her nightgown up over her head and flung it out of the way.

His hands closed gently over her breasts.

"Charlotte," he said.

Her name was a hoarse whisper in the shadows.

She fought to get rid of his T-shirt and then she started to work on the zipper of his trousers. He was fully aroused, his erection thrust firmly against the fabric of the pants.

The zipper resisted. She took a firmer grip on it and prepared to yank hard.

Max sucked in his breath and stopped her with his hand.

"I'll take care of it," he said.

She rolled onto her side so that he could deal with his trousers. He got up, stripped off the pants and then stepped out of his briefs. He lowered himself alongside her and gathered her to him. One of his hands moved on her, gliding over her thigh. When she touched him, she discovered that his back was damp with sweat.

He found her hot, wet core with his fingers, and she gave herself up to the wild, elemental thrill of pure sensation. A fierce urgency tightened her lower body. She was stunned to realize that she was on the brink of a climax. She hadn't even plugged in the vibrator.

"Now," she said. She clenched her fingers in his hair. "Do it now."

He moved between her legs. She raised her knees, welcoming him. He entered her slowly, pushing deep. She had never felt so tight, so stretched. He forged into her again and again.

Her release crashed through her in waves. She wanted to scream with the sheer pleasure of it all, but she could not catch her breath. Instead she dug her nails into Max's shoulders and held on for dear life.

The raw energy of her climax pulled him into the vortex. The muscles of his back and shoulders were as taut as steel bands. His skin was slick with perspiration.

The storm broke.

When it was over, he collapsed slowly along the length of her, crushing her into the bedding. She held him close and listened as his breathing returned to normal.

After a while he untangled himself and stretched out beside her.

"Charlotte," he said again.

"Shush." She levered herself up on her elbow and put her fingers over his lips. "Don't say anything that will ruin the moment."

"I don't think the announcement of the end of the world could ruin it for me." He watched her through half-closed eyes. "Can I ask if it was good for you, too?"

She smiled slowly. "It was good. Very, very good. The first time I've ever been able to finish without a small household appliance."

"Huh. You usually use a vibrator?"

"I keep it in the drawer beside my bed. Why?"

"Nothing," he said. "Just curious."

She wondered if she should inform him that he did not do innocent well.

"Why are you interested in my vibrator, Max Cutler?"

"You know how it is with us guys. We like to fool around with gadgets."

She stroked a finger slowly down his chest and smiled again. "You don't need to use a gadget."

"Doesn't mean I couldn't come up with

something interesting to do with one," he said.

"I'll think about it," she said.

CHAPTER 38

He awoke to dark skies, the gentle sound of rain on the window and the tantalizing fragrance of freshly brewed coffee. He tried to remember the last time he had felt this good. He wasn't sure how to describe his mood. Refreshed, maybe. Relaxed. Invigorated. *Good.* That was it. He felt good. He could get used to this feeling. He could get used to it in a hurry.

Memories of the night tumbled through his head. He thought about the vibrator and smiled to himself. Unfortunately, he was alone in the bed. On the plus side, Charlotte and coffee were not far away.

He shoved the covers aside, sat up on the edge of the bed and reached for his trousers. He and Charlotte had made a lot of progress with their relationship the previous night, but he was pretty sure it was too soon for him to wander naked into the kitchen.

He stood and closed the zipper with some

care. He was half-aroused.

Satisfied that he had met the minimal sartorial requirements for morning-after attire, he shoved his fingers through his hair and headed down the hall.

Charlotte was in the kitchen. She looked fresh from a shower. Her hair was caught back in a careless twist. Dressed in a pair of black jeans and a blue T-shirt, she somehow hit the sweet spot between sexy and innocent.

It wasn't an act, he thought. It was the natural Charlotte. There was an innate wholesomeness about her that could easily be mistaken for naïveté or vulnerability.

No wonder her stepsister had felt compelled to protect her. Maybe Jocelyn Pruett hadn't understood that it took a certain strength of character to hold fast to qualities like optimism and kindness and, yes, wholesomeness, in the face of all the hard evidence of evil in the world.

Charlotte smiled at him. "You're awake. Want to shower before breakfast?"

He rubbed his face and winced at the rough stubble of his morning beard. "Probably a good idea." He watched her open the refrigerator door. "I take it you're an early riser."

"I'm definitely a morning person." She

took a carton of eggs out of the refrigerator and set it on the counter. "You?"

"I think so."

"You think so? You don't know for sure?"

He lounged in the doorway, enjoying the sight of her bustling around the kitchen. "Mostly I'm whatever I need to be on a particular job. Sometimes that means getting up early. Sometimes it means staying up late or all night."

She nodded. "Your profession demands flexibility."

He smiled.

She shot him a suspicious look. "What did I say?"

"I don't think of my work as a profession. It's just what I do."

"What you need to do."

He thought about it. "Okay, what I need to do."

"That makes it a profession." She paused. "No, I take that back. That makes it a calling."

He chuckled. "First time I've ever heard anyone label my line of work a calling."

She shrugged. "It is what it is. Go take your shower."

"Right."

He went into the living room, collected his duffel and started back down the hall toward her bathroom.

Charlotte spoke again as he went past the kitchen door.

"Any more thoughts on how we move forward with the search for Jocelyn?" she asked.

"By the time I get out of the shower, I'll have a plan."

"Ah, you're one of those people who think more clearly in the shower."

"Wrong. Turns out I'm one of those people who think more clearly after great sex."

She gave him a ferocious scowl and cracked an egg against the side of a bowl with considerable force.

He went on down the hall, smiling to himself. He had been teasing her, but only a little. The truth was, he was discovering that it was easy to think clearly when he was with her; when he could talk to her.

A short time later he sat down at the dining bar. Charlotte placed a plate of creamy scrambled eggs, sausage patties and buttered toast in front of him. He took a closer look at the sausage.

"What is that?" he asked.

"Tempeh sausages," she said. "I make them myself."

"From tempeh."

"Exactly."

"Tempeh, I take it, is not meat."

"It's a fermented soy-based product."

"Huh."

"Let me guess. Real detectives don't eat tofu or tempeh," she said.

"Don't know what real detectives eat. I'm still new at the business. But I'll give the fake sausages a try."

"Excellent decision, considering that I don't have any other kind in my kitchen." She forked up a bite of her eggs. "How did the planning session in the shower go?"

"Would have gone a lot better if you had been in the shower with me."

"I doubt it."

He took a tentative bite of fake sausage and concluded that it wasn't terrible. It wasn't real meat, but it wasn't inedible. Luckily there was a really big pile of eggs and some toast. He would not starve.

"What I concluded is that it's past time we had a chat with Jocelyn's closest friends," he said. "The members of the investment club."

Charlotte considered that briefly. "All right. I'll ask my boss for some vacation time so that I can go with you. I doubt if they'll be able to tell us anything useful, though. As far as they're concerned, Louise died of an overdose and Jocelyn is on retreat somewhere in the Caribbean."

"Stuff has happened. Might be interesting to see if it changes their minds about the situation."

Charlotte paused her fork halfway to her mouth. "We should probably start with Madison Benson. She's the one who founded the club."

"What do you know about her?"

"Not a lot. She owns her own financial planning business. Quite successful. She donates regularly to the women's shelter where Louise worked and she's active in the shelter's fund-raisers. She recruited the other members of the club, including Jocelyn, from among the regular donors."

"So they all had a connection to the shelter."

"Right. But Louise and Jocelyn had a special friendship, not just because they were both passionate about funding the shelter, but because they had both been assaulted in the past. They understood each other in ways that no one else could. They thought of themselves as a small survivors' club."

"What do you know about the other members of the investment club?"

"Victoria Mathis is in marketing at a local

sportswear company. She seems nice, but I really don't know her very well. Emily Kelly is in human resources. Works for a local tech company. Again, I don't know much about her."

Max thought about that while he ate some of the tempeh sausage.

"Why an investment club?" he asked.

Charlotte had been about to drink some coffee. She stopped and gave him a quizzical look.

"Why not an investment club?" she asked. "After all, it was Madison Benson who brought them together and Madison's expertise is in financial planning and investing."

"But you said that the club has never made a lot of money."

"There hasn't been a big windfall. I think the club started out as an excuse for Jocelyn and the others to get together for drinks and conversation. But a few weeks ago Jocelyn told me that it looked like one of the start-ups they invested in is a good candidate for a buyout. She said that if the deal goes through, all the club members will make a very, very nice profit."

"Except for Louise."

Charlotte sighed. "Except for Louise."

"What happens to her shares in the club?"

"Hmm." Charlotte thought about that. "As I understand it, if a club member resigns, her shares go back into the club's pool to be split up among the others."

"And if a club member dies?"

Charlotte watched him with troubled eyes. "The same, I suppose. The shares are divided up among the rest of the club members. Jocelyn said something about not wanting to have to deal with heirs who might try to claim a share of the profits or dilute the value of the shares. It was intended to be a very exclusive, very private investment club."

"So now we have a situation in which there is one less person to share in the profits of the start-up buyout."

"Oh, crap." Charlotte put down her fork. "But if this is about money, what was Louise Flint doing in Loring?"

"We both know that there's only one logical answer. She was there because of what happened to Jocelyn all those years ago."

"Then her death is linked to the past, not to the potential profits from the club's investment in the start-up," Charlotte said.

"In my experience, it's never smart to ignore the money trail."

"Okay, you're the expert here. What's our next move?"

"When you're dealing with a group dynamic, you get better results if you don't start at the top. The leader usually has the most to lose and he or she can exert some control over the others. We'll talk to Victoria Mathis and Emily Kelly first and then circle back to Madison Benson."

"What, exactly, are we going to ask Victoria and Emily?"

"I won't know until we start talking to them."

Charlotte raised her brows. "That's how you work?"

"It's called turning over rocks until you find something interesting."

Charlotte started to respond to that, but her phone rang, visibly startling her. She jumped to her feet and grabbed the device off the kitchen counter.

"It's the doorman," she said.

Her disappointment spoke volumes. Max knew that she had been hoping that the call was from Jocelyn.

"Good morning, Phil," she said. "A visitor? I'm not expecting anyone. Are you sure it's not a delivery?" There was a pause. "Oh. I see. Huh. Well, as long as he's here, you can send him on up. Thanks."

She ended the call and put the phone back down on the counter.

"Sorry about this," she said. "It's my ex-fiancé. Evidently he told Phil, the doorman, that it was really important."

"Interesting."

She gave him a curious look. "Why?"

"Think it's a coincidence that he's back in your life at this particular juncture?"

"Wow. You really are the suspicious type, aren't you? Yes, I think it's just a co-incidence. He called the other day and told me that the woman he left me for changed her mind about leaving her husband. She dumped Brian. He's looking for a shoulder to cry on."

"And he immediately thought of you."

"Yep." Charlotte smiled an angelic smile. "And when Phil told me that Brian was downstairs just now, I immediately con-cluded that this was a golden opportunity to demonstrate that I have moved on. Sorry, partner, I'm using you."

He ate some more eggs. "I live to serve."

The doorbell chimed. Charlotte hurried around the corner and disappeared into the small foyer.

"Hi, Brian. Come on in."

Max smiled at her bright, vivacious tone.

"It's so good to see you again, sweetie. I've missed you."

Brian Conroy sounded warm, engaging,

sincere. There was even a note of humility. It was the tone of a man who knew he had screwed up; a man who was hoping to find his way back into a woman's good graces.

"We were just finishing breakfast," Charlotte said. "Would you like some coffee?"

She was sounding more cheerful and enthusiastic by the second, Max thought. If she got any more upbeat, she would break out in song. The lady was looking forward to her little taste of revenge.

"Someone else is here?" Brian sounded uneasy now. "Jocelyn?"

It was clear that he did not want to confront Jocelyn.

"No, Jocelyn's out of town," Charlotte said.

"Good. I mean, right, that's what I thought."

"Come in and meet Max," Charlotte said lightly.

"Who's Max?" Brian asked. "Did you get a dog?"

Max winced.

"Nope," Charlotte said.

She whisked Brian around the corner and into the kitchen.

The man went with the voice, Max decided. Pleasant, successful, clean-cut and sincere.

"Max Cutler, I'd like you to meet Brian Conroy," Charlotte said. "I believe I mentioned him once or twice."

"The guy who got cold feet five days before your wedding," Max said. "I remember."

He rose from the dining bar, but he did not offer to shake hands. Instead he picked up the coffeepot and poured himself another cup.

Brian got a deer-in-the-headlights look and then he turned to Charlotte, clearly shocked.

"What is going on here?" he said. "Who is this guy?"

"Not the dog," Max offered, going for helpful.

Brian ignored him.

"Max is a friend," Charlotte said. "A very good friend. He spent the night here and now we're having breakfast, as you can see. Would you like some coffee?"

"No, thanks." Brian lowered his voice, very earnest now. "Look, Charlotte, I really need to talk to you."

"Go right ahead. I have no secrets from Max."

"Well, I sure as hell do. Where did you meet him, anyway? Some kind of bar hookup? Or have you been hitting the online dating sites?"

"None of the above," Max said. "We started out as business acquaintances. Things progressed from there."

Brian drew himself up and squared his shoulders. "I'm not buying that."

"I'm not selling it," Max said. "Just stating facts."

"Just who the hell do you think you are?" Brian asked softly. "If you think you can take advantage of Charlotte —"

For the first time Charlotte seemed to realize that she was playing with fire. Alarmed, she put a hand on Brian's arm.

"That's enough, Brian," she said firmly. "What was so important that you felt you had to come and see me at this hour of the morning?"

"I am not about to discuss our personal business in front of some stranger."

"Then you might as well leave," Charlotte said. "Because Max and I have a busy day ahead. Places to go, people to see."

Brian flushed a dull red. "Damn it, Charlotte —"

She fixed him with a steely glare. "Here's the thing, Brian. I don't have time to waste giving you tea and sympathy because your married lover dumped you."

Brian abruptly changed tactics.

"Look, sweetie, I know I hurt you. I didn't realize what we had until I lost you."

"Until you dumped me and left me with all those wedding bills to pay off."

"I can make it up to you. I'll write you a check if that will make you feel better."

"Be my guest. I'll send you an itemized list of expenditures. But I can tell you right now that it won't change things. Say what you came to say and then leave."

"Charlotte, this isn't like you." Brian shot Max a fierce look. "Whatever you think you have going with this guy, it's just a rebound thing. It's natural under the circumstances. But he won't stick around for long. When it's over, you'll realize that what you and I had was something much deeper and more important."

"You've got it backwards," Charlotte said. "You're the one who's on the rebound. You're here because you got dumped and you want me to make it all better until you can find a new relationship."

"That's not how it is."

"People tell me I'm too trusting," Charlotte said. "And maybe that's true. However, it does not follow that I am stupid. Once someone has proven that he can't be trusted, I learn my lesson. I try not to repeat my mistakes. The bottom line is that I could never trust you again, Brian. You broke our relationship. There's no way to repair it."

"You're making a huge mistake," Brian warned.

"It's time for you to leave," Charlotte said.

She turned on her heel and went back around the corner, heading for the door.

Brian looked at Max, anger heating his blue eyes.

"I don't know who you are, you son of a bitch," he said, "but I know you're taking advantage of her."

"Charlotte wants you to leave," Max said. "It would probably be best if you did."

"Fuck off," Brian hissed softly.

He stalked out of the kitchen. A few seconds later the door closed quietly behind him. There was a long silence before Charlotte reappeared. Her arms were crossed very tightly and she looked worried.

"That," she said, "was one of the dumbest things I've ever done. I should never have let Phil send him up here."

"Relax. Pretty sure it will all blow over."

"Pretty sure?"

"I don't know Conroy as well as you do. What do you think?"

"I . . . I'm not sure. Before this morning I would have said he wasn't the type to make a scene."

"He got mad because the woman he thought he could come back to on the rebound had already moved on. He needs time to cool off."

"I hope you're right." Charlotte took a deep breath and let it out slowly. "Still, letting him come up here this morning was a really dumbass thing to do."

"Yeah, revenge has a strange way of backfiring."

She narrowed her eyes. "You seem to know something about the subject."

"I do — for a couple of reasons. One is that in the past six months I've learned that a lot of the people who hire a PI tell you that they just want answers, but what they really want is ammunition for revenge. I try to avoid that kind of work. It never ends well."

Charlotte watched him intently. "What's the other reason you think you know something about revenge?"

"In one way or another I've been looking for revenge since the night Quinton Zane set the fires that killed my mother. Look where it's gotten me — I'm divorced, damn near broke and, according to at least one shrink, burned out. I've got a failed career as a profiler behind me. A lot of people are predicting that I'm going to fail again as a

PI. They say I'm obsessed with the notion that Quinton Zane is still alive — and all because I want revenge."

"No, because you want to be sure Zane is dead. It's understandable. You want justice."

"Tell that to the therapist who diagnosed me."

She surprised him with a fleeting smile. "I will, if I ever get the opportunity."

A strange, comforting warmth stole over him. She believed him. She didn't think he was paranoid or obsessed. She trusted him and she trusted his intuition. Among those who knew something about his past, she was the only one outside his foster family who did have faith in him and his weird way of looking at the world.

"Thanks," he said. He couldn't think of anything else to say.

"Well, so much for the pleasures of revenge," Charlotte said. She moved into the kitchen and picked up the coffeepot. "Back to business. How much are we going to tell the other members of the investment club when we interview them?"

"We'll start with the truth — that Jocelyn is missing and that I'm investigating Louise Flint's death. We'll see how they react and take it from there."

CHAPTER 39

"I understand you're worried about Jocelyn," Emily Kelly said. "But I really don't think there's anything I can tell you that will help. I assumed she was at some convent in the Caribbean doing a tech-free retreat."

Max drank some coffee and tried to get a read on Emily Kelly. The only thing he was certain of at that moment was that she was tense and anxious. She looked as if she had not slept well.

She had initially refused to meet with them. When Charlotte had called her a half hour earlier, Emily had been quick to explain that she was on her way to a yoga class. It was only after Charlotte had said she was concerned for her stepsister that Emily had agreed to meet with them at her house.

The moment she opened the door it was obvious there was no yoga class. Two suitcases stood in the hall. Emily was preparing to leave town.

The house was an older home in a pleasant residential neighborhood. The interiors and furnishings were standard-issue contemporary, bland to the point of invisibility. There was no edge. No bold strokes of color. In a city noted for its gardens, Emily's front yard stood out because of its sheer ordinariness.

Emily suited her house, Max thought, attractive, neat and well maintained. But there was nothing unconventional, exotic or over-the-top about either the woman or her home. It was as if both were determined to blend into the background; as if they went out of their way to go unnoticed.

"Do you have any idea where Jocelyn might have gone?" Charlotte asked.

"None." Emily shook her head. "But this is Jocelyn we're talking about. For all you know, she simply decided to ditch the retreat and head for a high-end beachfront hotel. It wouldn't be the biggest surprise in the world."

"She hasn't been in touch with you, then?" Charlotte said.

Emily shook her head, her lips pressed tightly together.

She was lying, Max thought.

"You're worried, aren't you?" he said.

Emily stared at him with a helpless expression. Then she seemed to collapse in on herself.

"We all are," she whispered. "Because of Louise. I've been telling myself that I won't run. I've got a gun. Good security system. I've also got a great job. I will probably lose it if I just disappear. But I haven't been able to sleep. I can't go on like this. My nerves won't take it. So, yes, this morning I packed my things. I was about to put my suitcases in the car when you phoned."

"Thank you for waiting," Charlotte said.

Emily shook her head. "I only hung around because I hoped you might have some news or at least some information about what is going on."

"Will you at least tell us why you're so concerned?" Charlotte asked. "Jocelyn is my stepsister. I think I have a right to know whatever you can tell me."

Emily hesitated.

"Have you spoken with Victoria or Madison?" she asked finally.

"Not yet," Charlotte said. "I called Victoria right after I called you. I wanted to set up an appointment, but she didn't answer her phone. I left a message. I'll try again later."

"It would be better if you talked to them,"

Emily said. "I'm the newest member of the club."

"What is this all about?" Max asked, deliberately sharpening his tone.

Emily flinched as if she had been struck. She recoiled and turned to Charlotte.

"What is going on here?" Charlotte asked.

"I don't know," Emily said. Tears leaked from her eyes. "That's what I'm trying to tell you. I just don't know what is going on. None of us do."

"But you're afraid," Charlotte said. "Because Louise is dead and Jocelyn is missing."

"Yes." Emily used a tissue to blot her eyes. "I'll tell you what I know and then I need to leave."

"Talk to us," Max said.

Emily fixed her attention on Charlotte. "Madison started the club."

"We know that," Charlotte said.

Emily clasped her hands very tightly together on her knees. She was so rigid she looked as if she might shatter at the slightest touch.

"It's a legitimate investment club," she continued softly. "We do make investments. In fact, one of them might be about to pay off in a very big way. But at the start the investment angle was meant to serve as a cover."

Charlotte stared at her, speechless.

"For what?" Max asked.

"It was Madison's idea," Emily said quickly. "She said that we — the five of us — could do so much more than just donate to the women's shelter where Louise worked. She said we could punish the men who got away with abusing their wives and kids."

Charlotte sat frozen. "Punish them? How?"

"Madison said that we could perform what she called takedowns. The targets would be selected from the files at the women's shelter."

"Louise had access to those files?" Max asked.

Emily nodded. "She often interviewed the women. She was in a position to get the details we needed to go after the ones who got away — the men who went unpunished by the system. We were just trying to get some justice for the victims, you see."

"What kind of justice are you talking about?" Max asked.

"We did everything online. There's so much damage you can do and remain anonymous. We went into the chat rooms that the men used to find their victims and we did what we could to expose them. We ruined credit ratings. We even got two men fired from their jobs."

"You hounded them," Charlotte said.

"Yes." Emily raised her chin. "Our goal was to make sure the abusers never had a moment's peace. We wanted them to be afraid all of the time. We tried to ensure that they never got close to another potential victim."

"Jocelyn never told me any of this," Charlotte said.

She sounded as if she'd had the wind knocked out of her, Max thought.

"Of course not," Emily said. "Jocelyn considers herself your big sister. She thinks she needs to protect you. And, although we were careful, we all knew that what we were doing was potentially dangerous."

"Why did Jocelyn disappear?" Max asked.

"None of us knew that she had disappeared," Emily said. "Not at first. We really did believe that she was off at some retreat in the Caribbean. But after Louise died, Victoria and I started to wonder if something had happened to Jocelyn, too. Then someone sent the warning code. We assume it was Jocelyn. It has to be Jocelyn who sent it. Otherwise, it makes no sense."

"What is this warning code?" Charlotte said.

"Our biggest concern was that one day one of the targets might figure out who was behind the online takedowns," Emily said. "We worked out a code word to be used in such a situation. Last Friday all three of us — Madison, Victoria and I — got an e-mail from an anonymous address. We are sure it must have come from Jocelyn. There was only one word in the subject line. It was the code word."

"You think that one of the men you punished has turned the tables," Max said. "You think he's targeting you and the other members of the investment club."

Emily looked at him, her eyes stark. "That's what Victoria and I believe. Madison has . . . a different theory."

"What is Madison's theory?" Max asked.

"Ask her," Emily muttered.

"Where are you going?" Charlotte said.

Emily bit her lip. "No offense, but I'm not telling you or anyone else."

"I understand," Max said. He reached into his pocket and took out a card. "But if you need help, you can contact me at that number. Day or night. Got that?"

Emily nodded. She clutched the card and

got to her feet.

"I need to go now," she said.

CHAPTER 40

Neither of them spoke until they were back in Max's car, driving away from Emily's house. Charlotte tried to organize her thoughts, but she kept hitting a mental stone wall no matter which way she turned. She glanced at Max. He seemed lost in his own thoughts.

"I can't believe it," she said, more in an effort to break the silence than anything else.

"You can't believe that Jocelyn and her investment club pals were living out some sort of real-life female revenge fantasy?"

"Well, actually, I can see Jocelyn doing something like that," Charlotte admitted. "I suppose what I find hard to believe is that I had no clue she was living a secret life."

"Looking back, are you sure she never dropped any hints?"

"No. Well, in hindsight I guess the fact that she was so firm about refusing to invite me to join the club was a clue. But I didn't pick up on it. You must think I'm incredibly naïve."

"What I think is that you had no reason to suspect that Jocelyn was taking a huge risk."

"But what does any of it have to do with what happened all those years ago in Loring?"

"Maybe we'll get more answers out of Victoria Mathis," Max said.

Charlotte took out her phone and keyed in Victoria's number again. She was dumped straight into voice mail.

"She still isn't answering," she said.

"Either she's running, too, like Emily Kelly, or —"

He stopped. His mouth tightened. Charlotte's insides knotted.

"Or whoever murdered Louise has already killed her. Is that what you were going to say?" she asked.

"It's a possibility, but at this point I'm inclined to doubt it."

"Why?"

"Like I said, dead bodies have a way of showing up."

"Sometimes they do disappear forever, though."

"Sometimes," he agreed. "But this particular killer doesn't seem to be concerned with making his victims disappear. If we're right about him, his goal is to make it look like his targets OD'd."

"So he doesn't care if the body is found," Charlotte said. "He must be very sure of himself."

"Yes," Max said, thoughtful now. "Yes, he is very confident, isn't he? That's interesting."

"Why?"

"Ultimately it will make him more predictable."

"Well, alive or dead, Victoria isn't answering her phone."

"That leaves us with Madison Benson," Max said. "Unless she has decided to run, too."

CHAPTER 41

Madison Benson was not running. Not yet, at any rate. But Charlotte could tell that beneath her cool, controlled executive demeanor and her Armani armor, she was nervous.

"I agreed to talk to you," Madison said, "because you are Jocelyn's stepsister. But when you called a few minutes ago you didn't say anything about bringing an investigator with you."

She cast a grim look at Max.

"I told you, Max is helping me search for Jocelyn," Charlotte said. "And he's also looking into Louise's death. If what Emily told us is even partially true, it seems to me that you and the other members of the club need all the help you can get."

She and Max were standing in the living room of Madison's elegant home. The big house was perched on the hillside of the upscale Queen Anne neighborhood. It was surrounded by lush gardens. The windows commanded a panoramic view of Elliott Bay.

Madison had not invited them to sit down and she had not offered coffee.

She had initially refused to talk to them, but upon being informed that Charlotte and Max had just had a long chat with Emily she had changed her mind.

Madison was not happy about Max's presence, but it was clear that she wanted information from them. Fair enough, Charlotte thought. They wanted information from her.

"What, exactly, did Emily tell you?" Madison asked.

"She said that your club is a cover for an online operation that targets abusive men," Charlotte said. "Men that the five of you decide have gone unpunished by the law."

"She seems to believe that Louise was murdered by one of your targets," Max added. "Someone who figured out that your club was responsible for making his life a living hell. She said you and the others think that Jocelyn was the first to run and that she recently sent a message warning all of you."

For the first time Madison looked as if she had been caught off guard.

"Emily told you that?" Madison said.

"Yes," Charlotte said. "Isn't that what you believe?"

Madison did not answer immediately. She walked to the wall of windows that looked out over the waterfront and Elliott Bay.

"I know that Victoria and Emily believe that is what is going on," Madison said after a moment. She sounded as if she was choosing each word with great care. "Emily told you the truth about the original purpose of the club. We did target some of the men who, in at least one case, literally got away with murder. He beat his wife to death and managed to convince a jury that someone else did it. And, yes, we always knew there was a possibility that one of our targets might figure out who had destroyed his finances or his job or his social life. But I'm not so sure that's why Louise was killed — assuming she was murdered, which is still an open question, in my mind."

"What do you think is going on?" Charlotte asked.

Madison turned around, her eyes hardening. "You really want to know?"

"Yes," Charlotte said.

"All right, I'll tell you, but you aren't going to like it and I doubt if you'll believe me. Here's the bottom line. Our club was established to punish abusers we believed had escaped the law. But we wanted our cover to look good. So we did make legitimate investments. We focused on small start-ups, one of which is about to get bought out by a large tech firm. If the Keyworth deal goes through, the profits for the members of the club are going to be huge."

Max studied her for a thoughtful moment and then he nodded once.

"You think Jocelyn murdered Louise so that there would be one less person in the club," he said. "One less member to share the profits. And now you're wondering if she's going to try to take out the rest of you so that she'll be the last one standing when the big payday comes in."

"No." Outrage swept through Charlotte. "That's not true. You can't possibly believe that, Madison."

"I'm not saying it is true," Madison said evenly, her eyes sharpening. "I'm telling you that I think it's a possibility. Frankly, I've also wondered if Emily might have murdered Louise. But Victoria is convinced that it's Jocelyn we have to worry about. There is a great deal of money at stake. In my world, that makes for motive."

"It makes for a very good motive in my world, too," Max said.

"Jocelyn is not a killer." Charlotte tightened her hands into fists. "For God's sake, Madison, you know her. You're her friend. And Louise was her *best* friend. How can you think for even one moment that she would do something horrible like murder her closest friend?"

"I'm not saying she did." Madison's jaw jerked a little. "All I'm saying is that when there's a lot of money at stake, people become . . . unpredictable."

"Not Jocelyn," Charlotte said.

She was still furious, but her voice had steadied. She was very certain of her ground.

"If Jocelyn has decided to get rid of some or all of the rest of the club members in order to maximize her profits, why would she send you and the others the coded warning?" Max asked.

He sounded mildly curious, not like he was trying to push a witness for answers, Charlotte thought.

"Isn't it obvious?" Madison was visibly impatient now. "She wants to make us think that the danger is coming from a different direction — from some unknown target who is out for revenge."

"Seems like sending you all into hiding would only make things more difficult for her," Max pointed out. "She knows where you live here in the city, but how will she find you if you all leave for parts unknown?"

"You don't know Jocelyn very well, do you?" Madison smiled a thin, humorless smile. "Well, let me tell you, she's had over a year to get to know the club members. At one time or another she's probably figured out exactly where we would go if we had to run."

"But you're not running?" Max asked.

"No. This thing will be over in ten days. That's when the Keyworth buyout is set to conclude. In the meantime, I need to stay on top of it. Buyouts are fragile. This one could collapse if even one individual gets cold feet."

"In other words, if Jocelyn is trying to get rid of the other club members, she's on the clock," Max said.

Charlotte glared at him, but he didn't seem to notice.

"Exactly," Madison said.

"But what if neither Jocelyn nor Emily is the killer?" Max said quietly. "What if one of the targets, as you call them, really is hunting the members of the club?"

"I have a gun," Madison said. "I know how to use it."

"You and everyone else in the club, it

seems," Max said.

Madison shrugged. "We knew there was some danger involved. We just didn't expect it to come from one of the other members."

CHAPTER 42

Aunt Hildy had often claimed that the old trailer was a classic. Victoria didn't doubt it. In the distant past its aluminum shell had shone mirror-bright in the sun, but time had oxidized the metal to a dull gray color. The rounded front end had been state-of-the-art back in the day, designed to make the trailer aerodynamic and, therefore, easier to pull.

But the trailer had not been moved in decades. It had served as Hildy's home for as long as Victoria could remember. It had become a refuge for her and her mother after the nightmare of her mother's second marriage had finally ended.

The trailer was set on a parcel of land that overlooked the rugged coastline, a mile outside of the small town where Victoria had finished high school. During the summer months the community was populated with tourists, weekenders and others who came to the coast to enjoy the dramatic, windswept beaches. But the tourist season was over, and that meant there were few strangers in the area. Those who did show up for a fall beach weekend stood out.

After Hildy's death Victoria had told herself that she ought to sell the property. But the memories had been too strong. Besides, neither the land nor the trailer was worth much.

In the end she had decided to keep the trailer as a weekend place, at least until land values picked up. The trailer and the property it sat on were all she had left of the strong woman who had protected her and her mother.

She looked around the compact interior, remembering how safe she had felt there after she and her mother had moved in with Hildy. It had been crowded with the three of them in the small space, but Victoria hadn't cared. Hildy had said she would take care of them, and Victoria had trusted her to do just that.

The bastard who had married her mother had shown up only once. Hildy had met him at the door of the trailer with a gun in her hand. He had never returned. But Victoria knew that Hildy had slept with the gun in the drawer beside her bed every night until they got word that the s.o.b. had been killed in a car crash.

Before that summer was over, Hildy had taught Victoria how to fire the weapon and how to keep it in good condition. She had given Victoria a pistol of her own as a high school graduation present. Victoria had slept with the weapon in a bedside drawer every night of her life since.

Some people might have found the relative isolation of the trailer's location unnerving under the circumstances. But Victoria felt safer there where everyone in the community knew her than she had in the city where she was virtually anonymous.

It was the kind of small town where strangers asking for directions to the home of a local resident were automatically viewed with suspicion. There were other factors that ensured the safety of the trailer. The land around it was covered with scruffy, weather-beaten bushes and grasses. There were no tall trees to provide cover for someone who wanted to approach unobserved. Any vehicle coming up the graveled drive would make plenty of noise before it got near the trailer.

She was as safe here as she would be anywhere else, she thought. And if she did have to use the pistol, there would be a lot less explaining to do afterward than would be the case if she were forced to fire it in her condo tower. In this part of Washington State it was understood that a woman living alone had a right to protect herself.

CHAPTER 43

Max and Charlotte went to the same neighborhood restaurant where they had eaten the night Max had first visited her apartment. Charlotte was amused when he ordered the crab cakes.

"Again?" she said.

"I'm a creature of habit," Max said. "I did try to warn you. A one-foot-in-front-of-the-other kind of guy, remember?"

"Right. Personally, I'm going to take a walk on the wild side. Mostly because I'm starving." She looked up at the waiter. "I'll have the crab cakes, too."

The waiter left with the order. Charlotte turned back to Max.

"I owe Anson a dinner," she said. "Heck, a whole week of dinners. I can't tell you how relieved I am to have my bag back with my wallet and credit cards. And I can't believe my phone survived. I thought for sure I'd have to replace it."

"You lucked out because you had your phone in a decent case and because your bag was waterproof nylon."

"It's my street bag and I live in Seattle," she explained. "So, yes, it's waterproof. What do we do now?"

"We look for the one member of the club we haven't been able to interview — Victoria Mathis."

"How do you propose to find her?"

Max sipped some beer. "How would you characterize her financial situation?"

"I told you, I don't know any of Jocelyn's friends well. Everything I do know about them I've picked up from Jocelyn. She and Louise and Madison had the highest-paying jobs, I can tell you that much. I think Emily and Victoria were doing okay, but they certainly weren't rich. Why do you ask?"

"Because it costs money to go into hiding. Not everyone can pick up and leave for some no-name island in the Caribbean at a moment's notice."

"Oh, right. I see what you mean. Well, for what it's worth, Victoria probably qualifies as the one with the fewest resources."

"Then we should be able to find her."

"We've already talked to Madison and Emily. What more can Victoria tell us?"

"I have no idea," Max said.

His phone pinged. He took it out of the pocket of his jacket. Charlotte watched his face as he read the e-mail. His eyes tightened a little at the corners. He shut down his phone without comment.

"News?" she asked, unable to squelch her curiosity.

"Yeah, but not about your stepsister or this case."

"Another case you're working on?"

"Another case I *was* working on." Max drank some of his beer. "I've dropped it."

Charlotte waited to see if he would add any additional details. But he didn't. She could tell from his eyes and the set of his jaw that he had retreated into some other dimension again.

The subtle transition was jolting. It made her realize that ever since they had returned from the harrowing trip to the mountains, a sense of intimacy had infused their relationship.

Or maybe that was just her imagination.

She was suddenly consumed with the urge to haul him out into the light.

"Why did you drop the case?" she asked. "Did the client fail to pay his bill?"

For a moment she didn't think he was going to answer. But in the end he looked at her over the top of his glass.

"I never got around to sending a bill," he said. "Not that I had planned to send one."

"Ah. Pro bono stuff." Charlotte smiled. "Like a lawyer, you do some jobs for free. I suppose it's a private investigator's version of charity work. That is very nice of you."

"Just to be clear, I am not in the charity business."

"Oh."

Max hesitated. "This was . . . personal."

"I don't understand. Why did you drop the case if it was personal?"

Once again she was sure he was going to refuse to answer.

"Hey, it's not like you haven't learned a heck of a lot about my personal life recently, *partner,*" she said.

She was a little surprised when the tactic worked. Max set his glass down, leaned forward and folded his arms on the table. There was a dark, disturbing intensity in his eyes.

"You really want to hear more about my personal life?" he asked.

She refused to be intimidated. "Yes, I do want to hear about it."

"Fair warning. It's boring."

She smiled. "You're talking to the other plodder on this team, remember?"

Max contemplated her for a long moment.

"All right, I'll try to keep this short and simple. I told you my mother was a single mom."

"Right."

"She was a single mom by choice. When she decided to have a child, she used the services of a sperm donor clinic. I'm the result."

Charlotte gripped the stem of her wineglass. "I see."

"I grew up knowing that my father was an anonymous file in a clinic database."

"But eventually you went looking for him, didn't you?"

"Think so?"

"I know you well enough to know that is exactly what you would do. What's more, I'm willing to bet you found him, because you are very good at what you do."

"It's true what they say, you can find anyone online these days. So, yes, I found him."

"When?"

"A few years ago, right after I got the job with the profiling agency. I guess I had some vague idea that he might be interested in meeting me. I e-mailed him."

"How'd that go?"

"Not well. He e-mailed me back and accused me of stalking him. He said he had legal documents making it clear that he had no obligation to me and that if I ever contacted him or anyone in his family he would contact a lawyer."

She thought she had been prepared for anything in the way of an unhappy ending to the story, but she was stunned almost speechless.

"That was —" She could not find the right words. "Awful."

"No, it was clarifying. I had my answer. I promised myself I would never contact him again."

"Does he have other children?"

"A son and a daughter," Max said. "And they're not kids. They're adults now."

"Which means that you have a half brother and a half sister."

"Biologically speaking, yes. One of the sons is an executive in the family business, a commercial real estate development company in Portland. The daughter is an interior designer, a very successful one, I might add."

"In other words, your siblings are both entrepreneurial."

"You could say that."

She smiled. "None of the apples fell very far from the tree, did they?"

Max unfolded his arms and picked up his

glass. "Meaning?"

"Meaning you and your half sibs seem to have a lot in common."

"No," Max said. He set the glass down with great precision. "We don't. We have nothing in common. They both went to private schools and graduated from very good colleges. They're both successful in their careers. The son is married with a son of his own and the daughter has recently become engaged. I got my education in a war zone followed by some community college classes, followed by a few years spent hunting human monsters, followed by a failed marriage. I am now starting over as a private investigator who is just beginning to make enough money to pay the mortgage on a house that needs a lot of expensive work done."

"Here's the way I see it," Charlotte said. "You have established your own business and in time it will be successful because you are smart and you are good at what you do. You are showing the same entrepreneurial spirit that your siblings have demonstrated."

Max gave her a pitying look. "Just when I conclude that you are not nearly as naïve as everyone seems to think you are, you go and prove me wrong."

"I think that is an insult, but I will pretend

I didn't hear it. Let's get back to this case you say you dropped. What does it have to do with your family history?"

"If I tell you, will you let the subject go?"

"Depends," she said crisply. "I make no promises."

Before Max could respond, the waiter returned with the crab cakes. When they were alone again, Charlotte picked up her fork.

"Talk to me, Max," she said. "After all we've been through together I deserve some answers."

"What the hell," Max said.

"That's the spirit."

He ignored that. "After I got that e-mail from Decatur telling me to stay out of his life I respected his privacy. But from time to time I sort of checked in from afar. I swear I didn't stalk the family, but it's easy enough to keep track of business news."

"So when Decatur's name showed up in the press, you read the articles. That's not stalking. That's plain, old-fashioned curiosity. You've got a biological link to that family. You've got every right to be curious."

"Trust me when I tell you that Davis Decatur would not agree with you."

"Decatur." She frowned. "Why does that name sound vaguely familiar?"

"I told you, Decatur is in commercial real estate. He's a developer. The firm has been successful — very, very successful. They've handled some major projects here in Seattle as well as down in Portland."

"That explains it. I've seen the name go by in the press occasionally, too."

"For the most part the news that shows up in the business media is pretty ordinary stuff — ordinary for a highly successful firm, that is. But about three months ago, Decatur's daughter —"

"Your half sister."

Max exhaled slowly. "Her name is Brooke. She got involved with a hedge fund operator named Gatley. Simon Gatley. Now they're engaged. The name rang a bell and not in a good way. I took a look at him online."

"This isn't going to end well, is it?"

"No. I've got evidence that Gatley is a very sharp scam artist. He's been conning people since college. Amazingly good at it, too. Right now he's operating what looks like a Ponzi scheme. Not his first. It's eventually going to come crashing down, but meanwhile, he is moving his clients' funds into his own offshore account."

"You tried to warn your father — Davis Decatur — didn't you?"

"It was a stupid thing to do," Max said. "I couldn't warn Brooke. She doesn't know I exist. She'd probably think I was the real scam artist. So, yeah, I e-mailed Decatur and suggested that he have his financial and legal people take a close look at Gatley. I got an e-mail back informing me that if I made another attempt to contact anyone in the Decatur family, I would be looking at charges of malicious harassment."

"You did what you could to warn Decatur about Brooke's new boyfriend. Decatur chose to dismiss your warning. So now you've decided to drop the case?"

"There's not much else I can do." Max exhaled slowly. "That last e-mail I got a few minutes ago was just more confirmation that Gatley is a con man."

"You know," Charlotte said, "some people might see this scenario as a nice example of karma. Decatur ignores you for your entire life and now he's going to pay a price."

"Yeah." Max ate some of his crab cakes. He did not look enthusiastic.

"But you hate knowing that Gatley is using your half sister to get close to the Decatur family in order to get his hands on their money."

"Pisses me off that he's going to get away with it. Don't ask me why."

"You don't have to explain why it pisses you off," Charlotte said. "It's perfectly obvious. It's your family that's going to get hurt."

"It's not my family. There's a biological connection, but that's it."

"Fine. It's a biological connection. But after the fallout comes down on the clan, there is an innocent person — your half sister, biologically speaking — who is going to be left with an enormous load of guilt. She'll probably be convinced that the disaster was her fault because she's the one who brought the snake into the family circle."

"Assuming there is a disaster. It's possible someone will figure out that Gatley is bad news before things go south."

"Two words: Bernie Madoff. He managed to con people for years — some of them were very smart people. You and I both know you can't give up. We need a plan."

Max raised his brows. "What's this *we* stuff?"

"We're partners, remember? Don't worry, we'll come up with an angle."

"Be sure to let me know when inspiration strikes. Meanwhile, we've got other priorities."

"Victoria."

"Right."

"Where do we start?"

"After dinner you're going to water a friend's plants."

CHAPTER 44

An hour later Charlotte stood in the hallway outside of Victoria's condo and watched Max do something she was pretty sure was highly illegal to the lock on the door.

She was doing her best to look like she had every right in the world to be there with a man who was performing a small act of breaking and entering. But she worried that she was not much of an actress.

Fortunately, none of the other residents had paid any attention to them thus far. The security in the building was standard. There was no manager or doorman on duty in the evenings. It had been unnervingly easy to follow one of the tenants into the lobby. The techy young man leading the way hadn't even bothered to look up from his cell phone. Charlotte didn't think he was aware of them.

"There's always a lot of turnover in a big apartment complex," Max had explained on the way over, to alleviate her worries. "People are used to seeing strangers in the hallways. And in this case, you're a legitimate acquaintance of one of the tenants. The plant-watering story is just backup in case someone does stop us."

They had headed downstairs to the parking garage first. Victoria's car was not in the slot marked with her apartment number, more proof that she had fled. Now they were about to enter the apartment. Charlotte was so tense she was shivering. She hoped Max didn't notice.

There was a small, muffled click from the lock and then Max was opening the door. Charlotte hurried inside. Max followed and closed the door. She noticed that he took the precaution of locking it. If someone did knock, they would have a little time to make the plant-watering story look good.

Max switched on a lamp.

"Makes our visit look more legit," he said. "A couple of people moving around in here in the dark with a penlight might arouse curiosity."

"No kidding." Charlotte looked at the three potted plants on the window bench. The leaves were drooping. "Looks like the plant-watering story is going to be accurate. I'll give those poor things a drink before we leave. Meanwhile, what are we looking for?"

"Anything that might tell us where Mathis went."

"That kind of travel info would probably be stored on her phone or laptop," Charlotte said. "I don't see either one."

"She may have taken the hardware with her and is keeping the devices turned off. Or maybe she left her phone and computer behind altogether."

Charlotte surveyed the apartment. "Should we try to find them?"

"No, we can't risk tearing the place apart. For all we know she stashed the tech in an off-site location."

"How are we going to find her?"

"I think there's a good chance she drove to her destination," Max said.

"She might have just driven to the airport and left her car in the garage," Charlotte said.

"Maybe. But leaving a car in an airport garage for an extended period of time is very expensive. Most people who intend to be gone for a while would take a cab. And there's something else — Jocelyn aside, Mathis was the member of the club who got out of town the quickest. But you said she's the one with the fewest financial resources."

"I think so."

"Sounds like she had an exit strategy planned for a while. If she didn't have a lot of money to finance an expensive getaway, maybe she went to stay with a friend or a relative."

Charlotte looked at a photo on the wall. It showed a gray-haired woman dressed in baggy jeans and a faded shirt. She had a gardening trowel in one hand. Behind her was an old trailer.

A memory pinged.

"I don't know anything about Victoria's friends outside the investment club, but there was a relative — an aunt," she said. "Jocelyn mentioned that Victoria was very close to her. The aunt died a few months ago."

"Where did the aunt live?"

"She had a place over on the coast. Jocelyn said that Victoria used to spend weekends there, but then the aunt developed some serious health problems. She moved into an assisted living community here in Seattle for the last few months of her life."

Max looked up from the file drawer. "Did she leave her estate to Victoria? That could explain how Victoria got the money to disappear."

"Jocelyn told me that the aunt left everything to Victoria but that it didn't amount to much. The care she needed toward the end ate up most of her savings. I think there was some property over on the coast. Jocelyn said it wasn't worth much. She said Victoria intended to sell it eventually when the market improved."

Max plucked a file out of the drawer. "Looks like Victoria boxed up her aunt's financial files and brought them here to store. Lucky for us, the aunt was old-school. She kept paper files."

It didn't take long to find the tax records that related to the property on the coast.

"That picture on the wall was probably taken there," Max said. "I think there's a very real possibility that Victoria went there to hide."

"She's not answering her phone, so there's no way to find out if she's at her aunt's old place unless we drive to the coast. That's a hundred miles from here."

"No point heading out there this evening," Max said. "It would probably scare her to death if a strange car pulled into her driveway in the middle of the night."

"You're right. Not a good idea. Jocelyn says that Victoria has owned a gun since she graduated from high school."

Max whistled softly. "This is one well-armed investment club we're dealing with."

"A gun didn't do Louise any good," Charlotte pointed out.

"No, it didn't. We'll drive out to the coast first thing in the morning."

CHAPTER 45

Charlotte awoke to the steady patter of rain and the knowledge that she was alone in the bed. She opened her eyes and saw Max silhouetted against the window, steeped in shadows. He was in his briefs and the black crewneck T-shirt that he had worn to bed earlier. He seemed to be contemplating the night.

She knew that he was once again in that other dimension.

It was maddening, she thought; rather like reeling in a big fish that is fighting the line. That, of course, led to another question — why was she struggling so hard to land her catch?

"Hey," she said softly. "Everything okay?"

He turned his head to look at her. "Yes. Sorry. Didn't mean to wake you."

"It's all right. I wasn't sleeping well, anyway. Just sort of drifting in and out."

"Same here. I keep thinking that I'm missing something important in this case."

She sat up and wrapped her arms around her knees. "I'd say we're both missing something important. We're in this together, remember?"

"Yes, but this is my job. I'm supposed to be the one who can see the pattern."

"Is there any one particular element that is worrying you more than the others?"

"The road maps."

"The ones we found in that suitcase in Louise Flint's storage locker and in Jocelyn's safe-deposit box?"

"Right. Louise and Jocelyn both circled the locations where the three rapes took place and the two towns where the women supposedly died of overdoses. What was so important about those five cases?"

"Maybe Jocelyn and Louise were tracking one of their targets for the investment club."

"Maybe," Max said. "But Madison Benson and Emily Kelly both confirmed that the club selected their targets from the files at the women's shelter where Louise volunteered. There's nothing to indicate that the three rape victims or the two women who died were connected to the shelter. And then there's that note that Louise wrote to Jocelyn confirming that those five files were in hard copy only."

"Maybe Victoria will be able to give us some answers." Charlotte glanced at the clock. "It's four thirty. No point trying to go back to sleep. We might as well get ready for the drive to the coast."

Max turned away from the window. "Yeah."

She tossed the covers aside and slipped out of bed. "I'll shower first and fix us some breakfast while you shower and shave. Oh, by the way —"

"What?"

She paused in the doorway and looked back over her shoulder. "I had a thought about your family problem."

"I don't have a family problem. I've got a business issue involving some biological relatives."

"Call it what you want, I've got a suggestion."

He eyed her with unwilling curiosity. "What?"

"You said Decatur will not accept any contact from you; that he would be suspicious of anything you told him. But he's a successful businessman, right?"

"So?"

"He probably has a lawyer on retainer."

"Probably an entire firm. What about it?"

"Businessmen listen to their lawyers. Do

you know any lawyers?"

"I do some work for a couple here in town. One of them has become a friend. Why?"

"Why not take your file on Gatley to him? Ask him to contact Decatur's lawyers and show them the file. If they see the same red flags that you noticed, they'll talk to their client."

"Huh."

"That way you remain one step removed from the situation."

"Once he finds out that the file came from me, Decatur will probably decide I'm the scam artist and ignore the information."

"Yes, but at least you'd know that he saw the file. I think it's far more likely that if Decatur's lawyers take the file seriously, Decatur will, too. He'd be a fool to ignore the data right in front of his eyes. After all, the information can be verified, right?"

"Yes."

She waited for him to say something else, but he didn't. He just stood there, looking at her.

"Well, it was just a thought," she said. "I'll go take my shower."

She started to turn away.

"Charlotte."

She stopped and looked at him.

"Thanks," he said. "It's a logical approach to the problem. The obvious approach. Hell, I should have thought of it myself."

She realized then that he thought he had somehow failed to do his job; failed to live up to his own personal code.

She smiled. "The only reason you didn't come up with the plan is because you're too close to the situation. You're emotionally involved. Perfectly natural under the circumstances."

"No, it's not. I should have thought of the lawyer-to-lawyer angle."

"Cut yourself some slack, Max. You've got a right to some very complicated emotions when it comes to family. *Everyone* has complicated emotions when it comes to family."

He crossed the room to the doorway where she stood and stopped a few inches away. He raised his hands, gripped the doorjambs on either side of her and leaned in very close.

"My feelings about the Decaturs may be complicated, but my feelings about you are not complicated."

She held her breath. "Really?"

"Talking to you helps me clarify my thinking."

Okay, not exactly a declaration of love,

but coming from Max it seemed like a major statement of some kind. Before she could request a little clarification herself, he leaned in and kissed her.

It wasn't one of the slow, drugging kisses that left her clutching at his shoulders. It was a quick, deliberate, intensely intimate kiss. It was, she mused, the kind of kiss that a man gave a woman when he considered himself to be in a close relationship with that woman.

Or maybe she was reading far too much into a kiss.

He released his grip on the doorjambs and stepped back.

"Charlotte —" he said.

He stopped and just looked at her. She thought she saw a question in his eyes. Probably just a trick of the dawn light, she decided.

"We'd better get started on that road trip to the coast," he said. "I think we really need to talk to Victoria Mathis as soon as possible."

Charlotte raised her brows. "Something wrong?"

"Just got a feeling. It happens like that sometimes in a case."

Charlotte did not ask any more questions.

CHAPTER 46

"Thank goodness, Victoria is here," Charlotte said. She hadn't realized just how tense she had been during the long drive from Seattle until now. "There's a car parked in the driveway in front of the trailer. It must be hers. You were right, Max. This is where she came to hide out."

"It seemed reasonable," Max said. "When people get scared, they often retreat to familiar territory, someplace where they feel safe."

"I don't mind telling you I was getting a little nervous about what we would find when we got here," Charlotte said.

She had steeled herself against the possibility that they would not find Victoria at the end of the journey. Now, at least, they might get a few more answers.

Max stopped the car halfway up the drive and hit the horn a couple of times.

Charlotte glanced at him.

"What?" she asked.

"You said she had a gun and she knew how to use it. If she's running scared, the last thing we want to do is take her by surprise. She won't recognize this car."

They had made the trip in his gray sedan.

"Good point," she said.

He leaned on the horn a couple more times: quick, nonthreatening blasts designed to announce their arrival in a friendly manner.

Charlotte watched closely, but as far as she could tell there was no movement inside the trailer. No one peeked out from behind the curtains. The door did not open.

She unbuckled her seat belt and opened the door. "I'll get out and let her see me. She doesn't know you, but she has no reason to be afraid of me."

"Unless she thinks you're conspiring with Jocelyn to steal her share of the profits from the Keyworth buyout," Max said.

"Crap. I can't believe she would think that Jocelyn would want to kill her. I can't believe any of them would believe it. I'll try to talk to her — let her know that we think Louise's death may be linked to something in the past."

"All right, but keep the door between you and the trailer. Tell her who I am and why

I'm here."

Charlotte climbed out. The sharp winds of the storm moving in off the ocean lashed at her hair and sliced through her jacket.

"Victoria, it's me, Charlotte Sawyer," she called. "I know you're scared, but I'm scared, too. I can't find Jocelyn. I've got a private investigator with me. Max Cutler. He's trying to help. Please talk to us."

There was no reaction from the trailer. Charlotte held her whipping hair out of her eyes and leaned down to look at Max.

"I'm going to go knock on her door," she said. "She won't shoot me in cold blood."

Max did not take his eyes off the trailer.

"Get in the car."

It was an order.

"We can't leave," she said. "Not after having come all this way."

"We're not leaving. Get in."

Something about the grim set of his jaw told her that there was no point in arguing. She slipped back into the passenger seat and closed the door.

"You think something's wrong, don't you?" she asked.

"If she's in there and if she's okay, she should have at least looked out the window to see who was coming up the drive."

Charlotte did not respond. A bone-deep

dread settled on her. *Please,* she thought, *not another one gone. Not like Louise. Not dead.*

Max drove the rest of the way up the drive and stopped in front of the trailer.

"I'll take a look," he said.

He got out of the car and glanced back briefly when Charlotte opened her own door and started forward to join him. She knew he wanted to order her to get back into the vehicle. She just shook her head. He didn't like it, but he didn't fight it.

He went up the three old metal steps and rapped sharply on the door. There was no answer. He tried the handle.

"It's locked," he said. He paused, his attention focused on the aluminum panel beside the door. "Shit." His voice was very soft, very cold.

He vaulted down from the top step and pried open the panel. Charlotte caught a glimpse of mechanical apparatus, but before she could ask any questions Max was issuing orders again.

"Get back," he said.

Bewildered, she retreated a few steps. Max picked up a fist-sized rock and smashed it against the nearest window. Glass shattered.

Charlotte could have sworn that she heard the trailer take a deep, gasping breath. Max smashed another window and then he kicked the door again and again. There was a loud crack as the old lock snapped.

"Stay out here," Max ordered. "Call nine-one-one."

He took a deep breath and rushed inside the trailer. He reappeared seconds later with Victoria draped over his shoulder. He hauled her down the steps and put her on the ground.

Charlotte examined her quickly while she waited for the emergency operator to respond. There was no sign of injury. Victoria was alive, but she was deeply asleep. Unnaturally asleep.

Charlotte looked up, horrified. "Another overdose?"

"No," Max said. "Tell the operator we've got a woman unconscious from carbon monoxide poisoning. And tell her to send the cops as well as the medics. This was attempted murder."

CHAPTER 47

"Someone tried to murder Victoria by rigging the trailer's old heater box so that it didn't vent to the outside," Max said. "Carbon monoxide is odorless. The trailer didn't have a detector. Victoria went to bed and went to sleep. Over time the gas built up inside. Old trailers are notorious for that kind of accident."

Charlotte shuddered. "But this wasn't an accident, was it?"

"No. Someone who knew what he was doing sabotaged the heater. Went out of his way to make it look like an accident."

They were sitting in a small café at the edge of town. Victoria was in intensive care at the regional hospital. No one knew when she would wake up — if she woke up. And even if she survived, her memory of events would probably be foggy.

The local police had not been convinced that they were dealing with attempted murder. Charlotte had overheard one of them comment that old trailers were prone to carbon monoxide disasters. Someone else had remarked that the trailer had fallen into disrepair after the owner had moved to Seattle. Another officer had pointed out that it was possible some transients had moved in for a while and messed around with the heater in an attempt to make it function more effectively.

"If we hadn't arrived when we did, she would have died and the authorities probably would have blamed the death on a faulty heater," Charlotte said.

"Probably. She's still in grave danger. You heard the doctor. There's no way to know how long she'll be unconscious."

"At least she's got a chance," Charlotte said. "Thank goodness we decided to drive out here early today. If she lives, it will be because of you, Max."

But he wasn't listening. She could tell that his attention was fixed on something else now.

"She's been here a few days," he said. "But evidently the heater didn't go bad until last night."

Charlotte watched him closely. "What are you thinking?"

"I'm thinking that the killer showed up

yesterday."

"How could he sabotage the heater without alerting her?"

Max tapped one finger very slowly against the side of his cup. "Maybe by using the same method he used on Louise. Victoria was probably drugged first, but she wasn't given a lethal dose. Once she was out, the killer sabotaged the heater, hoping to make it look like an accident."

"No wonder the members of the investment club are scared," Charlotte said. "Someone really is trying to kill them."

Max looked at her. "Would Jocelyn have enough mechanical know-how to rig a trailer heater?"

"Don't say that. Don't even think it. Jocelyn is not the killer."

"I understand you're convinced that she's innocent. But I need to look at all the angles. Level with me. Could she have been responsible for screwing around with that heater?"

Charlotte forced herself to think about the question. "I don't know. How hard would it be?"

"Not hard at all if you knew what you were doing."

Charlotte sighed. "I wouldn't know how to do it, but Jocelyn is much more mechanically minded than I am. She's into the whole DIY thing. She keeps her motorcycle and her car in good repair and she has a boating license. She's not afraid to tackle all kinds of home improvement projects. She knows how to use a gun. Yes, I suppose it's possible she might know how to sabotage a trailer heater, but I know her. You have to believe me. She didn't murder her best friend and she wouldn't have tried to kill Victoria."

Max drank some coffee and lowered the cup. He looked out the café window, watching the storm that was now hammering the coastline. His eyes were very cold.

"Someone who knew that Jocelyn was good with the DIY stuff might have set things up so that anyone who suspected sabotage would leap to the conclusion that it was Jocelyn who tried to kill Victoria," he said. "Or the killer could have assumed that no one would notice the rigged heater. But either way, it feels like Victoria knew the killer."

"Max," she said, "if you really believe that Jocelyn has gone totally psycho, tell me now."

He met her eyes. "What I believe is that we need to go back to the start of this thing."

"Are you talking about Louise's murder?"

"No. I'm talking about your stepsister's rape. One thing we know for sure is that she was convinced her assailant was someone on the campus. The older detective we talked to at the Loring Police Department, Atkins, said that was his conclusion, too. He said they were starting to interview some of the men at the college when Briggs told him that the department was being pressured to drop the case and then the evidence box was lost."

"Which ensured that the case got dropped. So?"

"You said that Jocelyn has always been convinced that the man who attacked her was a student," Max said.

"Right."

"Why did she exclude the other men who would have been on campus at the time? Janitors? Groundskeepers? Security people? Academic staff?"

"A lot of little reasons. I can't recall all of them, but I remember she insisted that the attacker wore gloves — fancy leather driving gloves, not work gloves. When he was struggling to get the bag over her head, she caught a glimpse of his shoes. They were expensive, trendy running shoes. He didn't talk much, but when he did, she was sure he sounded like he was close to her age."

"Every new wave of young people in high school and college seems to develop its own accent and a certain pattern of speech."

"Exactly." Charlotte sipped her coffee. "And then there was the fact that he had planned the attack down to the smallest detail. He used a condom."

"He was trying to avoid leaving any evidence."

"Also, the path where he waited for her was a shortcut to the library that only the students who lived in her dorm used on a regular basis. He obviously knew that. Like I said, it was a bunch of little things, but when added together they convinced her that the rapist was a student at the college."

"Apparently Atkins was convinced, too." Max set the coffee mug down on the table. "We need to go through the names on that list that was in Jocelyn's safe-deposit box."

"There must be almost three hundred. What do you expect to find that Jocelyn couldn't?"

"Welcome to my world," Max said. "This is where an investigation becomes a slog."

"Ah, the one-foot-in-front-of-the-other thing?"

"Right. We're going to try to find out what

happened to each one of those men on that list."

"What are we looking for?"

"We want to know where they are now and what they're doing."

Charlotte exhaled slowly. "You're right. That could take a long time."

"Not necessarily. We'll be able to tap the resources of one of the finest, most efficient investigative organizations on the planet."

Charlotte stared at him. "You've got connections with the FBI?"

"I do, but we're not going to bother with that approach. The FBI is strictly second-string compared to the detailed files of the average college alumni records office. In my experience, no one does a finer job of keeping track of people."

Charlotte nodded. "Right. For networking purposes."

"That, too, but mostly it's all about the money. How do you think colleges build up those big-assed endowments that keep them going? Former students are a huge source of revenue. So, yes, alumni organizations keep very close tabs on former students."

"Got it. Still, it's going to take a long time to check out the whereabouts of a few hundred men."

"We'll have help."

"Who?"

"My dad."

"Mr. Salinas?"

"Anson Salinas was one hell of a cop in his day. And it just so happens he needs a job."

"Okay, I get the picture. But I still don't understand what we're looking for."

"A pattern," Max said. "There is always a pattern."

CHAPTER 48

"I see you managed to make my birthday reception," Marian Greenslade said.

Trey smiled. He kissed her cheek.

"I told you, I wouldn't miss it for the world," he said.

The reception was a formal affair. The venue was the Loring College faculty club. The college was always delighted to accommodate any member of the Greenslade family. It was, after all, the Greenslade endowment that paid for everything from faculty positions and classrooms to special collections for the library.

Marian Greenslade was the center of attention. *As usual,* Trey thought. Whenever she was in the room, everyone paid homage. She was the undisputed queen not only of the campus but of the town. Everyone knew she was the real power behind the throne of Loring-Greenslade. She took her role seriously.

She had been a beautiful woman in her younger days. Over the years she had transitioned gracefully from attractive to formidable. Today was her eightieth birthday celebration. Her mind was crystal clear, and it seemed to Trey that her eyes were as ice-cold as ever.

"Can I get you a glass of champagne?" he asked.

"Yes, please. By the way, Angela Carson is here."

"Of course she is. Angela wouldn't miss this reception, either."

Angela was the woman that Marian had handpicked for him to marry. Angela was even more ambitious than she was beautiful, which was saying a great deal. She had made it clear she was interested — not in him, but in the Greenslade money. He felt sure they could do business together.

He made his way through the crowd, stopping to greet various VIPs. Now that his father was gone, he was the new face of Loring-Greenslade. Like Marian, he had a role to play in the community, and he intended to play it to the hilt.

At the open bar he got a glass of champagne for Marian, but he ordered a whiskey for himself. He needed something to help him get through the long afternoon ahead.

He collected the drinks and turned around to find Angela smiling at him. He smiled back. She was a beautiful woman, but when she was dressed for a formal occasion, as she was today, she exuded an aura of pure glamour. Every man in the room was watching her out of the corner of his eye. A number of women were also taking covert second looks.

"I see you made it after all," she said. "I was a little worried that I might have to make excuses for you. Did your business in Seattle go well?"

"Everything is under control," he said. He surveyed her from head to toe and put a little heat into his smile. "You look fantastic. The most spectacular woman in the room. And also the most intelligent."

Angela laughed her light, appealing laugh. "Don't let your grandmother hear you say that. She's convinced that she's the smartest woman in the room."

He grinned. "Why don't you come with me and help me feed her ego? You know how she loves it."

"Of course."

They walked through the throng together. Heads turned. Trey allowed himself to savor the attention.

It wasn't just Angela who was drawing

every eye. Today he was making his first high-profile social appearance as the heir apparent to the position his father had held. He was no longer in the old bastard's very long shadow. He was poised to take over the helm of one of the most successful pharmaceutical research firms in the Pacific Northwest. *The king is dead, long live the king.*

"Don't look now, but your cousin is watching you as if he would like to see you fall off a cliff," Angela whispered.

Trey glanced across the room. Sure enough, Charles was looking daggers at him. Trey gave him a blinding smile. Charles turned away and resumed his conversation with a bearded member of the faculty.

"Nothing new there," Trey said.

"He wants to take your father's place, you know," Angela said casually.

"He hasn't got a chance."

Angela smiled, satisfied. "No, he doesn't, does he?"

Eventually he would sell Loring-Greenslade, Trey decided. He did not plan to follow in his father's footsteps and waste his life poring over sales graphs and charts in the executive suite. But for now the company gave him an excellent platform from which to control his destiny.

That was what he craved most of all, he thought; what he had always craved — total control and the power that accompanied it. Now, at long last, it was within his reach.

But first he had to find the evidence box and deal with the women who had complicated his life. Strategy was everything.

He glanced across the room. Charles still had his back to him.

Trey smiled to himself. *You don't stand a chance, cousin. Grandma always liked me best.*

CHAPTER 49

Max's phone rang, shattering the oddly companionable silence that had settled on Charlotte's living room. She looked up from her perch on the sofa where she had been making notes.

Max had been typing names into his computer. He stopped, picked up the phone and glanced at the screen.

"It's the Loring Police Department," he said.

He took the call.

"Cutler," he said.

He listened intently, frowning a little, and then he took his little notepad out of his pocket, picked up a pen and jotted down some notes.

"Right," he said. "I appreciate the update, Walsh. No, nothing concrete on this end. Yes, I'm still pursuing the investigation. I will. Yes. Thanks."

He ended the call and looked at Charlotte.

"Roxanne Briggs has disappeared," he said. "Walsh says he drove back up the mountain today to ask her a few more questions. She was gone. There were no signs of foul play. Evidently she packed up and left."

"She probably got nervous after her husband was killed. After all, she was married to him for decades. She must have known his secrets."

"I keep thinking about the issue of timing," Max said. "We're looking at a cascade of recent events that all seem to be connected to the attack on Jocelyn over a decade ago. It's as if a dam that had been holding back the past was suddenly breached."

"You think that some single event triggered the situation we're in now?"

"Yes. Whatever it was, it happened in the past few months. When we find it, we'll be able to see the complete pattern."

She looked down at her list. "You're right about the alumni records. There was no problem logging in under Jocelyn's ID. We're making progress but not very quickly."

"Time to call for backup," Max said.

She glanced up. "Who?"

"Anson is good at this kind of stuff."

CHAPTER 50

"You're sure you want me to handle this for you?" Reed Stephens closed the file that Max had placed on his desk. "You don't owe that family a damn thing."

Max had been distracting himself by leafing through the morning edition of the newspaper. He tossed the paper aside and got to his feet.

Reed's office was located in a downtown office tower. He specialized in business law. He was not one of the high-flying merger-and-acquisitions experts, but he had helped several local start-ups and small businesses get off the ground.

More to the point, Reed was well respected within the legal community. Max was counting on that reputation. Charlotte was right. Any halfway decent lawyer would be likely to pay attention to what Reed had to say.

"I can't think of any other way to get the

information in that file in front of Davis Decatur," he said.

Reed nodded once, stood and went to stand in front of the window. "You dug up a lot of solid information on Simon Gatley. There's more than enough in that file to take to the feds. Why not start with them?"

"You know how the feds work. If they actually opened a case, it would take them a couple of years to complete the investigation — assuming they ever did. Besides, they like big, headline-grabbing cases. Gatley has been smart enough to keep his operations under the radar. Sure, some investors have lost some money, and at some point in the future the whole Ponzi scheme will collapse. But taking him down at this point would not be a career-making move for a federal investigator."

Reed nodded. "You're right."

"Everything in that file can be verified by another investigator. I can't take it to Decatur myself. He'll assume I'm angling to find a way into the family, that I'm after a share of the Decatur money."

Reed turned around. "Davis Decatur will probably listen to his lawyer. He might even be convinced by what's in that file. But his daughter might not want to believe any of it. You know what they say about love being blind."

"In which case, there's nothing more I can do."

"All right. I'll find out who handles the Decatur family's personal legal interests and give him or her a call. But no guarantees that this will turn out the way you hope it will."

"Trust me, I'm well aware of that. Thanks, Reed."

Max headed for the door.

"By the way, I've got a job coming up," Reed said. "Corporate security. Are you available?"

"I'm a little busy at the moment."

"A word of advice, my friend. You're trying to build a business. You shouldn't be turning down the kind of work I'm offering. Corporate security is going to be your bread and butter."

"I'm a one-man company, Reed. You know that."

"Maybe it's time to think about expanding. And while we're on the subject, you also need to get yourself a full-time receptionist. If you don't have someone available to handle potential clients when they come through the door, you're going to crash and burn before you ever turn a serious profit."

"I know you're giving me good advice, Reed. It's just that right now I haven't got time to deal with the logistics of running a business."

"Make time. Soon."

"I'll do that."

CHAPTER 51

Madison Benson ordered another martini and checked her phone again. Maybe a text message had come in but she just hadn't heard it. Given the noise level in the crowded hotel bar, it was entirely possible.

There was no new message. She stared at the screen for a moment, trying to ignore the twisted mix of anger and jealousy that threatened to overwhelm her. All right. She was angry. She had a right to be angry. It looked like she was going to be stood up. But she must not allow herself to acknowledge the jealousy. Other women might succumb to that dangerous emotion, but she was not that weak. She was not jealous. She was furious. Big difference.

But they were supposed to be business partners, not just lovers.

How much longer was she going to give him? She had to draw a line and make it stick.

But she knew that it was unlikely that she would ever meet another man who was capable of arousing such passion in her. Everything about him excited her. He was strong — as strong as she was; willing to do what had to be done to achieve his objectives. He was charismatic and ruthless; her true mate. They came from very different backgrounds, but she was certain that, deep down, they understood each other. There was a bond between them.

She had grown up poor, the only child of a single mother who had been addicted to drugs and abusive men. One of the bastards had felt no compunction about raping his girlfriend's pretty, blond-haired daughter.

But she had overcome her past. She had learned very fast that her good looks and her intelligence gave her power. She had figured out how to use that power. She was a self-made woman who knew what she wanted and wasn't afraid to go after it.

She had run a number of scams in the course of her career, but the strategy of targeting abusive men had proven particularly satisfying. Each time she and the other members of the club took down one of their targets she had remembered the bastard who had raped her. He had been dead for several years now. She had taken great pleasure in confronting him in the parking lot of a bar one night. She had made quite certain he knew who she was before she shot him dead.

She sipped the martini and pondered her options. She would give her lover twenty minutes, she concluded. Just long enough for her to finish her drink. If he did not show up by that time, she would leave. She would have no choice. She was just as strong and just as ruthless as he was. She would not allow him to treat her as anything less than his equal. She was not her mother.

Thirty minutes later he walked into the bar. She was still sitting alone in the booth, having made up an endless series of excuses for not leaving at the twenty-minute mark.

She watched him make his way through the crowd. By the time he got to the booth, her pulse was skittering with anticipation.

"Sorry I'm late," Trey Greenslade said. "Got delayed at the old lady's birthday reception."

She kept her smile very cool. "I was just about to leave."

He sat down beside her.

"Good thing you didn't," he said. "It's been a hell of a day. I need a drink. I also need you. I need your help."

"What do you want from me?"

"I've got to get control of the situation before that damn investigator who's looking into Flint's death causes any more trouble. That means we've got to find a way to bring in Jocelyn Pruett. You said you might be able to do that."

"Maybe." She could negotiate, too. "What's in it for me?"

He smiled. "How about a seat on the Loring-Greenslade board?"

She thought about that. The Keyworth buyout was going to be big — far and away the biggest deal she had ever done — but the profits paled in comparison to the kind of money that sloshed around the pharmaceutical industry. And Loring-Greenslade was a prime takeover target.

"I'll take the seat on the board," she said. "I also want shares in the company — a controlling interest."

Trey's brows rose. "You play hardball." He smiled. "I like that about you."

"Then we have a deal?"

"We have a deal."

Too easy. Did he think she was a fool? He was convinced he was playing her. But the reality was that she was playing him.

A thrill of passion and excitement snapped through her. Trey might be the most exciting man she had ever met, but she did not trust him. She could never trust any man.

She was wearing a tiny, state-of-the-art digital recorder under her very short skirt. When she got home that night, she would copy the contents into the computer file she had created on Trey Greenslade.

With luck she would never need to use the file to protect herself, but a woman couldn't be too careful. When you slept with the devil, it seemed like a good idea to have some leverage.

CHAPTER 52

"Damn, but it's good to see you, Jocelyn," Madison said. "I was afraid you were dead — just like Louise. You do know that Emily has disappeared, don't you? I have no idea where she is or even if she's alive."

"I sent the code," Jocelyn said. "She's probably in hiding. That was the plan — your plan. What is going on?"

"The plan didn't do Victoria any good. She's in intensive care at a hospital over on the coast."

"Oh, shit. What happened? How did he find her?"

"I have no idea. They're calling it a carbon monoxide accident — something about old trailer heaters being prone to that kind of thing. But given what's been going on, I'm not buying it."

"I'm here because you used the code word that we agreed would be used only if my stepsister was in danger," Jocelyn said. "But

I made an anonymous call to the door station at Charlotte's apartment building. I said I wanted to deliver some flowers to Charlotte. The doorman didn't seem concerned. Said he would make sure she got them. Charlotte's okay. So what the hell is going on?"

Jocelyn had been very careful to arrive ahead of the agreed-upon meeting time. After driving past the roadside restaurant, she had left the car she had rented with a fake ID on a side road. She had made her way back through the woods and waited for Madison.

She had been the first one in line when the library had opened that morning. The coded message had been waiting in her email inbox. It had been sent during the night. She had responded immediately and then driven hard and fast to make the rendezvous point. It was now late morning. There weren't many cars in the small parking lot. When Madison had arrived it was clear that she was alone. No other vehicle had pulled into the parking lot behind her. When Jocelyn had walked out of the woods to join her, Madison's relief had been unmistakable.

Now they sat at one of the small tables, drinking bad coffee out of cheap paper cups. Jocelyn was vaguely aware of being hungry, but the smell of stale grease emanating from the kitchen was not appetizing. She reminded herself that she had a wedge of cheddar cheese and some bread and dill pickles in the rental car.

"Here's the problem," Madison said. "I don't know what is going on with Charlotte, but I think she may be in real trouble. She was nearly killed a few days ago."

Jocelyn's stomach knotted. "What are you talking about?"

"Did you know that Charlotte has hooked up with a private investigator?"

"Why? She thinks I'm in the Caribbean."

"She knows you're not at that convent."

"Damn. This is all getting so complicated. I wanted to keep her out of this mess. What made her think I wasn't at the retreat?"

"You can probably blame Cutler. He's the PI. He's the one responsible for dragging Charlotte into this thing. Louise's cousin hired him to look into Louise's death. I guess Cutler somehow connected it to your disappearance."

"How? It makes no sense."

"All I can tell you is that he has dragged Charlotte into his investigation," Madison said. "It gets worse. For some reason the two of them drove to Loring."

"What? Why?"

"Evidently they went there to talk to Egan Briggs. That's how Charlotte almost got killed."

Jocelyn's head was starting to spin. It was her worst nightmare, she thought, and somehow she had given Charlotte a starring role.

She tried to concentrate, to focus.

"Why would they go to see Briggs?" she asked.

"Apparently they wanted to interview him about Louise."

"What could he possibly know about her? Briggs and Louise never even met."

"I don't know, but evidently when Cutler and Charlotte attempted to drive down out of the mountain, Briggs deliberately used his vehicle to push theirs into a river."

"Oh, my God," Jocelyn whispered again.

It was too much. Overwhelming. She had put all of them, including Charlotte, in danger.

The snowballing disaster was her fault. She was the one who had been unable to let the past stay buried.

"I'm on my way to Sea-Tac," Madison said. "I'm going to Mexico. I would have caught an earlier flight, but I felt I had to warn you first."

"Thank you. You're a good friend." Jocelyn rubbed her temples, but the spinning sensation was getting worse. "At least . . . at least Charlotte has that investigator — Cutler — with her. She's not alone."

"No, but you should know that the bastard who is hunting us is doing his or her damnedest to make it look like you're the killer. I think Cutler is convinced that is the case."

"What?" Jocelyn raised her head so quickly she nearly fainted. "Why? What possible motive could I have for murdering Louise and the rest of you?"

"The Keyworth deal," Madison said.

Jocelyn felt a great weight crushing her. "I don't . . . I don't understand."

"Back at the start it was going to be a five-way split. Now it's a four-way split. If Victoria doesn't survive, it's a three-way split."

The shock stole Jocelyn's breath for a few seconds.

"You can't possibly believe I'm the one who murdered Louise and tried to kill Victoria," she finally whispered.

"Of course not. If I thought that was the case, I wouldn't have asked you to meet me here. But I've been going crazy thinking about what happened to Louise and what almost happened to Victoria. I know this is going to sound like some kind of wild conspiracy theory, but I've come to the conclusion that we have a traitor in our midst. She's been there all along, waiting for her opportunity. I think she's decided to score big with the Keyworth deal — by getting rid of the rest of us."

Jocelyn closed her eyes. "Emily."

"Think about it. If Louise and Victoria and I are dead, you and Emily will be the last ones standing. And if Emily manages to make you look guilty of murdering the rest of us, she can kill you, too, and claim it was self-defense."

"No." Jocelyn opened her eyes. "Emily isn't the one behind this. It's him, the bastard who raped me. I've got to find him, Madison. I have to pull him out into the open and finish this once and for all."

"I wish you all the luck in the world, but I can't help you. Like I said, I'm getting as far away from this mess as possible. From where I'm sitting it looks like neither of us will be safe until after the buyout happens."

Jocelyn shook her head, trying to clear it. But her thoughts were chasing each other in tighter and tighter circles.

"Cutler," she said, trying to focus on the name.

Madison frowned. "What about him?"

"You said he was hired to investigate Louise's death and now he's looking for me."

"Because he thinks you killed Louise."

Jocelyn drank some coffee, hoping the caffeine would steady her nerves. "Maybe my best option is to come out into the open. I'll contact Charlotte. Let her know I'm safe. Then I'll talk to the PI. Tell him everything I know. We can pool our resources. Maybe if we work together we can find the bastard before he kills again."

Madison's expression tensed. "Do whatever you think is best, but I'm warning you that at the rate this thing is going down, there's a good possibility that you're the one who will be arrested for murder. I know that Charlotte will believe you're innocent, but Cutler won't. He struck me as pretty damn cold, to be honest."

"I'll have to take my chances," Jocelyn said. Another wave of dizziness swept through her. She really needed to eat. "This is my fault. I brought the devil out of hiding."

"What do you mean?"

"Long story. I can't go into it now. I've got to contact Charlotte, try to find a way to protect her."

"Do what you have to do." Madison

glanced at her watch and slipped out of the booth. "I have to move. I brought some extra cash with me. Figured you might be running low and I know you don't want to use your credit cards."

"I don't know how to thank you, Madison," Jocelyn said.

She used both hands to set her cup down on the table and pushed herself up out of the booth with an effort of raw will. She was exhausted, she realized. She'd been sleeping poorly for days now and it was catching up with her. Getting the coded warning from Madison had been the last straw.

She followed Madison out of the restaurant, stumbling a little over the front step.

Madison took her elbow to steady her. "You okay?"

"Yes." Jocelyn took a deep breath. "I'm just tired."

"No wonder, given what you've been through. Where's your car?"

"Parked it a little ways from here. Wanted to make sure you weren't followed."

"No one followed me. Trust me, I kept an eye on my rearview mirror all the way from Seattle."

Jocelyn realized she was feeling oddly numb. "I need to sit down, Madison."

"Here you go." Madison opened the back door of her sedan and eased Jocelyn into the seat. "I'll drive you to where you parked your car."

Jocelyn tried — and failed — to focus. A shock of understanding cleared her brain for a few seconds.

"Bitch," she whispered. "You drugged me. The coffee."

"Stop fighting it and go to sleep, Jocelyn."

"Am I going to wake up?" Jocelyn asked. She was acutely aware of the fact that she was slurring her words.

"Of course you're going to wake up. But first you need to sleep. Why don't you lie down?"

Madison accompanied the suggestion with a slight shove. Jocelyn collapsed onto her side. For a few seconds she stared, bemused, at the back of the front seat, trying to understand how she could have been so stupid.

I always thought that Charlotte was the naïve one, the one who was too trusting.

So much had gone wrong. She could only hope that the unknown Max Cutler would be able to take care of Charlotte.

Sorry, little sister. I screwed up.

CHAPTER 53

Max leaned back in his chair and examined his notes. He and Charlotte and Anson had divided up the remaining names on the list. Then they had cranked up their laptops and gone to work, tracking down each and every man.

They had gathered in his office to do the painstaking work. It made for a crowd because it was a small space and there were only three chairs — his desk chair and the two intended for clients. The door was open to the small reception room, which was empty due to the fact that there was no receptionist.

Charlotte had made no comment when he had opened the door and ushered her into the office a couple of hours earlier, but he was very conscious that it, like his only remaining vehicle, was not very impressive.

The potted plant in the corner had been left behind by the previous tenant. It did not look like it was going to survive much longer. The furniture was rented and looked it. The walls were bare and the small bookcase was empty.

Reed Stephens was right, he thought, he needed to hire a receptionist. Okay, he needed a more upscale office to go with the receptionist. And he needed money to pay for both. He had to bring in more corporate work.

But first he had to find the needle in the haystack — one man on a list of three hundred who looked like a viable suspect for three rapes and two murders.

The work was time-consuming, but it wasn't tricky — just old-fashioned investigative work, the kind that old-school journalists and cops did. The college yearbooks were available online and they made for excellent starting points. There was a wealth of data on each individual. Alumni bulletins and the published lists of those who had donated to the Loring College endowment fund had provided a trove of additional data.

They had filled in the gaps with social media and the powerful online search engines. In virtually every case they had current addresses and Google street views of the homes of the individuals. After all, it wasn't like any of the three hundred men was trying to hide.

As he had told Charlotte, if you looked hard enough, you could find anyone.

"Looks like these men all have a few things in common," he said. "They were all attending Loring College the year that Jocelyn was there. And they are all still living in western Washington."

Charlotte looked up from her notes. "She probably considered the locations of their current residences important because the three rapes and the two murders all took place on this side of the Cascades."

"Several of the men on that list have an address here in Seattle or nearby," Anson said. "A lot are over on the Eastside — Bellevue, Redmond, Issaquah, Kirkland. A few never left Loring."

"Most are married with families," Charlotte added. She tapped her pen against her notebook. "About twenty percent are divorced and many are remarried. Careerwise the men on the list are all over the place — engineers, tech guys, sales reps, counselors, architects — you name it. One's a fitness trainer with his own studio. Some went on to law school and three are doctors."

Max got to his feet and went to stand at the small window. The view was the brick wall of the building on the other side of the alley. He really needed a more impressive office, he thought.

"All the reports of the three rapes and the two murders that Louise Flint and Jocelyn collected and marked on their maps had a few things in common," he said. "Drugs were involved in every instance. And each of the victims fit a profile that matches Jocelyn's profile as it was a little over a decade ago. Same age. Same blond hair. Very attractive young women."

"Not quite the same profile," Anson said. His eyes tightened at the corners. "None of them were in college."

Max turned around. "You're right. They weren't in school; but they were all employed, which means that, most days of the week, they had a regular routine."

Charlotte looked at him. "A predictable routine."

"What kinds of jobs?" Anson asked.

Max went back to the desk to check his notes. "Of the three rape victims, one worked the front desk at a hotel. One was a cocktail waitress. One worked at a hospital. They all worked evening shifts."

"So they were all vulnerable at night," Anson said. "What about the two women who supposedly OD'd?"

"I can answer that," Charlotte said. "One

was a receptionist at an urgent care medical clinic. The other was a librarian."

"Again, both worked evenings," Max added. "They went home around nine o'clock."

"So, all of the victims had a few things in common, even if the men on Jocelyn's list of suspects don't have much in common," Charlotte said.

"The more you know about the victim, the more you know about the perp," Anson said.

"Okay," Charlotte said, "based on the information we've got about the victims, what do we know about the killer?"

"In each case the assailant was familiar with the terrain," Max said. "He chose his sites with care. And yet those locations are, literally, all over the map. How does one bad guy become so intimately familiar with so many different places?"

"He spends a fair amount of time in each place," Anson suggested.

"Doing recon and selecting his targets," Max added. "He's not in a rush. He has plenty of time to get familiar with the terrain and yet no one notices him."

"Like a wolf with a territory," Charlotte said.

Max felt the familiar ping of knowing.

"Or a sales rep," he said softly.

Anson whistled tunelessly. "Sales rep. Damn. Max is right. A sales rep has a legitimate excuse for getting to know a territory very well. He stays in the same hotels. Eats in the same restaurants. Drives the same routes. What's more, most sales territories, especially those here on the West Coast, are big. Plenty of room to hunt."

"There are several sales reps on Jocelyn's list," Charlotte said. "All kinds."

"I think we can weed out most of them if we consider the one other factor that is common to all the murders and each of the three rapes," Max said. "Drugs."

"Drugs are widely available everywhere these days," Anson grumbled.

"True, but these drugs seem to be fairly exotic — not stuff that's common on the street. Anyone on our list with access to that kind of designer drug?"

Charlotte grabbed her notes. The name leaped out at her as if written in hellfire.

"Trey Greenslade," she said. "He graduated from Loring College a year after Jocelyn left. And based on the lists of major donors, the Greenslade family practically owns Loring College. He went to work in the family business — Loring-Greenslade Biotech. He's been with the company ever since. In fact, he recently inherited it. He worked as a sales rep for several years, but a year ago he was made vice president."

"He's had a lifetime to become familiar with a wide variety of drugs, and his connection with Loring-Greenslade would provide him with a perfect cover," Max said. "As a pharmaceutical rep, he would have a reason to travel all over the state calling on doctors. And as a vice president, he still has an excuse to go out into the field to entertain accounts."

"Feels like a real possibility," Anson mused.

"Yes, it does," Max said.

Charlotte looked up. "You do realize we have absolutely no proof that he's the killer. I would point out that the Greenslade family controls a pharmaceutical firm that employs a huge percentage of the town of Loring. It also controls just about everything else that goes on in that town, or at least it did a decade ago. I doubt if much has changed."

"That means the family would definitely have had the clout and resources to shut down an investigation," Max said.

"We need to send a message to Jocelyn and hope that she is checking her e-mail," Charlotte said. "We've got to warn her."

"I agree," Max said. "We also need to warn the other two women in the club — Emily Kelly and Madison Benson."

"We know Madison is still in town, but Emily and Jocelyn Pruett are in hiding," Anson pointed out. "Are you sure they'll be checking for messages?"

"They're running and they're scared," Max said. "Benson is on edge, too. Trust me, the Internet is their lifeline. One way or another, all three of them will be clinging to it."

CHAPTER 54

"Jocelyn Pruett. After all these years, we meet again. Wake up, bitch."

She knew that voice. It had haunted her for over a decade. It was the charming voice of a man who could sell flamethrowers in hell. It sent a jolt of fear and adrenaline through her, arousing nightmares and rage.

She used the energy of fury and fear to push through the oppressive weight of an unnatural drowsiness. She fought to open her eyes and succeeded, only to shut them immediately against the glare of a powerful flashlight.

He slapped her face, hard.

"I said, wake up."

She opened her eyes again, cautiously this time, looking down and off to the side in a bid to avoid the dazzling light. She realized she was lying on a cold, hard surface. Concrete, she decided. Instinctively she tried to get to her feet — and discovered that her wrists were secured in front of her.

She managed to sit up against an ice-cold concrete wall.

"You certainly complicated things," the man said. "I'll give you credit for that. But you never stood a chance. I've been in control from the beginning. It was just a matter of time. You see, I've kept an eye on you all these years. You were my first, after all. And you were very nearly my last. I admit I was worried for a while after you went to the cops and I found out you'd made them take you to the hospital to prepare a rape kit. I'd always heard that most girls — *smart* girls — kept quiet afterward. But you weren't smart, were you? Luckily the evidence disappeared."

"Wasn't that a curious turn of events?"

He slapped her again, harder this time. "Unfortunately for you, that evidence box has reappeared, but the evidence seems to have disappeared. And you're going to help me find it."

"What the hell are you talking about?"

"You really don't know what's going on, do you? Stupid woman."

She tried to look past the flashlight, but she could not make out his face.

"Who — ?" she managed.

"You never knew, did you? All these years

you've wondered. I'll bet you've thought about me every day since then. It's never been as good with any other man, has it?"

"You are one sick bastard."

He slapped her again. The side of her head came up hard against the wall. She tasted blood in her mouth.

"Want to know a little secret?" He was almost crooning now. "Until recently it's never been as good for me with anyone else, either. They say you never forget your first. But I finally found a way to recapture the magic."

"By murdering the last two women you raped."

"The game had become boring. It was just so damn easy. I decided to try to inject a little more excitement into it. But it was the deaths of those two whores that caught your attention, wasn't it?"

"Yes," she said. "I realized you were escalating, you see. For years you were able to maintain control, weren't you? But a few months ago you really lost it. You went over the edge. Now you're a flat-out crazy killer. That means you're making mistakes. I realized there was a connection between the murders and the serial rapist who attacked those other women. It's just a matter of time before the cops figure it out, too. Because you can't stop, can you?"

He struck her again, with a closed fist this time. She had braced herself for the blow, but the pain exploded through her, leaving her light-headed and sick to her stomach.

"I'm in control," he hissed. "Don't doubt it for a minute. I am always in control."

"Good for you. I'm not. I think I'm going to throw up."

He jumped to his feet and retreated hurriedly.

"Oh, wow. You're afraid of a little vomit," she said. "Good to know."

She managed to suppress the nausea. She made a note of his alarm and promised herself that, in the end, if vomiting was her only weapon, she would use it.

"Where is the evidence?" he raged.

"Ah. So that's what this is about. It really has come back to haunt you. Where's it been all this time?"

"Briggs hid it. He used it to blackmail my father."

"So it was your father who paid off Briggs to make sure the evidence disappeared."

"I didn't know, myself, not until recently. My old man never told me about the arrangement he had with Briggs. Probably afraid that I'd do something drastic like kill Briggs to make sure he kept quiet. Dear old

Dad didn't want me getting arrested for murder, you see. Bad for the family name. Bad for Loring-Greenslade. And really, really bad for Gordon Greenslade's personal reputation."

"Well, damn. You're Trey Greenslade."

"You never figured it out, did you?"

"Don't worry, you're on my list. After I'm gone that list will go to the cops, by the way."

Okay, she was mostly bluffing now — yes, his name was on her list, along with three hundred other men — but, no, that list would probably never end up in the hands of the cops. Even if it did, they wouldn't do anything with it. But she had nothing left to lose.

"What list?" Trey said.

She managed a cold smile and did not respond.

"You're lying, bitch."

"You bet," she said.

"You're lying. Admit it."

"Right. I'm lying."

He hit her again. Her ears rang.

"You shouldn't have come looking for me," he said hoarsely. "You should have just continued to savor the memory of the real-life fantasy we had all those years ago."

"Hard to forget a guy who can't get off

unless he's got a knife to a woman's throat. How did you know I was searching for you?"

"I didn't. Not at first. I didn't realize that you were building a fucking file on me until I paid some hacker on the other side of the world to get into your computer and your phone and give me the keys. I've been watching your every move online for a couple of months now. And through you, I discovered that little investment club you and your friends set up."

"When I went dark, you realized that I knew I'd been hacked. But why did you murder Louise?"

"Because she went to Loring, and we both know that there is only one reason she would have done that."

Jocelyn stopped breathing. "What reason?"

"She went there to buy the evidence box from Briggs."

"You really are crazy."

"You say that one more time, I'll slit your throat and be done with it. I'm telling you, Flint bought the damned evidence. But she hid it. I searched her condo, her car, her storage locker — everywhere I could think of — but I couldn't find it. Next thing I know I get a call from Briggs offering to sell the box to me. I thought maybe I'd been wrong about Flint. Maybe Briggs had scammed her. So I met Briggs. He had that old evidence box, all right. But it was filled with *garbage.* I'm the one he cheated."

"He tricked you."

"Which means I was right the first time — Louise Flint did get that box the day she went to Loring. Briggs sold her the contents and then, because he was a stupid bastard and a bad con man, he tried to sell the box of trash to me. But he paid for that."

"Maybe he cheated Louise, too. Did you ever think of that? The bottom line seems to be that you don't have the evidence box."

"No," Trey said through his teeth, "the bottom line is that you're going to help me find the contents of that damn evidence box. Because someone you know has it. It's the only explanation. Flint gave it to someone to hide. Maybe one of the other members of the investment club. Maybe your stepsister. Doesn't matter. You and I are going to find it."

"Leave Charlotte out of this. She has nothing to do with any of it."

"That might have been true back at the beginning, but she's in it up to her ears now," he said.

"No, I'm telling you the truth. Charlotte doesn't know anything about the things in that box."

"Let's hope she does — for your sake and hers as well. See, here's the deal — if I get what was in that box and destroy it, I can let you go. You're no threat to me without it, just as you've never been a threat. My lawyers can make your claims go away. But if I can't find the evidence, I'll have no choice but to get rid of you and your interfering stepsister. It will be the only way I can make certain you never use the evidence against me."

He was lying. She knew it in her bones. He intended to kill her. But for now it seemed best to let him think that she at least wanted to believe him.

"I might be able to help you figure out what Louise Flint did with the contents of the box," she said.

It wasn't difficult to keep her voice tremulous. She had never been so afraid in her life, with the exception of the night that he had attacked her. But this was even worse because now she had put Charlotte in danger.

"As a matter of fact, that's exactly what you're going to do," he said.

She heard him rustling around in his clothing. A second later there was a blinding flash of light and the unmistakable click of a cell phone camera.

"Why?" she gasped.

But she knew.

"Proof of life, I think it's called," he said. "I need to convince Charlotte Sawyer that I really do have you."

"No. Wait. Don't hurt Charlotte."

"I'm afraid it's her own fault. She shouldn't have brought a private investigator into this."

Boards creaked as Trey went up the wooden steps. At the top he opened the door. A man appeared silhouetted against the grayish daylight.

"Did she tell you where the box is?" he asked. "Well, did she?"

Whoever he was, he sounded unstable. Jittery. As if he was overly excited, maybe desperate.

"Take it easy," Trey said. "We've got work to do."

"I need a hit."

"Then get it."

Trey didn't bother to conceal the disgust in his voice. He paused long enough to flip a switch at the top of the steps. A weak bulb in an overhead fixture came on. It cast a dim, shadowy light around the basement.

He closed the door. Jocelyn heard the muffled sound of a key in the lock.

She tried to breathe through the panic.

She needed to think. To plan.

Her head ached from the blows. She forced herself to ignore the pain. She staggered to her feet and took a closer look at her surroundings.

Like most basements, the one in which she was trapped had clearly served as a storage room for years. She walked slowly around the shadowy space, taking inventory. There was an ancient fold-up camp cot in one corner and a chair with a broken leg. A rolled-up sleeping bag that smelled of must and mold occupied another corner. One large box was filled with yellowed newspapers.

She knew she probably wouldn't find anything she could use as a serious weapon against Trey, who was armed with a gun. But she made herself go through the process of searching because it distracted her from the horror of knowing that there was now nothing she could do to protect Charlotte.

CHAPTER 55

Charlotte's phone pinged, startling her. She grabbed the device and looked at the screen.

"It's a text from Madison Benson," she said. "You were right. She's certainly paying attention to her messages."

"What does it say?" Max asked.

Charlotte read the text aloud. " 'Urgent that I meet with you and Cutler.' "

Max folded his hands on the desk. "Ask her where and when."

Charlotte entered the message and hit send.

The response came back almost immediately. Charlotte read it silently and then looked up.

"She wants to meet us after dark at her home."

Max considered that for a moment. "She feels safe there because of her security system."

"And her gun," Charlotte reminded him.

"And her gun," he agreed.

"Jocelyn had both of those things and she still chose to run," Charlotte said.

"Yes, she did," Max said. "It's interesting that Madison doesn't feel the need to hide."

"I think it would be very hard to scare Madison Benson," Charlotte said. "You've met her. She's tough."

Anson spoke up. "And judging by what you told me, she wants to keep her finger on the pulse of that buyout deal."

"Yes," Max agreed. "And there's one other thing we know about Madison Benson — she wants us to think that Jocelyn might be trying to kill off the members of the investment club."

Charlotte went very still. "Yes, she does."

Max took his holstered gun out of the desk drawer. "Maybe she's got a reason to be pointing us in that direction."

Charlotte eyed the gun. "Where are you going?"

"To talk to Madison Benson."

"But she set the meeting time for tonight."

Anson looked amused. "You never let the subject dictate the time and place of the meeting — not if you can help it."

"Right." Charlotte jumped to her feet. "I'm coming with you."

CHAPTER 56

Charlotte and Max Cutler were convinced that Trey was the man who had murdered Louise.

It was a breathtaking turn of events.

Madison paced the floor of her vast living room while she tried to decide what to do with the information. They had no doubt sent the same warning to Emily, but that wouldn't be a problem. Emily was a nervous little rabbit of a woman. The news that someone really was hunting them would put her into a state of abject fear. She would stay hunkered down. There would be time to deal with her later.

The real question was whether or not Cutler had gone to the cops with his theory. It seemed highly unlikely. He'd want proof or at least something more than mere suspicion.

She needed more information, too. That was why she had set up the meeting with

Charlotte and Cutler.

She stopped at the wall of windows and looked out across Elliott Bay. She was on fire with excitement. Adrenaline flooded her veins. A woman could get addicted to this kind of rush, she thought. There was nothing else like it.

Unfortunately she had nearly three hours to kill before Charlotte and Cutler arrived. Time seemed to stretch out to infinity. She reminded herself that she had preparations to make. Victoria and Jocelyn had never hesitated when it came to drinking the coffee. Charlotte and Max Cutler would drink it, too.

The problem, of course, was what to do with the bodies. But she had that handled.

The knock on the back door sent a shock through her, rattling her nerves. She hurried down the hall, her pulse spiking again.

Until she had met Trey she had gotten her thrills from scoring in the financial world. She'd always had a talent for manipulating others. There was a huge rush in knowing that you were the smartest person in the room.

But now she was playing with fire and she did not want to stop.

When she reached the back door, she peered through the peephole. A whisper of alarm crackled through her when she saw who was on the doorstep.

She deactivated the alarm system and opened the door.

"What are you doing here?" she said. "It's too early. We're going to do this after dark. We can't risk someone seeing you take the bodies away."

She didn't see the gun until it was too late.

The killer fired twice, but the second shot was unnecessary.

Madison's last conscious thought was that she wasn't the smartest one in the room after all.

CHAPTER 57

Charlotte, struggling to suppress a wave of dizziness, looked down at the body on the floor. Madison Benson lay in a pool of blood that was already starting to dry. She looked somehow smaller in death.

"He got to her," Charlotte whispered. "Trey Greenslade found her and murdered Madison."

Max crouched beside the body. "Call nine-one-one."

He got to his feet and went swiftly down the hall.

"Where are you going?" she asked.

"I want to take a quick look around before the cops get here."

He disappeared into the big house. Charlotte turned away from the sight of the body and fumbled with her phone. The emergency operator answered on the first ring. Charlotte made her report.

"Yes, I'll stay on the line," she said.

A short time later she heard sirens in the distance. Max didn't reappear until the first responders were pulling into the long driveway. She started to ask him if he had found anything, but she closed her mouth again when she realized the emergency operator was listening.

"The police are here," she said into the phone. "I'm going to hang up now."

She ended the connection before the operator could argue. She looked at Max.

"Well?" she said.

"No signs of a computer or her phone. But here's the real news — Anson just texted me. He says Greenslade has an ironclad alibi. He's been in Loring all afternoon taking meetings. He's still there, according to his administrative assistant."

"That can't be. We were so sure."

"We'll tell the cops the truth — that I'm looking into the death of Louise Flint. Madison Benson texted us to say she had information for us, but when we arrived, she was dead."

"What do we do now?"

"We go old-school again. We follow the money."

CHAPTER 58

"They really think Madison was the victim of a home invasion robbery?" Charlotte collapsed on the sofa and contemplated the abstract print on the saffron gold wall of her apartment. "We tell them the whole story and they go with that dumbass theory?"

"As a rule, cops like the simplest answers best because they are usually the right answers," Max said. "There's been a rash of robberies lately in which the robber uses a repairman's uniform. He knocks on the back door of the house."

Charlotte sighed. "The homeowner opens the door because most people intuitively trust a guy who's wearing a legitimate-looking uniform."

"Right. None of the other victims were murdered, but the cops said they were afraid that it was just a matter of time before the robber escalated. The bottom line is we can't prove otherwise. Benson's neighbors were gone for the day. No one saw anything suspicious. No one heard the shots. No one saw anyone running away from the house. The house has decent security. But here's the interesting thing — Benson's computer and phone were missing."

"Greenslade got to her," Charlotte said. "It's the only explanation."

"I told you, he was at the headquarters of Loring-Greenslade at the time of the murder."

"Then what in the world is going on here? Why hasn't Jocelyn or Emily Kelly checked in? And why did Madison Benson set up that meeting with us?"

Max stopped his pacing.

"We've been focusing on the men on that list that we found in Jocelyn's safe-deposit box," he said. "Anson's right: the more you know about the victim, the more you know about the killer. We need to take a closer look at Madison Benson."

"How?"

"In my experience administrative assistants usually know more about their bosses' private lives than the bosses' spouses and lovers do."

CHAPTER 59

"Look, I'm still in shock, okay?" Drew Irby ran his well-groomed fingers through his highlighted hair. "My boss has been murdered and I'm out of a job. I should be working on my résumé, not talking to you two."

The three of them were sitting in a coffee shop a block from the tower where Madison Benson's office was located. Charlotte had ordered a decaf latte. The last thing her nerves needed was a heavy dose of caffeine. She was certain that time was running out for Jocelyn.

She had slept very little during the night, but she was sure that Max had gotten even less sleep. Each time she'd surfaced from a restless anxiety dream she had found herself alone in the bed. He had spent much of the night in front of his laptop, trying to find as much information as possible about Madison Benson's financial affairs.

But his reaction to the stress of the situation was much different from hers. He was energized and focused. He was not exactly enjoying himself, she decided — not in the usual sense of the word — but he was definitely exhilarated by the hunt. This was what he was born to do, she thought; what he needed to do.

It had been his idea to corner Madison's administrative assistant first thing that morning. They had been waiting for him in the lobby of the office tower when he had arrived to clean out his desk. Irby had been wary at first, but when Max had removed a few bills from his wallet, Drew had agreed to talk to them over coffee.

"Take it easy," Max said. "We just want to ask you a few questions about Madison Benson."

Charlotte tried to come up with a reassuring smile. "It's very important, Drew. My stepsister has gone missing and I think Madison might have had some information. She sent a text shortly before she was killed saying she wanted to talk to Max and me. But by the time we got there, she was dead."

Drew frowned. "Are you saying there's a connection? I heard that it looked like Ms. Benson was the victim of a home invasion robbery."

"She opened the door to her killer," Max said. "But that's all we can be sure of at the moment. Given the fact that two members of the investment club are now dead, one is in intensive care and two are missing, we think the home invasion story is wrong. We think this may have something to do with the investment club. We want to ask you a few questions about it."

Drew grimaced. "I don't see how I can help you. The thing is, Ms. Benson never talked much about the club. Once in a while she mentioned that she was going to have drinks with the other members, but that was about it."

Charlotte leaned forward. "Madison founded the club. She handpicked the other members from among the women who took an interest in the shelter she helped support. Do you know how she went about choosing certain members?"

Drew shrugged. "I heard her say that each member of the club brought a specific skill set to the table. That's all I can tell you."

"Yet in spite of those skill sets, the club doesn't seem to have been highly profitable," Max said. "Everyone made a little money from time to time, but there were no major hits — not until the Keyworth buyout popped up."

Drew put his latte down with both hands and fixed Max with a grim expression. "I'm not so sure about that."

"About the buyout?" Max asked.

"No, about there being no other profitable investments."

Charlotte took a quick breath. "What do you mean?"

Drew hesitated and then exhaled a long, deep sigh. "I guess I don't owe the boss any more confidentiality. Look, I don't know a lot about the investment club, but I can tell you that Ms. Benson always insisted on handling the club's spreadsheets personally. A couple of times I offered to help with the updating and she always refused. She said she liked to keep the club's records completely separate from those of her regular clients."

"So?" Max prompted.

Drew's jaw firmed. "She was sort of secretive about the investment club records, so I admit I got a little curious. You work with someone long enough, you get to know their ways. Sometimes when she was out of the office I took a closer look at her files. I can tell you that she often transferred some significant sums of money out of the club's brokerage account into a numbered account. At first I assumed that she was moving the club's profits offshore to avoid taxes. She wouldn't be the first investor to help her clients shield money in an offshore account. But sometimes I wondered . . ."

"Wondered what?" Charlotte asked.

Drew looked at her. "Sometimes I wondered if the other club members knew about that numbered account. I can tell you that there is a lot of money sitting in it."

Charlotte looked at Max. She shook her head.

"Before you ask," she said, "I'm quite sure Jocelyn didn't know anything about excess club profits being funneled into an offshore account."

"Sounds like Madison Benson was routinely skimming off profits from the investment club," Max said.

Drew cleared his throat. "For what it's worth, I don't think those were the only profits she was transferring offshore. Lately I've begun to wonder if she was scamming her regular clients, as well. In fact, I was getting so nervous I was thinking about handing in my resignation even though it was the best-paying job I'd ever had."

"Now that I know where to look, it shouldn't be hard for the police to figure out if she was scamming her accounts," Max said. "But that's not important to me, not yet, at any rate. What I really want to know is, was Benson seeing anyone?"

Drew looked surprised. Then he shrugged. "Yes. But she was keeping it off the radar. I figured the guy was probably married."

"Was it serious?" Max asked.

Drew snorted softly. "I'll say. She went to Maui for a few days about six weeks ago."

"With the man she was seeing?" Charlotte asked.

"She traveled alone," Drew said. "But I'm pretty sure he was there at the same time."

"What makes you so certain?" Max asked.

"You had to know Ms. Benson. She almost never took time off. She was a confirmed workaholic. She loved her business. Occasionally she did spa weekends, but while I was with her she went to Hawaii only that one time. She wasn't even there a full week."

"The trip surprised you?" Max said.

"Are you kidding? She took off for the islands just as the Keyworth deal started to come together. I couldn't believe it. The situation was very delicate. A couple of her biggest clients had some serious issues at the time, too. It wasn't like Ms. Benson to leave town when she had fires to put out. All I can say is that she must have really had a thing for the guy."

CHAPTER 60

"Ethel, I realize you want to go for a more dramatic effect with your memoir," Charlotte said.

"It's what they call high-concept," Ethel explained.

"I understand," Charlotte continued. "But as we discussed last time, you are writing your personal history — not fiction. Your children and your grandchildren and your great-grandchildren will want to know that they are reading the truth about their ancestors."

It was late morning. Ethel Deeping had waylaid Charlotte in the hallway to argue her case for the shocking ending to the chapter on her marriage.

"Trust me, my kids will get plenty of truth," Ethel said.

"Yes, but if they see one very dramatic element in your memoir that they know isn't true, they'll be inclined to doubt all of your story — including the really thrilling parts such as your work as a military nurse. You saved lives in war zones. You were a true heroine. You don't want to give your descendants any reason to doubt those facts, do you?"

"There's plenty of ways they can verify my military service."

"Yes, but will they even bother to do that if they doubt some of the other details? I'm afraid that if they read that you killed your husband, they'll conclude that the entire memoir is fiction."

Ethel looked as if she was prepared to argue further, but Charlotte's phone pinged. She looked down at the screen. The number was unfamiliar, but the photo and first line of the text turned her blood to ice.

If you want to see her alive, come outside. Alone. Bring your phone. Tell no one. Gray car parked on the street out front. You've got two minutes.

"Are you okay?" Ethel asked in sudden concern. "You look like you just saw a ghost."

Charlotte turned off her phone. For a moment she stared at Ethel, trying to think clearly. She grabbed the notebook and pen that Ethel carried in the basket of her walker and wrote Max's number down on a page in the notebook.

"Something very bad is happening, Ethel," she said. "Please call that number and tell Max Cutler that someone came to pick me up. Tell him that person says he's taking me to see my stepsister. Tell him he sent a picture of Jocelyn."

"Sure, I'll tell him. But you don't look good, dear."

"I don't feel good, either." Charlotte paused at the door, trying to think. "Would you do me another favor?"

"Of course."

"The person who is picking me up is driving a gray car that is parked in front of this building. Before you call Max Cutler, I would really appreciate it if you would use your cell phone camera to take as many pictures of me getting into the car as you can. Try for a photo of the license plate. But whatever you do, don't go outside. Take the shots through the lobby window. Understood? Promise me you won't let the driver of the car see you."

Ethel's eyes narrowed. "You're in danger, aren't you?"

"Yes. And so is Jocelyn. Whatever happens, the driver of the car must not see you take the photos."

"You're being kidnapped."

"Yes."

Ethel didn't argue. She rummaged around inside her bag, which was attached to the walker, and pulled out her cell phone with a shaking hand.

"Don't you worry," she said. "I'll get the picture. Hell, I used to hold bleeding wounds together with my bare hands while we were taking fire."

"I know. Call that number right after you take the photos."

Charlotte opened the door and hurried through the lobby. Ethel clanked along behind her, making excellent speed on her walker.

Two minutes, Charlotte thought. She did not dare take time to alert anyone else. There were only seconds left.

She rushed outside, barely noticing the snap of the chilly wind. She saw the gray car waiting at the curb, its engine idling. An eerie, light-headed sensation swept over her. Part of her could not believe what was happening.

The windows of the vehicle were tinted, but when she got closer she could make out the impression of a man behind the wheel. She opened the passenger-side door.

She barely had time to register the fact that he looked familiar before she saw the gun.

"Get in the back," he ordered.

She slammed the door shut and opened the rear door. For the first time she realized there was a second man inside the vehicle. He, too, held a gun. Something about him was off. He looked excited. His eyes were a little too bright. His face was flushed.

"You're not as pretty as the other one," he said. "Give me your phone."

He was high, she thought. In that instant she realized that he, too, looked vaguely familiar.

She gave her phone to him.

"What do you want me to do with it?" he said to the driver.

"Toss it out the window. Cutler might be able to use it to find her. Can't have that."

The jittery man with the gun lowered his window and threw the phone into the street.

"Don't make any sudden moves," the driver said. "Nolan, here, is a bit unstable. If you make him nervous, he'll pull that trigger. You'll be dead long before Jocelyn Pruett is."

"I recognize you," Charlotte said. "You were here at Rainy Creek Gardens the other day. You stopped me just as I was leaving.

You asked questions about the community. Who are you?"

She was almost certain she knew the answer, but there didn't seem to be any reason to let him know that she had figured out his identity.

"Trey Greenslade," Trey said. He pulled away from the curb. "I'm touched that you remember our meeting the other day. I wanted to get a good look at you because I realized you might be the bait I needed to force Pruett to come out of hiding. This would have gone a lot more smoothly if you hadn't brought that damned PI into the picture."

The jittery guy with the gun wiped the sweat from his forehead.

"I think I need another hit, Trey," he said.

"Take it, but don't take your eyes off her," Trey ordered.

"Okay, okay."

Trey met Charlotte's eyes briefly in the rearview mirror.

"His name is Nolan Briggs, by the way," he said. "He's been assisting me in exchange for some very good meds."

"I thought I recognized him," Charlotte said quietly. "There are photos of him on the mantel in the Briggses' cabin." She looked at Nolan. "You do know your father is dead, don't you?"

"Yeah." Nolan popped a couple of tablets into his mouth and swallowed hard. "No loss."

CHAPTER 61

Max studied the maps and the timelines he had spread out on his office desk. After all the murk and confusion, the picture was finally starting to come into focus.

There had been a Loring-Greenslade sales rep convention taking place on Maui during the time period that Madison Benson had traveled there. One more data point had just fallen into place. Madison had gone to the islands to meet her lover — Trey Greenslade. Greenslade was not married, as Drew Irby had speculated, but he certainly had an excellent reason for keeping his relationship with Madison off the radar.

The real question was whether Madison Benson had ever realized that the man she was seeing was a stone-cold rapist and murderer.

Max took out his phone and texted a message to Charlotte. May have a new lead. She would be excited, he thought. That knowledge buoyed his spirits.

When she didn't return the text, he started to get the old edgy feeling that told him something was very, very wrong. She was probably busy, he thought; but he had never been good at lying to himself.

He tried a phone call — and wound up in voice mail.

He took the gun and holster out of his desk drawer, pulled on his windbreaker to conceal the weapon and headed for the door.

His phone rang just as he emerged from the lobby elevator. For a few seconds he knew an almost overwhelming sense of relief. Then he saw the unfamiliar number on the screen.

"Cutler," he said.

"Mr. Cutler, this is Ethel Deeping, *Lieutenant* Ethel Deeping."

The voice on the other end was hoarse with age but firm and resolute.

"I remember you, Mrs. — I mean, Lieutenant Deeping. What's the problem?"

"A couple of bastards in a gray car just kidnapped Charlotte. Charlotte said to call you."

Everything inside him went ice-cold.

"I'm on my way," he said.

"I've got pictures."

CHAPTER 62

"You shouldn't have let him take you," Jocelyn said.

But she didn't sound angry or even fearful, Charlotte thought. Instead Jocelyn's voice was dulled with bleak despair — and for some reason that was more worrisome than anything else that had happened.

She had seen Jocelyn in a variety of moods. Anger, excitement, delight, outrage, laughter — Jocelyn did them all well. But never had she sounded like a beaten woman.

A fresh wave of alarm swept through Charlotte. "Is he keeping you drugged with something?"

Jocelyn frowned. "What?"

Charlotte studied her closely. In the gloom cast by the low-watt bulb in the overhead fixture, Jocelyn appeared exhausted.

"I asked if he had drugged you," Charlotte repeated. "I've never seen you like this."

"Madison Benson drugged me. That's how I wound up here. But Greenslade hasn't used any more drugs on me."

"You do know that Madison Benson is dead, don't you?"

"He murdered her, too?"

"Well, Greenslade has a perfect alibi. He was in Loring at the time. But now that I've met Nolan Briggs, I think I can understand how he pulled it off."

"He sent Nolan to kill her?"

"Evidently. She was shot twice."

"She must have been working with Greenslade all along. Why kill her now?"

"Maybe because he didn't need her any longer. She had become a liability. She probably knew too much about him."

"Louise and Madison are both dead. I'm sitting here in this basement with you. What about Victoria and Emily?"

"Victoria is still in the hospital, but according to the last report, she's going to recover. As for Emily, there's been no word. Max says that's probably a good thing. He says it indicates she's still alive."

"Charlotte, I am so damned sorry. The last thing I wanted was for you to get sucked into this quagmire."

"Yeah, well, what are sisters for, right? Anyhow, the good news is that Trey Greenslade needs to keep both of us alive until he can figure out how to get rid of Max Cutler. And that won't be easy."

"Why does he have to get rid of Cutler?"

Charlotte felt a rush of icy certainty. "Probably because he realizes that Max won't stop looking until he finds me."

Jocelyn's eyes tightened. "You're sure of that?"

"Positive."

"For all the good it will do. The problem is, I'm pretty sure Greenslade has gone crazy and his partner is a junkie. That is not a good combination."

"Jocelyn, why did you try to disappear and make me think you were on some sort of tech-free retreat? What scared you?"

"I freaked out one day when I realized my computer and probably my phone had been hacked. Someone was watching me — Greenslade, as it turns out. But at the time I had no way of knowing who was spying on me or how long he had been doing it. I didn't even know why someone was watching me. But I was convinced it had something to do with the past."

"Your past in Loring."

"Yes."

"What made you think that?"

"The two murders that I was investigating," Jocelyn said. "Both occurred in recent months. I was sure they had been committed by the same man who had attacked me all those years ago. The question was, why, after all these years, had he suddenly started killing his victims?"

"He was escalating."

"Yes."

"You should have told me what you were doing."

"You would have worried about me."

"No shit."

"I'm sorry," Jocelyn said. "I thought I was protecting you. The only person I told was Louise."

"Why only her?"

"She was my closest friend in the club. She had helped me do some of the research on the two murders and the three most recent rape cases. We were trying to find some sort of pattern — methods and locations. I didn't tell the others because I didn't want to drag them into it."

"Just like you didn't want to bring me into it. Jocelyn, I love you like a sister, but at times you are an idiot."

"Look, there was nothing you or the other members of the club could do and every chance that someone would slip up and accidentally alert whoever we were hunting.

It's so easy to get careless with a text message or an e-mail."

"Okay, I get that. I don't like it that you felt you had to keep secrets from me, but I understand it."

"I'm sorry."

"Never mind," Charlotte said. "What did you hope to accomplish by disappearing for a while?"

"I thought that if I went off the grid I could somehow force the bastard to reveal himself. I wasn't sure how that might happen, but I assumed that when he couldn't find me online, he would come looking — expose himself. And then, the next thing I knew, Louise was dead."

"So you sent the coded message warning the other members of the club."

"I had no choice. I thought that I'd been wrong all along. I decided that it was one of our targets who'd hacked my computer. After Louise was murdered I was afraid everyone in the club was at risk."

"When did you realize Trey Greenslade was the killer you were hunting?"

"I didn't realize it until I woke up in this damn basement." Jocelyn groaned. "He was always on my list, but I could never find a way to tie him to any of the rapes that occurred in the years after I was attacked. He was too careful. I knew I had to have some solid evidence before I could go to the police. The Greenslades are still the most powerful family in Loring."

"Did you know that Louise went to Loring the day she died?"

"Not until Greenslade told me that he was sure she had picked up the old evidence box that day."

"Max and I assumed she went there to talk to Briggs, but Briggs denied it."

"You can't believe anything that bastard told you," Jocelyn said.

"Yeah, we figured that out right after he tried to kill us."

"Oh, God, Charlotte, I swear I didn't want you to get involved —"

"You shouldn't have kept secrets from me — starting with that stupid investment club. Whatever made you think you and your pals could get away with playing female avengers? Didn't it occur to you that sooner or later one of your targets would figure out what was going on?"

"Yes, that's why we set up the escape plan."

"Oh, yeah, that worked well, didn't it?"

"You know, I could do without the lectures."

There was some real energy in Jocelyn's

voice now. She no longer sounded so despondent, Charlotte thought.

"Sorry." She looked around. "So, you've been here longer than me. Any thoughts on how to complicate the lives of those two creeps upstairs?"

Jocelyn hitched herself up against the wall. She held up her bound wrists. And then, like a magician pulling a rabbit out of a hat, she separated her hands. Charlotte saw that she had slit the duct tape. In the shadows it had not been apparent.

"Ah," Charlotte said. "I knew you hadn't been sitting around down here feeling sorry for yourself."

"I found an old fishing tackle box in the corner," Jocelyn said. "There was a knife inside."

"Where is the knife now?"

"Tucked into the waistband of my jeans under my shirt. The problem is that we're dealing with two guys who have guns."

"Lucky for you I was a Girl Scout."

Chapter 63

"There were two of them in the car." Max studied the photos on Ethel Deeping's phone.

"Yep." Ethel watched him anxiously. "I saw the other man when Charlotte opened the rear door to get into the backseat. One man at the wheel, one in the back. What's more, I think the s.o.b. in back had a gun. Can't be sure, but if you enlarge the photo you can see something in his hand."

"It's a gun," Max said. "You got the license plate. Good work."

"Figured you might need it. You're a PI. You can run a license plate, right?"

He looked at her. "Don't believe everything you see on television."

"But you can find out who owns that car, can't you?"

"There are ways, legal and illegal. But the fastest way is legal." He took out his phone.

"Who are you calling?"

"The Loring Police Department. There's a detective there who has an interest in this case."

Detective Walsh took the call.

"Trey Greenslade? Damn. Are you sure?"

"Yes."

"Are you absolutely certain we're talking about a kidnapping?" Walsh said.

"I'm sure," Max said. "If you can't help me, say so."

"And you'll go find some illegal online outfit who can get you into the DMV database for a price, right?"

"Not necessary," Max said. "I've got a few connections. If you can't get me the plate, I'll call someone I know who can get it."

"Hang on," Walsh said.

He came back on the line a short time later.

"This doesn't make any sense," he said.

"Just give me a name."

"The vehicle is registered to Nolan Briggs. I told you about him. He's the fucked-up son of Egan and Roxanne Briggs. How the hell is he involved in this thing?"

"You know junkies," Max said. "They'll do anything to get the cash they need for their next fix."

He nodded a quick thanks to Ethel and went swiftly outside, still on the phone as

462

he headed for Anson's SUV parked at the curb. Anson was in the front seat, waiting.

"But junkies are unreliable," Walsh said. "If you're right about Greenslade, he's a strategic planner. Why would he take the risk of employing an addict to help him kidnap a woman?"

"Maybe he thinks he has some leverage he can use to control Briggs," Max said. "Maybe he has a reason to think that he can trust him, at least for the time being."

"What reason?"

Max thought about the pictures on the mantel at the Briggs house. Then he thought about what Detective Atkins had said about Roxanne Briggs. *A fine-looking woman in her day. But she got pregnant the year after she graduated from high school. Never could figure out why she slept with Briggs. He was too old for her and with her looks, she could have done better.*

"We can go over the details later," Max said. "Right now we need to find Charlotte. At this point Greenslade doesn't know we've ID'd him."

"Unless Charlotte Sawyer told him."

"Charlotte is smart. She'll keep quiet. Obviously Greenslade took a few precautions, though. He used Nolan Briggs's car — probably hoping that would throw us off the trail if someone did get the license plate."

He opened the driver's-side door of the SUV and got behind the wheel.

"I've got to go, Walsh. I'm headed for Loring. I'll be there in a couple of hours."

"Wait, any idea where Greenslade might have taken Charlotte?"

Max fired up the engine and pulled away from the curb.

"Someplace where he feels secure," he said. "A location where he thinks he can control the situation and the environment. He was a sales rep for years. He likes to know the territory."

"Why would Nolan Briggs help him? Because Greenslade can supply him with an unlimited supply of drugs?"

"I'm sure that's a factor, but there's something else at work here," Max said. "Pretty sure Nolan Briggs is Trey Greenslade's half brother."

CHAPTER 64

"This had better work the first time," Jocelyn said. "We won't get a second chance."

"It will work," Charlotte said.

But she knew that Jocelyn was right. The plan, such as it was, absolutely had to work the first time.

"You know I've always admired your optimistic attitude," Jocelyn said.

"Bullshit. You've always considered me naïve."

They were standing in utter darkness because a short time before, Jocelyn had succeeded in smashing the low-watt bulb in the ceiling light fixture. It hadn't been a simple task because she had been trying not to make any more noise than necessary in the process. By positioning herself halfway up the wooden stairs she had been able to use the handle of an old mop to shatter the bulb. The faint tinkle of broken glass had evidently been muffled by the heavy plank flooring overhead because their captors had not bothered to check on the situation.

They had taken up positions on either side of the old wooden steps, not daring to move because there was no way to know when the door would open and one of their captors would appear. They had to be in position and ready.

"I've never thought of you as naïve," Jocelyn said. "Just, you know, maybe too inclined to look for the good in other people."

"Uh-huh."

"I still can't believe you hired a private investigator."

"I thought I made it clear. I'm not a client," Charlotte said. "Max and I are partners in this thing. His client is Louise's cousin."

"Still, I can't believe you got involved with a private investigator," Jocelyn said.

"It wasn't like there were a lot of viable options. Your best friend was dead under what both her cousin and I considered mysterious circumstances and the police were not displaying any great interest in the death. And then I find out that you are not in that Caribbean convent learning to think tech-free metaphysical thoughts. What was I supposed to do?"

There was a short silence from the other side of the stairs.

"Louise was a very good friend, but she wasn't my best friend," Jocelyn said after a while.

"No?"

"You're my best friend."

"That's very touching, but we both know it isn't true."

"What do you mean?" Jocelyn sounded hurt.

"If I was your best friend, you would have told me about the risks you were taking playing Lady Avenger with your pals in Madison Benson's so-called investment club."

"I didn't tell you about the club's activities because I didn't want to put you at risk. I was trying to protect you."

"Yeah, well, that doesn't let you off the hook. Best friends don't keep secrets like that."

"I can't believe we're arguing about the definition of friendship," Jocelyn said. "Not now, at any rate. In case you haven't noticed, we've got a few problems on our hands."

"Max will sort things out."

"You've got a lot of faith in him, don't you?"

"I trust him, yes," Charlotte said. "But in addition, he's very, very good at what he does."

There was another deep silence from the other side of the stairs.

"Damn. You're falling in love with him, aren't you?" Jocelyn asked after a while.

"I think so, yes."

"You think so?"

"After the fiasco with Brian, I'm trying to be very cautious when it comes to relationships."

"That's my little stepsister, all right," Jocelyn said. "Cautious."

"We don't all have your sense of adventure."

"You can see where a sense of adventure got me. And it's nice of you not to remind me that I'm the one who kept telling you that Brian Conroy was perfect for you."

"Yes, it is nice of me not to point that out."

A sudden flurry of heavy footsteps thudded on the floor overhead.

"Shit, it's him. Cutler." Trey's muffled voice was strained with rage and panic. "How did he find this place?"

"Never mind that. You heard what he said, he's got the evidence," Nolan shouted. "He wants to see the women before he'll make the trade. Get 'em. Bring 'em up here. Show him they're both alive."

"You get them," Trey ordered. "I might get a shot at Cutler. Go on, hurry, you stupid junkie."

Once again footsteps pounded on the floorboards overhead. A few seconds later the lock on the door at the top of the stairs rattled and clanged and the door slammed open. Nolan stopped short when he realized he was gazing down into an unlit basement.

He groped for the light switch and flipped it several times in a frenzied manner.

"They fucked with the light," he shouted over his shoulder.

"It probably burned out," Trey said. "Use the flashlight."

Charlotte stood very still in the dense darkness under the stairs. She sensed Jocelyn doing the same thing. Each gripped an end of the length of fishing line they had found in the tackle box. The line stretched across a stair tread halfway down the steps.

A couple of beats later the brilliant beam of a flashlight speared the darkness.

"I can't see 'em," Nolan shouted, clearly starting to panic.

"Pruett, Sawyer, get up here," Trey yelled. "Do it now. Cutler's here to make the trade. You only get one chance. Move."

Charlotte had to remind herself to

breathe. Fear and adrenaline surged through her. She knew that Jocelyn was equally wired.

Neither of them moved in response to Trey's orders.

"They're gone," Nolan said, voice shaking. "Somehow they got out."

"There is no way out of that basement except the stairs," Trey said. "They're down there. Go get one of them."

"I don't see Jocelyn or Charlotte," Max called from somewhere outside. "If either one of them is dead, the deal's off."

"No," Trey roared. "They're both here. Both alive. I'll show you."

Charlotte heard him cross the room to the top of the stairs.

"Get out of my way," he snarled to Nolan.

There was some scrambling overhead as Nolan obeyed. And then Trey was coming down the stairs, flashlight in hand. The beam of light arced back and forth across the basement, but it could not reach the darkness under the stairs.

The fishing line was all but invisible in the shadows. Certainly Trey never saw it.

Charlotte tightened her grip on the fishing line. On the opposite side of the staircase, Jocelyn did the same. They had torn off strips of their shirts and wrapped them around their hands to protect them from the bite of the line.

She felt the sharp tug when the toe of Trey's shoe caught on the fishing line. She heard a harsh gasp and a choked shout of raw panic. For a dizzying instant, she thought she was the one uttering the horrified cry.

But it was Trey whose scream ripped through the deep well of night in the basement. The flashlight flew from his hand, the beam spiraling wildly. Charlotte heard the gun clatter on the floor.

Trey tumbled down the steps, flailing wildly in a frantic effort to catch his balance. He landed on the concrete floor with a jarring thud, a sound that Charlotte knew she would hear in her nightmares for years to come.

Shivering, she unwound the fishing line from her hand.

Jocelyn rushed to the flashlight, grabbed it and swung it in wide, sweeping arcs. Charlotte realized she was searching for the gun that Trey had dropped. The beam of the light passed over Trey, who lay very still. There was a dark pool forming under his head.

"Trey?" Nolan looked down from the top of the stairs. "What the fuck?"

Jocelyn switched off the flashlight.

Nolan freaked. He fired wildly into the basement.

"Stay back," he shouted. "Don't move. I'll shoot anyone who tries to come up the stairs."

He retreated and slammed the door shut. Charlotte heard his running footsteps overhead.

Jocelyn switched on the flashlight. "He's going out the back door. Probably hoping to escape through the woods."

"Charlotte." Max's shout was somewhere between a desperate prayer and a command.

"Down here," she called, raising her voice to be heard through the closed door. "The basement. We're okay."

Jocelyn finally pinned the gun in the beam of the flashlight.

"There it is," she said.

She scooped up the weapon.

Charlotte heard muffled shouts. There were more thudding footsteps. The door at the top of the stairs slammed open. Max stood there, a gun in his hand.

"Charlotte," he said again.

"I'm here," she said. "So is Jocelyn. We're both all right. But I think Trey Greenslade is dead."

She ran up the stairs and straight into

Max's arms.

"Charlotte," he said.

He spoke her name in a raw, grinding voice that was infused with some fierce emotion. He sounded like a man who had just had a narrow escape from hell. He wrapped her close and tight against him.

"I knew you'd find us," she said into his chest.

"I'm glad one of us was sure of that. For God's sake, woman, don't ever scare me like that again. I don't think my heart could take it."

Anson approached, a gun held alongside his leg. He looked every inch a lawman.

"You ladies okay?" he asked.

"Yes," Charlotte said. "Yes, we are."

She was vaguely aware of other voices and people moving around inside the cabin. Someone was giving orders. She recognized Detective Walsh's voice. He sounded buzzed on adrenaline.

"Get the damned aid car here," he said to someone.

She heard Nolan Briggs whining earnestly in the background, explaining to an officer that he had been one of Greenslade's hostages.

Incensed, Charlotte gave Walsh a fierce look. "Don't believe a word that bastard says. He was working with Greenslade all along."

"Yeah, we figured that out," Max said.

He eased her out of the way so that Walsh and a uniformed officer could descend the basement steps.

Charlotte looked down and saw that Jocelyn was still standing over Trey Greenslade. Her hand was clenched around the grip of the gun.

Walsh went down the steps and gently took the gun from her.

"You're Jocelyn Pruett?" he asked.

"Yes." Jocelyn did not move. "Is he dead? I really hope he's dead."

The officer crouched beside Trey and checked for a pulse.

"He's alive," Walsh said.

"Too bad," Jocelyn said.

She started to cry.

Charlotte freed herself from Max's grasp and went down the steps. She took Jocelyn's hand.

"It's all right, Jocelyn," she said. "Come with me. Let the police do their job."

"We got him," Jocelyn said. "Didn't we?"

"Yes, we did," Charlotte said. "It's over. Finally."

She tightened her grip on Jocelyn's hand

and drew her up out of the basement into the daylight.

CHAPTER 65

They bought four coffees and four hamburgers with fries at the drive-through window of a fast-food restaurant near the campus. They needed the basic food groups, Max thought — caffeine, carbs and protein. They had to fortify themselves before they gave their statements to Detective Walsh.

He drove to the nearest city park. It was late afternoon and too chilly to use one of the picnic tables, so they settled for eating the meal in the car. Charlotte was in the passenger seat. Jocelyn and Anson were in the backseat. Max was behind the wheel.

"Let me guess," Charlotte said. "We're here to get our stories straight before we give our statements to the police, right?"

Max had been about to take a bite of his hamburger. He paused to look at her, everything inside him tightening at the realization that he had almost lost her. For a second or two he could not speak, let alone eat.

Then she smiled at him and he was able to breathe again.

"You don't have to make it sound like we're a bunch of coconspirators," he said.

"Why not?" Jocelyn said. "That's pretty much what we are."

"Yeah, that does describe our situation," Anson agreed.

"Yes, I know," Max said. "But when Charlotte says stuff like that, somehow it sounds so much worse than it actually is."

"That's Charlotte," Jocelyn said. "Why do you think I never told her about the investment club?"

Charlotte turned in her seat. "If you had, I would have advised you not to get involved with people like Madison Benson and her little band of online vigilantes."

"Okay, I think that's enough squabbling, ladies," Max said. "We don't have a lot of time. Just so you know, the number one rule in situations like this is —"

"There are rules about giving statements?" Charlotte asked, frowning.

"The rule," he repeated patiently, "is that you don't lie but you don't volunteer any more information than absolutely necessary. Right, Anson?"

"Right," Anson said around a mouthful of hamburger.

"Good rule," Jocelyn said. She eyed Max. "How did you figure out that Trey Greenslade was holding us at the old hunting cabin?"

"Greenslade had a pattern," Max said. "He was into planning and he was obsessed with having a thorough knowledge of his territory. Also, he needed to feel that he was in control. In the course of researching him I'd checked his tax records. He inherited some property in the town of Loring and he has an apartment in Seattle. But of all the places he controlled, his father's old hunting cabin in the mountains seemed like the only one that could be used to hold a couple of captives. No nosy neighbors to ask questions."

Charlotte nodded and munched a French fry. "You're good. Really, really good."

"Yep," Anson said. "He is good."

Max looked at Jocelyn. "Do you know what happened to the contents of that old evidence box?"

"No," Jocelyn said. "And I don't know why Louise made that trip here to Loring the day she died, if that's what you're going to ask next."

"Trey Greenslade must have had some

reason to think that she got the evidence box in the course of that trip," Charlotte said. "He killed her hours later that same day."

"But she died of a drug overdose," Anson pointed out. "How did he get close enough to her to drug her?"

"Probably the same way he got close enough to me to drug me," Jocelyn said. "He used Madison Benson."

"Who helped him because she saw a golden opportunity to increase her share of the profits from the Keyworth deal," Max said. "Maybe she had even higher aspirations. Maybe she thought she could somehow get a slice of Loring-Greenslade."

"Why did Greenslade cut her out of the herd?" Anson asked.

"Once he discovered that I was closing in on him, he realized he had a problem," Jocelyn said. "At that point he couldn't know how much the other members of the investment club knew about my investigation. He realized that Madison Benson was the one in charge of the club, so he went after her first."

"Probably recognized another sociopath," Charlotte said. "Takes one to know one."

"Exactly," Max said. "Figured he could do business with her."

"He seduced her," Jocelyn said. "But knowing Madison, she probably thought she was in control."

Anson shook his head. "Two sick sociopaths, each trying to manipulate the other."

"Getting back to the contents of the evidence box," Jocelyn said, "Trey Greenslade thinks that Briggs scammed him. He thinks Briggs sold the evidence to Louise and then tried to sell the empty box to him."

"If that's true — and there is some logic to it," Max said, "we have to figure out where Louise hid the contents of the box."

"Here's what's bothering me," Jocelyn said. "If Briggs did decide to sell the box, why did he call Louise? I'm the one who would have paid whatever he asked for that damn box."

Charlotte looked at her. "Maybe he couldn't get hold of you because you were out of town and off the grid."

"Oh, shit," Jocelyn said. She looked stricken. "You're right. If he called my office, Louise would have taken the call. She would have recognized the Briggs name. She would have understood that if he was desperate to get in touch with me, it was about something very important — something related to the past."

"She must have told him that she knew

about your past," Charlotte said. "When he told her what he had to sell, she agreed to the deal. She took ten grand out of her own bank account and went to Loring to collect the box."

Jocelyn's eyes were haunted. "Louise died because of me."

"No," Charlotte said quickly.

"Yes," Jocelyn said evenly. "It's my fault Louise is dead."

Charlotte looked at Max. He could feel her willing him to assure Jocelyn that she was not responsible for her friend's death. This was going to be the hard part about his new line of work, he thought. Finding the right words at the end of the case was not his strong suit.

"Louise took a risk," he said.

"But she couldn't have known how big a risk," Jocelyn said.

"Maybe not," Max said. "But her motives might not have been entirely altruistic."

"What are you talking about?" Jocelyn demanded.

"She was the one member of the club who knew that you weren't on that Caribbean island," Max said. "She knew that you had gone off the grid because you were afraid someone had hacked your tech. But she had to know that you would be watching your e-mail."

Charlotte looked at him. "The same way that you assumed Jocelyn was watching."

"Louise and I established a code," Jocelyn said. "She was supposed to use it if there was some sort of emergency. But she never sent it. Maybe she didn't think she had time. Maybe Briggs told her that she had to bring the money immediately."

"Or maybe she had her own plans for that evidence," Max said.

Jocelyn looked stunned. "What?"

"She had to know that it was worth a fortune to your rapist," Max said. "She knew that he would have paid a lot more than ten grand for it."

"No," Jocelyn said. "No, she was my friend."

"Hold on," Anson said. "If Briggs was looking to score big-time, why didn't he contact Trey Greenslade first? Greenslade was in a position to pay a lot more money for the evidence."

"That," Max said slowly, "is a very good question. Briggs most likely would have tried to do the deal with Greenslade first, not Jocelyn. That leaves us with only one other individual who would have had access to the box and a reason to sell it. If I'm right, Trey Greenslade would have been the last person she would have contacted."

Charlotte's eyes narrowed in faint surprise.

"Roxanne Briggs?" she said.

"I can't prove it, but I think so, yes," Max said. He thought about it. "It feels right."

"But why?" Jocelyn asked.

"Because Gordon Greenslade was killed in an alleged hunting accident a few months ago," he said. "And Trey Greenslade inherited everything. Roxanne's junkie son — Gordon's *other* son — got nothing."

Jocelyn raised her brows. "Are we going to tell the Loring police your brilliant theory?"

"No," Max said. "We are not."

Anson peeled the lid off his coffee cup. "Remember rule number one — stick to the truth, but don't volunteer anything."

Charlotte looked at him. "What's rule number two?"

"See rule number one," Anson said.

CHAPTER 66

"I was right," Daniel Flint said. "Louise was murdered. I knew it. So it was that bastard, Trey Greenslade, who killed her?"

Daniel was grim and somber and he looked a lot older than he had at the start of the case. But Daniel also appeared satisfied in a bone-deep sort of way. Sometimes a man needed answers, Max thought. He knew the feeling.

The four of them were gathered in Max's office. He was sitting behind his desk. Daniel was in one of the two client chairs. Jocelyn had taken the other chair. Charlotte was watering the half-dead plant in the corner. Anson lounged against the wall, his arms folded.

At Daniel's comment, Charlotte straightened, watering can in hand, and looked at him.

"Yes," she said. "Greenslade murdered her with Madison Benson's assistance."

"Greenslade's still in the hospital in Loring," Max said. "But he started talking this morning, according to Walsh. Trying to cut a deal. So is Nolan Briggs. And it gets better — Madison Benson is talking, too."

They all looked at him.

"How?" Charlotte demanded.

"Got a call from the homicide detective in charge of the case here in Seattle. The cops found Benson's computer and phone at the cabin. The forensics people got into both today. Turns out she was keeping digital audio recordings of her conversations with Greenslade. There is more than enough material to make sure he goes away for a very long time."

Daniel frowned. "So Madison Benson was his accomplice right from the start?"

"Yes," Max said. "Somehow they found out that Louise had picked up the evidence box in Loring. They assumed it was still in her possession when she returned to Seattle. Madison went to see her and slipped the drug into her drink. Madison took Louise's keys and gave them to Greenslade, who went into the condo, gave Louise a lethal dose of another drug and then searched for the evidence box."

"Imagine his surprise when he couldn't find it," Charlotte said. "And his panic. He

485

actually broke into the carry-on Louise had used to store her copy of the file on him, but he obviously didn't bother to take a closer look."

"He was fixated on locating the contents of the evidence box," Max said. "He wasn't interested in a road map. He never even bothered to open the envelopes. He knew that as long as that old evidence box was out there, somewhere, it was a threat to him. He needed Madison's help to locate it."

"He assumed that I was the one person who might know what Louise had done with the box, but I had dropped off the grid," Jocelyn said. "They didn't know where I was. And then, before he could figure out his next move, I sent the code word that caused Victoria and Emily to go into hiding."

"That must have made Madison really nervous," Charlotte said. "She wanted both of them dead because she wanted their shares of the Keyworth buyout. But she had to know that if they all died in suspicious accidents the police would start investigating, so she tried to make it appear that you and Emily were the ones with motive."

"How did she get to Victoria so quickly?" Jocelyn asked.

"Victoria woke up and started talking,"

Max said. "Turns out she actually told Madison Benson where she planned to hide — her aunt's old trailer on the coast. Madison probably intended to let a little more time elapse before she murdered one of the other club members, but after Charlotte and I talked to her, she realized she had to move fast. She got into her car and drove straight to the coast."

"Victoria let her in because she thought Benson was a friend who had brought some news," Charlotte said. "She served coffee. She doesn't remember anything at all after that. Obviously Benson drugged Victoria's coffee. Then she sabotaged the heater and left."

"Madison was raised in a trailer park," Jocelyn said. "She would have known how to rig the heater."

"She took a risk," Anson said. "The sabotaged heater might not have done the job, but she knew that if it worked no one would link her to the murder. She almost got lucky. If Max and Charlotte hadn't decided to make the drive to the coast early the next morning, Victoria Mathis would have died."

Daniel looked at Max. "Louise was like a big sister to me. She joined the investment club because she was trying to right some wrongs. I think she went to Loring that day because she wanted to get the evidence box before Roxanne Briggs changed her mind. I'm sure she planned to give it to Ms. Pruett."

"That's possible," Max said.

It was not his job to shred Daniel's memories of his cousin, he thought.

Jocelyn and Charlotte kept silent.

"Thank you, Mr. Cutler," Daniel said. He got to his feet. "You got answers for me. That's all I wanted. I promise you'll get your money after I sell Louise's condo. But it might take a while. The real estate agent warned me that a lot of people won't buy a place if they know someone died in it."

"I've heard that," Max said. "I can wait for my money."

"I'd better be on my way." Daniel glanced at his watch. "I'm due at my job in twenty minutes."

Max got to his feet, crossed the room and opened the door. He shook Daniel's hand and then closed the door and turned around to face Charlotte and Jocelyn.

"My client is satisfied," he said. "But we've still got a couple of unanswered questions."

"Right," Anson said. "For instance, what the heck did Louise Flint do with the evidence that she bought from Roxanne Briggs?"

"The Loring cops say that Trey Greenslade is going to live," Jocelyn said. "They assured me that he'll be going to jail for the murder of Louise Flint as well as other crimes. But I'd really like to get my hands on that old evidence. There must be something in it that proves he's the one who attacked me or else Briggs would never have been able to blackmail Gordon Greenslade all those years."

Max walked back across the room to stand behind his desk. He took out the Washington State road map that Louise had marked up and opened it.

"Here's what we know," he said. "Daniel Flint is quite certain that Louise Flint had no friends or relatives between Seattle and Loring. We know that between the time she met with Roxanne Briggs in or near Loring and the time she was murdered that night she managed to conceal a package containing what must have been a large quantity of crime scene evidence."

Charlotte studied the map and shook her head. "Nothing but small towns between Seattle and Loring. And you said that the GPS and odometer readings indicate she didn't make any big detours."

"According to the cameras in the condo garage, she did not take anything out of her car when she returned from Loring," Max said. "The trunk was empty. There was nothing hidden in her storage locker except her copy of the file that she and Jocelyn were building around Trey Greenslade."

Jocelyn looked up. "What are you saying?"

"I'm saying that obviously she did stop somewhere between Loring and Seattle. Maybe her intuition was warning her that she was involved in something very dangerous. Maybe she was afraid that Roxanne Briggs would lose her nerve or have regrets and tell someone what she had done."

"Someone like her husband," Charlotte suggested.

Max looked at Jocelyn. "Maybe she just wanted to protect the evidence out of an abundance of caution. Whatever the case, she stopped long enough to ditch the package."

"But where?" Jocelyn demanded.

Max folded the map. "Got the keys to your office at the foundation, Jocelyn?"

"Yes, why?"

"Let's go take a look."

A short time later they stood around Jocelyn's desk and studied the contents of the package that had been waiting for her.

"She didn't hide the evidence somewhere between Loring and Seattle," Max said. "She entrusted it to the U.S. Postal Service."

" 'Neither snow nor rain nor heat nor gloom of night . . . ,' " Charlotte quoted softly.

Jocelyn looked up, tears in her eyes. "She addressed it to me. Not herself. Me. She wanted to be sure I got it in case something happened to her."

"By then she knew that the situation was very dangerous," Charlotte said. "She also knew that I was collecting your mail and that you would not want me to be involved in whatever was going down."

"She mailed her condo keys to my place before she left town," Jocelyn said, "because at that point she was concerned but not really scared. She was just taking precautions. But after she picked up the evidence package, she knew it was very hot and that someone might come looking for it. She didn't trust the security at her building or mine. We're talking about condo towers, after all. It's not that hard to get past the door stations. But she knew that the security here at the foundation is very good. She had every reason to believe that evidence would be safe in my office until I returned."

Charlotte smiled. "You were right. Louise wasn't going to try to scam you or use the evidence for her own benefit. She was a good friend."

"Yes, she was," Jocelyn said. She smiled a watery smile. "But I meant what I said in that damn basement. You are my best friend."

"No more secrets, friend?" Charlotte said.

"No more secrets."

CHAPTER 67

Max opened a couple of beers and set them on the kitchen table. He sat down across from Anson.

Anson picked up one of the bottles and took a healthy swallow. Then he lowered the bottle and looked at Max.

"You said you had an update on the situation?"

"Emily Kelly reappeared today, safe and sound," Max said. "She was hiding out in eastern Washington and staying off her computer and her phone. But, like Jocelyn, she kept an eye on things using the resources of the local public library."

"Everyone's accounted for, then." Anson looked pleased. "Except for Roxanne Briggs, who is a woman on the run. Probably scared as hell."

"Trey Greenslade and Nolan Briggs are recovering. They've both lawyered up, but both are talking."

Anson nodded. "Trying to cut deals."

"Right. There are one or two loose ends to tidy up, but things are under control."

"Congratulations." Anson clinked his bottle against Max's. "Always said you had a talent for chasing down bad guys and finding people who don't want to be found."

"Thanks. Unfortunately, this particular case did not conclude with a big payday. I can't charge the client full freight for time and expenses, not only because he can't afford me, but also because I spent a good portion of the time working another angle."

"Searching for Jocelyn Pruett."

"Exactly. Here's the bottom line: I need more corporate business and consulting work."

Anson squinted a little over the top of the beer bottle. "You'll never attract that kind of work with that little rinky-dink office you're in now. Hell, son, you don't even have someone to answer the phone."

"I'm aware that I need a flashier office. I also need staff. But I can't afford both, not yet."

"I can help out a little."

Max smiled. "Thanks, that's exactly what I'm about to suggest."

"You want a loan? I can cash in a CD, no problem."

"Thanks, but I don't need a loan. What I need is a really cheap receptionist — someone to take phone calls and deal with clients and manage the files."

Anson's bushy brows rose. "You got someone in mind?"

"You."

Startled, Anson put his beer bottle down very slowly. "Me?"

"You need a job and I need someone who can handle my office. I need someone I won't have to train or manage. Someone who understands the investigation business. Most of all, I need someone I know I can trust."

"Me," Anson repeated.

He sounded thoughtful now.

"I also need someone who will work for low pay until business improves."

"Me," Anson said.

This time he sounded certain.

They drank a little more beer. After a while Anson took out his notebook and a pen.

"I'll start shopping around for better office space tomorrow," he said.

Max smiled. "Thanks. I'll help you."

"No, you won't," Anson said. "You need to focus on bringing in the business. You've got contacts and connections from your old days at the profiling agency. It's time you got serious about networking."

"Networking?"

"And while you're at it, think about bringing in another investigator. One-man firms never impress high-end clients or big businesses."

"Another investigator? Who would want to work for a small investigation business like mine? Maybe when business picks up —"

"I'm telling you, business won't really pick up until you look like a bigger operation."

"I can't afford to pay another investigator."

"So offer him a piece of the action. Make him part owner of the business. That way he'll be responsible for bringing in new clients."

"Him? You've got someone in mind?"

"Yep, as a matter of fact, I do."

Anson told him.

"Huh." Max considered for a while. "That's an interesting idea. I should have thought of him myself."

"That's why you've got a receptionist — to think about stuff like that."

"While we're on the subject of thinking about stuff, I want to run something by you."

"What?"

"Charlotte says that my obsession with finding out what really happened to Quinton Zane isn't going to go away."

"She's probably right," Anson said. "Doubt if Cabot and Jack will ever be able to let it go, either. See, if you three really could let go of it, none of you would have turned out to be good investigators."

"Wonderful. Are you telling me that being obsessive is part of the makeup of a good investigator? You're saying I'm in the business because of a personality disorder?"

"What you have — what all three of you have — is a passion for finding answers to certain kinds of questions. Call it an obsession if you want. All I know is, you're gonna go on looking for answers, come what may."

"Charlotte says I need to allow myself to spend some time looking for Zane."

"She's right," Anson said. "Because that question isn't going to go away."

CHAPTER 68

It was raining lightly when Charlotte left Rainy Creek Gardens on Monday afternoon. She pulled up the hood of her anorak and hurried home along the familiar route.

Mentally she made a list of what she needed for the meal she planned to serve to Max that evening. It would be the first time she had actually cooked dinner for him. She wanted it to be perfect. The menu included roasted Romanesco and grilled salmon, so she made a quick detour through Pike Place Market to pick up the veggies and the fish.

The early dark of the autumn night was descending fast by the time she got to her apartment tower. The warm light of the streetlamps glowed on the damp pavement and the sidewalks. Raindrops sparkled on the windshields of passing cars.

I love this town, she thought. *And I love Max.* Everything about Seattle felt like home.

She fumbled with her key fob to open the door and let herself into the lobby. The front desk was vacant. The concierge had gone home for the day.

She took the elevator up to the twelfth floor, got out and went down the hall. She opened the door of her apartment, flipped on the hallway light and went into the kitchen to set the groceries on the counter.

She was about to open the refrigerator when she felt a subtle shift in the atmosphere behind her. Her pulse was suddenly beating very fast and her breathing felt constricted. *Too much excitement lately,* she thought. *My nerves are on edge. I need to meditate.*

But instinct overrode the soothing self-talk. She turned quickly and looked out across the breakfast bar into the darkened living room. A figure stirred in the shadows.

"I've been waiting for you," Roxanne Briggs said.

The light from the kitchen gleamed on the gun in her hand.

Charlotte tried to breathe through the panic.

"How did you get in here?" she managed.

"It wasn't hard. I arrived a couple of hours ago. I didn't know exactly what time you would be home, you see. I wanted to be here first. I told the nice man at the front desk downstairs that I was your new cleaning lady and that I needed the key to your place."

Roxanne waved the gun rather casually at a janitorial bucket on the floor of the living room. Charlotte could see some brushes and a mop sticking out of the bucket.

"He believed you?" Charlotte asked.

"He took some convincing because you hadn't notified him that I was starting today, but everybody trusts a hardworking cleaning lady. Besides, things were quite hectic in the lobby. The afternoon deliveries were coming in. Contractors were asking for keys. It was all a little chaotic. Your concierge gave me the key to get rid of me, I think."

"Why are you here, Roxanne?"

"I've been thinking about things," Roxanne said. "I finally decided that everything went wrong because of you. You're the one who got that damned PI involved. Now my son is facing prison because of you."

"You can't blame Max or me for a disaster that you helped create," Charlotte said. "You're the one who killed Gordon Greenslade, aren't you?"

"He lied to me," Roxanne said. The hand holding the gun shook a little. "I kept his

500

secret all those years and in return he promised he would take care of our son."

"You and Gordon Greenslade were lovers."

"Back at the start, yes. He told me he loved me at the beginning. Said he would divorce his wife and marry me. I stopped believing that lie years ago."

"Why, after all that time, did you decide to kill him this past summer?" Charlotte asked.

"Because my son needed to go back to the hospital for rehab again and Gordon refused to pay for it. It costs thousands, you see. Gordon had paid for two treatments, but he refused to pay for a third. He said he didn't care if I told everyone the truth because he'd met the woman of his dreams — on an online matchmaking site. Can you believe it?"

"I've heard people do things like that sometimes."

"He was obviously having some sort of delayed midlife crisis. I knew that if he was planning to run away from Loring and his responsibilities, he would probably also change his will. I couldn't risk letting that happen."

"So you killed him before he had a chance to do that. But he lied about the will, too, didn't he?"

Tears of fury filled Roxanne's eyes. "Nolan was never in his will. Gordon left everything to his *other* son."

"Trey."

"That was not right," Roxanne said. She seemed to regain some control. "My Nolan had an equal claim on the Greenslade money. If he'd had all the advantages that Trey had, Nolan would never have become addicted to drugs."

"So you shot Gordon Greenslade for nothing. Greenslade left nothing to Nolan."

"That bastard didn't leave my son — our son — a dime. He never even acknowledged him."

The intercom buzzed, startling both of them.

"What's that?" Roxanne hissed.

"Max Cutler. He's downstairs. He knows I'm up here. I'd better let him in."

"No."

"If I don't, he'll get suspicious. Trust me, he'll get a cop and make a very big scene."

Roxanne hesitated. "All right. Do it."

Charlotte went to the intercom. "Max?"

"I've got the wine. I've also got news."

"Come on up." She pressed the lock release. "We've got company."

"Who?"

"Surprise."

"I'm on my way."

She looked at Roxanne. "I think you want him to hear the rest of this. You want us to know your side of the story, don't you?"

Roxanne looked uncertain now. A couple of minutes later, there was a knock on the door. She flinched.

"Open it," she ordered, the gun shivering in her hand. "Do it."

Charlotte held her breath and went down the hall. She opened the door. Max stood there. He had the bottle of wine in one hand. He held his gun, concealed against the side of his leg, in the other hand. His eyes were ice-cold.

"Who?" he asked quietly.

"Roxanne Briggs," Charlotte said, careful to keep her voice pitched in a normal tone. "She's telling me how everything went wrong."

He mouthed, "Armed?"

She nodded, then turned and led the way down the hall. Max put the pistol into the pocket of his jacket. He kept his hand wrapped around the grip, making it look casual.

"Hello, Roxanne," he said. He acted as if he did not notice the gun in her hand. "Are you okay?"

"Don't move," Roxanne said nervously. "I swear, if you move, I'll shoot."

"I won't move," Max said.

"Roxanne was just telling me that she was desperate to raise cash for another round of expensive rehab for her son," Charlotte said. "You were right — Nolan is Gordon Greenslade's son."

"I shot that lying son of a bitch because years ago he promised to leave my son his fair share of the Greenslade money," Roxanne said hoarsely.

"Obviously he lied about that," Max said. "Is that why you decided to sell the contents of the old evidence box? To get enough money to send Nolan back to rehab?"

"I had no choice," Roxanne whispered. "Egan had been slowly bleeding Gordon for years by threatening to let that evidence box suddenly get discovered — maybe in a closet at the old police station or some such nonsense. But the truth was, he'd hidden it in our basement."

"Gordon Greenslade paid blackmail all those years to protect Trey?" Charlotte said.

"No." Roxanne shook her head. "Gordon Greenslade didn't give a damn about either one of his sons. But he did care about his family's reputation in Loring. Or, at least, he did, until he went crazy and decided to run off with that woman he met online."

"Did your husband know that you killed Gordon Greenslade?" Charlotte asked.

"No, of course not. Egan never gave me credit for having the guts to do something like that. Besides, he didn't know I had a motive."

"You mean Egan never suspected that Nolan was Gordon's son?" Max asked.

"No." Roxanne smiled a thin, cold smile. "I'm a woman of my word. I promised Gordon that I would keep quiet so long as he made sure that Nolan was in his will. The only times I asked Gordon for money were when Nolan needed treatment. Egan refused to pay for rehab, so I went to Gordon for the money. He gave it to me the first two times. Everyone, including Egan, assumed both occasions were acts of charity. Gordon was very big on charity if it made him look good to the community."

"Trey continued to pay blackmail after his father's death, didn't he?" Charlotte said.

"Yes. Egan contacted him — anonymously — and Trey paid up the first couple of times. But I knew that Trey was far more dangerous than his father."

"Did Egan know that Trey had escalated from rape to murder?" Max asked.

"Of course," Roxanne said. "I'll say one

thing for Egan — he was a pretty good cop. He kept an eye on Trey over the years. Whenever there was a new rape case with elements that were similar to the Jocelyn Pruett case, he made notes. Egan figured out right away that Trey had switched from blindfolds to drugs to keep his victims from being able to identify him. Recently Egan was also certain that Trey had started murdering the women he raped."

"Trey started escalating after his father was killed, didn't he?" Max said.

"Yes." Roxanne frowned. "It's weird, but on some deep level I think Trey was afraid of his father. Once Gordon was dead, though, it was as if someone had taken a lid off a boiling pot."

"Did Egan know that the evidence box he tried to sell to Trey was filled with magazines and books?"

"No." Roxanne looked disgusted. "The fool never bothered to check. Why would he? He was in a terrible rush to leave that day. He went down into the basement, grabbed the box and stowed it in the SUV. The box felt full because after I removed the evidence I stuffed it with the magazines and books. I resealed it exactly the same way that Egan had the last time he opened it to add some data about Trey's latest crimes."

"You were afraid of Trey Greenslade, even though you knew he could have paid the most for the evidence," Max said. "So you tried to contact Jocelyn Pruett. But you got Louise Flint instead."

"It's not like there were a lot of potential buyers," Roxanne said. "Yes, Louise Flint took my call. She said Jocelyn was out of town for a month. She said she was Jocelyn's best friend and that she knew Jocelyn would want her to buy whatever I was selling. I told her I needed ten thousand dollars. She said she could get her hands on that much money and meet me in a few hours."

"Ten thousand would have covered another round of rehab for Nolan," Max said.

"Yes. I met Flint at a fast-food restaurant just outside of Loring. She gave me the money and I gave her the package containing the contents of the evidence box. That should have been the end of it. But it wasn't. Everything went wrong."

She started to weep. In a moment she was engulfed in great, wracking sobs. She never even noticed when Max crossed the room and gently took the gun from her hand.

Charlotte went forward and touched Roxanne's shoulder. Blinded by tears, Roxanne turned toward her. Charlotte put her arms around her. Roxanne cried harder.

Max watched quietly for a time. He did not speak again until Roxanne began to grow calm.

"One thing we've been wondering," Charlotte said. "How did Trey Greenslade learn so quickly that Louise Flint had gone to Loring to pick up the evidence box? He found out that same day and, with Madison Benson's help, murdered her that night."

Roxanne raised her head from Charlotte's shoulder. "I told you there weren't a lot of potential buyers for that box of evidence."

"Right," Charlotte said. "There were only two — Trey Greenslade and my stepsister."

"There was a third," Roxanne said. "I called her first."

"You contacted Trey's grandmother — Marian Greenslade, didn't you?" Max said quietly.

"Yes." Roxanne wiped her eyes with the sleeve of her flannel shirt. "I went to see her. I approached her as one mother to another. I thought she would pay to protect her son's good name — the good name of the family — especially now that Trey was in line to take charge of Loring-Greenslade. Everyone knew that Trey was her favorite grandson."

"But you guessed wrong," Max said.

"Marian Greenslade told me to go to hell. I warned her that if she didn't come through with the money, I would offer the evidence to the victim, Jocelyn Pruett."

"Marian Greenslade called your bluff," Charlotte said.

It was Max who answered.

"Yes, she did," he said. "That was my news. Walsh just called with an update on Trey Greenslade's story. Turns out that right after Roxanne left her, Marian Greenslade got on the phone to her grandson. She told Trey to clean up the mess he and his father had made or else he would not get control of Loring-Greenslade."

CHAPTER 69

After the police left with Roxanne Briggs, Charlotte contemplated the brilliant green Romanesco and the fresh wild salmon. She decided she no longer felt like cooking. She opened a bottle of wine and sent out for pizza instead.

When the pizza arrived, she and Max sat at the dining bar and talked.

"What do you think will happen to her?" Charlotte asked.

"They're going to hold her for the Loring police," Max said. He ate a bite of pizza. "They've got her on a suicide watch. I talked to Walsh for a few minutes. He's driving into Seattle with an officer to pick her up tomorrow and escort her back to Loring."

"You were right back at the start when you said that once we knew the triggering event, everything else would fall into place."

He nodded and drank some more wine.

"That's how it usually works."

"Do you miss being married?"

He paused in midchew, startled by the question. She didn't blame him. She'd had to work up her nerve to broach the subject and in the end she hadn't come up with a particularly elegant segue.

"What I miss is what I used to think marriage would be like," he said.

Walking on eggshells, she thought. Well, so was she.

She smiled. "In other words, you're a romantic."

He gave a crack of laughter, effectively restoring a sense of reality to the conversation.

"Sorry, but you're way off base there," he said. "When I said I miss what I thought marriage would be like, you need to understand I'm talking about the boring parts. I would rather have a tuna fish sandwich and a beer at home than go out to dinner. I'm not the cocktail party type. I'm not good with a lot of emotional drama."

"Understandable."

He started to take another bite of pizza and paused. "It is?"

"Sure. In your work I'm sure you see a lot of drama, and I imagine that very little of it is joyful. There is also bound to be a fair amount of frustration involved in what you do."

"That, too," he agreed. "Someone hires you to find answers and then gets upset with the answers."

"But you go looking for the answers anyway."

"Yeah. Sounds like the classic definition of insanity, doesn't it? Doing the same thing over and over again and expecting a different result."

She leaned forward and helped herself to a slice of pizza. "So why did you become a profiler in the first place and why have you opened your own investigation business now?"

"Probably because I'm good at it. I don't seem to be good at anything else."

She munched some pizza. "And probably because you aren't interested in doing anything else."

"There is that," he agreed. He contemplated her with an unreadable look. "Speaking of my small business, you might be interested to know that I hired a receptionist."

"Is she cute? Blond? A redhead? Do I need to be jealous?"

"Probably not. The new receptionist is Anson."

"Ah." She gave that some thought. "Great idea."

"He needs a job and I need someone to handle things when I'm out of the office. Seems like a win-win."

She smiled. "Definitely."

"I'm going to need a new office, too. It looks like I'll be getting a partner."

"Really? Who?"

"One of my foster brothers — Cabot Sutter. I talked to him today. He's been a police chief down in Oregon for a while now. Stuff has happened. He's looking for a change. Thinks he might like to try Seattle and the PI business."

Charlotte smiled. "In other words, you are about to double the size of your business — triple it, if you count adding the new receptionist."

"That does not guarantee that the number of clients will double or triple," Max warned.

"It will," she said, serenely sure of herself. "So, what with all those big business plans you've got going, I guess you probably won't have a lot of time to miss being married — or to miss what you thought marriage would be like."

He pushed his plate aside and folded his arms on the table. "Correct me if I'm wrong, but, ace detective that I am, I have the feeling that I am not quite following the thread of this conversation."

She gulped some wine, lowered the glass and met his eyes across the table. "I was just wondering if you think that, at some point in the future, you might want to consider getting married again."

"I have been considering it since the day I walked out of the elevator in Louise Flint's condo building and saw you."

She almost stopped breathing. "Really?"

"Really. What about you? Ready to consider marriage again?"

Her heart was so full she was afraid she might cry. "Yes. Yes, I would absolutely consider marrying you. I mean, it's way too soon for either of us to be sure, of course."

"Of course."

"We've been through a lot of drama together. We need time to really get to know each other before we do anything drastic."

"You mean you need time to find out if I'm going to bore you to tears," he said.

"No. That's not what I meant, not at all."

He got to his feet, caught her by the shoulders and gently hauled her up out of the chair. "We've both been burned, so we've both got reasons to take this slowly. But for now can we just go back to the first question? My answer is yes, I would consider marrying you."

"And I would consider marrying you."

"Let's stop right there for tonight."

She put her arms around his neck. "Okay," she said. "We can stop there. For tonight."

"I won't change my mind," he said.

She smiled. "Neither will I."

CHAPTER 70

He awoke to the gentle sound of rain on the window. It was still dark outside, but dawn was on the way. He could feel it. He turned on his side and gathered Charlotte close against him.

She stirred and stretched. "Morning yet?"

"Almost," he said. He levered himself up on his elbow and kissed her tumbled hair. "I've been thinking."

"About your new business plans?"

"No, about us. Will you marry me?"

She turned a little and opened her eyes. "I thought we were going to take our time. Get to know each other."

"I know everything I need to know about you," he said.

She smiled and touched the side of his face with her fingertips. "Do you?"

"I told you, one of the tenets of my work is the fact that people don't change — not deep down at their core. You are the woman

I want to marry now and you will always be that woman."

"Is that a way of saying I'm predictable?"

"No, it's a way of saying I love you."

"That will work out nicely because I love you. But, then, you probably already knew that, didn't you? What with me being so predictable and all?"

He smiled. "Sometimes it's important to hear the words."

"Yes, it is."

She pulled him down to her and kissed him.

CHAPTER 71

Max stopped on the sidewalk outside the restaurant.

Charlotte looked at him. "You don't have to do this."

"Yes," Max said, "I do. But you two don't have to go in there with me."

"Sure we do," Anson said. "Family."

"He's right," Charlotte said. She glanced down at her hand. Max's fingers were locked around hers, covering her engagement ring. She raised her head to meet his eyes. "Family doesn't let family do this kind of thing alone."

"Damn straight," Anson said.

"There's something else to consider," Charlotte said. "In addition to feeling very curious about the half brother they never knew they had, your brother and sister may also be feeling really, really awkward. Maybe even guilty."

Max frowned. "Why would they feel guilty?"

"They may be afraid that you'll resent them because they got the father you never had," Charlotte said.

"They'd be wrong." Max looked at Anson. "I got the father I was supposed to have."

Charlotte smiled. "Exactly. And that's what we're going to show them today."

Anson grunted, but Charlotte thought he looked quietly pleased.

"Are we going to do this?" he said. "Or are we going to stand around out here on the sidewalk until it starts raining again?"

"Let's get it over with," Max said.

He opened the door and led the way into the crowded restaurant. He did not release Charlotte's hand. He gripped her fingers as though she was a talisman.

She spotted the two people they had come to meet almost at once. There was an aura of tension around the booth at the back where a dark-haired, well-dressed man in his late twenties sat across from an attractive woman who was a few years younger. There were two cups of coffee on the table but no food.

She knew that Max saw them at the same time. A kind of stillness came over him.

Anson fixed his cop eyes on the booth

where the two people sat.

"Reckon that'll be them," he said.

Max did not say anything. He started forward.

The dark-haired man in the booth was seated facing the door. He saw the trio coming toward him first and said something to the woman, who turned her head to look over her shoulder. She was tense, Charlotte thought — anxious and nervous.

The man got to his feet. He was built a lot like Max and he had the same gold-and-brown eyes. He looked wary but determined.

"Max Cutler?" he said.

"Yes," Max said.

"I'm Ryan Decatur. This is my sister, Brooke. Thanks for meeting us today."

"Thanks for making the drive from Portland," Max said.

He held out his hand.

Relief warmed Ryan's eyes. He shook Max's hand.

"Let me introduce a couple members of my family," Max said. "Charlotte Sawyer, my fiancée, and Anson Salinas, my dad."

"A pleasure," Brooke said quickly. "Will you please join us for lunch? Or just coffee, if you prefer."

She appeared braced for rejection.

"Lunch sounds good," Max said.

"Yes, it does," Charlotte put in quickly.

"About time someone mentioned food," Anson declared. "This is a restaurant, after all."

There was some scrambling around to rearrange the seating. When the dust settled, Brooke and Ryan were on one side of the table. Charlotte and Max sat on the opposite side of the booth. A waiter brought a chair for Anson, who was positioned at the end of the table. Anyone walking in the door would have assumed he was the patriarch of the clan, Charlotte thought, amused.

Once the food had been ordered, the floodgates opened. They talked about everything except the past — the traffic on the interstate, the weather, how Seattle had boomed in recent years. Ryan and Brooke bombarded Max with questions. He answered them patiently.

"Were you really a criminal profiler?" Brooke asked.

"What's the investigation business like?" Ryan wanted to know.

And then Brooke looked at Max. "I owe you more than I can say. I would never have been able to forgive myself if I had allowed that con man, Simon Gatley, to worm his way into the family."

"Forget it," Max said. "I'm sure you and the rest of the Decaturs would have figured it out sooner or later."

"It would have been later," Ryan said. "A lot later. Gatley was good. I'll give him credit for that. He even had Dad fooled."

"At first Dad didn't want to believe what his lawyer was telling him about Gatley," Brooke said. "He knew the information had come from you. He said we couldn't trust any of it. He said you probably had an agenda."

"But Dad is too good a businessman to ignore hard data," Ryan added. "He keeps a security firm on retainer. He asked them to look into Gatley. They confirmed everything that was in your report. Can't believe Gatley got away with the con for so long."

"He's still getting away with it, as far as we know," Brooke said. She shook her head. "He's moved on, but I hate to think of all the people he'll be able to scam before the authorities finally manage to nail him."

"Brooke was afraid you wouldn't show up today," Ryan confided. "I was afraid that if you did show, you'd be angry."

"No," Max said. "Curious, but not angry."

"I'm sorry Dad didn't come with us," Brooke said. "I know he's grateful because you saved the family from Gatley. But to be honest, he's having trouble processing this whole situation. Mom is handling things better than he is. She told him he should come with us and meet you."

"Probably better this way," Max said.

"His loss," Brooke said.

"Or not," Ryan said quietly.

His attention was riveted on the front door of the restaurant. Charlotte and the others turned in their seats to follow his gaze.

A grim-faced man with silver-gray hair and hard-to-read eyes walked toward the table. He moved at a steady, deliberate pace, as if he wasn't certain that things would end well when he reached his destination. At the same time it was clear to Charlotte that he was committed to the journey. One foot in front of the other, she thought. She smiled to herself.

"I didn't think he would change his mind," Brooke whispered. "Dad must have gotten into his car right after we left Portland."

Anson pushed himself up out of his chair and stood back, giving Max room to get to his feet.

Davis Decatur came to a halt in front of Max and looked at him.

"I came to thank you for what you did," Davis said. "You didn't owe us . . . me . . . anything."

He put out his hand.

Max took it. "It's okay."

The handshake was a bit stiff, but it was a handshake, Charlotte told herself.

"He did it because that's the kind of thing he does for a living," Anson said.

"I understand," Davis said. He surveyed Anson. "And you are?"

"This is Anson Salinas," Max said. His voice resonated with pride. "My dad."

"I see." Davis extended his hand to Anson. "I understand Max lost his mother when he was young. He was lucky to find you."

"You've got it backwards," Anson said. He shook Davis's hand. "I was the one who got lucky. Plenty of room at the table. You hungry?"

"Yes," Davis said. He smiled at Ryan and Brooke and then his gaze settled on Max. "I believe I am hungry. It was a very long trip."

CHAPTER 72

Charlotte was in the Fireside Lounge, chatting with some of the residents who were waiting for happy hour, when she got a pleasant little whisper of awareness. She turned and saw Max standing in the doorway.

She smiled at him. His usually cold and unreadable eyes heated — not with passion, she thought, although that was surely part of it — but with promise; with love.

It would always be like this, she thought. The sense of connection was real. It wasn't just the by-product of the danger they had shared together. She knew now that it had been there from the beginning and it had only grown stronger.

The residents greeted Max with enthusiasm. They were getting to know him quite well. He responded and then looked at her.

"Ready to leave?" he asked.

She glanced at her watch. "Yes. I'll just

get my things."

Ted Hagstrom, the engineer, winked. "Got plans for the evening, eh?"

The others chuckled in a knowing way.

"As a matter of fact, we're going to spend most of the evening looking at paint chips," Max said. "Got a lot of work to do on the house."

"I'll meet you in the lobby," Charlotte said.

"Right," Max said.

He edged aside so that she could slip through the doorway and then he turned back to his conversation with the residents, who were all suddenly buzzing with remodeling tips and tales of DIY projects gone bad.

She hurried down the hall to her office to collect her jacket and bag.

When she arrived in the lobby, she saw a familiar face — Ethel Deeping's son, Richard. He smiled and greeted her.

"How are you doing?" he said. Concern marked his face. "We read about the kidnapping in the press. Mom told us all the details. What a nightmarish experience."

Charlotte smiled. "You do know that your mother helped save my life and the life of my stepsister, I hope."

"Mom said that she took some photos of

the car the kidnappers used and that your fiancé used them to help track down the bad guys."

"All true," Charlotte said. "Needless to say, my stepsister and I are extremely grateful to her. Ethel was a real heroine."

Richard smiled. "She loved every minute of it, believe me. She approves of the new fiancé, by the way. Says you're going to hold the reception here at Rainy Creek Gardens. She's very excited."

"So am I," Charlotte said. She turned and saw Max coming toward them. "I'll introduce you. This is Max Cutler. Max, this is Richard Deeping, Ethel's son."

The two men shook hands.

"A pleasure to meet you," Max said. "Ethel was brilliant. She got the pics and she made the call that alerted me to the kidnapping. Can't thank her enough. Charlotte and I took her out to dinner the other night. She wanted to hear the whole story."

Richard chuckled. "She'll be talking about dinner with you and her part in the adventure for a long time to come, believe me. Glad she was there for you when you needed her."

"She was," Charlotte said earnestly.

"It will certainly make for an exciting chapter in her memoirs," Richard said.

Charlotte took a deep breath. She would never get a better opportunity to give Ethel's family a gentle warning about the memoir they would soon be reading. She glanced around the lobby, checking to be certain that there was no one within hearing distance.

She turned back to Richard. "Do you have a moment to discuss Ethel's memoirs?"

Richard's eyes lit with enthusiasm.

"Sure. She loves that class. Great idea, by the way. Got to capture the details about the past while we still can, right? Once the older generation is gone, a lot of history is gone, as well. Luckily, Mom's memory is still sharp."

"Yes," Charlotte said. She lowered her voice. "Ethel's memory is very sharp. And so is her imagination."

Max looked at her. "Charlotte, you may not want to go down this road. It's Deeping family history and it might be a little more complicated than we know."

Richard's brows shot up. "Define 'complicated.' "

Max winced. Charlotte ignored him.

"It's just that your mother has decided to sprinkle a little fiction into her plot," she said. "I mean, into her personal history. I don't want you to be surprised by some of the more . . . imaginative parts, that's all."

"What is she fictionalizing?" Richard asked.

Max shook his head, but he had evidently decided that it was too late to interfere. He kept quiet.

"The part that may seem a bit . . . *sensational* is the chapter on her marriage," Charlotte explained. "She writes glowingly of your father, of course. She mentions what a fine businessman he was, for example. She talks about his service to the community. She's very clear that he was well respected and a good provider. She even says he was an excellent golfer."

Richard nodded. "All true, as far as I know. I was quite young when he died, though. Just nine years old, so I don't remember a lot about him. My sister was barely seven. That's why Mom's memoirs will be so interesting."

Charlotte cleared her throat. "I'm afraid they may be a little more than interesting. Here's the problem — after telling us about your father's accomplishments and how he had the respect of the entire community, she says she, uh, killed him."

Richard looked at her, his face expressionless. "Mom wrote that in her memoir?"

"I'm afraid so. She feels it makes for a

more dramatic ending."

"Well, I'll be damned." Richard started to grin. "Does she, by any chance, say how she did it?"

"I believe there is a brief reference to putting some sort of medication into his oatmeal the morning of the day he collapsed on the golf course."

"Ah, so that was it." Richard nodded, satisfied. "We always wondered how she pulled it off. No one ever questioned the heart attack. But, then, Mom was a nurse. She knew how to make it look good."

It was Charlotte's turn to stare. "What?"

"Sounds like Mom told you the truth about Dad," Richard said. "As far as the community was concerned, he was the perfect husband and father. But the reality was that he was an abusive monster at home."

"I see," Charlotte said. She couldn't think of anything else to say, so she decided it was time to take Max's advice and shut up.

"Mom wanted to take my sister and me and leave, but the bastard threatened to murder all of us if she did. He would have done it, too. And then, one day, he conveniently dropped dead on the golf course. My sister and I didn't understand it at the time. Mom never talked about it. But later, when my sister and I were older, we pieced it together."

"Your mother actually did kill your father?" Charlotte managed.

"Probably," Richard said. "No one else could protect us — hell, no one else would have believed there was even a problem. A restraining order wouldn't have worked. So Mom did what she had to do to protect my sister and me and herself."

"Oh, my," Charlotte whispered.

She noticed that Max was giving her an amused I-told-you-so look. She pretended to ignore it.

Richard looked at her. "Family secret. Got a problem with that?"

"Nope," Charlotte said. She looked at Max. "Do you?"

"Nope," Max said. "I hear most memoirs are part fiction, anyway."

"Right," Charlotte said. "Lot of fiction in the memoir genre. Everyone knows that."

"I've heard that, too," Richard said. He smiled and looked across the room. "There's Mom now. If you'll excuse me?"

"Yes, of course," Charlotte said, aware that her voice was somewhat faint. "Enjoy the evening."

"We will," Richard assured her. "It's a birthday party for one of her grandkids.

Mom loves parties."

He went forward to greet Ethel.

Charlotte narrowed her eyes at Max.

"Did you know Ethel's story was true?" she asked.

"I had a hunch it might be," he said. "Ethel Deeping is a very tough lady."

"I suppose this will all seem very amusing one of these days," Charlotte said.

"Probably. Ready to go home and look at paint chips?"

Charlotte took his hand. "I can't think of anything I'd rather do more."

ABOUT THE AUTHOR

Jayne Ann Krentz is the author of fifty New York Times bestsellers. She has written contemporary romantic suspense novels under that name, as well as futuristic and historical romance novels under the pseudonyms Jayne Castle and Amanda Quick, respectively. She lives in Seattle.

Printed in the USA
CPSIA information can be obtained
at www.ICGtesting.com
JSHW011103121124
73438JS00005B/77

9 781432 834302